Dan Jakel spent 30 years as a police officer with the Royal Canadian Mounted Police. He enjoys travelling, which has been broad and varied through the years. This include several evenings exploring the Tango venues of Buenos Aires with his wife, Nathalie, and enjoying the culture of Seville and Madrid. These particular places have informed a number of scenes in the novel, in combination with hours of research ensconced in textbooks, journal articles, archives, videos and photographs. He resides in Ottawa. This is his first novel.

To my wife Nathalie, the love of my life.

Dan Jakel

MADAM JOSEFINA'S SOCIAL HOUSE

AUSTIN MACAULEY PUBLISHERS™

LONDON * CAMBRIDGE * NEW YORK * SHARJAH

A CIP catalogue record for this title is available from the British Library.

ISBN 9781035813032 (Paperback)
ISBN 9781035813049 (Hardback)
ISBN 9781035813056 (ePub e-book)

www.austinmacauley.co.uk

First Published 2024
Austin Macauley Publishers Ltd®
1 Canada Square
Canary Wharf
London
E14 5AA

This book was conceived in Buenos Aires in 2017, during a semi-obsessive study of Tango within the milonga's that sprout up nightly, and further refined in the flamenco bars of Seville in 2019. Although many of my initial concepts fell to the side during the outlining process, scenes involving these dances miraculously escaped the axe. In fact, much of the plot relies on cultural artefacts, as the reader may notice, be it dance performance, evading the horns of a charging bull, Shakespearean profanity, or Italian opera, to provide a richer background.

Most agree that Tango began developing organically in the city's brothels in the late 1800s. If you're wondering how I came upon the idea of a brothel being a gathering point for spies, police officers, rogues in high office, a refugee from the Spanish authorities, and a Tango aficionado, there you have it. That and a book written in 1928 by Albert Londres, *The Road to Buenos Ayres,* describing his inquiry into cross-Atlantic human trafficking, somewhat analogous to the road taken by the character, Sofia Montserrat.

Other sources of inspiration include the book *Paradoxes of Utopia: Anarchist Culture and Politics in Buenos Aires 1890–1910,* by Juan Suriano. For a couple of years, this book never left my side, an excellent account of the role adherents to anarchism played in advancing the cause of Argentina's working class.

And Professor David Rock, author of *State Building and Political Movements in Argentina 1860–1916,* which holds endless, factual, titbits to serve as background, think any mention of railway profiteering, dubious banking practices, corrupt elections, political scandals, and coup d'états. Similarly, Professor Donna Guy's journal article *White Slavery, Public Health,* and *the Socialist Position on Legalised Prostitution* in *Argentina, 1913–1936,* was highly instructive on the factors that drove women into the brothels of Buenos

Aires, and their regulation by municipal authorities. I hope to have passed along some of her observations, albeit in fictional form.

I also made liberal use of the journal article *Casual Workers, Collective Action and Anarcho-syndicalism in Southern Spain: Jerez de la Frontera, 1882–1933*, by Enrique Montañes and James Simpson, to inform about the scenes taking place in Jerez de la Frontera. The GJENVICK-GJONVIK Archives, available freely on-line, holds a repository of first-hand accounts of crossing the Atlantic in steerage class, stark reminders of the problems migrants faced at the time. John E. Hodge provides a detailed and dramatic account of the Teatro Colón in *The Construction of the Teatro Colón*.

Next, my thanks to Nathalie, my wife of thirty years, for volunteering to be my first editor. Ruthless proof reader, caller outer of poor English, sentence structure, repetitive phrasing, and bad literary ideas in general. Thank you, my love, you get the first read, always.

Those of you who courageously volunteered to read early versions of the manuscript, and give it to me straight, I owe you my gratitude. There were several, however, those that weighed in by putting pen to paper include my stepmother Betty Jakel, my sister Cathy Thibault, Kasia Majewski, and Karl Morton, voracious readers all, and I emphatically trust their judgment.
Three last mentions. Toronto editor and author Damian Tarnopolsky, for his encouragement and kindness to a stranger in need. His referral led me to the services of Jane Warren, who cast her extraordinary editorial eyes upon the manuscript and provided sage developmental advice. Thank you, Jane, you're a true professional.

My very last thank you to Austin Macauley Publishers for bringing the novel to life. Upon receiving your offer, we uncorked a bottle of *Pol Roger*, a good champagne, and drank the whole darn thing.

Table of Contents

Chapter 1
A Discreet Inquiry

Wednesday, 27 May, 1908, Buenos Aires. Ernesto Torrente, lawyer and long-serving functionary of the Ministry of the Interior, stepped onto the cobblestone sidewalk outside of the ministry building on Avenida 25 de Mayo. He looked upward to take stock of the grand clock imbedded in the tower on its fourth story, as if to make sure he had not mistaken the time, which he had not, and took a much-needed breath of fresh air. 'The last five days had been as trying as any he had previously experienced in his adult life time,' he thought, 'yet here he was, still kicking.' 'Not bad for a 60 year old.'

While awaiting the appearance of one Sofia Montserrat, if she appeared, he was doing his best to keep his mind off of an unrelated preoccupation, but one that would consume him, and threaten his sanity if he let it. In order to do so, he had wandered outside of his office to look at things, touch things that were real, and he reached out and trailed his fingers along the grooved sandstone exterior surrounding the massive double wooden doors. 'I'm alive and things will be alright.'

But Ernesto's mind wandered back to last Sunday. He had not known then what he knew now. Hadn't even imagined the burden Monday evening's bizarre event would bring, weighing deep in his mind, a place he held in reserve for the love of his children, and their children. That people would think to threaten—brutally extinguish—other's very lives to advance their grievances. How could that even be possible? Yet now he knew it was. But it was another matter for another time. 'Concentrate on your task.'

On Sunday, he'd been sought out at his home, interrupted during a game he'd been playing with his grandchildren, summonsed to meet with Minister Avelleneda himself. Another crisis threatening a fragile presidency. It had to be managed, but he'd been resentful at being rousted on a Sunday, which he normally dedicated to the church and his family.

"Why me," Ernesto had demanded, sounding unprofessional even to himself, and regretting it. 'That would be his one and only protest,' he thought.

The Minister looked up sharply, as if ready to admonish, but then obliged this brief and uncharacteristic petulance. "Because I trust you Ernesto. That's not something I can say to everyone around here, is it," he said, his voice raised.

The question was rhetorical and Ernesto remained silent.

"Many of your colleagues—and that undoubtedly includes all the youngsters in your shop—were part of the conspiracy to overthrow the President three years ago. None of them can be trusted to remain discreet on a sensitive issue that might expose this President to a scandal. They'd be too happy to do such a thing. His enemies are many and they're lying in wait. My good sense is telling me that if there were ever a time to have a steady hand of experience look into something, now is that time. What has it been, thirty-five years of loyal service?"

"Thirty-five indeed," Ernesto said. 'A lifetime,' he thought.

"Then neither of us can count the number of times you could have been enticed into sedition—yet you were not. Therefore I trust you." The Minister was pacing his office, fidgeting with every decorative object he passed. "And because you're competent."

A compliment as an afterthought, but Ernesto knew what the Minister said about him was true, and was now growing intrigued as to what he was getting at. He was not exaggerating about the President's enemies lying in wait. Jose Figora Alcorta had inherited the final four years of President Quintana's six year term, the latter having passed away with Alcorta in the Vice Presidential position. The unruly provincial governors had schemed against Alcorta, and since they controlled their respective congressional members, they filibustered any spending measures Alcorta proposed. But Alcorta had fought back, dismissing the congress and declaring an election. He issued a presidential decree, and took control of the nation's finances. The governors were then forced to accept his own congressional candidates to represent their jurisdictions, and now he was preparing to return the financial powers back to congress, where the constitution had put them. The governors were furious, bested by Alcorta, and politics were taken very personally in this country. A tenuous time for the President indeed, Ernesto thought. 'No scandals, not now, they lie in wait.'

"Have a read of this," the Minister said, shoving a folded newspaper into Ernesto's hand, the Worker's Rebellion, an anarchist publication. One of the more popular, and strident. There was a front page article circled in red ink. "Published yesterday," the Minister added.

J'accuse! As the French high military command illegally conspired against the Jewish officer Dreyfuss—one of their own brothers—falsely condemning him of treason—so to the insidious stench of fratricide has infected the Police of the Capital. Senior officers contrived to assassinate their leader Colonel Falcon! This occurred in front of us all, during International Worker's Day celebrations last year, when a mounted officer resembling Falcon was shot. This caused Colonel Falcon to order the poorly informed rank and file police officers to fire into the crowd and kill several innocent people. But information has been suppressed by the President and the blame for the slaughter has been cast on a rogue cell of anarchists.

It was no rogue cell of anarchists—it was a rogue cell of clandestine police agents! This can no longer be swept under the rug for the sake of President Alcorta's political fortunes. There are eye witnesses now willing to come forward—

'The Enraged Prostitute'

"Clever don't you think? Making reference to the Dreyfuss affair, which cost the French Prime Minister his job. This woman, the Enraged Prostitute, has been particularly incisive with her articles, they're of a quality not normally found in the anarchist rags," the Minister said. "Last year she grew popular amongst the working class throughout the course of the rent strike. 120,000 residents in the affected tenements, they said, nearly a 50 percent increase in their rents—how can you blame them? Fortunately for us it mostly impacted immigrants who can't vote. Nevertheless, those responsible for collecting their rents were indeed our voters, whom she referred to as heartless and un-Christian like. She was starting to cut us deep—impressively deep. With such influence, I've been paying heed to her articles myself—but nothing we couldn't handle until this. The President and I were pondering the subtext Ernesto. There's the implied threat of course, but is there a message? What is she telling us?"

"In any case, we can't just ignore it—she's got a large following, even outside of anarchist circles. You know what comes next—there needs to be a discreet inquiry led by this ministry. No involvement of the police for obvious reasons. You'll conduct the inquiry personally, you alone—quickly."

Ernesto was rubbing his temples. 'What the devil is going on with our police department?' International Worker's Day 1907 had been a disaster, and the press coverage had been relentless in its criticism of the police response. The chief of police, Colonel Ramon Falcon, had been hauled in front of the President to explain himself. He'd been adamant that an extreme element of anarchists had opened fire first, and that the response had been necessary, commensurate with the threat posed to his men. In any case, the President was stuck, as he had personally appointed Colonel Falcon to the position. They had needed a military man in charge of the Policia de la Capitale, to deal with the growing number of strikes and riots, and their fortunes were tied together for better or for worse. The President had endorsed Falcon's explanation, and then his reasoning to increase the numbers of uniformed officers on the streets and in the riot squads, to the detriment of their acclaimed investigational division, the detectives doing the unseen work, with whom the papers had an odd fascination. The budget of the Police of the Capital was modified significantly, funding a new cadet academy and uniforms. Cuts to the budget of the investigative division paid for them.

Personally Ernesto had thought the strategy was a mistake. As chief legal counsel for the ministry, Ernesto had been at the centre of consultations for the Residency Act, passed in 1902. Ernesto had spoken at length with Felipe De La Fuente, the commissioner in command of the investigative division, to ensure the police were in a position to enforce it. The act was in response to the growing number of anarchist agitators immigrating to Argentina, and more often than not, front and centre during the strikes and riots. It allowed for an immediate deportation, under the signature of the minister, once Ernesto had reviewed the case presented by the detectives. On receiving the minister's authorization, the police put the subject onto the first steamer back to the European continent, steerage class of course. Ernesto had a grudging admiration for De La Fuente, whose men he thought to be efficient and effective at their work. He would have made a better chief of police than Falcon, but the minister had insisted, although he'd recently expressed reticence about it.

"Unfortunately it was I that convinced the President to appoint a former military man. My God—the President had asked me if I thought Commissioner De La Fuente wouldn't have been more suited to the position. He was a confirmed loyalist through two coup d'états that nearly succeeded—a police officer bred from the rank and file with the loyalty of his men. He was there waiting to be picked—and a presidency in this country relies on the police department for stability." The minister brushed unruly tufts of hair back, and continued. "He just didn't have the pedigree, I'd said. The ladies talked poorly of him at our parties. He owns a brothel you see Ernesto—amongst other morally questionable endeavours just waiting to be discovered. I felt the President couldn't afford a scandalous nomination. But now I see the error of my ways. Falcon is a bull in a China shop, lining up cavalry charges and rifle volleys against men and women with sticks. He's using a bloody sledge hammer to crack walnuts!"

It was quiet for a moment, as the minister took a seat at his desk, and then fixated Ernesto with a cold stare. "She claims there was a rogue cell of clandestine police agents. This ministry has heard of no such thing—unfortunately something about her accusation rings true to my ears. De La Fuente is an ambitious rogue if ever there was one, and this has his signature all over it. He's used all manner of clandestine activities without us knowing about it. Get on it—and make no mistake about the Presidents fragile position."

It had taken Ernesto's young aide Nicolas Morales all of two days to identify the woman writing under the nom de plume the Enraged Prostitute as one Sofia Montserrat, bookkeeper at a brothel called Madam Josefina's Social House, and arrange for her attendance today. How exactly he had done it remained unclear, and his explanation had been vague. But it was not Ernesto's overriding concern at the moment. Nor was it lost on him that Commissioner De La Fuente happened to own the premises on which Madam Josefina conducted her business, a fact that had been lost on the Minister. 'And it was nothing more than coincidence,' he thought, that 25 years ago he had in fact met Josefina briefly, an actress in a former life, to congratulate her on a performance. She was a woman that could not be forgotten.

"Señor Torrente?"

"Indeed that is I Miss Montserrat." He had not been expecting a young woman in her late twenties. 'Her articles reflected sophistication beyond her years,' he thought. "Please come this way."

He led her through the doors, down a flight of stairs, and along a hallway. He had arranged for a small office, not far from the stenographer's pool, where the collective rattle of typing caused a dull, metallic chatter. He opened the door and ushered her in. He had arranged for a stenographer himself to take notes, the spouse of a trusted colleague, and she was already seated inside, at the ready. A sparse office, the glazed window of the door barely allowing light, and relatively quiet. A notepad sitting for him on the desk, a fountain pen and ink.

It suddenly occurred to him she was taking a big risk with her public allegation against the police, and now attending the ministry in person. 'They could be vindictive,' he thought. The incident was over a year ago, long displaced from the ever searching eye of the news cycle. It hardly seemed worth it. Why now?

"Is there something I can offer you to make you comfortable, tea, use of the ladies room?"

"No—thank you but my time is very limited," she said. Then, once seated inside the small office, "I have an Orsini bomb."

Chapter 2
Mercenaries

September 1904. Commissioner Felipe De La Fuente, commander of the investigative division of the Police of the Capital, had convinced his boss, Chief Francisco Beazley, that he should attend the international police conference concerning the transnational problem of violent anarchists. It was being hosted in Madrid. De La Fuente was now halfway across the Atlantic, on the steamship's upper deck, having a discussion with a man he secretly despised. The man was what psychoanalysts were calling insane without delirium. He could kill another human being without the slightest remorse, and he'd done so now on several occasions, to De La Fuente's knowledge.

The man was also devout, an unexplainable contradiction of De La Fuente's layman's diagnosis of his personality disorder. Was it a pretence? He didn't believe the man was diabolical enough for that. He just had faith, so be it. But the man was powerful, and he held De La Fuente's future in his hands, so he suppressed his irritation.

"Tell me about the anarchists again Felipe, because I know you follow these things closely," Senator Hugo Montserrat said, "I can't tell them apart from the socialists. Tell me who's most dangerous to Argentina. They do the same things—organise general strikes, pick fights with the police, and complain about their jobs. Every year there are more strikes—they're costing us far too much money."

Owing to his elevated position within the police department, De La Fuente had educated himself on the ideologies at play within the labour force of Buenos Aires, which caused his police department so much work. He'd read Marx and Engels, the Communist Manifesto, and Capital, amongst others. Their works were foundational for the socialists. From each according to his ability, to each according to his needs, the final stage of communism, having evolved from the necessary transitional state of the dictatorship of the proletariat.

Of the anarchists he'd read Mikhail Bakunin, Principles and Organisation of the Brotherhood, a rejection of all forms of authority over individuals—state, religion, laws, police, religion, and morality. The forebears of socialism and anarchism had fallen out with each other. However, the means to obtain their goals, violent overthrow of those controlling the means of production, were the same. Sometimes they were natural allies.

"Where do these anarchists come from?" The Senator asked.

"Spain and Italy for the most part Senator."

De La Fuente knew that the staggering influx of European migrants into their labour force brought with them the competing ideologies of socialism and anarchism. But the largest number of migrants came from Italy and Spain and were more inclined towards anarchism. According to the theorists, the backwards, rural nature of the two countries was more likely to foster sentiments towards anarchism. But he didn't give a damn about any of that, because he was a highly practical man. What mattered was how this impacted his job. 'And why was the Senator suddenly interested in the academic nature of all this?'

The intelligence reports of his detectives dedicated to political crimes and public order, indicated that it was anarchist agitators who controlled the Argentine Workers Federation. The federation in turn controlled the pugnacious unions of port workers, stokers, and sailors. It had also learned that coordinating strikes by these unions increased the pressures put on the country's exports, and the businesses that fed them, giving them more negotiating power. The number of strikes had increased substantially over the last three years. Senator Montserrat had become wealthy from the beef exports produced by his ranches, slaughterhouses, and meatpacking operations. 'That's why he took such an interest,' De La Fuente thought, 'it was just business.'

"They're difficult to distinguish that's a fact Senator, because they run in the same pack—the unions. They both envision a collectivist society whereby workers control the means of production. That would include your new meat processing plant—and ranches in Baha Blanca and wherever else you've hidden them. The cheap land you've acquired would also have to be usurped for the benefit of their collective. 'That should set the bugger off.'"

"Most are just trying to improve their pathetic lives. The last time I wandered through a tenement, they were packed five men to a room—or a large family in a single room. It's a bleak existence. That's why all the workers are out chumming it up at their union halls—or at my brothel if they've some spare change they've managed to hide from their wives. It's their escape."

"Men need a distraction, and you'll never hear me say they shouldn't make enough wages to have a little fun," the Senator said. "But they're making more than enough for that."

"Quite. As I was saying, the socialists aren't as much of a danger, so there's no need to focus my resources on them. They've made progress the traditional way—having now won voting power in the congress. As you're more than aware, a deputy that proclaims himself to be a socialist is now representing the rabble in La Boca and Barracas. That should counter any revolutionary fervour on their part."

De La Fuente thought he'd better remind the Senator of an unrelated preoccupation of his detectives. "We can't be complacent about other adversaries. Remember, there were no anarchists, socialists, or unions involved in the attempted coup of 1890. That was all the doing of our so-called intellectuals, professionals and academics—who managed to convince senior military officers—generals in fact—to lead their men in revolt. Then these fine citizens had a grand old time shooting from the windows, helping the rebel troops kill loyal soldiers and police officers by the dozens."

The Senator grunted an acknowledgement. De La Fuente wasn't certain he was interested in this but persisted.

"It was 14 years ago, but they're scheming again. Irigoyan and his followers in the Civic Union are outraged with this last election. Another President hand-picked by Roca maintaining the status quo. They claim it was rigged—which, Of course, it was. My detectives still need to keep an eye on them—but that's another matter I suppose." De La Fuente took a long draw on his cigar while wondering what the Senator was trying to get from him.

"But from what we hear from our informants, the anarchists have won the hearts and minds of the workers. This concerns me because their zealots have now managed to kill an Italian King, an Austrian Royal, a French President, an American President, and a Spanish Prime Minister—along with hundreds of innocent bystanders of course."

"That's what I'd heard—that they're vicious murderers," the Senator said, now lighting himself a cigar as well. 'He seemed quite satisfied with his conclusion,' De La Fuente thought. "Their nonsense aside, my senate colleagues and I are concerned—the President as well. They've found our weak spot—they're coordinating their strikes very effectively now Felipe. This impacts our profit margins—something we take very seriously."

"As you should—the sheer numbers they can mobilise on International Workers Day and during strikes makes them our biggest threat, and because they don't play by any rules," De La Fuente said, wagging a large hand in the air—bringing the Senator's attention to the scarred knuckles of a former boxer and hard-nosed street cop.

"It's one thing for us to line up with truncheons and face off with the union's hardest men—it's another thing if they start leaving women and children dead on the streets from indiscriminate bombs and stray bullets."

The Senator seemed ready to make his point. "I've seen war myself as you know. I've had to settle things the hard way. That's how it was 30 years ago when I arrived in this country, if you wanted to get ahead. If a neighbouring ranch was causing you trouble, you went to war—killed as many as you could. You ruled your town by fear, and you controlled the local bank. Loans went to friends and allies—never to your enemies. We played for keeps. I suppose you were living in the city back then?"

"Yes."

"In the provinces that was the way of doing business until not so long ago. It's friendlier now, but you still have to know who your friends are—that's how this country is run. You form alliances with strong, ambitious men but you watch your back. Our presidents have always won elections by having the support of the governors—who control the justices of the peace, the local police and the voting booths. It's simple—the men have to say who they're voting for. When they're making the wrong choice—well," the Senator shrugged, "—they're corrected. Once the President takes office, he nominates loyal allies to key positions. By my reckoning, the most important are those that control the country's finances. This way the governors and the select few required to repeat the process will always receive the loans they need from the national bank. It's a good, reliable system," he said, "for those of us that understand it."

He paused for a moment, thinking. "We would hate to see that system end. These anarchists, their bombs, you'd better have a plan for such eventualities Felipe. You're hanging out on a limb. As the head of the investigative division, you control all the detectives—you're the obvious one to blame if something goes wrong. But don't let this scare you—you just need to prove yourself. I want you in that position. The President can be convinced given the right circumstances—it's your job to make sure those circumstances arise. Otherwise, the President seems insistent that a former military officer will succeed Chief Beazley."

De La Fuente looked at the Senator and thought about the death of the prostitute at Madam Josefina's Social House, as described to him by his Lieutenant, Vicente Machado. Naked, splayed indignantly in the iron wash tub—dead. She'd bled out from the cuts—erratic, deep, stab wounds to the neck, breasts, and genitals—evidently from the broken, bloody whiskey bottle nearby. The blubbering Senator sitting on the bed, cradling his head with his blood covered hands. He'd been angry with a woman called Maria—God help her if he ever found the real one, De La Fuente thought. 'Tiring as it is I have to play his game.'

"I've done discreet favours for other well-placed people as well as yourself Senator. I can call those favours in when the time is right. As you say—I'm in a tenuous position if something goes wrong. Although commanding the detective division has been central to my utility as an ally—I'll be infinitely more useful as the chief of police," De La Fuente said, with a smile he hoped was convincing.

"Tell me," the Senator said, "Lieutenant Machado, the man you've got in charge of your brothel—do you trust him?"

De La Fuente felt the need to defend his Lieutenant, upon whom he depended. "I'll tell you something about Vicente, who is dear to me. I discovered him as a raw-boned 16-year-old stowaway, fresh to our shores from Pigalle Square in Paris—a tough neighbourhood if there ever was one. His mother was a whore, that's what the ladies do in Pigalle—all of them. She had a pimp—a brute of a man," much like myself he thought wryly, "he was a gang leader. He beat her and Vicente every day. I know this because I had it checked out by the Sûreté at the Paris prefecture," he said.

"They knew Vicente well and felt badly for him. But then he grew—a large man even as a 16-year-old. He killed the pimp one day in front of his mother—when he'd finally had enough. His mother—God bless her loving soul—told the Sûreté that she'd done it. But it was impossible for the small woman to plant a butcher knife clean through the ribcage and heart of a large man—the blade sticking out the front," De La Fuente said.

"She gave him money she'd hidden—told him to get to the coast, Le Havre. He managed to stow away. The ship's Captain placed him into our custody at the docks, but he gave two of our finest a very hard time," he said, with a fond smile. "Broke the nose of one with a headbutt—put a nasty beating on the other until a truncheon took the fight out of him. I knew these two policemen—they weren't smart," De La Fuente laughed.

"They really should have seen it coming. They were angry with him, so they put him in a cell with a regular con—big and tough—to teach the kid a lesson. I was the desk sergeant. The con was very dead when I checked the holding cell the next morning. He'd tried to cosy up to the lad that evening—might as well have cosied up to a feral cat. I had it cleaned up. Another bruised, beaten body to the busy morgue—no big deal. I told the men Vicente was our next member— once he could shave. Until that time, he was Madam Josefina's to manage— room and board. A couple of years later, he was our new recruit."

"You looked after him," the Senator said, nodding with respect.

"I've looked after him all right. It wasn't hard. He took well to life at the brothel. He'd had a lot of experience with that sort of thing. The recurring issues of drunken transgressions were conveniently settled. He was always there and never drank. He despised drunken behaviour—it reminded him of his mother's pimp. Imagine—100 kilograms of street brawler waiting to be moulded in my vision. It was a dream come true. Of course, I asked him about the trades—I wouldn't have stopped him from going into one if he'd shown any interest. The stone masons would've wanted him, or the butchers at your meatpacking plant. He's got the strength in his arms."

"But I suppose I influenced him. He'd become a cop when he was old enough, he said. In the meanwhile, he was the muscle at the brothel. I was never called again to deal with unruly men. A 12-hour day of hard labour and three whiskeys will make any man a fighter. But I never passed judgement, and neither did Vicente. It's a good quality not to bear grudges—and its good business."

"He learned on the streets of Montmartre that a beating should only be given when it serves a purpose. A demonstration to discourage similar behaviour or quick justice for the prostitutes—hell, let them throw in a smack or two if they felt the need. But the man is still a client. We wanted them to return. The trick is to keep it proportionate to the transgression."

De La Fuente looked upward at the sky, obscured only by the black, furling smoke escaping from the four stacks of the ocean liner.

"A few years later, after his military service, I had him assigned to my squad—uniformed work in the tough south quadrant. The men showed him the ropes. Everyone liked to partner up with Vicente, he was tough, smart and streetwise—it's not common to have all three traits."

The Senator looked wary. "I don't want to be blackmailed by some streetwise gangster."

"Hear me out Senator. And then came the revolt of 1890—a test of my own loyalty. We were told there were 2000 rebel troops in the heart of the city and on the march under General Campo—who'd just escaped from police custody rather miraculously."

"Not everybody in your police department was as loyal as you."

"Indeed. General Campo's troops were armed to the teeth, coming from the ammunition arsenal stored at the Parque d'Artillerie. There was a panic and we had to hurry. For some reason, General Campo stopped the rebel's advance. This allowed us to organise our defence—doesn't make sense to this day. The General easily had enough men to make a rush for the institutions on Avenida de Mayo, they could have captured the President. But they stopped, and that was our chance. I volunteered my police squad to go face them alongside the soldiers that remained loyal. It was an even match of numbers. We were supposed to be behind the soldiers as we moved towards the battle lines—but things got mixed up as we moved north through the city and closed in on the Parque d'Artillerie. Then the shooting started and all hell broke loose."

"My squad got pinned down in the street in a crossfire—the worst possible situation. The rebel soldiers had Gatling guns set up on the rooftops and they cut my squad of police officers to pieces along with a platoon of soldiers. I took a rifle shot in the thigh. It hurt so bad I couldn't fight—couldn't walk—could barely think. I resigned myself to die right then and there."

"There was myself and Vicente left, protected behind a pile of corpses torn up by the Gatling guns. Vicente was still shooting his rifle God bless the lad—it gave me time to crawl to shelter. But I was done in. I told the lad to run and save himself. In my dying moment, I went all sentimental—and I'm ashamed of myself to this very day. Instead, he hoisted me on his shoulders, and carried me for three kilometres to the hospital. As you can see, I'm a heavy man Senator. It's conceivable I was a few pounds lighter then—but still—not an easy task. That's my story of loyalty. I was loyal to the President—Vicente was loyal to me. That's still how it is."

The Senator looked circumspect. "That's a touching story, Felipe. It makes me feel more confident about the Lieutenant," he said, a shortening cigar clamped in his teeth, something else evidently still bothering him. "Why haven't you married Madam Josefina?"

'He's looking desperately for a weakness,' De La Fuente thought. "A fine woman Senator. British roots—like myself on my mother's side. We shared a passion for the arts—literature mostly and Shakespeare in particular. She was an actress—and had all the lines memorised. Why aren't we married? For one, she didn't see herself as a wife or a mother. She was brought up in London's East end and knew what poverty meant—prostitution. Her mother had been in the business. When I acquired the property, I convinced her to start the brothel. We've been successful business partners and that's where it stayed. It's true we were lovers once," exhaling a melancholy stream of cigar smoke, "—still are on the odd occasion. For two, I had a prospective career. The Chief told me this himself. It's best you let that one lie for appearances sake Felipe. Didn't want to see her on my arm at his gala parties for the officers."

"We all have to make regrettable choices." The Senator had grown bored.

"Indeed," he said, dwelling on the Senator's comments.

The international police conference in Madrid had gone well. Despite himself, he'd enjoyed the pomp and circumstance. An obsequious host had introduced the gaggle of ambassadors and ministers in attendance, and each had stood from their chairs in the auditorium for a round of applause. The Spanish Minister of the Interior gave a rousing speech, summarising the progress Europe had made in coordinating its respective legislative provisions on deportation and policing strategies. They'd been formalised at the recent diplomatic gathering in St Petersburg. He hadn't been high enough in the chain to receive an invite, but one day he would be.

He nevertheless received a lavish introduction as a guest presenter from Argentina. He played up his limp and use of his cane as he ambled to the podium to provide an overview of his country's response to the anarchist threat. He described his country's practical solutions, for the sake of any actual police officers present: creative use of the gambling law that allowed police entrance to places without a warrant, the fettering out of subversive presses—which had no bearing on gambling whatsoever—and deportation of individuals on the basis of the evidence found within, pursuant to the residency law.

He'd listened attentively to a presentation of an officer from Spain's Guardia Civil, the head of their intelligence unit that concerned itself with internal threats.

It had been alarming. He was reminded of the number of instances where improvised bombs, infernal devices, had exploded in the busy squares and train stations of Europe. There'd been a show and tell with bomb fragments laid out on tables; neatly labelled with the location in which it had exploded, the name of the culprit, and the number of victims.

He suffered through the predictable fillers—a professor giving a long lecture on the major influences of the anarchists, Proudhon and the 1848 worker-driven revolutions across Europe, the socialist experiment of the Paris Commune in 1871, and Mikhail Bakunin's epochal disagreement with Karl Marx. The speaker had a sympathetic view of Bakunin's argument, "It's merely replacing the bourgeoisie oppressors with another, the dictatorship of the proletariat."

De La Fuente found himself dozing. He was re-invigorated with a break, a coffee and pastry, 'To make me even bloody fatter,' and he listened with renewed attention to the presentation on the assassination of McKinley, the American President, by an out of work factory migrant just three years prior. The motive was revolution. The perpetrator, a young man called Leon Czolgosz, hadn't given the slightest thought to escaping. 'He assumed he'd just be applauded on the spot?' 'My God we have droves of such young men in Buenos Aires,' he thought.

The words of the last lecture lingered in his thoughts while he mingled outside the doors of the lecture hall. He made eye contact and nodded to a professional acquaintance, meeting him was the real reason he went to such lengths to attend the conference. He manoeuvred through huddles of men speaking animatedly and making their arrangements for drinks and dinner. He needed to make his own such arrangements with the former military attaché of the Spanish Embassy in Buenos Aires, Colonel Benito Gimenez.

Prior to leaving Buenos Aires, De La Fuente had cornered the division's paymaster with Vicente in tow. "Tell me—just how many sergeants are we short right now?"

"There are three positions that can be filled at that particular rank sir. We're always short a few personnel."

"Indeed—take the sum of three sergeants wages from the salary account and place the exact same amount into the general slush fund. Salaries will be paid to three men without identifying them by name into accounts held at the national bank. Lieutenant Machado will give you the details."

"Sir—that is highly unusual."

"And?"

"It could be noticed. Someone might think I'm stealing."

"But you're not stealing, are you?" Vicente had said.

"No."

"It was a rhetorical question."

"I see," the diminutive paymaster had said, intimidated by the towering Lieutenant.

"Keep this to yourself."

Now it was time to use that money. "Colonel Gimenez, I'm glad you found your way in," he said.

"Yes—I had to rekindle an old friendship within La Guardia Civil to get an invitation. I'm finding it informative. Will you join me for dinner?"

"I'd be delighted." He didn't want to discuss their business at hand within the earshot of present company.

'The noisy brasserie had been a prudent choice for their conversation,' De La Fuente thought. No sense skulking around looking suspicious. With the steady hum of conversations and people walking to and fro, they could talk freely. Just two old acquaintances catching up over dinner.

"I appreciate your making the arrangements Colonel—I knew I could rely on an old friend," De La Fuente said.

"Come now Felipe—we both know I owe you a debt."

"Indeed," De La Fuente said. "It's worth repeating—there was never any judgement on my part. For God's sake, I've operated a brothel for 30 years. 'Let those without sin cast the first stone.' Yours was a regular occurrence—no need to feel shame."

"Not shame Felipe—resentment. You can't blame me for having been suspicious of your involvement in the matter. The sordid affair begins and ends at your brothel—the inestimable Madam Josefina—your very close associate— sent me upstairs with one of your finest looking ladies, I was stupidly drunk from the several whiskeys that came my way free of charge, and in the midst of things we're joined by a young man I'd thought was a waiter—not a prostitute."

"You'd been flirting with him all evening, Colonel. I recognised the sentiment and thought you'd appreciate the gesture. You can trust me—I'd never meant for it to go that far. When I heard about the blackmail note, you received, I knew exactly who it came from. I had Vicente look after the matter. He won't bother you again, I assure you. But do my methods trouble you?"

"Au contraire Felipe. I have a lot to lose—my military title, my wife's affluent family and the inheritance, the children. All for a night of debauchery in the most reputable—or should I say disreputable—fleshpot of Buenos Aires," he laughed raising his glass of draught beer and clinked De La Fuente's glass.

"You deciphered my telegram without too much trouble?"

"I've made the arrangements. These men have no connection to Argentina and no interactions with the anarchists in Spain, so they won't be recognised," Gimenez said, putting a forkful of fish into an already full mouth and speaking in spurts. "For the sake of my good conscience, however, I want to warn you what kind of men they are—former infantry soldiers of the Barcelona regiment and bloodied veterans of the war in the Philippines. A sergeant and two privates. All three of them were dishonourably discharged over a scandal the army managed to keep quiet. A man disappeared—the son of a French diplomat—last seen drinking in a tavern with these men. He was later found in a shallow grave—multiple stab wounds. There was no evidence tying them to the grave, but when they were interrogated by the Municipal Guard, they didn't quite get their stories straight. A couple of years of hard labour for dishonourable conduct was the best the military could do, and then the discharge."

"Since then, they've been doing unsavoury jobs at mining operations within our zones of influence in North Africa. I'm told they've been useful making troublemakers disappear when strikes get out of hand. The military attaché that covers the protectorate is a friend of mine. He deals with them directly. I thought of them when I got your telegram. They've progressed in their professionalism—but spirits are their downfall—like many of us."

"Indeed," De La Fuente said, raising his glass to the Colonel, thinking of the problems that streetwise mercenaries, acting in the capacity of clandestine agents, could resolve for him. Foremostly, his department's inability to infiltrate the inner circles of the anarchists. It was the circles that promulgated acts of terror, that concerned him. On two occasions, he and Vicente had the novel idea to use young trainees, men that had never been seen in uniform, and sent them into the heart of the beast.

The first had grown contemptuous and indiscrete after only a few weeks, and was spotted drinking in a tavern frequented by police. He was followed home and beaten within an inch of his life by two surly dockworkers using lead pipes. They left him sitting slumped against a whitewashed wall and painted the word Policia above his head with his own blood.

In search of payback, off-duty police officers wielding trudgeons then raided a tavern frequented by dockworkers and beat any man found within—message received.

For De La Fuente and Vicente, the incident only provided unwanted publicity.

They'd put more thought into the second attempt—lodging the officer in a tenement and having him apply for union jobs, before sending him into the waiting arms of the halls, the rallies, and the study groups. He'd found employment as a baker, and since he listened attentively when others talked, he was a likeable sort. Things were progressing spectacularly well, until the young officer fell in love with his boss's daughter. She'd snuck him into her father's bedroom and he confessed all of his sins to her during a passionate encounter. She promptly whispered an embellished account of those very same sins into the ear of the lead baker during a similar romantic encounter later that day.

Unfortunately for the love-struck young officer, the lead baker was also an enforcer for the district baker's syndicate. The officer was also beaten within an inch of his life, the lead pipes exchanged for rolling pins, and his misadventure is now gleefully recounted in police friendly taverns with a curious mixture of respect, disgust, and hilarity.

Following this incident, they gave up on infiltrating anarchist circles, and reverted back to traditional bribes, threats, or beatings to squeeze information from those in the know. But this sort of intelligence was superficial, and unreliable more often than not. It brought the Senator's warning to mind, 'It will be you that is held responsible Felipe.'

However, giving the task to former hardened soldiers, relying only on themselves when things went bad—that was another matter. They could operate without legal or moral constraints—at the very heart of things.

De La Fuente supposed they didn't really need a military background. But there was another reason he wanted that particular skill set, affirmed by the Senator during their conversation on the ship. He'd heard grumblings circulating amongst the other district commissioners. President Quintana had decided that a former military officer would be appointed as the next chief of police. It was odd that the executive power would do the choosing, and not the minister of the interior. But the absolute loyalty of the chief was essential for the political survival of a President, in a country where coup d'états were always a real possibility. So be it, De La Fuente resigned himself. But President Quintana was known to be deathly ill, and the Vice President Jose Alcorta would succeed him, and likely institute another change. Who would he appoint—another soldier? Or a man from the rank and file? De La Fuente felt his bad leg throbbing from the September humidity that gripped Madrid. Soldiers had tried to kill him. If the Senator failed to come through, and if President Alcorta also decided to appoint a former military officer, De La Fuente had no quandaries about killing a military officer. The chief of police was the perfect target for an anarchist.

Colonel Gimenez was talking, bringing De La Fuente back to the present. "They will want reassurances regarding financial compensation. I told them the money would be deposited in a bank, here or over there, whatever's expedient. They'll undoubtedly raise this point with you."

"They'll want top dollar for what I have in mind and I intend to see they get it—what they believe to be top dollar that is. A police salary, sergeant level. They won't be able to use it during the operation—they'll have to make their own money in one of the factories or whatnot. But they'll have themselves a nice little nest egg when they finish.

The bloody paupers will think they've struck it rich."

Chapter 3
An Unconventional Young Woman

Sofia Montserrat eased her mare into a canter on the cattle path leading to Jerez de la Frontera, 10 kilometres to the west of the family estate. The dawn sun was peeking up behind her, warming her back. She had a long day ahead, starting with a meeting with the local farm workers' union representative, as she needed to hire seasonal labourers to harvest their fields. She was determined to avoid the previous year's acrimony, when the union had threatened a strike unless better wages were offered. The union had a strong negotiating position, as excellent crop yields and high prices had been profitable for the estate owners.

Believing the owners would panic if they thought their crops wouldn't get harvested—the union overplayed its demands. Sofia had been forced to offer the work to a union representing Arcos de la Frontera, a village to the east. She'd cursed herself when three villagers were ambushed and brutally murdered on the road, returning home from the harvest. The Civil Guard had investigated the incident, and claimed it was the work of anarchists, who had left a warning note on the corpses. But Sofia believed it had been a spiteful act of vengeance, as opposed to an ideological statement.

Sofia had discussed the meeting with her father at dinner the evening before. Her mother had reached across the table and grasped her father's hand fondly.

"This is what the education of our daughter has resulted in. It's a good thing you listened to me. She was the best in her class in arithmetic—after all, she had to beat the boys."

"Of course, I listened to you, my dear—and then I gave her responsibility for the affairs of the ranch—where she could apply her education."

"Listen to the two of you. It was I who insisted that I continue my studies. And father it was I who insisted I come along with you. You needed someone that could negotiate and not fold so easily. Then both of you tried to marry me off to a lout that couldn't even read. The buffoon would have insisted I stay at home, raise children, and shut my mouth."

"Is that so bad?" Her father asked. "We do wish to be grandparents someday."

"That day is still a long way away—I have much to accomplish first."

"Maybe you have a little too much on the go," her mother had said, hoping for any sign of domestic ambition and receiving none.

It was true Sofia was eternally pressed for time. She practically ran the estate. With occasional guidance from her father, she managed the operations of the permanent ranch hands. She met with the foreman Rodrigo every day to organise their work. Old Rodrigo had been there since she was a little girl and had readily adapted to her practical style of management. There was always something to do with their cattle, be it calving, branding, driving them to auction, or those that were ready, to the abattoir in Jerez.

But their wheat fields were tended by temporary workers, and their numbers depended on the season. To hire them, she dealt with their union representatives in Jerez, men that had openly declared themselves as anarchists. They had become more sophisticated in their negotiations, and took into account the state of the crops, the prices they fetched on the market, and the crops importance to the financial health of the estates. But this was fine with Sofia. They'd had several productive seasons, and she was happy to see conditions improving for the workers and their families.

If that wasn't enough, she still practiced every other day with the Jerez flamenco troupe led by the gypsy woman Mirella, who she'd also known all of her life. To save time, she stayed at her grandfather's apartment in Jerez, although he had now passed.

He had been a perceptive man, critical of the backwardness of their rural province, and had encouraged Sofia to study and think more deeply about things. But he was gone now, and before falling asleep in the empty apartment, she missed the conversations she'd had with her grandfather, and his kindred rebel spirit.

She harboured grand aspirations, unleashed by a challenge from her grandfather three years ago. After supper one night, he'd shuffled to his habitual resting place, a Victorian-style, leather-covered chair, having adapted a matching end table as his footstool. He'd been reading the daily newspaper El Correo, the

Mail. His bovine snort distracted Sofia from her handbook she used to write down endless calculations and notes for the following day.

"What do you think of this dear Sofia? It appears that Australia—a British Commonwealth country—just held a national election in which women voted."

"And why would women vote in that country," she'd asked, with all sincerity.

"To have a say in who gets elected. When you have a say in politics, you can change things—sometimes."

Nightly consumption of her grandfather's daily paper ensued, along with spirited debate, her grandfather not letting any ill-founded opinions escape scrutiny. She had just turned 21 years old and had discovered yet another endeavour to throw herself at.

"Would you mind if I read my newspaper before you tear it to pieces?"

"I would mind because you're too slow," she'd teased.

"Alright—give me the financial section and I'll let you read your headlines. What are you looking for?"

"Any articles on women's suffrage. There hasn't been one for a while. I've thought about it a lot. I would like to be able to vote."

"Then you'll have to change things. Perhaps you should write an article yourself."

With that remark, the beast was set free. She started with a flurry of letters to the suffragette idols of the day, proclaiming her loyalty to the cause. A letter, poorly addressed, to the Women's Christian Temperance Union was returned to sender. A more carefully addressed letter to the International Woman Suffrage Association went unanswered.

Individually addressed letters to Britain and America were similarly met with silence. As a means to emulate the firebrands she read about, leading the charge overseas, she moved on to other strategies. Twice she was featured as the guest of honour for early grade school classrooms at her former school in Jerez. But when parents complained of the radical ideas she was engendering in their children, the school principal intervened.

"Perhaps you could change your radical tone—our school's conservative parents are resistant to ideas of change. They might be less concerned if the children weren't so young. Why don't you speak to the older classes?"

She'd fought back. "If I speak to the older classes, there will be less girls to listen to me—won't there? In fact, there might not be any girls at all because the parents are too entrenched in their ways to keep them in school passed the sixth grade," she'd said, to a chastened principal.

Smelling victory, she continued. "How is that so radical—telling the girls to stay in school and learn arithmetic, rather than chase boys and get pregnant?"

Later, recounting her humiliating exchange with the principal to her grandfather, "Maybe it's your means of persuasion that needs refining." Upon which Sofia ruminated for the rest of the evening.

Next was the meeting, and it had to be a grand affair. She envisaged a parade of vocal women marching through the streets with placards and grim determination. She hadn't dared tack her posters over the anarchist propaganda, displayed on the wooden poles protruding from the earth in every part of the town and countryside. It seemed unwise to deliberately pick a fight with them. 'But the advertisement peg board at the bullring Plaza de Tores was perfectly reasonable,' she thought. Everyone went to the bullfights, and many women, would pass by it. The sitting room at their nearby family stable, if a little rustic, would do for a location.

She rehearsed in front of the bathroom mirror, much to the annoyance of an incontinent grandfather. But to her disappointment, while waiting nervously to give her speech, only two elderly ladies had shown, widows both. They weren't interested in a voting institution. They preferred to focus on re-instating the authority of the Catholic Church amongst the working class, who were breeding like rabbits.

"What's the matter with you?" Her grandfather had asked, noticing her agitation.

She was pacing back and forth, muttering to herself.

"It was a complete failure! The women are cowering in their houses—afraid to venture into the night and voice an opinion of their own. Those that showed—well I admit there was only two—failed to grasp my point. I think they were actually spying for the priest bishop, I'll hear it from him, I'm sure."

"This idea is new to the peasants and not their priority. It's year to year survival for them and they're still cynical about the universal male vote. It was hailed as a great step of progress. But most of the peasants can't even read, and don't pay attention to issues unless they're at their doorstep. So they don't bother voting, or, they vote for who the landowners they work for tell them to."

"What else can I do?" She'd asked in despair.

"Building support for women's suffrage will take time. But, remember that women will be considered a voting block. If a politician believes he will win an election on an issue supported by women, he will be very motivated to pass a law for women's suffrage. For example, if a politician is opposed to war for financial or moral reasons, all women—landowners and peasants alike—would be supportive of him. For the simple reason that they don't like to see their sons going off to war to get killed."

"And if they were able to vote against such wars—"

"I'm sure you'll encounter other important issues in which women could be unified as a voting block."

"Yes, I see!"

"The Catholic church is important—if you can convince them that women will vote for policies supported by it that would help."

"I haven't attended as of late. Every time I went, mother and father tried to introduce me to an eligible bachelor, with whose parents they had conspired behind my back."

"I'll say it again—why don't you write an article for the paper? The owner of The Mail is an acquaintance of mine and we talk after Sunday mass. Why don't we attend church together?"

But the meeting with the newspaper's owner was yet another disappointment for Sofia. She'd kept the article short and to the point. She'd asserted that the enlightened attitudes of New Zealand and Australia led to their extraordinary acceptance of women's political engagement, that Britain and America would most certainly follow suit, and that Spain would be next—reasons to follow in a forthcoming article.

"It's not the right content for our readers Sofia—nor am I convinced of your conclusion. This is all rather revolutionary—and we've enough radicals shouting for that already. Women are the purveyors of morality and pass our values on to our children. How can they do that if they're running around worried about business and figuring out who to vote for like the men?"

She hadn't the heart to argue with the old curmudgeon, she wasn't going to change his mind. However, he reinforced something her grandfather had said. 'Somethings that matter to women are not dependant on social status or wealth.' Well, the anarchists had wrangled control over the working-class peasants of Andalucia from the church, so what did the anarchists think about women's suffrage? It was time to find out.

At Mirella's flamenco salon, the old man with creased, sun-weathered skin, played a battered guitar while the dancers prepared and got blood flowing to their muscles. Sofia believed he was Mirella's husband, but nobody had ever worked up the courage to ask. He was their tacoar, who wrung dark-toned scales and sharp accents from his instrument that so inspired Sofia, helping her focus and put life's trivial distractions aside.

The tacoar's music overtook and consumed her very soul until she manifested its essence—duende—in turns of joy, dread, hope, anguish, and acceptance, through the sum of the elements of flamenco. Then, having churned this emotional array through her mind, she would sleep deeply within the security of her home and loving presence of her parents, and awaken renewed.

But this particular evening she resisted the call of the tacoar as she had a mission. She needed to get the attention of Manuel, in order to instigate a reconciliation of sorts. They had danced together for years, having both grown up dancing under Mirella's tutelage.

Manuel was a talented flamenco dancer, whose parents worked the farms ceaselessly in order to pay for his indulgences, for which he showed no gratitude whatsoever. But he was their best dancer by far, and was always a main feature of their show. He might be hard for Sofia to approach because all the other girls also wanted his attention, and more. He wouldn't get anything like that from her, but she needed to talk to him nonetheless.

The problem was that she'd loudly rebuked him once before, to his embarrassment, after he'd made a crass remark and an unwelcome lunge to kiss her on the lips. A stomp to his insole and a kick to the shin with her metal tacked shoes, made him yelp, and he'd limped away cursing her. But that was a few years ago, so why wouldn't he be open to a simple conversation? She'd heard him bragging about his older brother being an anarchist, who produced leaflets and newsletters to promote their ideas. She wanted Manuel to introduce her to him.

But since the incident he'd been contemptuous of her in public, and just ignored her if they were alone together. She supposed she had given him similar treatment, and now had a plan to change that. It rested on her reminding him she was his equal as a bailaor, a dancer. For a few years, she'd been happy to let other girls take prominence in the routines they practiced for their shows. But in the past she'd been his equal, and if she reminded him of such, he would treat her with due respect, she hoped, and they could talk.

Sofia wore her best practice skirt, a deep red, its bottom half comprised of four overlapping layers, each with a frilled edge. She added a white blouse with small polka dots that fell low on her shoulders, exposing her exquisite olive-toned skin, which she believed to be an attractive feature. 'He was a man and it wouldn't hurt to look her best,' she thought. The dress was loose enough so that it could be held high with her hands, and swished from left to right without going too high on the leg. She added a shawl, which she could use in similar fashion, pinning it to one side or the other, and discarding it at an opportune moment to feature her shoulders.

She started her routine, long since ingrained in her muscle memory, snapping her fingers in time, rolling her wrists through their fullest range, getting her taps going, adding toe heel flicks, and her eyes sought out Manuel, who was paying her no attention whatsoever.

She moved with practiced ease amongst the other dancers on the small floor. Each dancer knew to pass with enough distance that no unintended physical contact interrupted the rhythm of another dancer. There were silent acknowledgments as she moved amongst people that she'd danced beside for many years. She suddenly realized that she knew very little about their personal circumstances, although she had a deep understanding of each's sense of musicality and particular flamenco style. 'She would have to rectify that,' she thought, 'these were her people as well.'

On hearing the guitarist pick up the rhythm, she improvised a flutter of syncopated taps, executed a precise rotation of exactly 180 degrees to survey the floor, and was disappointed to find that Manuel had moved away from her. He'd somehow danced his way to the opposite side of the floor and had a flirtatious gaze going with a pretty teenager. She realized it had been a ridiculous plan, unlikely to succeed now or later. But she was feeling invigorated and decided to abandon it. Instead she let herself drift into the state of concentration required to produce flamenco, a trance that invoked an interplay of her spirit with the spirits of the other dancers and musicians.

Sofia watched from the corner of one eye as Mirella positioned herself beside the guitarist. His fingers weaved an intricate arpeggiated pattern using an exotic phrygian scale. Mirella lined the dancers along the outskirts of the floor with a wave and began chanting softly in the Romani dialect used by the gypsies of Andalucia. Commanded by a gesture of Mirella's arm, eyes or fingers, the dancers took the stage in ones and twos, practicing their entrances and exits. She was a puppet master, working their strings to combine their movements into a unified, mysterious force.

Waved off the floor, Sofia joined in the rhythmic clapping. Mirella increased the tempo by having the tacoar break into a more light-hearted song. There were longer solos now for the dancers, the men amongst them beginning to sweat profusely. It was the opportunity to impress one's peers amongst the cuadro, the troupe, spontaneous shouts of 'si' and 'hassa' indicating their approval and encouragement. Sofia was unusually animated, encouraging her fellow dancers, 'vamo ya!' with more enthusiasm than she'd felt for a long while.

After an hour of intense practice in which Mirella appeared possessed, the dancers felt the soreness and cramping in their calves and feet. They welcomed the transition into the slower song that typically marked the final dance of the practice, only to find they'd been cruelly duped by Mirella. The tacoar broke into an unexpected bulerias, the fastest flamenco tune, testing the determination of their young spirits.

Sofia took the stage, flicking and stamping her tap shoes, lifting her dress just enough to show off her footwork. Encouraged by the shouts of her fellow dancers, she continued front and centre, until the guitarist's fingers fluttered across the strings with percussive staccato, their crescendo coming to a stop, their breathing the only sound to be heard in the stillness.

"What the fuck are you doing Sofia? That donkey's ass is who you fall for? Five other single men your age on the floor—two of whom can read—one of whom is tolerable—yet you pick him?" Having singled out Sofia with a come-hither crooked finger.

"I need some information from him and I can't get his attention."

"And that is why you're trying to distract him?" Mirella barked at the guitar player to stop playing. "What do you need to know?"

Sofia now wondered why she hadn't thought to consult Mirella. Sofia admired her directness, and she seemed to know everything that went on in Jerez. "I have an idea—well it's quite radical apparently. I want our country to allow women to vote—"

"—Ha! Allow women to vote—why would we vote for cretinous politicians? They wouldn't know a horse's ass if it shit on their boots. Why would we give them the satisfaction?"

"Well said—but my goal is to be able to vote for women politicians as well. I want to meet with anarchists who are influential with the working people."

"Why?"

"I want them to publish an article I wrote. I want to see if the idea will gather support amongst working families."

"What does this have to do with Manuel?"

"His brother is an anarchist and publishes their newspaper. I don't know anything about him—where he lives, how to contact him, or even what his name is for heaven's sake. I want to ask him to publish my article and see what the peasant women think."

"Next time just ask me. I'll arrange it. His name is Francisco. He's a smart man—not like his brother. He can read."

"Mirella speaks highly of you Sofia. I was surprised to hear her say you had an impressive work ethic. I found it ironic speaking of the work ethic of an estate owner," Francisco said. He was wearing a fraying waistcoat, and had his shirtsleeves rolled up past a pair of skinny biceps.

Beads of perspiration dripped from his nose. It was hot in the small room, its space occupied mostly by the newspaper press, typesetting machinery and papers bundled together with twine. He lit a rolled cigarette, using up what was left of the breathable air. "We consider you a bourgeois oppressor. Why would you want to join us?"

"I have no intentions of joining you. However, I believe that we share a common goal. It's a benefit for everyone if we travel down the road to women's suffrage together—workers and employers alike."

He stared at her without expression, cigarette held expertly between his teeth, smoke bellowing from mouth and nostrils.

"Your project is—how shall I say this—offensive to me Sofia. Nobody speaks of women's suffrage around here—this is Andalucia. Most of the women are old-stock peasants. They cook, do laundry, and have babies when they're not tending the fields—and even then, they have babies. You want them to vote?" Sensing he'd upset his visitor, he added, "The men are no better. They can barely read. We have to keep the messaging simple," pointing to a pile of stacked, thin newsletters, two pages thick at best.

"I think they'll find a way to read what I have to say."

"That's possible." He gave in quickly, Sofia observed. "It would have to be placed behind other priorities. These farmhands already have a hard time understanding what is required without confusing them more—and their women grow suspicious the minute we mention revolution."

"Do you oppose the idea of women voting?" Sofia said.

He adjusted a pair of spectacles sitting crookedly on a Roman nose, revealing soft brown eyes like his brother Manuel's. "Your question is of fundamental importance. Section 9 of the Principles and Organisation of the International Brotherhood—speaks to political organisation. It proclaims complete equality of political rights for men and women, including universal suffrage—once we've achieved our ideal society. On the other hand, we'll only attain that society by violent revolution and for that we will need the assistance of women. But the idea of women voting prior to its establishment might distract us from other practical considerations. I'm probably overthinking this."

He started heaving bundles of newsletters onto shelves. "My colleagues might object. But I could convince them that it might help attract women to the cause."

Sofia waited patiently. She found his contrary nature and obvious intelligence endearing.

"What do you propose," he asked.

"I'll provide you with an article to publish in your newsletter. The Mail refused to publish it."

"You tried them?"

"It was the first place I went to."

"They're a daily—several pages thick. I publish a weekly, two to four pages at the most—most times two—and sometimes I don't publish at all if I don't have any content." He said, crushing the cigarette butt into the floor with a dusty boot. "I can't give you the same public exposure."

"I'm glad they refused to publish it. Since it's such a revolutionary idea it should be printed in an anarchist newspaper. I'm not afraid to ruffle feathers. In fact, that's exactly what I intend to do—and this will get you the support of your women!"

"I met with a man that publishes a newspaper grandfather. He's going to include my article," she said.

"Really? Well done. How did you convince him?"

"I appealed to reason," she said. "He's an anarchist, so his newspaper will be read by the peasants."

"Is that what you want to do—help the anarchists woo the peasant women into their cause? As I mentioned before, women are suspicious of revolutions, and I'm not sure we want to see that change."

"It's the only avenue I have at the moment—it seems that politics make for strange bedfellows."

Her grandfather laughed. "Indeed, it does Sofia." Then he grew serious. "Aren't you worried he could be dangerous?"

"He didn't seem like the dangerous type," she said. "He's very different from other men I've met. He's educated and dedicated to his cause. I wasn't expecting such a man to be from Manuel's family."

"He might not be dangerous, but he will know those that are. They've killed people you know."

"I'll be careful. This is my town as well grandfather. We've all grown up side by side, gone to school together at some point, and danced together in the halls. Think about the people from all walks of life that my flamenco troupe has entertained—and the different backgrounds of the dancers. There's no need for me to be afraid of anyone."

"That's very true—you've done well Sofia," he said, and promptly fell asleep in his leather chair.

Meeting Francisco for the second time, she found herself fussing with her hair and straightening her dress. It was unusual for her to be concerned about her appearance. He'd been waiting for her, and on this occasion, he too had made efforts to improve his appearance. Hair combed with pomade, almost holding a recalcitrant forelock in place, a fresh shirt under his tattered waistcoat. It smelled a little better in the claustrophobic space she noted. Then it dawned on her what was happening, and she fought off the unwelcome romantic distraction— annoyed at herself.

"Here's the article. It's a very concise version. Exactly what I submitted to the Mail."

"Let me see."

Their fingers touched briefly when she passed him her typed article, and her eyes met fleetingly with his in response. 'Dear Lord, what's happening to me? Pull yourself together foolish woman!'

"Is this it?"

"Yes," she said, sensing his disappointment. "Is something wrong?"

"It's too short. Look at the space I have for you," pointing to an empty block of the typeset mould. "If you're truly serious, go home and write some more."

"I can put the typeset in place right now—I know exactly what I wish to say."

Four weeks, eight visits, and three articles later, Sofia found herself in the first official affair of her young life. She'd had a couple of romantic trysts a few years ago. Boys and girls in her flamenco troupe had reached the age where their respective hormones produced shocking physical events. The teenagers had split into two separate encampments—girls versus boys. They dared each other to cross to the other side and attempt manoeuvres on a sliding scale of seduction: a kissing on the lips or the neck, 'Use your tongue Manuel,' groping across advancing levels of intimacy, 'do you even know how babies are made, you moron?' Achievements were subsequently compared for bragging rights.

Sofia herself had been attracted to a funny boy, gangly and not very confident. She had lured him into the hayloft at her parent's stable near the bullfighting arena. Later, she'd described the wondrous encounter as an experiment to her horrified mother, who'd discovered red hickeys on her neck and above her breasts. Her furious mother put a swift end to the experiment, in order to prevent a more fulsome encounter, through an emergency message and intervention by their family priest.

Her affair with Francisco was different. The many kilometres she rode to and from the Montserrat Estate were filled with thoughts of their last tentative embrace, and of the next to come. Francisco was a warrior ideologue for the under-privileged, someone she could admire for that quality alone, except that he also listened to her intently, encouraged her, contradicted her, consoled her. 'Do you expect this to happen tomorrow Sofia? It will need a decade. But every day that you do nothing—that decade is extended by that day if not more.'—to her riposte, 'Do you think women aren't interested in voting? They're told as children that their only concern is to raise a family. Give them hope for a career, and they'll stay in school. If they stay in school, they'll read. If they read, they'll want to vote.'

Francisco was a man with a vision of a better future, and if that vision wasn't exactly shared, the need for change certainly was. Although, 10 years her senior, Sofia's mind was equal to the task, and they now found reasons to extend the length of her visits.

When she exhausted her stable of far reaching-hopes, Francisco stepped in with tales of revolutionary brotherhood. He was neither hurt nor offended by her unyielding scepticism.

Wanting no more favours from Francisco, she would don her pinafore, hitch up the sleeves of her blouse, and lend a hand on the production line. Content received, start typesetting. Typeset done, justify margins. A final proofread— roll the press and mimeograph copies. At times, she would anguish and lose confidence, but Francisco was there in those moments. 'Francisco—I can't get it right!' He would hold her head and look into her eyes, 'Keep trying. It will come to you, Sofia.'

With each visit—another talk, another tentative embrace, a brush of the lips, and a stolen kiss before tearing themselves apart, 'We can't!'

Until it all came undone, bursting through their long simmering desire, on a makeshift bed of blankets lay over the small square of rubble floor lying fallow in the corner. Afterwards, enjoying the smell of Francisco's rolled, brown tobacco cigarette against a cocktail of cooling lead, ink, oil, and dust—naked with her knees tucked in her arms and leaning into his chest under the single blanket, she gazed up at the byzantine machinery casting ugly shadows by the light of their candles, and thought it had been perfect.

"I want you to meet my colleagues, tomorrow evening. They're bringing articles for the newsletter that couldn't be sent by telegraph."

"What are they like?"

"They're dedicated members of the brotherhood. They will expand your bourgeois perspective Sofia."

"Are they atheists?"

"Yes."

"What will they think of me? Won't they be hostile?"

"No—they're open-minded individuals."

"You weren't exactly open-minded when I first approached you."

"I've learned something from you Sofia—to be open-minded. You'll need to persuade them of the utility of your endeavour if you want to continue with your articles. They're the final decision makers when it comes to editorial direction. But I think that you'll be able to convince them, and it will make it easier for me."

Sofia wasn't sure what she thought about atheism, or going so far as to officially reject the church, as those in the international brotherhood were required to do. All of the Montserrat family were either truly devout, or at least moderately, like herself. They attended church regularly, favouring the grand cathedral where the head priest presided. She told herself compromises had to be made to further her cause, however, she didn't want to harm anyone in the process. That was her line in the sand—and she would make sure of it.

Convince them she did. Sofia had honed her ability to rationalise and explain her best ideas through countless hours of discussion with Francisco. They'd dispensed of the outliers, and separated the wheat from the chafe. In a word, education. It needed to be universal across class, age, and include girls as well as boys. Francisco's purist colleagues couldn't argue with that, it fit perfectly with their utopian dream.

'I'm making sense and they're listening!' They nodded their heads in agreement here, disagreement there, exasperated sighs and rubbing of temples. Finally, worn down by her persistence, 'It's highly unorthodox, but does anyone adamantly oppose a partnering of class opposites, for the practical purpose of bringing women's suffrage to the fore?'

But my goodness, nothing is that easy Sofia. How can we trust you not to betray us? Will you sell us out to the authorities that have us under constant surveillance, paying their spies with the devil's silver? 'It's a metaphor—I'm an atheist.' What do you tell your family? Who do they tell after that? We don't wish any harm to befall your beloved grandfather Sofia but there are hotheads within our ranks. And what of your church? History's abound with its cunning and abject cruelty. You can be part of this circle for the purposes of this one cause only Sofia—for your own good as well as ours.

Our decision? A firm maybe Sofia. For such serious men, they were incredibly indecisive. They had asked her to wait outside while they convened in private. All in favour say aye. Aye! But—there's a condition. It's a compromise Sofia. We can't be observed openly associating with someone of your bourgeois class. We could lose the hard-won farm workers unions to the socialists and that—dear Sofia—is out of the question. No articles can be written by Sofia Montserrat, heiress to the exploitive Montserrat Estate, rallying our anarchist women to her cause. You'll have to use an alias. It can be of the female persuasion, but it must reflect the views of the international brotherhood. What say you?

It was as easy as that. A deal was done, the consequences of which she couldn't imagine. 'I agree!' Sofia went home to the apartment late again, a plate of cold supper waiting on the table, a snoring grandfather slumped in his chair. She shook his arm gently to wake him and cajoled him to bed. She ate her supper under the dim glow of a single lantern. She looked at the mahogany escritoire that had accompanied her from the estate to the apartment, at which she'd spent countless hours on reading assignments and math tables.

More recently, it was where she spent her time accounting for her father—cattle, horses, sheep, ranch hands, farm labour—costs, wages, feed, slaughter—profits. It had also served as her place of solace, thoughts, and dreams. She looked at the black and white photograph in its weathered wooden frame, Mirella the profane gypsy woman, chin held high and clapping, a group of dancers and musicians posing in a line. She started to write.

That was two years ago. Now, nearing the stables in Jerez, she pushed her mare to a canter while trying to take her mind off the events of the past. Her grandfather was gone now. Last night, she and her father had worked out the number of field labourers they would need for the seasonal harvest. It was the highest number ever as they were enjoying another bumper crop year and expected high prices for their goods. The ranching operations could run under the supervision of old Rodrigo, they were not her worry for the moment. The sun rose higher in the east, warming the morning air, final few moments of tranquillity before her work.

Again, her mind drifted back in time. Two events had put a stop to her arrangement with the revolutionary anarchist cell of Jerez that published the newspaper. In retrospect, the first was less concerning than the second, an event she reckoned likely happened to many women with matters of the heart.

It had been foreshadowed by an oddity during the flamenco practice at Mirella's studio. Catching her eye, Manuel had cast her a look of utter contempt, something he'd never done before. 'What's this now?' The contemptuous look had preceded a refusal to take the stage with Sofia, and Mirella had waived another man in, with a stream of profanity.

Later Sofia had cornered him. She was not one to let such behaviour pass. "You missed your chance to show me up Manuel. Did I scare you away?"

"You're nothing but a cheap whore! I won't share the floor with you anymore."

"Be careful little man, I'll slap your face and stuff your mouth with horse dung. Is that how you treat a woman?"

"Does my brother Francisco treat you differently?"

Sofia was instantly deflated. She and Francisco had agreed to keep their relationship a secret. "What did he tell you?"

"He didn't tell me anything. His wife is at home all day and evening with their children. He never comes home anymore. She asked me to check on him. I saw you two together so don't say it isn't true."

"He has a wife and children?" Sofia asked softly, her world disintegrated to pieces. 'How very naive of me.'

As hurtful as the first event had been, the second was destined to be far less forgiving. Her path of recovery from the anguished spell cast by Francisco's betrayal, lay in throwing herself with even more abandon than usual, at the three pillars of her existence; the estate, the flamenco, and her cause. A teary-eyed Francisco had been mocked by his anarchist companions when he suggested that their association with Sofia be discontinued, after she'd broken off their affair.

'Really, Francisco? Marital fidelity is so bourgeois—you have nothing to be ashamed of. We were happy to see you enjoy a little freedom from the yoke of your marriage. That's our goal—liberty! You were miserable—Sofia's feminine charm cheered you up. There's no question of expelling her we're afraid.' Her cause was too important to let Francisco's duplicity stop her, and she insisted that their alliance continue.

'Resuming their search for her nom de plume with a suitable cloak of symbolism, their suggestions became comical,' Sofia thought. The Vanguardess, 'Is that even a word?' A Free Woman, Woman of Liberty', 'I'll take either of those two,' Queen of Fire, 'Too Sturm und Drang for me.' In the end, they were generous enough to give her the final decision.

"A Free Woman it is."

Several editions later, Sofia was desperate for feedback from somebody— anybody! She thought it might be easy to approach some of those employed on the estate. "And what did you think of the anarchist weekly this time around?" to the lead ranch hand, old Rodrigo.

"I can't read very well Miss Montserrat so I can't comment on it myself."

"What about your wife—does she read it?"

"Our children keep her very busy when she's not doing laundry or work in the fields. She doesn't have time to read such things."

"But she can read?"

"I don't think so. She never went to school at all."

This had only made Sofia more determined. Having gradually resumed a normal working relationship with Francisco, she let her curiosity overcome her.

"What have you heard Francisco? What are the women saying?"

"It will take more time Sofia. The workers have very basic lives. Just getting through one of their days is a lot of work. From what I can tell, chasing several children around is exhausting enough. It would be a rare sight to see one of the peasant women reading a newspaper."

"What does that do for your revolution if most of your intended audience can't read? What about your wife—does she read?"

"Is it necessary to speak about my wife?"

"You have a beautiful wife Francisco, and she was smart enough to marry you. I'm asking earnestly—does she read the newsletter?"

"Yes."

"What does she think?"

"She likes your articles. She gets very excited about them—you should continue."

That was all Sofia needed. If just one woman had taken interest in her articles, there would be others.

The event that reversed Sofia's fortunes occurred a year later. Articles by a Free Woman, were creating a mild stir amongst the region's women, peasants and property owners alike. Sofia was excited to learn that the main anarchist press in Madrid, La Ravista Blanco, had a small cohort of female contributors, whom she followed, although she didn't care for their tone. Doing away with the marriage contract seemed like an open invitation to men to father children without any obligations, and be happily on their way. No matter.

Sofia penned a harsh critique of the directive emanating from the recently formed Ministry of Education, which required children to attend school up to age nine. She decided to attack the policy from two angles. The age should have been set higher, to master the necessities of reading and arithmetic. Countering the tiresome logic of the rural peasants who advised that their children didn't require education to sharpen a hoe, she suggested educated children would help the family bargain the prices of goods and labour, and negotiate their rents.

Next, she'd suggested that landowners be fined if children under the age of 14, were found toiling their fields or shovelling the manure in the barns. The age was much higher than the present standard, and most significantly included girls. Sofia aimed to upset the sensibilities of both the property owners, by suggesting they should face fines, and the peasants by reducing their ability to collect wages as a family unit. 'That should get them thinking.'

Sofia had the hand-written article in her leather bag, creased and stained from exposure to scorching sun and torrential rains, which she slung over her neck while riding. She tethered her horse at the stable, and walked several streets to the building that housed the small newsletter press. Her mind had been on the impending discussion she would have with Francisco, wanting the article to be prominent in the weekly. 'Is the front page too much to ask, for a change?'

"Second page, Sofia. It's the best I can do. Madrid is ambivalent on the utility of your views. They give me an earful every time."

"Will you read it?"

"Of course—"

The door had burst open, and three men of the Civil Guard rushed in. They were holding clubs, ready to strike anyone that resisted.

"Mother of Jesus! What is going on?" Sofia hadn't been able to restrain herself.

One of them went straight for Francisco, another began searching through papers. A third remained at the doorway.

"This is the place Captain. That's a press."

"I can see that for myself. What's your name?" Looking directly at Sofia.

"Sofia—Montserrat."

"Dear Lord—of the Montserrat Estate?"

"Yes."

"I didn't recognise you—you've become a woman. What are you doing here with this man," he said, looking at Francisco contemptuously, who was pinned against a wall with a truncheon across his throat. Francisco was too terrified to speak and was having difficulty breathing.

She looked at Francisco, worried that whatever she said would get him into trouble. Then she decided that neither of them had done anything wrong. Certainly not enough to deserve such treatment by the Civil Guard. "Why should I tell you that? Who are you and why are you here?"

"My name is Captain Rafael Dominguez. I'm in charge of gathering criminal intelligence for the region of Andalucia. My job is to know every anarchist in my jurisdiction—it's been that way since the killings. We're quite familiar with

Francisco—he publishes our favourite newsletter. We read every edition. We've been watching this place for a while. Nobody we ask seems to know who this writer is, a Free Woman. It's a complete mystery. I suppose it's you?"

"That's none of your business."

"I just told you it was." Losing his patience, he waived at one of the enlisted men who grabbed her bag from her hands. "Check inside of it!" The enlisted man opened it and pull out a sheet of paper.

"What does it say?"

"I don't know—I can't read."

"Idiot! Give it to me." He read it to himself, and laughed at the soldier. "How ironic. It says children need to learn how to read—by God I completely agree with you!" He circled her malevolently. "I know your parents. I went to school with your father and his brother. Do they know you're an anarchist?"

"I'm not an anarchist."

"But you write for their newspaper?"

"Yes"

"So, you're the author a Free Woman?"

"Yes."

"Good—mystery solved. We can keep this incident between us if you like. There's no need for me to tell them, is there?"

Sofia thought of her parents. Why hadn't she told them? Because they simply wouldn't understand, and she couldn't ask them to. The estate owners were the declared enemy of the anarchists, who were the union representatives. She'd accompanied her father many times to bargain with the union for their field workers. Sometimes ill will had ensued, and she and her father had been cursed, sometimes they'd been threatened. Her father would feel betrayed.

"No—there's no need to tell my parents. Let him go—you've accomplished your business here," she said. With that decision, Sofia could hardly complain publicly of receiving ill treatment by the authorities.

She'd nevertheless continued to write her articles under the pen name a Free Woman. Nothing more had seemingly come from the encounter. The previous night she'd had discussions with her father about the state of the fields—how much grain they would yield, the prices they expected to command, the wages paid the year previous—and they'd worked out a range of potential wages around which to negotiate.

They would offer more than last year, a gesture of good will to the peasants, the landless field workers who lived hard lives. They could afford it as crop prices were up. She was looking forward to meeting the union agent in the town square.

It had been time well spent with her father Antonio, time that they'd both enjoyed together, ever since her father had discovered her mercantile talents to his immense relief. "I'm so very proud of you—your mother and I are both so very proud of you and we love you," he'd said, and given her a rare, heartfelt embrace. "Good luck tomorrow—the negotiations are in your hands."

But she would be dining with her parents again that evening, and so would have to make the ride back later. They were having a special supper for her father's brother, her Uncle Hugo. He'd made a trip from Argentina, where he was a Senator. 'An actual politician!' They wanted her to meet him and she was excited to do so. Her father and him would be in discussions during the day to finalise inheritance matters, following the passing of her grandfather six months ago. Considering he was living so far away; they were willing to pay out his portion of the inheritance. They hoped he would accept their offer, as it would simplify the proceedings considerably.

Chapter 4
Anarchists of Jerez

Having bid De La Fuente goodbye at the train station, Hugo Montserrat planned to stay in the port city Cadiz until he was ready. His parents had moved from their inland ranch estate to Cadiz to benefit from the cooler daytime temperatures owing to its proximity to the ocean, and it was where his mother had spent her final years. But his reason to stay was not sentimental. He had business to take care of, part of which was to assess the value of an inheritance. His father had grown lonely after Hugo's mother had passed away, and he had moved back to the town of Jerez de la Frontera to be closer to the Montserrat ranch and the family. He'd shared a small apartment in Jerez with his granddaughter Sofia, Hugo's niece, whom he'd never met.

To his knowledge, she was still living in the apartment now that his father had died, freeloading. His older brother Antonio lived on the estate with his wife Maria. Staying in Cadiz was a precaution, far enough away to discreetly conduct his inquiries.

Although, he'd received many letters from his parents over the years since he'd been sent to Argentina, he'd never responded. His consuming bitterness over their betrayal of him remained even after three decades. His father had arranged for him to apprentice at a ranch on the southwest frontier of the province of Buenos Aires, with a former military acquaintance who needed a stout ranch hand that could shoot a rifle. It was an unforgiving life. He'd survived the long-running battles between the ranch owners that supported opposing candidates for governor. The battles seemed to alternate with the night raids conducted by the Ranqueles Indians under the feared Chief Calfucurá. 'They hoped I'd be killed!'

His father had told him his strength was in ranching, that he knew Hugo would do well if he stuck to that. 'That was true,' he thought. He loved everything about ranching growing up on the Montserrat Estate—the calving season, the auctions, and herding the cattle to the abattoir. Unlike his sentimental brother Antonio, he wasn't bothered by the slaughter. He never grew attached to their animals. He'd been resentful when Antonio pulled him away from the grisly scene, 'Quit watching! You like seeing them die don't you.'

His father had let him breed bulls—the particularly aggressive kind for the bullfighting arenas in Jerez, Seville, and Grenada. It was the only thing his father had gotten right about him. Unlike his brother, he needed to work with his hands, remembering his envy of his brother's business acumen and his head for mathematics. Hugo had not been good at math, compounded by deliberate absences from school, and business had bored him. But his outlook changed drastically when he arrived in Argentina, where he realised that land ownership meant wealth, and with wealth came power and respect.

On the other hand, Hugo was devout, which pleased his mother. He was always keen to report his sins to the priest in Jerez so that he could be absolved, pay his penance, and then forget about them. Confession helped diminish his fears, notably of a recurring nightmare where he was trapped in a room on fire, with no doors or windows. 'Hell!' The confession ritual was a welcome solace to the teenager who was otherwise loath to express his emotions.

It was at church that he'd met Maria. She was a local anomaly, well-educated for a woman in Spain, 1875. He'd been smitten. When he'd mustered the courage to blurt this out to her, she'd been contemptuous. "I could never love you Hugo. I need a man closer to me in faith and intellectual development," she'd said. He'd made himself vulnerable to the statuesque beauty, and she had scorned him. Later, Hugo realised she'd been referring to his brother.

The more he thought of her rebuke, the more he fantasised of her supplication to him. Submissive and eager to please, like the 15-year-old daughter of some local peasants had been. She'd gotten pregnant, and a confrontation between the offended parents and his own ensued. His mother had been shocked and humiliated, his father only slightly less so. Arrangements for a discrete allowance were made on the condition they kept the arrangement a secret. The priest had been sympathetic and forgiving during confession. God forgave him.

His anger rose as he thought about his final year on the Montserrat ranch. At 18 years old, he was still young in mind, in body a grown man, and physically daunting. The conflicts between the two brothers had gradually begun to boil over. Having put on muscle over the year, he was waiting for the right opportunity to put Antonio in his place, and wipe the smug smile from his face.

The final humiliation for his father occurred when Hugo had drunk too much wine at the supper table, and became brooding and unruly. Joyous talk of the pending wedding between his brother and Maria sparked his temper, and he'd made a crass joke pertaining to Maria's virginity. His brother immediately punched him in the jaw, which left him dazed on the floor. Hugo got up and rushed at his brother like a raging bull. Antonio deftly sprung away from his path and struck Hugo again in the jaw, leaving him on his rear end.

This time he was unable to rise. His brother, who he considered to be mentally weak, had felt badly. Antonio lifted him up, slung an arm over his shoulder and dragged him to his bed. 'I'm sorry Hugo—I'm sorry!' He knew his brother loved him, but the harder Antonio tried to express his brotherly love, the more Hugo had despised him.

Remembering the incident that occurred over 30 years ago focused his rage. There was a lot to do in Cadiz before taking the train northward to Jerez de la Frontera and then a coach to the Montserrat Estate. With both his parents dead, its ownership was now in question. He needed to examine the will, a copy of which had been graciously forwarded to his lawyer in Cadiz. The letter he'd received from his lawyer compelling him to return to Spain, insinuated that a generous inheritance was due, to be split with his brother. But he had no intentions of sharing an inheritance.

He checked in to the hotel and watched closely as two bellhops in red jackets and matching pill box caps struggled to carry his trunk up the winding stairs to his room. He didn't want any of his precious cargo to disappear or be discovered.

The Senator paused at the door stencilled Abogados Señor Adelmo Vega and Associates, then went in. A curvaceous, middle-aged woman in a dark skirt and polka dot blouse greeted him, and led him to a boardroom decorated in Moorish styles. Dark hardwood panelling, scarlet carpets, and ornately carved mahogany chairs with lattice and inlaid mother of pearl lent an aura of sombre contemplation, 'a place for serious business.' There were two piles of legal documents stacked neatly on the table.

"I'm very sorry for your loss Senator," Vega said. "It must have been difficult to learn of the passing of your father while you were so far away."

"We weren't close."

Vega quickly moved on. "I've laid out the will for you. There's a considerable amount of reading, but I can take a few minutes and explain the salient points."

Montserrat nodded, opened the humidor of complementary cigars, and helped himself to one. He inserted it into a decorative cutter that looked like a small guillotine and watched the fine steel blade slice its end off cleanly.

"There's bad news and good news Senator. The bad news is that there are many valuable assets in the way of property, so it gets complicated. The good news is that there are many valuable assets in the way of property, so it gets complicated." His attempt at humour rebuffed by a dull stare, he continued. "You'll have to come to an agreement with your brother, and I'll await your instructions."

"My brother has a daughter of age—how does she fit in?"

"It's a moot point since the parents are still alive. However, there's a clause in the will that explicitly states she will inherit all of their assets and property in the case of their demise, being an only child—sometime in the future presumably."

"She's illegitimate—my brother's wife had intimate relations with another man during their marriage. He isn't aware."

"My God—how awful for him. That certainly could change things upon their death. But it has no bearing at this point."

"And if the daughter becomes a prostitute? Let's just say her real father doesn't come from reputable pedigree."

"You're well-informed of the civil code I must say. It addresses this very point—to encourage marriage and discourage immoral behaviour. The inheritance is very likely forfeit in such circumstances. It might be yours to claim if the daughter lost her way and turned to prostitution for some unfortunate reason—again, that's if you were to outlive them."

"I heard it was something like that," Montserrat said, blowing cigar smoke into his face, pleased with the confirmation. "Have your assistant fetch me a brandy while we go over it."

The lawyer nodded and sent her away for a brandy, as well as a small coffee for himself.

"Señor Vega—I presume our conversation is confidential?"

"Of course, Senator. I'm your legal counsel on this matter—bound by professional secrecy. Our communications are sacred."

"That includes your beautiful mistress." He watched Vega's face redden. He could always spot an affair. "Take me through it."

Hugo sat in the restaurant awaiting his guest. He looked longingly at the bottle of fine brandy he'd ordered, but was determined to keep it at the ready, to ply his guest. His childhood friend was now a ranking officer of La Guardia Civil, and he'd sent him a note at their headquarters to meet him. He recognised his friend Rafael Dominguez approaching the table in the distinctive uniform, a dark double-breasted tunic, leather holster and shoulder strap, and a black tricorn hat.

"How impressive my old friend—an officer of the guard," waving his hand up and down the uniform. He put a fatherly hand on his shoulder. "You've done well with yourself—Captain is it?"

"Yes—my God Hugo, it's been 30 years—and you're a senator now." They embraced in a manly hug, patting each other's back. "I was wondering if the death of your father would bring you back—and then I got your letter."

"I have a few things to clear up with Antonio and Maria."

"Is there still bad blood?"

"It's water under the bridge. I was too immature to appreciate the many talents of my older brother. There was too much pride and young blood flowing through my veins." It hurt him to give his brother praise.

"Come now—we can speak honestly between us. I saw him beat your brains out several times. Remember the day he found us in the hay barn with the peasant girls?"

"How could I forget," Hugo chuckled. "But he was only doing my father's bidding. I can't hold it against Antonio any more. As I recall, we both deserved a beating. We weren't supposed to be anywhere near those girls after the incident," moving his hand in an arc near his stomach to indicate a pregnancy.

"It's all forgotten now, and I'm spending a few days with them at the estate." Hugo watched Rafael closely, to see if he'd detected Hugo's insincerity. Satisfied, he poured them both a generous glass of brandy.

"Isn't brandy what always got us into trouble?"

"I'm in the company of an officer of the Civil Guard—who would dare put a stop to our shenanigans now?" Hugo said, noting the capillaries on Rafael's bulbous nose. Rafael emptied the glass in a single swallow. "So, did you marry one of those randy peasants' girls we used to frolic with—or did you nab yourself one of the reputable Catholic girls from our school?" Hugo already knew it was the latter.

"Yes, Therese. She has been a good wife and given me several children."

"A fine catch indeed—a beautiful, pious woman as I recall."

'She was a shrew.'

"I will love her to the end of my days," Rafael said, looking sad.

Hugo thought he must be feeling guilty for not being at home with her. 'She can't have you back just yet.'

"Here is to your wonderful family—may you have many grandchildren," refilling his friend's glass. "Join me for dinner. It would be my pleasure to buy supper for an officer of the guard."

"I'm famished," Rafael said.

Hugo had guessed correctly that he would accept. Even at the rank of Captain his wage would not be high. Nor would he have entered the police force had his family passed on any of its wealth to him.

"Tell me about your adventures in Argentina Hugo. How did you become so successful?"

"I landed in Argentina at a good time. My father's associate Luis Pedro looked after me, and my father had made some money available for me to buy land—and start a ranch of my own."

"The land was cheap?"

"There were deals to be had, but it wasn't as simple as that. Luis Pedro's ranch was on the frontier—100 miles to the west of Bahia Blanca—the closest town, and the Indian raids were fearsome. They hated the settlers who move into their territory. They attacked farmhouses and set them on fire. They killed the men—mutilated and burned their bodies. Sometimes they took women as prisoners. On Luis Pedro's ranch we carried rifles, and stood guard at night, if the moon was showing."

Rafael's eyes had grown wide. "Indians! Like they say in the newspapers?"

"Yes," Hugo said, hiding his bemusement at Rafael's ignorance of the world. 'He could be easily fooled,' Hugo thought. "Luis Pedro was a charming and persuasive man. Politicians often wanted his support. Roca—who later became President—came through our area. He was raising money to clear the plains of marauding Indians. He was issuing bonds to fund his expedition—against land that would be freed up for ranching. Luis Pedro got Roca's guarantee that he would get his pick of land near the railroad—which would become very valuable.

I invested all of my money into these bonds. And Luis Pedro rallied all the ranchers and farmers in the province of Buenos Aires to support the expedition."

"And it worked?"

"Yes—Roca moved his army into the area quickly by train, and the conquest took just two months. I was one of the first to obtain prime land before its value shot up. I left Luis Pedro's ranch when I married into another ranching family. Then Luis Pedro committed a foolish error."

"How so?"

"He betrayed Roca. Roca became so popular he ran for president. Luis Pedro supported his opponent, Governor Tejedor. But Tejedor misjudged the support Roca had obtained from other governors."

"How did this help you?"

Hugo smiled at him slyly. "I knew Roca was the choice of most governors. I pretended to support Tejedor and kept on good terms with Luis Pedro. He told me everything that Tejedor was planning. Then I went to Buenos Aires, and met with Roca's men. I warned them that Tejedor had armed supporters who planned to kill Roca. Roca's men moved him a few kilometres north to Belgrano with the national army. When Roca won the election, Governor Tejedor declared war. Luis Pedro sent his men to fight with Tejedor's militia, who held positions in the city. The national army attacked them and won—and I'd made a powerful friend."

"What happened to Luis Pedro?"

"He lost most of his men and suddenly found his access to bank loans dried up. But I now had access to loans from the national bank, as an expression of gratitude from the President. Eventually Luis Pedro had to sell his ranch before the sheep and cattle starved. I bought it very cheaply knowing how desperate he'd become. I also knew it would increase in value—it was situated on a natural land corridor that a railroad could be built on to access the pampas."

"That's very impressive, Hugo. I always knew you had a sharp mind for business affairs. Would you consider employing my two younger sons? There is nothing for them here—and I won't be able to give them much—if anything."

'This really was going well,' Hugo thought. "My friend," he said, with a hand held over his heart, "I would be honoured. You need just send them my way."

"How did you become a politician?" Rafael asked, now glassy eyed and starting to slur his words.

Hugo had only sipped on his own brandy. He needed to keep a clear mind. He was happy to kill time answering Rafael's questions. When he was drunk enough, he would answer Hugo's questions, and then forget them.

"I decided to enter politics once I realised it was the pathway to power and wealth. My connections in President Roca's government confided to me that they planned to offer land grants to foreign railroad construction companies. I knew from my experience with Luis Pedro's ranch what that meant for land values along any new railroad routes. I also saw how the politicians who were astute businessmen, profited from knowing such information in advance. So, I decided to run for congress."

"By then, I'd become a citizen and met the constitutional requirements to be nominated on the ballot. I met my future bride Camila at church while I was still working for Luis Pedro—and I managed to impress her father, who also owned a large ranch. Naturally, he asked me what my ambitions were."

"As any father would," Rafael said, nodding with approval.

"Precisely. I mentioned my interest in becoming the area's deputy in the congress. It had entered my mind when I met the representative myself and thought he spoke utter nonsense. The day I married my beloved Camila, my father-in-law arranged for my full citizenship through his lawyer. It was a quick process once the bribes were paid."

"I had wondered if you married—did you have any children?"

"Luck was not with me Rafael. Just one year later, my Camila was killed by Indians during a raid on our ranch. My heart and my dreams of a family died with her on that night." Hugo feigned a sorrowful countenance for this part of his story, as he'd done when he'd described it to the police and coroner from Bahia Blanca, and Camila's sobbing father. The account was only partly true. "She was their only child and I became like a true son to them afterwards."

"My God—the heathens!"

"Savages," Hugo said, recalling the horrific scene, and how happy it had made him.

"To assuage my grief, I threw myself into my political career," Hugo continued. "They were a fine, church going Argentine family—and knew the right people. My father-in-law convinced Governor Roche that I was the right man to represent his interests, and the province of Buenos Aires, in congress. I won the next election cycle as the deputy for Bahia Blanca. I moved to the city of Buenos Aires and learned quickly how to play the game, supporting bills that would increase my land values, and would keep Governor Roche happy."

Rafael was engrossed in his story. Hugo could read Rafael's mind—he was desperately trying to think of how he could benefit from Hugo's good fortune, which was exactly what Hugo wanted. So, he continued.

"I did two terms as a congressman, and became eligible for the senate when I turned thirty. When I won my position as a senator, I realised I'd obtained true power. I was now included in the President's meetings, and could influence his advisors. I was sought out by British railroaders who wanted to expand past Bahia Blanca, into the fertile prairie in the province of La Pampa. I threw my support behind all of the British railway endeavours who were expanding in every direction. Since I knew of their plans in advance, I took my pick of opportunities to buy land cheaply—before its value became known. The British really knew how to throw money around—which I admired," he said, winking at Rafael. "And attracting foreign capital to develop the country further was what the President wanted."

"But my biggest opportunity came with the new port—British money once again. Four docks in a row—allowing more ships to unload and load quickly. They would enter from the north and exit from the south. No need to turn them around. I saw right away that export volumes would increase significantly— beef, mutton, grain—all of it. So, with the support of the finance minister overseeing the national bank—who was also benefitting from land investments thanks to me—I obtained a large, low-interest loan. I built a new slaughterhouse and a meat packing factory close to the port and closed the loop on my ranching operations."

A quick topping up of Rafael's glass. "I was happy to deliver politically, you see, Rafael."

'Did the bumpkin see or not?' No matter, Rafael was enthralled and right where Hugo wanted him.

After their meal, Hugo led Rafael next door to the bar. "One more drink and then I'll let you return home to your lovely wife," he said, deciding Rafael was sufficiently inebriated to start plying him for the information he needed.

"What can you tell me about the unrest with the peasants I've been hearing about, Rafael?"

"Many troubling things have happened. A few years after you left—I had just joined the Civil Guard—anarchists arrived in our province. The peasants ate

58

their anarchist manure up like it was their dinner. Suddenly there were secret societies everywhere—meetings, talks, drinking and fights. They got themselves all riled up and started beating up landowners they ambushed along the roads. Then along came the Black Hand in Jerez and there were killings," he said, shaking a rigid hand comically, making Hugo laugh.

"The Black Hand! Sweet mother of Mary—revolutionaries?"

"Yes—and they had many members. They killed farmworkers who they thought had colluded with landowners and the priests. Then they killed a few of the smaller estate owners. We found some out—a cell of about eight men and women—and interrogated them until they confessed. We used the water cure. Myself and other junior men held their arms and legs—the old Sergeant forced their mouths open with his club and poured water over the mouth and nostrils— making them drink until they passed out. They were rolled over and would spew the water out. It seemed very painful and I was sickened—I was still naive and idealistic—but I understood it had to be done. They were murderers after all."

"I understand completely." Hugo suspected Rafael was embellishing the crimes in order to justify the torture. It affirmed that Rafael was still as gullible as ever, and the incompetency of the Civil Guard. "What did they tell you exactly?"

"They told us how they'd killed their victims. They told us that the farm hands had become anarchists. The arrests slowed them down for a while. There had also been a drought, and some of us thought that the lack of food was making them a little crazy. But the rains returned—there were good harvests and bellies were full again. Presto! No more Black Hand."

"That was a while ago you say?"

"A good 20 years ago. It had become dangerous to travel on the roads at night. There were robberies—killings if someone resisted. This improved with the disappearance of the Black Hand. But 10 years ago, the anarchists came back and organised an uprising in Jerez. They killed a tax man—no loss there—but then they also killed a wine salesman—and Hugo, between you and me," he said leaning in close, "nobody kills a wine salesman in my town."

He broke into laughter, and Hugo joined along. "We had to make an example of those responsible. There were five in total—four of which were put to death by way of the garrotte, and the last committed suicide the day before. I can't blame him—the garrotte is a brutal way to die."

"How are things now?" Hugo asked, soaking in every detail.

"Now the anarchists are sprouting everywhere. It's become the fashionable thing to do if you're a stupid young peasant trying to impress your friends—but even the old ones are joining in now. There are occasionally murders—with claims pinned on the corpse. They call this propaganda by deed, oppressors this, proletariat that—what I call revolutionary talk. They prefer this to strikes which—as you well know—are ineffective when there are always people desperate enough to work. Three times now there has been a murder of a landowner or their family. You'll need to be careful in Jerez after a certain time of night, dressed as you are. If they think you own a latifundio, a ranching estate—which Of course, you do—they might single you out."

"It's that serious is it?"

"I'm sorry to be the bearer of bad news."

Hugo smiled at him, and finally allowed himself a large swallow of his brandy. 'To the contrary, it's not bad news at all—just a few more seeds to plant into the idiot's head.'

"My brother's daughter—"

"—Sofia—she's quite a trouble maker."

"How so?"

"She's too smart for her own good."

"What makes you say that?"

"She stayed in school longer than the other girls, and it obviously went straight to her head. I told your brother he needed to watch her more closely—find her a good Catholic husband. My son was perfect for her. Antonio insulted me—said she was too smart for my son. She has funny ideas that no one likes—the authorities, the church, the other land owners—and she upset the apple cart when she proclaimed women need the right to vote. Can you imagine?"

"Good Lord. Where would she get such funny ideas?"

"She comes up with them all on her own. The owner of the Jerez newspaper told me that she'd submitted an article and wanted him to publish it on the front page. He refused her request of course—so she turned to the anarchists."

Rafael said nothing more, so Hugo prompted him. "Do you suppose this is why she began associating with the anarchists?"

"Yes—so that they would publish her funny ideas in their treasonous newspapers. We read them ourselves—to gather intelligence. El Anarquismo is the local one."

"Tell me—how has my brother fared with the anarchists influencing his workers on the estate?"

"Surprisingly well—the army has never had to intervene there. Even when we were forced to arrest all the working men in the village Estela—the year before last—he managed to find workers and avoid trouble."

That was not what Hugo had wanted to hear. "Maybe Sofia is the reason they haven't caused trouble at his ranch. Do you think my brother is in any danger?"

"I think any landowner is in danger. They're anarchists after all, and will stop at nothing."

"Indeed Rafael—indeed."

Chapter 5
A Trail of Breadcrumbs

The anticipation of seeing Antonio and Maria in his gunsights suppressed his usual fury whenever he'd thought about them before. He felt very alive, to the point his entire body was tingling, and he envisioned today's events with acute clarity. He'd reviewed every step of his plan during the train ride from Cadiz to Jerez de la Frontera. So far everything had gone in his favour, but there was still a couple of things he needed.

In his hotel room in Cadiz, he cleaned his guns, checking for rust from the voyage, and made sure the Mauser C96 pistol was functioning properly. Fascinated with the awkward looking weapon, he pulled back the slide repeatedly, working the spring and ejecting all six rounds held in the built-in magazine in front of the trigger guard. He examined each round, wiped it clean, and placed them in the stripper clip, a quick loading device, and reloaded the magazine. He prepared the stripper clip with six more rounds in case a reload was needed.

The 7.63 mm rounds travelled at high velocity, shattering when they struck bone, sending bullet fragments and bone shards chaotically into nearby vital organs, causing horrific wounds. It could be fired accurately and rapidly with a single hand. Most importantly, it was the kind of weapon an anarchist in the south of Spain would be in possession of. 'They're everywhere.'

As anticipated, his brother had sent old Roberto, the Montserrat's lead ranch hand. 'I'll send Roberto to fetch the Civil Guard, and tell them to send Captain Rafael Dominguez.' Roberto had been hired when Hugo was a child and had been like a second father to Hugo. He had originally worked as a vaquero on a neighbouring estate where the owners bred fighting bulls, which roamed the fields freely until the vaqueros corralled them. They used long poles from their mounts to prod the bulls, which took formidable skill to avoid injuries.

Roberto had been slow to react to a bull's charge one afternoon, and the tip of the bull's horn caught his thigh. He had nearly bled to death and now had a permanent limp from the muscle damage. The Montserrats had hired him to handle their own ranching operations due to his skill and experience. Unbeknownst to Hugo's father, Roberto used to take him on horseback to the fields, to taunt the bulls until they gave chase. Hugo had been enthralled.

"Roberto, old fellow. It warms my heart to see you."

"Gracias, Señor Hugo. These are my two sons. They are *vaqueros* on the estate."

"You must be very proud. Have them load my trunk into the coach and don't let them tip it."

"Of course."

"Have you shown them how to corral the bulls?"

Roberto grinned from ear to ear. It was his favourite topic. "We play with the bulls from time to time."

"Can they handle the coach?"

"Yes."

"Give them the reins. I need you to sit with me—tell me everything about the estate. Were you aware of the warnings about the anarchists?"

"I've heard no such thing."

"I was just warned by the Civil Guard. There is an armed group of anarchists planning to kill landowners. They want to start a revolution and seize the properties for themselves. Has there been any such talk amongst the ranch hands?"

"No, Señor Hugo. They're treated well, they have lodgings, and they're happy to have jobs—not like the field workers."

"What have you heard the field workers saying?"

"They're never happy. They don't make enough money and sometimes they go without proper food. I think that's why they support the anarchists. Today Miss Sofia is hiring workers at the square as the fields are ready for harvest. They'll be demanding higher wages—just like last year when Miss Sofia held out and hired workers from another town—it created bad blood. There were beatings and killings. She wants to avoid that this year."

"It's the anarchists Roberto. It's the way they work. They want to change everything through revolution. Now Roberto, I need you to tell me the truth about something I was told by the authorities. Is Sofia still associating with anarchists?"

Roberto looked shocked. "I didn't know she ever was."

"Really? Well the authorities are very concerned—she works at their newspaper. They haven't told my brother or his wife about it. Now tell me about the cattle and the crops. I'm expecting my beloved brother to make me an offer—to buy out my share of the inheritance. I will take him up on it as that would be what's best for the estate honestly. But I can't let him fleece me. He's lucky to have you and your sons, Roberto. One day, you should send them to Argentina to work on one of my ranches. I can always use good lead hands—if you were ever so inclined."

"Gracias, Señor Hugo—Gracias." Tears were welling in Roberto's eyes.

Hugo now had the final piece of information he needed to go ahead with this plan. Sofia would not be there. He also knew Roberto would be thinking about what Hugo had told him when he was sent to fetch the Civil Guard, the power of suggestion was everything.

Roberto stuck his head out the open window and banged his hand against the coach.

"Eduardo, let's go," he said to his oldest son. Eduardo snapped the reins and spurred the horses westward on Calle de Medina towards the town's centre. When the coach turned and headed north, Hugo caught a glimpse of the cathedral peeking overtop of the whitewashed walls facing the road. As he gazed at it, he experienced an all-consuming nostalgia, and reached for the rosary in his pocket. In his youth, it was the only place where he experienced solace, freedom from his nightmares. He wouldn't have time to attend the cathedral before returning to Argentina unfortunately.

'Hail Mary, full of grace, the lord is with thee, blessed art thou among men'—he found himself reciting in his head the short prayer he found so soothing. He shook himself back to the present, to find Roberto looking at him quizzically.

"Do you attend church, Roberto?"

"No, Señor Hugo."

"You've lost your faith then?"

"I can't remember ever having faith."

'Typical peasant—godless worshippers of anarchism.' If Hugo had felt any kinship with old Roberto, it disappeared at this moment. "What of the ranching operations then?"

"The ranch is doing well. There are more than 500 head—about the maximum for our available land. Sometimes the fighting bulls from the neighbouring estate cross into our fields and we have to herd them back. My sons have taken well to this."

"Will you be in the fields today?"

"Yes—do you need anything?"

"Later in the afternoon I'll need to look around the estate—have the horses ready for 4 pm." 'That should be about the right time to send him back to Jerez and fetch the Guardia Civil.'

As the coach turned eastward onto Calle de Arcas he looked to the north and saw the Plaza de Toros. It made him reminisce about the young matador that had tormented him. He couldn't even remember his name now. 'You're too fat Hugo, he'll shove a sharp horn right up your ass!' He'd been right. Hugo had been stocky at a young age. He was slow and lumbering, not suited for a pastime dominated by lithe men. The arrogant teenage matador had not made it to full adulthood. He'd cut it too close with a bull of unpredictable temperament. He was impaled near the groin by a razor-sharp horn and was flung high in the air with a flick of the bull's powerful head—to the horrified cries of the audience.

Hugo, watching from the stands, had jumped to his feet with glee, bringing looks of disapproval. Hugo revelled in the teenager's comeuppance. A field doctor desperately tried to tame the spurts of oxygen rich blood from the femoral artery to no avail. He died from the blood loss soon after in front of the crowd. There'd been no time to get him to the hospital. 'It had felt good,' Hugo thought, as today's events would feel good. He settled in for the ride, thumbing his rosary. 'Hail Mary, full of grace—'

There was an awkward reunion on the veranda of the estate. The two brothers shook hands and embraced, examining the lines the years had etched into their faces. Although, Hugo was a large man, Antonio was bigger, leaner, and his body had not softened a bit. There were tears in his eyes, legitimate tears of joy, and Maria evidently shared in what they thought was a joyous moment. Hugo also had tears in his eyes, which were mistaken for joy.

"It's good to see you my brother. We feared you would not come as you had not answered our letters."

'How I despise him. Look at him—consumed with guilt for how he treated me. He wants to make a deal and see me disappear again forever.'

"I was young Antonio. To my shame, I grew busy and forgot my past. I never saw mother and father again. They would have wanted me to make amends in their time. I failed them."

"Father missed you terribly. You were the impetuous one. Not afraid to mess around with the bulls. He was so proud of you."

'He was a cruel bastard and sent me to die.'

"Maria—thank you for letting me to stay in your home." It pained him to say this, but he needed to throw them off of their guard. This charade of contrition would make his plan easier and all the more satisfying.

"I will have the boys bring my trunk to my room."

"Of course, Hugo. Settle in and then join us for lunch. Maria will be preparing our meal." Antonio was looking at his wife with fondness. 'He's still in love with the shrew. How very convenient.'

Hugo watched Roberto's sons unload his trunk. He was tempted to yell at them, but restrained himself. "Bring it to my room and be careful." He couldn't help himself.

Hugo walked into the two-storey house, taking into account every pertinent detail that he could. There was a single maid tidying. She stopped and curtsied.

"How long have you worked here, Señorita?"

"Three years now."

"Do you work alone?"

"Yes, but I help Señora Maria cook and there will be two of us tonight to help prepare the supper. The other maid is in school and will arrive later."

"I'll look forward to supper. Where are your quarters?"

"On the far side of the house, the servant's room, on the bottom floor." Her eyes were down and she appeared to be alarmed by his question.

'She's hiding something. Is it possible she's Antonio's lover?'

"Do you live there alone?" Checking for the presence of a spouse that might complicate his plan considerably, her feelings be damned.

"Yes."

"Very good then," he said, dismissing her. When the two sturdy teenagers left his room, he went to the window and watched them take the coach away towards the outbuildings a kilometre away, lower in the valley. The house itself was perched on a highpoint, giving an excellent view in all directions. He walked into a room on the other side, opened the shutters and looked out. It was an impressively large estate of 500 acres, although small compared to some estates in the area.

The wheat fields were far in the distance. There were no stragglers milling about. Give Roberto and his sons about an hour to go about their business, and then he would execute his plan.

He opened the lock on his trunk, foraged amongst the clothes, and removed a tightly sealed jar of red paint and a thick brush. He took out the gun belt with the Colt revolver in its holster, and then he took out the C96 automatic pistol, feeling its weight in his hand. He chambered a round, making it ready to fire.

In the late morning, Captain Rafael Dominguez of the Civil Guard sat high in his saddle watching the throngs of people milling around the Plaza de Escribanos towards the centre of Jerez de la Frontera. He occasionally peered through an extending brass telescope when something caught his interest. The labour exchange that occurred every fall prior to the harvest was an ideal occasion for him and his men to gather information.

A gauge of the rising influence of the anarchists was the fact that they were entrusted by the field workers to negotiate their contracts with the estate owners. The peasants far and above preferred piece rates, affording them the opportunity to work quickly, and make more money. It also meant that the more family members they had to work the fields, children included, the more money they could make. It mattered little to the anarchists, but Captain Dominguez wondered how long it would be until his Civil Guard became glorified truant officers chasing kids that were supposed to be in school, a task that didn't interest him in the least.

But that was not why they were monitoring the square. In past years, the contracts with the field workers, or lack thereof, were harbingers of trouble when they went badly. If the anarchists asked too much of the estate owners, they might go to an outlying village to contract workers. If the agents bargaining for the estates sought workers that were not represented in the square, the estate owners and their workers would become the targets of assault and robbery.

The secluded roads around Jerez, Seville and Granada, which was as far as his knowledge went, were renowned for acts of piracy, and murder. It would just take the wrong set of circumstances and he knew he could be removed from his Captain's position or transferred somewhere less pleasant. He also knew it was impossible to put a complete stop to such events, but if he could reassure his chain of command that he had things under control, he wouldn't be bothered by them. He liked his job and he intended to keep it.

Things had been fruitful. He had a steady stream of street urchins at the ready, waiting for him to snap his fingers. For a few centimes, the urchin would report back to him, the name of an unknown bargaining agent, anarchist or socialist? 'Anarchist Señor!' Where is he from? 'Jerez,' or 'Cadiz,' or 'Sevilla,' or some village he had never heard of.

It was unusual to see a woman in the labour negotiations, and peering through the telescope he recognised the unmistakeable figure of Sofia Montserrat. According to his wife the articles by a Free Woman were quite good. Why she chose to publish them in an anarchist rag was beyond him. A do-gooder and a rabble-rouser, he supposed. She harkened from a wealthy family, she was educated, she was an excellent flamenco performer—yet the status quo was not good enough for her. He snapped his fingers at a boy in rags watching him intently.

"Go see how the bargaining is going with the woman. I want every detail you can get," and sent the boy dodging through the crowd.

A few minutes later the boy returned, stood to attention and gave him a sharp open-hand salute. "I don't think it is going so well mon Capitaine."

"Why not?"

"She is taking a really long time."

"What's the problem?"

"She wants the Señor to tell the workers they can't bring children that are supposed to be in school. He said he couldn't do that because they wouldn't agree. He is frustrated with the woman."

"Are they making a deal?"

"I don't know."

"Are you going to find out by talking to me? Hep Hep," which sent the boy scurrying away again. Captain Dominguez pondered his information. He didn't want an incident at the property of his newly rediscovered friend Hugo, who had generously offered to employ one of his sons, if not two. He wanted to take the Senator up on that offer. 'This impetuous bitch will ruin everything if one of her family gets accosted.'

Sofia agreed to the deal. She had pushed the boundaries of negotiations to see if they would agree to keep the children out of the fields. She had started high. 'No children under the age of 14!' In the end, she saw that they would not agree to it. They agreed no children under the age of nine, simply because that was the law. 'They will simply tell their children to say they are nine or 10 or 11 when they are actually seven or eight.' But she had relented when her interlocutor began raising his voice.

'What is this? Are you negotiating in bad faith on purpose? To say you tried so then you can go try at one of the villages?' He'd played his trump card with many lookers on, so she decided to close the deal, to the immense relief of the union negotiator. She turned and was amused to see a street urchin with large puppy dog eyes looking up at her.

"I suppose you plan to be working this year? You had better be able to read and write if you want to work in my fields." She had only meant to tease him, but he seemed offended, 'I should apologise.' She watched him as he dodged back and forth amongst the crowd and then lost sight of him. She walked in the direction the boy had ran, as it was on the way to her apartment. Then she saw the boy again, standing at attention like a soldier, saluting to a tall familiar figure on horseback. 'Captain Dominguez—he was spying on me.' As she realised this she grew angry, and walked intently towards the Civil Guard officer. His eyes locked onto hers defiantly as she approached.

"Señorita Montserrat—I'm told you were giving the union negotiator a hard time. Aren't you afraid they will target your family if you offend them?"

Sofia glared at the boy in rags, who slunk away. "You pay these boys to spy, do you?"

"I give them a few centimes to help them buy food."

"Did you get all the information you need about me? You could have just asked—or is it the anarchists you're spying on?"

"Both. Remember our encounter two years ago and our arrangement—and as I told you before, this is my job. How many union representatives did you deal with today?"

Sofia hesitated before answering, wondering if she should answer his questions at all. She decided not to provoke him. "Four or five."

"Anarchists?"

"There are no socialists in these parts Captain if that's what you're wondering. They're only strong in the cities, they don't think rural peasants are worth their time. They consider them too uneducated to understand their concepts. Didn't you know that?"

"Of course, I knew that."

"Is there anything else you wish to know?"

"Give my regards to your father and the Senator," leaving Sofia again with a veiled threat of exposing her activities to her family. She wasn't sure if she cared anymore if her parents found out about her articles. 'Perhaps it's time to stop writing anonymously.' She was certain she could explain herself to her parents, and perhaps they would actually be impressed. She would consider it later. Now she needed to change and rest, and then ride back to the estate to meet her Uncle Hugo, the senator from Argentina. She thought she should arrive earlier than normal for their supper and to be social.

Hugo Montserrat was spattered with blood. He had shot his brother twice in the stomach first, one-handed from close quarters, while looking him directly in the eyes. The two high velocity rounds hadn't enough time to lose much of their kinetic energy before striking their intended target, shredding their way through the organic matter that lay unsuspecting in their path.

Even at age 60, his brother Antonio was an extremely fit man, unfortunately in this case. His abdominal muscles slowed the bullets down so they didn't exit his body, rather, every bit of their kinetic energy transferred into his body, causing a traumatic temporary cavity that made his brother stagger backwards into the wall, making his desperate grab for the pistol futile. He slid down to the ground, and landed in a sitting position, holding his stomach which was bleeding profusely. He met Hugo's eyes, shocked at the cruel betrayal.

Hugo turned to Maria, who was stunned, holding her face and hyperventilating. He shot her once in the stomach, knowing it would be extremely painful, without causing immediate death. She was gasping in pain and shock. He turned again to his brother, who was weeping from pain and anguish, and mocked him by rubbing his eyes and pouting to emulate a child crying.

Feeling exalted, Hugo turned his attention to finding the maid who would be in the bedroom at the far west end of the estate house. He walked into the bedroom and looked at her, curled in a foetal position on the floor near her bed. She saw the pistol aimed at her head and sobbed. Hugo pulled the trigger; he just wanted her dead. The bullet struck the bridge of her nose, blowing blood, skull, and brain matter onto the wall behind her.

He walked back into the grand living room, looking upon his work with satisfaction.

"Well dear brother—I finally have a few moments to talk without interruption." He tried to lock eyes with Antonio, barely alive, tears streaming down his face mouthing apologies to his dying wife. Hugo raised the pistol towards Maria, but was surprised to find he couldn't bear to shoot her in her pretty face. Antonio coughed and drew Hugo's attention. He was pleading with his eyes, his arm extended forward, shaking his head no to Hugo, 'For God's sake no my brother—don't do it!' Hugo looked back at Maria and shot her through the heart.

"I put her out of her pain. I assume that's what you wanted. I've waited 30 years for this moment. Dear brother—I guess I hold a grudge. Life is cruel isn't it?"

But mercifully Antonio could not hear him gloat anymore as he had passed into another world. His last undeserving memory was that of his spiteful younger brother murdering his beloved wife Maria in cold blood, and thinking of his daughter Sofia.

Hugo peered out the front and back windows to see if any alarms had been raised—as expected, there were none. He ran back to his room and retrieved the sealed bottle of red paint and the brush. 'Damn it—what were the words again?' He fished in his pants pocket with his free hand and pulled out the folded newspaper clipping. He looked around to find a suitable tableau to paint a message. 'This will throw them off the scent.' His eyes found the large mahogany table in the formal dining room. 'Perfect.'

La revoluçion comienza ahora! The revolution starts now! Then, with his message crudely painted on the table, he drew one of the Colt revolvers from his holster and shot all the rounds in its cylinder at the door and the wall nearby. 'When I heard the shots and screams, I took cover and recovered my revolver from my trunk. Then I snuck down the stairs and saw someone near the door. I started shooting and they ran out and escaped on their horses!'

It was fast approaching 5 pm and Sofia found she had let time get away from her. She had needed to wind down from the long hours of work she had put in. The day's events had been a success, and she would enjoy recounting the experience at dinner with her parents and her Uncle Hugo. She needed to speak to her parents about being watched by the Civil Guard. It was not fair to them that they did not know about her writing articles for the anarchist newspaper, and that the Civil Guard was now spying on her. That sly Captain was up to something, she was certain.

She dressed hastily—riding breeches, a fresh blouse, her jacket and her black felt hat, the type with a wide, flat brim that protected her face and neck from the overhead sun. The brisk 20-minute walk along the cobblestone streets from the apartment to the stables where her mare was kept cleared the mental fog of her afternoon siesta, and she looked forward to the ride along the cattle trails that led to the estate. A kilometre away from the Montserrat Estate, she slowed the mare and gazed at the golden-brown shoots of wheat swaying in the breeze along the rolling hills. For a few precious minutes, she was at peace.

As she trotted towards the stables, she noticed the ranch hands in the field being guarded by two soldiers wearing the black tricorn hat of the Civil Guard. Old Roberto stood up, and moved towards her, to take charge of her horse, but was roughly shoved to the ground. One of his sons stood up to protest but was punched in the gut by the largest of the two soldiers, while yelling at the group to sit still and shut up. Sofia spurred her mount towards them to see what was going on, but then saw a third soldier bearing towards her at a full gallop.

She held her mount steady as the soldier pulled up to her, and he aggressively grabbed her reins, almost making her fall.

"Stop that you fool, you'll make her panic!"

"Sofia Montserrat—I am placing you under arrest. These are the orders of Captain Dominguez. You are to be questioned and you will ride back to Jerez with me to the jail."

His grip on her reins was tenuous, and she spurred her mount away from him. His horse was spooked and was resisting his attempts to close on her again.

"What is this foolishness—why would he want me arrested?"

"The anarchists have been to the house. It's a massacre. Whatever you did to help your friends, you will have to tell us. Get over here!"

Sofia turned her horse and spurred it towards the house, but the soldier reacted immediately and was rapidly gaining ground.

"Stop where you are, you filthy whore!"

He stood in the stirrups and punched her across the jaw, knocking her from her horse. She hit the ground rolling. Coming to a stop, she was dazed. Her face hurt badly and she'd had the breath knocked completely out of her lungs and wheezed desperately for breath. It was possible she'd broken a rib. The soldier ignored her injuries and dove and landed on her. He tied her hands in front of her, while she rasped desperately for breath.

"Now you will do as I say, you murderous bitch—you're going to get on that horse and come with me to Jerez!"

It could be midnight, or 4 am, she couldn't tell which. The straw strewn on the jail cell floor stank of urine, faeces and bile of the prisoners that had been lodged in it before her. The white light from a quarter moon pierced the small barred window and fell on the heavy wooden doors that wouldn't budge when she shook them. She sat on the iron bed, the only fixture in the room, with her arms around her knees as she didn't know what else to do. But feeling she had to do something, she replayed every word of the interview by Captain Dominguez in her head. 'What had he said?'

"Your anarchist companions have really had a field day Sofia. They must be very proud of themselves celebrating right now."

"Just tell me what has happened." She was overcome, sobbing intermittently, an image of her parents in her head. She coiled her body and readied herself to attack the captain out of frustration—instead she just yelled. "What has happened to my parents?"

He was not calm either, switching from anger and yelling to anguish—while on the verge of tears himself. The murder scene had been horrific.

"You must tell me what you know first Sofia. Otherwise, I will not help you. I will not intervene. You saw how the anarchists died the last time this happened—death by the garrotte. It's a slow, painful death—horrific—is that what you want?"

"I have no idea what has happened Captain. Don't you remember watching me in the square? I've been in Jerez since early this morning."

"Don't think me foolish woman! That was a clever alibi I'll admit. But I know how the anarchists work—first you gave them the information they needed to plan the murders. They did their dirty work while you were being seen at the square. It would be a perfect alibi if I had not caught you with your anarchist friends that day and knew of your association."

The interrogation went on for many agonising hours of grief and desperation. She didn't give him any incriminating information, as she had nothing to give. He had grown frustrated and tired, and gave up trying to coerce a confession, which he had seemed certain was coming. As she sat now, instinctively curled up to preserve her body warmth against the cold evening temperature, she contemplated the fact that her parents were dead and there was no sense pretending otherwise.

She sat like this, shivering uncontrollably, until the sun pierced through the small window and lit a small corner of the cell. She moved to it and let it fall on her bruised and muddied face. She took long slow breaths. She had no more tears to shed—and fell into an exhausted sleep with her head and body propped up by the wall.

She awoke to orders being barked at her by a nameless soldier.

"Get away from the door!" and with that the iron girded wooden door was slammed open, banging against the wall. "There's someone here to see you." Why the soldier was angry at her, she couldn't say.

As she was being led from the cell area to the front, she caught a glimpse of Captain Dominguez standing with a heavy set, well-dressed man. He bore some facial resemblance to her father, and she caught her breath, stopped herself from breaking down again. 'Stay in control. Figure out what has happened.'

"In here." The soldier ushered her into an office with a desk and two chairs and closed the door. Shortly afterwards the man she had seen with Captain Dominguez entered holding his hat in his hands. He stood while she sat on a chair.

"Good day, Sofia. I'm Hugo—your uncle. I'm sorry to see you this way. There has been a tragedy. Have these men told you anything about what happened?"

"No."

"Captain Dominguez told me he has kept you in custody since yesterday. He was going to bring you to the courts to see a magistrate. They were going to charge you with being an accomplice in the murder of your parents, Antonio and Maria, and the young maid. They were killed by the anarchists yesterday, I'm afraid."

"Why would the anarchists kill my parents? They were not disliked. They were fair—we were fair. Why would they kill a young teenager?"

"The anarchists do not care about that Sofia. They wanted to kill landowners. They want a revolution and they want to seize and control the estates."

"I want to see my parents—their bodies."

74

"That's impossible Sofia. The bodies have been taken away for examination by the coroner. The estate is under guard right now. I have convinced Captain Dominguez that there isn't sufficient evidence to charge you, and that you should be set free until such time as that changes," he said, giving her a minute to absorb this information. "The Civil Guard are determined to find evidence that you are involved in this, although I would never believe it. You cannot return to the estate. And it seems—"

"What?"

"They have information that the anarchists will kill you as well—they believe you will betray them," he said. "Captain Dominguez has told me everything. You've been writing articles for an anarchist newspaper under the guise of another person. His theory is that you have become rebellious against your class—your parents. That you set them up as targets for your anarchist colleagues. Did you do this to your parents Sofia?"

"I loved my parents with all my heart. I would never do such a thing. How could they think that?"

"They will do everything in their power to bring someone to justice. I don't think they'll stop until they can prove you had something to do with it and see you executed by the state. Do you understand the gravity of your situation?"

"Yes."

"You must return with me to Argentina—escape from this place—until such time as they capture those that are actually responsible."

Chapter 6
Crossing

Sofia placed her hands on the steamship's handrails and gazed at the open ocean. Her usual joy for life was muted, and she wondered if she could ever get it back. Nevertheless, the endless shimmering mass of water underneath the cloudless blue skies improved her mood slightly. Two weeks following the death of her parents, she could not yet accept the bitter twist of fate that led to her present circumstances. 'It was true,' she thought, 'that she had nurtured friendships with the anarchists.'

'Francisco could it have been you, or your impetuous brother Manuel perhaps? None of them seemed like killers.' Then there were the authorities who would rather see her die in their insatiable quest for justice, without so much as a thought for the truth—her innocence. Her parents, the estate, her apartment in Jerez, flamenco, her independence, all was lost.

Her Uncle Hugo had warned her to stay close to her apartment in the remaining time she had left in Jerez. The authorities would track her every movement. If they grew suspicious, she risked being arrested again, and this time he wouldn't be able to intervene.

'Don't speak to anyone—not a soul—do you understand?' Her Uncle Hugo had said.

But she'd been able to see the gypsy woman Mirella one last time, and express sympathy for the senseless loss of her daughter. Mirella's face had been a mask of anguish and grief. She had gripped Sofia's arms tightly. 'I see a dark fog in your soul my child. It will be there for a long time, but you must find your way through it. Be careful who you trust. Seize any opportunity to make your life better. Survive at all costs.' It had been typical of Mirella to give advice in prophetic terms, but Sofia had understood.

The following day, her uncle had ushered her discreetly onto the train to Cadiz, and they had boarded the steamship that same afternoon. There indeed was a dark fog in her soul, she'd thought as she watched the colours of the shoreline turn dull and grey, until her country grew small and disappeared in the distance.

"Good day, Señorita."

She looked up and saw a good-looking man, well attired, moustache groomed to a sliver. He held his hat politely in his hands. She hadn't seen him approach.

"My name is Joaquin Cuéllar. I couldn't help but notice that you seem despondent—so I thought I should talk to you. Is it not a splendid view?"

"It's very beautiful, Señor Cuéllar."

"I've seen you dining with an older gentleman. Are you travelling with your father per chance?"

Sofia looked down. It was an innocent question, but it had struck her as hard as the first of the young Civil Guard that had knocked her off her horse. "Not my father. He's my uncle—Hugo Montserrat. He's an Argentine Senator. I'll be staying with him for a while."

"I've heard of him—he started as a rancher," Joaquin continued cheerfully. "You're travelling to Buenos Aires then—as am I. I have a business at the port— the Madero docks. It's commercial export and import, an extension of my family's business in Madrid."

Sofia took a breath and quelled her annoyance. She didn't feel sociable, but he'd piqued her interest speaking of his export business. The rationality of commerce appealed to her. She'd read, The Wealth of Nations, by Adam Smith, and found it fascinating. His explanation of the natural and market price of commodities and on the wages of labour, had made sense of the business operations of the estate. She'd returned it to the bookshelf, corner leafed at her favourite passages.

Supply and demand; affecting the choices of millions of people, negotiating prices in their own interest. Market price; striking the balance of a fair price covering the cost of production, including the requisite profit to continue a business. 'How we set our prices.' Wages of labour; a contract between two parties, masters offering the littlest possible and labourers demanding the most possible. 'How I negotiate for field workers in Jerez.'

"How did you come to have this business in Argentina?"

"It was my father's idea. My family have been merchants for generations, supplying Spanish goods to the British and other places in Europe. He'd heard of the incredible potential for growth in Argentina—their goods are in high demand. But I think his real reason was that I had just come of age and he wanted to get rid of me." Sofia almost laughed. "So, we started a business in Buenos Aires. That was 10 years ago. Now I'm afraid I've become part of the Argentine establishment."

Sofia smiled despite herself. 'Don't trust anyone.'

"Good day, Joaquin Cuéllar."

"Good day—" He stood there for a moment, hesitating.

"Sofia—Sofia Montserrat."

"Good day, Sofia Montserrat."

On the second day at sea, she was approached by the ship's Captain, a man in his sixties, tall and trim, with a bushy, grey beard worthy of a lifetime spent at sea. He was in a crisp naval uniform—a dark blue double-breasted tunic with gold buttons.

"I'm Captain Juan Perez. I'm an acquaintance of your uncle, Senator Montserrat. He told me what happened to your parents. I wish to extend my condolences. When I received his telegram, I made sure two spots were made available in 1st class. It's a terrible tragedy."

"Thank you, for making room for me. I haven't been good company to my Uncle Hugo and others on the ship, as you've probably noticed. I'm finding it very difficult to be sociable right now."

"That's completely understandable. Have you ever been on a steamship before?"

"Never."

"Her name is Sirio. I was made captain of this ship 15 years ago. She isn't old as far as steamships go. It's slightly older than yourself, I would guess," evoking a tentative smile from Sofia. "We left Genoa six days ago and stopped to board freight and passengers in Naples and Barcelona, and of course, Cadiz. We'll be following a route, along the coast of Africa, near Tenerife and the Canary Islands. Then we'll cross the Atlantic directly to Montevideo, and finally proceed to Buenos Aires. That will be 16 days from now, I should think. For some, that will make it a 22-day voyage. How has the food been?"

"The food is excellent—it's like being in the dining room of a fine hotel."

"Good. It hasn't always been that way. We're able to refrigerate our food stocks now, so it will be fresh dining for the entire voyage—at least for the 1st and 2nd class passengers. Just a few years ago, we would all have been eating from tins starting tomorrow."

"Can you tell me about all of the people I see on the lower decks—it seems very crowded."

"It is indeed. There are roughly 1200 people travelling in steerage. It will be a rough journey for them—some will perish, I'm afraid."

"How so," Sofia said, startled.

"They're living together in extremely close quarters—it makes them vulnerable to intestinal diseases like cholera and typhoid. Those in poor health will be susceptible to sickness and death. We try to prevent it by cleaning out the living areas when we can. But in bad weather and rough seas this becomes impossible. There are over 400 adult women in steerage—a good many pregnant. Childbirths at sea are often deadly for the mother or the child."

'I had no idea.'

"Why do they make this dangerous journey?"

"For better lives. Steerage class is full on every ship that sails from Europe to Argentina. There's work waiting for them in Buenos Aires. It's growing so quickly that they're needed for practically everything—construction, loading the ships, the slaughterhouses and meatpacking factories, the railroads—I could keep going. Some of them will eventually be able to purchase a home away from the city centre. It's their dream."

"How did you come to know my Uncle Hugo?"

"We're merely acquaintances. I speak with him at the horse races at the hippodrome, and we've enjoyed the odd drink together at gentlemen's establishments." He'd been hesitant about answering that question, Sofia observed.

"Thank you, for the information Captain. I found that very instructive."

"There will be music in the lounge tonight. The musicians we hired are quite good.

It might take your mind off things. Good day, Miss Montserrat."

Sofia hadn't been in the lounge yet and decided she would take a look. It was mid-afternoon, so it would still be quiet. She didn't think she was ready to sit with people who were drinking and enjoying themselves, and she had avoided it, knowing her Uncle Hugo was there. On their first two evenings, he'd excused himself after dinner to play cards and gamble. He had played all evening—and consumed a lot of liquor. It was just as well, as she was not completely comfortable around him yet. She had dearly wanted to discuss the world of politics with him, when her parents had told her he was coming to visit.

But she found he was taciturn and unfriendly when she broached the subject. She decided to put off such conversations until they'd both recovered from the tragedy of her parent's murder.

The lounge was exquisitely decorated; polished wood tables, a bar with gleaming brass rails and ornate beer taps, and a variety of trophy pelts hung on the bulwarks. Stewards and stewardesses were cleaning and preparing for the late afternoon onslaught. A small gathering of people was close to the stage, equipped with a piano and musical instrument resting on their stands. Tango Lesson was written on a folding chalk board. Middle-aged parents with children and teenagers were huddled around the instructor. She was surprised to hear the voice of Joaquin Cuéllar speaking to them.

"Tango is the dance of the working-class, so you won't see it on display in the main theatres. As far as I know, it is only practiced in Buenos Aires and Montevideo, where it originated." He held up one finger with a comedic flourish that brought laughter from his small audience. "Some people will tell you it is danced in the brothels—I don't know what those are and neither should you—but you'll see it danced in the cafe's and bars of the barrios—where the working class live—La Boca, Barracas, Constituçion, and Once. The music tells a story of the heart—such as a lost love, or family left behind in the old country."

He waived the musicians to their instruments, a piano player and two violin players, with one ready to sing, and mimicked an orchestra conductor with his hand. The band ignored him, and then he sang loudly and out of tune, drawing more laughter—some of it hushed and pitying. But then the band struck up, and he adjusted to a melodious tenor, that could only have been developed through years of choral instruction at a church.

The relieved audience applauded. "A demonstration with my gracious volunteer now." He held his hand out to a well-dressed, middle-aged woman. Her bemused husband and her children clapped and cheered her on, and he led her to the middle of the floor.

The clamour of the audience gave way to a hush. The band played quietly, and an apparent act of magic occurred before them. They held hands, his left to her right, and he slid his right hand under her left arm and deeply across her back, so as to guide her in the intended direction of the dance. A series of forward-weighted steps were taken by Joaquin, his volunteer responding elegantly with backward steps, until he shifted his weight slightly to his left, making her backward moving leg cross the other.

This led to a pause, or seemingly a pause, as his lady volunteer unwound her crossed leg and improvised some amateurish, but roundly applauded, figures—a backward flick of the heel, toe taps and a seductive brush along Joaquin's leg—the latter causing shocked women and children to bring their hands to their mouths and giggle. Joaquin aided her balance, Sofia observed, as the woman did a series of swivels, and Joaquin rotated in place on one leg, the opposite toe pointed forward, arcing like a geometry compass across the floor.

And again, he pressed forward with the music, long pronounced steps, again a pause for improvisation, taking their turns, a leg flicked backwards, a swivel over one leg, ankles brushing as one foot passed the other. Sofia was enjoying herself watching it. Although, it didn't match the polished performances her flamenco troupe put on in the theatre and outdoor stages of Jerez, it was nevertheless appreciated by the onlookers and children. She stayed until its end when Joaquin spoke.

"Thank you, for your attention everybody. Now I hope you will stay and participate in the lesson. If everyone agrees, we will practice every day at this time and put on a grand show next week."

She decided to continue watching. It was a welcome distraction. The dance had its merits. It pushed the boundaries of prudish, fin-de siècle social norms; the close hold of the couple, the licentious nature to its movements, legs brushing and entangled briefly, coupled with the lyrics of a lusty romance gone awry. 'It made for questionable viewing, at least for the socially conservative viewers amongst them,' she thought. But it was also mysterious, a dance of the heart, a story—a courtship.

Then the weather turned. The Captain had been on the bridge, observing the storm developing in the distance. There was no way around it without significantly deviating from their course, which would delay their arrival. He had issued a warning to the ship's passengers to expect rough seas, but not in a fashion to cause alarm, even if it was warranted. Through the evening the steamship pitched and shuddered evermore severely, while her screws propelled her towards Montevideo, and into the eye of the storm.

Having found her sea legs, Sofia was surprised to find she was not prone to the motion sickness that plagued most of the passengers and a good portion of the crew.

She spent much of the time seated in the semi-deserted lounge. Its complement of bustling stewardesses was depleted to the few that were still mobile. Daylight was muted by the low, sullen cloud cover. It spit bolts of lightning intermittently to further alarm the ship's passengers, if the size of the swells pounding the hull hadn't done so already.

She had a welcome conversation again with the ship's Captain Juan Perez. "I'm glad to see the weather doesn't have you confined to your cabin. Your uncle is not faring so well."

"I suppose not. I haven't seen him in three days. Mind you, there hasn't been many people well enough to show up for dinner."

"Unfortunately, the only news I have since we last spoke is bad news. I've seen worse storms, but they've been few and far between. I had to issue an order to close the outside decks two days ago. The passengers travelling in steerage haven't been able to get fresh air, and we haven't been able to clean out their quarters."

"How awful," Sofia said.

"Indeed. The medical officer has informed me his two nurses are exhausted from dealing with emergencies, and the sick bay is full. Only pregnant women are being admitted now. There's been three deaths in as many days. Burials at sea are hard on morale on the lower decks, and there's no end in sight to this weather."

"Will you let me know if I can assist the medical team in any way? I grew up on a ranch and have helped birth calves many times. I've seen midwife's deliver babies as well."

"That's a gracious offer. I'll advise the medical officer to call for you if it's necessary."

As he left a woman who she recognised as the volunteer Tango dancer, leaned closer, from the table next to hers. "It's much worse than he described."

"How so?"

"Imagine the berths of the families down there right now. There is only a couple of feet between them, they are practically sleeping on top of one another.

Now imagine that one of them is sick. They can't go outside on the decks to escape the smell. They are stuck with it, and then they all get sick. There aren't enough toilets so there are accidents and there aren't enough sinks to wash properly. I hope they can bear with it. They desperately need a change in the weather to clean themselves and their quarters. Otherwise, cholera will inevitably take hold."

"That's terrible."

"My husband is a doctor. He's been helping the medical team, but even he is sickened by the conditions down there."

Sofia decided to change the topic. "I saw you dancing in the lounge. I thought it was an excellent performance. It's the first time I've seen Tango."

"With young Cuéllar—yes. He's been a godsend, keeping us all amused. Did you see how quickly all the volunteers were picking it up? We were hoping to put together a performance for everyone—maybe once the weather turns again. I'm going to take advantage of it while I'm on the ship."

"What do you mean?"

"Respectable ladies can't dance Tango in Buenos Aires—it just isn't done."

"Why not?"

"My dear," she said, touching Sofia's shoulders, "it's danced in the brothels—you'll be mistaken for a prostitute. But I have to admit—I'm quite enamoured with it."

Sofia was woken up abruptly by sharp knocking on her cabin door. The ship was pitching and rolling without cease. She heard the knocking again and someone calling her name loudly.

"Yes—what is it?" She saw a steward there and a man in a rumpled suit, who she recognised as the husband of the woman she had spoken to, the doctor.

"I need help delivering a baby. It's unexpected and early. The ship's medical team is completely beyond its capacity—as am I now quite frankly."

"I'll be right there." Sofia tied her hair back and was dressed within a minute. They followed the young steward down metal stairs and through hatchways, stumbling against the bulwarks when they lost balance.

The sick bay was small, with only three beds, constructed of wood and fastened to the deck. The beds were occupied and the pregnant woman was lying in the middle, her legs up on metal stirrups that were clamped to each side. An older woman was holding her head and her hand, concerned, a mother reassuring her daughter. The steward gently ushered her out, it was too crowded for even one extra person, and Sofia rubbed her back as she passed.

"We'll look after her," Sofia said, with more confidence than she felt.

"The baby's dead! It stopped moving days ago—please just save my daughter."

Sofia looked at the doctor. He'd heard the mother and had a hand on the belly. He confirmed it with a nod. He leaned towards Sofia so the woman wouldn't hear.

"She's ready. She has to push it out—there's no other way. This place is too unsanitary. If I have to make any incisions, infection will take hold—she'll die of sepsis."

Sofia took the woman's hand, and held her head, so that she could see the doctor at the same time. Her eyes were wide with fear and she was taking shallow breaths.

"Breathe slower—now take a deep breath. You have to push—push!"

The next day the weather began to break for the better. By the following day, the pitching and rolling diminished enough that people began to recover and the Captain allowed passengers to get fresh air on the outer decks. Sofia had begun to accept her circumstances and was thinking of what life would be like for her in Buenos Aires.

Her Uncle Hugo had said he lived in a nice house in the neighbourhood of Recoleta, wherever that was. He said he would find a way to keep her updated on the murder investigation by the Spanish authorities. She had no experience with such matters and realised she was entirely dependent on him, which left her uncomfortable for reasons she could not explain. But he was her family, and a senator. He would have all the necessary contacts to acquire news. Would she even be able to attend the Spanish Embassy? Her uncle had cautioned her not to, they might arrest her.

'This needs to be resolved,' she thought. I'm an only child and will have inheritance rights, another topic she knew nothing about. That would be something she would have to depend on her Uncle Hugo as well. Helping the doctor perform the stillbirth two nights ago had reminded Sofia of something she knew about herself. She had fortitude. When she knew something had to be done, she would do it, no matter how difficult. She had held the woman's head and hand for hours, taking her cue from the doctor, encouraging her, reassuring her, or giving orders.

The baby had emerged lifeless, but the woman had survived. It had been wrapped in hessian sacking and the medical officer had given last rites from memory in front of the woman and her mother, a small act of decency to reassure their Catholic faith. Then it was jettisoned overboard, a sad but necessary procedure. She had not seen Joaquin Cuéllar approaching.

"In my six prior occasions crossing the Atlantic, I've never experienced a storm so bad. How are you faring?"

"I seem to have endured it better than most. I'm glad to see we've finally passed through it."

"I've been discussing putting on a Tango performance with the volunteers. I think it would cheer people up. The Captain has agreed to a show in the 1st class lounge—but won't allow us to do a show on the lower deck for the steerage passengers. Yet they need it more than anybody. What do you think?"

"It's a wonderful idea—I'm sure everyone will like it."

"Would you like to join us?"

"No—I can't I'm sorry." She decided she would confide a little more information to Joaquin. She had to tell somebody. "I'm grieving the loss of my parents. They died suddenly—they were murdered actually. The Captain of the Civil Guard detachment thinks it was the anarchists. 'But refused to tell me why.' For my safety I will be staying with my Uncle Hugo."

"My God—that's horrible! I'm terribly sorry for your loss. This must be a very difficult time for you. How long do you have to stay in Buenos Aires for?"

"I don't know just yet—I'll have to figure it out when I get there."

"I completely understand your decision not to participate. If I'd known, I wouldn't have been so forthcoming."

"I will watch. Perhaps I will mention to the Captain that it would be good for the steerage passengers. I wonder if he will change his mind. I agree they need some entertainment more than anybody." Sofia was thinking of the many children suffering below decks, and the woman who had given stillbirth.

The Captain was a man of stern disposition, Sofia thought. 'Not to be trifled with, but I suppose that's what it takes to assume such responsibility.'

"What are you proposing to do exactly?"

"A performance—by the group of volunteers that have been practicing Tango. There are about 10 of them including some children which would cheer up the children in steerage—the musicians would be required as well."

"To be honest with you it's the security that troubles me. There are some rough characters in that lot. I've had to place a few in the brig already for taking allowances with the single women."

"There are many women and children living down there without the benefit of security while we speak. Surely we can entertain them for an hour without too much fuss."

The Captain looked worried, but smiled. "You're right that they need some cheering up. I'll have the chief steward make arrangements."

Two days later, the intrepid volunteers put on their first show for the 1st and 2nd class passengers in the lounge. It had been well received, with exclamations of appreciation in the tradition of the flamenco. 'Ola! Si! Asi se baila! That's dancing!' Sofia had led some of the encouragement, giving the young dancers a boost of confidence.

Four of the five couples were either young teenagers or children, each of them having one partnered dance and a solo to enact the Tango story. Joaquin ended the performance partnered with his volunteer that built into a crescendo and ended abruptly for the entranced audience. He was obviously an accomplished Tango dancer. The professional musicians added to the quality of the show, singing immigrant stories with tragic endings, which resonated with the ship's passengers. 'Those travelling in steerage, would surely appreciate the tales, except for those mirthless endings,' Sofia thought.

The following day, with only two more days of sailing until they reached the shores of South America, the performers navigated the labyrinth of hallways, metal stairs, and heavy-hinged doors and filed onto the lower, outer deck of steerage. As the performers filed through the dense crowd of curious passengers, they were assailed by the odours of people who had endured long bouts of sea sickness and hadn't been able to wash. Joaquin was walking at the front and turned to see how his volunteers were handling the situation. He flashed a smile at the youngest volunteers as he could see the alarm in their eyes and the hesitancy in their steps.

The ship's stewards placed rope barriers in a square to provide a space for the musicians and dancers at the behest of Joaquin, who was waiving, and pointing. He was dressed sharply, the same outfit he had donned for the previous performance—a dark pin-striped double-breasted suit that sat wide on the shoulders and a wide brimmed fedora that curved downward at the front to shade the eyes. He stepped forward to speak to the audience, unsure for a moment as to how their presence would be received. 'With his most charming smile, he gave the introduction, sensing the variety of attitudes—hostility, suspicion, annoyance—all to be ignored,' he thought, as he also sensed wonder, anticipation, and relief from the misery of the moment. He glanced at his intrepid troupe of volunteers and gave them a nod.

"Showtime!"

Matias Del Pino took another sip of vodka from the flask, watching the commotion from the railing. At Del Pino's side were the two others; Javier Alamar, a skinny, talkative man, and Emilio Campaverde, who was short, stocky, and—in stark contrast to Alamar—generally kept silent. They'd been conscripted a decade ago into Spain's military forces, assigned together to the rifle battalion garrisoned in Barcelona, and were battle-hardened veterans of the Spanish-American war waged in the Philippines. In 1901, following their return to Spain, and two years of hard labour in a disciplinary regiment for their involvement in the murder of a French diplomat's son, the military declined to extend their contracts. Even for infantry soldiers they were simply too much trouble, often drunk, often violent.

Del Pino remained their unofficial leader in all things, as old habits die hard. He'd been promoted early in the regiment to the rank of Sergeant, due to his size and his mean streak. The commissioned officers had appreciated his ability to ensure the men followed orders. For 10 years, he had dragged the other two into his petty criminal schemes, but in the Philippines things had gotten serious.

A Spanish Colonel commanding an artillery brigade in Manila's walled city was secretly conspiring with his American equivalent, when it became obvious the Spanish would lose. In a gentlemen's agreement to keep their casualties low, they planned to move American troops into the walled city and keep the Philippine troops out, a bitter betrayal by their American allies. For this agreement to remain a secret, two Philippine officers serving as observers with the Americans would need to die in battle. The Spanish Colonel spoke with the officer in command of the infantry regiment, who in turn chose Sergeant Del Pino, the only NCO he had that wouldn't question such a morally dubious endeavour.

Del Pino brought along Campaverde, who was a crack shot with the service issue Remington Model 1871. Having been advised of the exact location that the two Philippine officers would be posted, with a description of their uniforms, they easily dispatched of them amongst the chaos of the battle.

The effectiveness of the venture had gotten the Spanish Artillery Colonel thinking. He correctly gauged the temperament and greed of Sergeant Del Pino, and offered him money to make a concubine disappear. She had accused the Colonel of getting her pregnant, and was blackmailing him to bring her to Spain. This time, Del Pino brought along Alamar, who was good with a knife and hated women. On the day their regiment shipped back to Spain, the concubine was found dead, her throat slit with such savageness that the vertebrae had been severed and she'd been practically beheaded. A local prefect concluded it had been the act of a jealous client, attached to one of the three armies serving in the region. As one army was shipping out, it was hopeless to investigate and he closed his file.

Following their discharge, it turned out there was a small cadre of senior military officers and their acquaintances who required such nefarious services, ranging from petty thuggery to assassination, in order to protect business interests or resolve romantic indiscretions. And of course, there were the key troublemakers stoking anger during the strikes in the Spanish areas of influence in North Africa. But other than that, they drank, they fought, and they spent a lot of time in jail. Commissioner De La Fuente's description of Buenos Aires with its brothels, bars, and gambling venues appealed to him. He decided they would do it, and the other two didn't complain.

The long voyage in the ship's steerage class was something they'd experienced before, so they knew what to expect. They had both bribed and intimidated a ship steward, and had managed to keep their flasks filled with vodka to keep the voyage interesting. Ironically, all three of them had been sea sick for the week, and hadn't consumed a drop the entire time. Having recovered with the help of the fresh air and access to the outer deck, Del Pino started feeling himself again. The three men sipped from their flasks, growing louder and more hostile towards other passengers. Then his eyes fell on the smug bastard in a pin-stripe suit and fancy hat.

"Ladies and gentlemen, boys and girls, my name is Joaquin Cuéllar. We have a show for you today—we thought you could use a little entertainment!" Joaquin had positioned himself in a far corner of the area the stewards had cordoned off for the show. There was only a smattering of clapping from the densely packed audience, a bedraggled collection of unwashed men, women and children. But he continued unabated. "This courageous group of volunteers has practiced hard for many days to give you a great show. Today is the day I give you the Tango," and giving a conductor's wave to the band he started his solo with a terpsichorean about-face and a clownish walk that transformed itself into a graceful glide, and he took the outreached hand of his first volunteer dancer.

Sofia was standing to the side, her hands on the shoulders of an eight-year-old boy and girl, ready to coax them onto the cordoned stage when their time came. Joaquin had changed the order, anticipating the young dancers could engage the audience better than the older dancers from the start. But firstly, he intended to use his own routine, loosely choreographed, so that he could concentrate on a spoken word introduction to the Tango.

'What is unique about Tango? It is a symbiosis of storytelling, music, and dance. You will experience sadness and yearning—just as life has its triumphs and disappointments. You will see the man use his inner force to guide his partner gracefully through a series of figures that are unique to Tango—ochos,' Joaquin said, while guiding the doctor's wife in a figure eight pattern in which she stepped forward onto a weighted and pivoted around it, brushing her ankles while her feet passed.

'Volcadas,' Joaquin announced while taking a step slightly backwards, causing the doctor's wife to fall slightly forward. He then used her momentum to guide her sideways, causing her outer foot to sweep across and between the couple. Light clapping came from the adults in the audience. 'Ganchos,' Joaquin said while making his volunteer make a full backward leg movement from her hip that hooked into his outstretched leg, making her leg curl up and around it slightly. This time the clapping was louder and accompanied by oohs and ahhs.

He continued his demonstration through a few more figures, made eye contact with Sofia and nodded. She lifted the hanging rope barrier rope and guided the youngest couple in. As predicted, the audience warmed to the two children, who were concentrating fiercely on their number. 'Si! Olay!'

'It was going much better,' Joaquin thought, and the young children and teenagers in the audience had now taken a keen interest, smiling and clapping. The pair received a respectable ovation, and the next couple was waived in—a pair of teenagers. She was more woman than girl and had mysterious curves belying her innocence. The boy was oblivious to the budding woman in front of him, the adults exchanging amused glances.

But the children in the audience were held in awe as the teenagers started a routine that was commensurately more complex than the preceding one. The mysterious romantic Tango ethos that Joaquin had tried to suppress in their choreography refused to cooperate, and the awkward teenage boy, that most of the audience had ignored given the youthful sensuality emanating from his female partner, stood straight and took command.

Joaquin himself was surprised by the electric charge of the moment, when the boy took the girl's hand and drew her close. He saw that the lead musician had taken notice of the unexpected dramatic intensity, easing the band into the music to match their first movements. To Joaquin's amazement, as this had never happened during practice, the quietness of the music was reflected with subdued movement, and the crescendos accompanied by abrupt and forceful steps. Joaquin was elated, seeing that the teenagers had completely won over the sceptical audience.

The boy concentrated single-mindedly on his task and sensing the unexpected confidence of her partner, the girl danced her heart. She embellished her footwork with taps and flicks, swept the inside edge of her foot along the floor through her swivels, and brushed her ankles demurely as they passed. Following their execution of each figure, she made eye contact with the boy, instead of looking at the ground shyly as had been their habit during practice.

Joaquin glanced at Sofia, who had also noted the elevated performance, and she met his eyes and gave him a nod, causing his heart to beat a little faster. Joaquin smiled and felt good. All of their work had paid off, entertaining people exhausted by the travails of their sea voyage, and lifting their spirits. He cinched and straightened his tie knot, and pulled his shirtsleeves out from the sleeves of his jacket, to show off a pair of sparkling cuff links.

He watched the teenagers bring their dance to a close, the boy drawing a leg backward sharply, causing the girl to lunge forward and look upward into his eyes at the same time the music ended with two accented notes. They held their pose until the audience realised the routine was finished and this time broke into a thunderous applause. 'Ole! Ole! Well done—bravo!' The boy held the girl's hand high as they faced the audience, and they bowed together. He then promptly resumed his adolescent slouch, dropped her hand, and walked out of the square, leaving the girl to fend for herself.

Joaquin suppressed a chuckle and went to guide her out of the square toward Sofia, but someone's hand from the audience had a skeletal grip on his arm and was pulling him off balance. Joaquin turned and got a whiff of sour liquor on the breath of a thin faced man who held his face uncomfortably close to his own. He hadn't expected it and was startled.

"Hey fancy pants—don't leave her out there too long. We haven't had the pleasure of a woman in three weeks—" The man broke into a droning cackle that caused flecks of disgusting vodka-inflected spittle to land on Joaquin's nose. Two other men had suddenly appeared at the thin man's shoulders, one of whom was a hulking menace.

"Hey moustache—those kids were pretty good dancers," the hulking menace said. "They don't need a fancy suit and hat like you, do they?" The utterance wasn't the least bit funny to anyone, but the thin faced man broke into a droning cackle anyway.

Joaquin pulled his arm to dislodge the man's claw-like grip to no avail, then jerked it free forcefully. He looked at the three men on the other side of the cordon with concern, which was not a barrier at all if they decided to push this further, and tried to think how to resolve the situation and continue the show. Looking around, Joaquin saw that the chief steward, an impressively sized man himself, was watching the three men from the other side of the audience and started moving closer to see what was going on.

"I'm fucking talking to you, fancy pants," the hulking menace said. Joaquin saw that he had cocked an arm back, and stepped back out of reach, just in case. He knew he had to do something to regain the momentum of his show—'anything!'

"Ladies and gentleman! I have three volunteers from the audience who wish to entertain you with their dancing skills as well. Come up here and take the stage—yes you three. Come now—no need to be afraid." It was a risk that they might take him up on his offer, but as hoped they did not. The three men didn't appear to like the sudden attention, and they shoved their way to the back.

"Don't be shy gentlemen—or scared! This drew some ridicule of the men from the audience. Joaquin continued, unnecessarily. "Gentlemen, even the children weren't so intimidated—come now—don't be so afraid." He laughed with the audience heartily until he noticed a reproachful look from Sofia, and realised he'd taken things too far. He gathered his thoughts, looked to see if his partner was ready at the far corner of the dance square, and nodded at the lead musician.

Sofia had watched the interaction with alarm and annoyance. 'What a foolish thing for him to do—he humiliated them in front of everyone. He has made some dangerous enemies for the sake of his ego.' She watched them whispering amongst themselves. The largest of them had a particularly malevolent countenance, and that man nodded almost imperceptibly to a short, stocky man. 'Were they a gang of criminals?'

The men shuffled back through the crowd toward Joaquin, who had his back turned and was preparing to go on stage for the final routine. She saw something metallic in the hand of the stocky man who was in the lead, and he moved aggressively toward Joaquin.

"Joaquin look out!"

Her warning made Joaquin look up and duck his head away from the piece of lead pipe the short, stocky man had swung at his head. It struck him on his upper back and he grunted in pain.

The chief steward had seen it and ran forward from his position near the stage to intercept him. He grabbed the man's collar and shook him.

"You're drunk. Take this man to the brig." Two other stewards now also had a hold of the man and struggled with him until they had his arms firmly behind his back.

Sofia saw that Joaquin was alright. He was moving his arms.

"Ladies and gentlemen, I confess—this was not intended to be part of our show. But we will continue." He waived at the musicians to continue the Tango music, and the violinist began singing again. Scuffles were part of a lounge musician's life, nothing to get overly upset about. Joaquin coaxed another pair of awaiting teenagers onto the cordoned stage, and they too provided their best performance, to the appreciation of the audience.

Meanwhile, Sofia continued to watch the two other men. They were upset and swearing now at Joaquin, who also heard them. He again decided to ridicule them, to her dismay.

"Apparently, there are still two enthusiastic volunteers to make our show even better. Gentlemen please come up. Oh my goodness—they're too afraid to dance with my volunteers." Some of the audience again laughed at the men, happy to see their discomfort, but then quietened under the menacing stare of the hulking one.

'Why is he taunting them, the fool! They're going do something rash,' Sofia thought. She watched the two men gesturing animatedly with their eyes on Joaquin. 'This isn't over.' She watched them as they pushed their way through the crowd and had a conversation with a ship steward, nodding toward Joaquin. The steward was nodding in comprehension to their question. 'Now they are planning something sinister—Joaquin is in danger.'

The vicious attack occurred much later in the evening. They'd lain in wait near his cabin. The hulking man's slap to his temple left him dazed, and he had barely been able to stay on his feet. A slew of invective came from the skinny one—and he broke Joaquin's nose with a punch fortified by a piece of pipe clenched in his fist. Several kicks to his ribs then ensued, causing Joaquin sharp pain when he tried desperately to suck air back into his lungs.

But Joaquin had the sudden realization he would be killed if he didn't fight back, and he mustered enough force to heave himself into the large one. Joaquin surprised him, and he watched the man stumbled backwards and fall across the door hatch. But the skinny one now had jumped on Joaquin's back, bringing such pain to his ribs he screamed and collapsed.

The large one had picked himself up and charged at Joaquin, roaring with rage.

"You're going overboard you little weasel!"

Joaquin braced himself for the impact, briefly realizing that his life was over. But the impact didn't come. From eyes swelling shut, he saw the Chief Steward strike the charging man forcefully with something heavy, and the man rolled to a stop in front of him. Other stewards hauled the skinny one away easily, while the Chief Steward placed manacles on the large one.

"Give this man a hand to the infirmary," he said to someone, and Joaquin was helped to his feet. He stumbled along being guided by someone he thought was a steward as well. But he couldn't see anything at this point through the blood and his swollen eyes.

"Thank God you came—thank you for helping me," Joaquin croaked. "How did you know?"

"The Captain sent us to check on you after your lady friend advised him you would be attacked. An incident like this seems to happen on every voyage. A tryst of jealousy or a gambling loss, and some blighter parks himself outside the cabin of his intended victim waiting for him to show. We're well prepared for such instances. They'll spend the rest of the trip in the brig—so you'll be safe."

Joaquin spent the remainder of the voyage in the sick bay, prone on a bed, on the advice of the medical officer. The broken ribs made it too painful to rise. Damn my impetuous utterances to those thugs. How stupid of me. And to think I told Sofia Montserrat that her concerns were ludicrous. He was giddy to have survived and he wondered if Sofia might visit, as he was in too much pain to seek her out. But then he considered his situation more realistically. He had burned his bridges with her, dismissing her warning as foolishness. She had been insulted, but thought to warn the Captain anyway. Damn! He had to find a way to see her and apologize.

Senator Hugo Montserrat observed Sofia's conduct on the ship with growing concern. 'I've underestimated her—she's smart and has courage. This could unravel all of my work—she's already questioning the circumstances of Antonio's and Maria's deaths. I don't want her questions to reach the ears of the Civil Guard in Jerez. She has to be dealt with, but killing her now would be too suspicious.' He thought of Commissioner De La Fuente. 'That's why I have allies. She won't be able to communicate with the authorities in Spain, nor at their embassy—I can control her.'

He knew what to do with this loose end. His telegram to Commissioner De La Fuente read: Return to Buenos Aires expected afternoon of October 2. Your assistance required. I have temporary custody of female relative, 24 years old, who was living in unfortunate circumstances and is somehow involved in the murder of my brother and his wife. But for reasons of my security she will need accommodation away from my own residence. Suggest Machado take charge of relative as of arrival in port. Subject willing and able to earn keep.

He smiled at his own cleverness. He recalled the words of the lawyer in Cadiz. 'The civil code was devised to encourage marriage and discourage immoral behaviour by our daughters. The inheritance is very likely forfeit in such circumstances.' 'The Montserrat Estate in Jerez de la Frontera was within his grasp,' he thought. It was a highly valuable acquisition that he could leverage against large bank loans. It would take a long while for the lawyers to settle matters, but there really was no need to press things as he was in an excellent financial position, and it might raise suspicion in itself. He would let that process take its natural course. He had won, and it was time to celebrate.

Chapter 7
A Team Made in Heaven

Police Commissioner De La Fuente read the missive. It was a letter with an official embossment forwarded urgently from the Spanish Embassy to his attention. He had only returned from Spain a few days ago, and his first thought was that something had already gone wrong with his clandestine hires, who were arriving shortly themselves. But it was nothing of the sort. Colonel Gimenez had thought it prudent to have De La Fuente notified of something he had learned in Madrid. The diplomatic note, however, was in factual plain language of a typical police nature—not something that would normally have been the subject of urgent diplomatic correspondence. 'Colonel Gimenez wanted him to read between the lines,' he thought.

Incident involving anarchists and Argentine Senator Hugo Montserrat. The investigative division of the Buenos Aires Capital Police is advised as follows: In September, 1904, anarchists are believed to have struck at the Montserrat Estate located 10 kilometres East / NorthEast of Jerez de la Frontera, Andalucia, Spain.

Anarchists seeking to destabilise relations between estate owners and estate field labourers have brutally murdered estate owners Antonio and Maria Montserrat, and an unfortunate servant who was present at the time they were ambushed in their home. Anarchist propaganda was left on the property and witnesses are believed to have seen the perpetrator's fleeing on horseback.

Antonio Montserrat is the older brother of Argentine Senator Hugo Montserrat, who was visiting Jerez de la Frontera at the time of the murders. Civil Guard is investigating and pursuing all leads. Several anarchists located and placed under arrest.

De La Fuente snorted out loud. 'Maria? Maria Montserrat—his brother's wife! Anarchists my bloody arse—you ruthless son of a bitch! You heartlessly cut down your own brother and his wife? Is there anything you are not capable of?' He recalled Vicente's description of the bloody murder scene at Madam Josefina's Social House. Although, a prostitute, the victim had been barely 20 years old with her entire life ahead of her. Her name was not Maria, but now he knew who the Senator had been thinking of when he butchered her.

De La Fuente had sent another trusted detective to the brothel, to help Vicente cover up the Senator's mess. The detective escorted Montserrat to his home in a carriage and gave him instructions to clean himself up. 'Don't say a fucking word about this to anybody!' Vicente had wrapped her corpse in a blanket and brought it in his coach to the overflowing city morgue.

The coroner stored it in refrigeration, awaiting further instructions. Vicente did the leg work, confirming the prostitute had arrived a year earlier from Poland. She had no family on record, and no husband to report her missing. The coroner was advised to dispose of the body, no longer required as evidence, no further investigation, no further details. He didn't make a fuss; she was just one more of many clogging up his over-flowing morgue.

De La Fuente was also holding the telegram the Senator had sent from the steamship. 'I'll continue to play his game. Sofia Montserrat has drawn some terrible cards. Too bad for her. Vicente can bring her to the brothel. She can make her own decisions from there. There are worse things than becoming a prostitute—like starving on the streets for example. Eventually the Senator will want her dead, that is certain—and he'll ask me to look after it. He already knows my price.'

Joaquin could now walk, but he had to slouch to lessen the muscular stress and the sharp pain in his mending ribs. He was desperate to catch a glimpse of Sofia, although he had no idea what he would say. A ship's steward had been assigned to carry his suitcase, as he had found it impossible with the pain. He found himself in a long line of people on the outer deck waiting to step onto the gangplank and walk off the ship. The line-up inched along at an agonisingly slow pace and his eyes drifted to the wooden plank docks where masses of people from another passenger ship were milling about and getting themselves organised.

The sight of the three thugs that had ambushed him at his cabin room and beaten him senseless made him flush with anger. 'The bastards! I hope they get their due.' He watched as the chief steward, distinguishable by his height and his uniform, led the three along the dock. They were met by two uniform police officers. But something seemed wrong. They all appeared to be laughing together.

Then the chief steward removed the manacles from all three men and walked away with another sailor that had accompanied him. The chief steward was shaking his head in annoyance. Joaquin watched in disbelief as the three men shook hands with the uniform cops and moving their wrists to get the blood flowing into their hands. Then one of the cops offered cigarettes. 'For Christ's sake—they must have bribed the cops.'

He watched as an authoritative figure joined the group, and things appeared to get more tense at that point. The man was sharply dressed—a bespoke suit, a bowler hat adding to an already impressive height, and a hefty club disguised as a gentlemen's cane. Joaquin could make out an angular face underneath the bowler and the outline of a beard accentuating the jawline, but that was about all he could see from a distance. 'The two policemen slinked away guiltily,' he thought, as if they'd been caught by their boss doing something wrong.

Joaquin watched the bowler hat man disappear into the crowd, closely followed by the three thugs. 'So be it. There's nothing more I can do.'

It wasn't unusual to see police officers around the port in uniform or in plainclothes, thinking of the violent general strike just a few months previous. In his case, he'd been grateful for their presence. Just prior to last Christmas, the stevedores at the port had called a strike.

Eventually, other unions—masons, bricklayers, painters, and carpenters had joined the strike as a gesture of union fraternity. Things went downhill for the many businesses at the port and for their supply chains. He'd had overseas customers concerned about delays and goods had arrived and built up in his warehouse, with no-one to move the merchandise. In a state of desperation, he'd agreed with other businesses at the port to employ non-union labour, to get things moving again.

The workers, however, could only make it to his warehouse under the close protection of the police, and even then, there had been fights. They'd had to cross some of the most vicious picket lines he'd ever seen. He'd caught sight of some of the men he himself employed, and almost didn't recognise them through their vitriol and hatred, while they threatened the wide-eyed workers. They had made a difficult choice, as they were just husbands and fathers desperate to feed the hungry mouths dwelling within their crowded tenement rooms.

His mind was wrenched back to the present when he caught sight of Sofia Montserrat waiting on the dock with her luggage. 'What a remarkable, beautiful woman—she may have well saved my life.' Joaquin agonised at his position while the line inched forward, he couldn't even yell to her such was the pain of his mending ribs.

She was turned away from the ship as if expecting someone and had an air of uncertainty. 'Unusual that she is alone. I would have thought to see her accompanied by her uncle the Senator. She looks so vulnerable.' His instinct to protect her was taking hold, and he reminded himself to expel such feelings. She certainly wouldn't have appreciated it from what he had seen of her. 'The imaginings of a man desperate for the attention of a woman.'

To his surprise, she was then approached by the bowler hat man he had seen lead the three thugs away, the one he thought to be a plainclothes police officer. He watched as the man appeared to introduce himself, and then lead her to a single horse closed carriage. He took the reins himself and snapped the gelding forward.

'Why am I torturing myself with such conspiratorial thoughts? There is nothing unusual about this. The Senator is busy, she was probably brought to his house by the authorities. He will have access to such privileges as a public figure. Perhaps I will send a note to thank her via the Senator—but he may not choose to provide it to her—damn it! A shame I didn't take the take time to introduce myself to him.'

Life had not been all business for Joaquin in the 10 years since he'd arrived in Buenos Aires. He'd initially become an ardent follower of the opera, his evenings spent at the Teatro Opera on Corrientes. The sheer numbers of Italian immigrants to the city ensured regular attendance of Italy's finest opera singers. He enjoyed watching the swimming galas on the Lujan River, marvelling at the stamina of the young athletes and grace of the springboard divers. He tracked the rise and fall of several horses in the newspapers and occasionally took the tram north to the Hippodrome in Belgrano to see Don Salvador, Etoile D'Or, Great Scot, or Rhodesia, confront its destiny.

He reassured his parents in Madrid by attending mass occasionally, at the Metropolitan Cathedral facing the Plaza Mayo. When he'd first travelled to the city with his father to set up the Buenos Aires branch of the family business, his teetotaling father had been dismayed by the profligate drinking establishments, many of them poorly disguised brothels. Prostitutes were evident on street corners, cafes and bars. His father had befriended a priest, Father Devechio, whom he'd entrusted with Joaquin's immortal soul before returning to Madrid.

Now, many years later, knowing a report would be forwarded to his parents, Joaquin made sure to follow the rite of confession with Father Devechio, even if it missed the mark on a few indulgences of a minor nature.

But he was adrift in the sense that he had yet to find a central feature to his existence. Then one evening while courageously strolling eastward along Avenue Independencia, an insalubrious area, he came across a nondescript cafe, with a few tables placed outside. Men, women and a smattering of children were listening to a lone musician. He was singing in Italian, and accompanying himself with an accordion of sorts, a bandonéon. Joaquin could understand the Italian words—a song of a lonely immigrant struggling in a new land, missing his family, knowing he would never see them again, never feel the comfort of his homeland.

When it ended, the audience was subdued, as if they were pondering the words, as if they'd been living the words themselves. The song made Joaquin think of his family back in Madrid, something he rarely allowed himself to do. The musician played a few staccato notes on his instrument and began singing again.

A couple got up from their table and stood facing each other. Joaquin found himself as entranced as the others by the intimate scene unfolding before him. He watched as they took a hand and leaned forward into each other in a close embrace. They danced, manoeuvring more or less on the same spot, in between tables, lost in the music and each other. Joaquin had discovered Tango.

Although, disappointed that he hadn't been able to say goodbye to Sofia, he was happy to be back and anxious to check on a few things. He was in no shape to walk his usual distance to the docks, so he took a taxi in the form of a single horse caleche. He arrived at his warehouse several blocks south of Plaza Mayo and a couple of blocks west of dock 2, the second of four contiguous docks that all together served as the shipping centre of the country, and saw from a distance that they were a hive of activity.

Ships were being loaded and unloaded simultaneously. Streams of dockworkers carried heavy sacks of goods up gangplanks on one side in ant-like fashion, while offloading goods down another. Pulleys and guy lines criss-crossed the horizon, wheeling the larger boxes of machinery from dock to ship or vice versa.

He had a contingent of stevedores that he employed at his warehouse full time. They had it easier than the longshoremen who waited in line daily, to be chosen based on the arrivals of the ships and availability of work. Joaquin had learned that he was better off hiring workers that were happy to show up on time, who had the re-assurance of wages for a day's work, and would put in a long day when needed.

Joaquin had taken the time to meet most of the men working in his warehouse. He knew which of them had a wife and kids to support, knew which of them worked with whiskey on their breath and would stop at one of the bars on their way home, and knew which of them took things too far during strikes. He did his best not to hold a grudge when he heard them curse at him, but he was only human and had fired a few of them, whom he suspected of sabotage in his warehouse. But generally, he was on good terms with them.

Joaquin entered the large warehouse and saw that goods were being loaded and moved to the ships. 'Excellent.' He nodded as he passed the men that said hello or tipped their cap in greeting. The warehouse was sturdy, its framework using thick timber. Guy lines and rope hung from rafters. There was a refrigerated area in which beef carcasses were hung on large hooks that could be pushed along an overhanging rail system.

He climbed the wooden stairs to his office area and shook hands heartily with his bookkeeper Pablo, a quick-witted native Argentinian who was good with numbers and names.

"Patron were you hit by a quick moving ox in Madrid? You look even worse than normal." Pablo said.

"You don't want to know what hit me, Pablo." He didn't feel like explaining the story right now, "How are things going?"

"Things are on track. We've managed to keep all our contracts, and I didn't fire any of the soft-headed dimwits you call employees."

"They're not all that bad Pablo. Some of them are family men."

"What about that one?"

Joaquin saw Pablo looking down over the rail. There was a staring match between him and Diego, a tall and muscular stevedore that was a constant source of trouble. "What has he done now?"

"He's just being his usual bastard self."

"I suppose you wonder why I keep him employed. To tell you the truth, I'm not ready to deal with the consequences of firing him just yet. The men follow him, and he carries more than any other man."

"Joaquin, I need to be honest with you about something—in case you don't know."

"What is it?"

"Diego's an anarchist—and there are others like him working for you."

Joaquin skimmed through the ledgers, refreshing his memory as to the terms of his contracts. He made mental notes if he felt he should speak with a particular client or supplier. In the afternoon, his thoughts turned to his friend Tony, a husky, gregarious Italian, and a gifted musician. It was Tony who'd been playing the bandonéon in the cafe, where he'd seen the couple dance Tango many years ago. Joaquin had returned the following evening, and spoken to him during his breaks, pestering him with questions.

"I'm quite intrigued about this music you play. Where did you learn it?"

"I'm a professional musician and I have to play at several places to make a living. I guess I heard it somewhere along the way."

"That's very vague."

"Yes, it is."

"Aha, I apologise, I didn't mean to offend. The music is wonderful, but the dancing is also intriguing isn't it?"

"Yes, it is."

"I suppose I'm annoying you with these questions."

"Not at all. I'm happy to make your acquaintance actually. Are you a musician or a performer?"

"Not really—but how would I learn about this dance?"

"Valentina the waitress will show you." He waived over the heavily made up, buxom figure clearing the empty tables. "This is Joaquin. He wants you to teach him Tango."

The waitress finished her task and spoke briefly with the bartender. She walked towards Joaquin holding a cigarette, and looking him up and down. 'She was almost pretty,' he thought, and as she got closer, he saw she was older than he had thought.

"We can go to a place around the corner. There's a room."

"Can't we dance here?"

"I think he really wants to dance," Tony said to her.

"Don't you want to sleep with me?"

"I was hoping you would show me Tango."

"That's an unusual request," her eyes on Tony's as if she was worried, they were playing a prank of some kind. Tony played a few notes on the bandoneon and started singing.

That had been a few years ago. Joaquin had since become a regular feature of the cafes, and people attended to watch him dance Tango spontaneously with the waitress or another volunteer. Eventually, Joaquin, Tony, and a married waitress and aspiring actress called Costanza Moreno began performing together exclusively in order to provide more polished performances. Tango filled the gap that was missing in Joaquin's life, and added spiritual fulfilment.

After a while, he and Tony grew tired of repeating the same old songs. Joaquin began experimenting with lyrics and storytelling himself. Soon enough another door opened for his artistic creativity, and he began exploring themes he thought were important to the people that loved Tango—the immigrant men and families living in the tenements, the broken-hearted, longing for the old country. Then more original themes—ambition to become an actor, or the Mayor for that matter—as long as it entailed fame and fortune.

Tony, in turn, expanded his repertoire of musical instruments, adding the likes of a peeling flamenco guitar and a violin that had seen better days. They added variety to the musical accompaniment of their acts, which appealed to the younger children now sitting in their audiences.

'Our goal is to keep their blessed little hearts entertained for an hour Tony— not one second more!'

Next, they decided to add two more men and women to the act.

'With the right actors, the show will become more popular Tony. We can include more characters and expand the choreography.'

But this they had found elusive. The actors and actresses were generally part of a transient community, hopping from job to job. They were hard to find and harder to keep. They went through a spate of mediocre debutantes that chafed under Joaquin's demand for perfection.

'It's a work in progress Tony—don't despair.'

'And Tony grew to be a close and sympathetic friend,' Joaquin thought. A true confidante. The two were from infinitely different backgrounds; Tony's parents had immigrated to Buenos Aires 30 years ago, and raised Tony and his two brothers in the slums in the centre of the city. Somehow, they had survived the outbreaks of cholera and yellow fever, although Tony's mother lost several children to illness along the way.

Like so many other European immigrants, Tony's parents had been opera enthusiasts and Tony's father had been thrilled to see that he possessed more than a modicum of musical talent, unlike his brothers. His parents had indulged him, finding him piano and singing lessons, while his brothers toiled in the slaughterhouses where their father worked. His brothers were proud of their little brother and bragged about him to the other Italians. God help anyone they heard denigrate their little brother. They had become hard men, ensnared into the one-upmanship of their union's culture. They were ardent front-liners, battling with the cops during the strikes and International Worker's Day protests.

Indeed, Tony's blue-collar background added a depth of street savvy to their lyrics. He filled in the gaps that Joaquin's privileged upbringing in Madrid did not expose him to. Joaquin had had a lot of time to think about an epic Tango play during his trip to Madrid, and he was anxious to discuss it with his friend. They worked best when Joaquin was drafting lyrics and Tony was experimenting with musical accompaniment.

It was a balancing act with Joaquin shooting for the stars, hoping to see their Tango in the finest opera theatres of the city, and Tony gently reminding him that Tango was working class, best received in the union halls, cafes and bars, sipping through the bubbles of a pint of frothy draft, sherry or hesperadina for the ladies.

Now, Joaquin hoped to find him in one of the cafes, as his home was too far, and dangerous, for Joaquin to visit. As he walked to the haunts he knew Tony frequented, he pushed something disconcerting to the back of his mind, a complicating factor he was not ready to face. There was at least one active anarchist working in his warehouse. How many others were there? What new trouble would result from this?

Chapter 8
Madam Josefina's Social House

Sofia climbed into the coach as Lieutenant Machado held the door, feeling foolish about the ostentatious means of transport. 'I'm not a royal princess.' She was unnerved by the sheer bustle along the waterfront, confused passengers darting right and left, the acrid odour of burned coal from the stacks of the steamships mixed with the sewage that streamed raw into the ocean.

The sights and smells of Buenos Aires were a stark contrast to the rural peace and quiet of Jerez de la Frontera. She'd been briefly disoriented, standing beside her suitcase and trunk, wondering what had become of her Uncle Hugo. She was startled by the apparition of a tall man in a bowler hat, who had conjured himself in front of her speaking her name.

"Señorita Montserrat I presume? My name is Vicente Machado—Lieutenant Vicente Machado."

"Yes. What's going on—why are you here exactly?" Sofia said, thinking she was about to be arrested again.

"I'm an acquaintance of Senator Montserrat. My boss and he are good friends so I've been asked to bring you to your residence. Come—I have a coach waiting. I'll take that trunk for you—it looks heavy." He hoisted the trunk effortlessly onto a very wide shoulder before she could object.

"Did you say you were a Lieutenant? Are you in the army?"

"Police of the Capital—investigative division. The Senator's protection forms part of our purview."

"Where is he? Isn't he coming as well."

"He's been called to attend to some urgent business," he threw her trunk onto the coachman's seat and tilted it on its side to make room for himself. Sofia heard its contents being thrown from side to side, but thought better of asking him to be more careful.

"I see—you said you were a police officer—do you have some sort of identification if you don't mind?"

"Of course—rude of me not to properly identify myself." 'If he was trying to be charming, he had failed miserably,' she thought. He opened his suit jacket and showed her the silver badge pinned to his vest. It was as genuine as the large revolver in a leather holster hanging under his armpit.

Convinced, she got in with her suitcase and he closed the door behind her. She'd had a hard time not asking more questions. She had the uneasy feeling she was losing control of her life, and she didn't like it. This feeling of dependence was irritating, despite her uncle's gracious offer to accommodate her. She would have to make arrangements to be independent as soon as she could. Exactly how, remained to be seen.

As she peered out the side windows of the coach, she marvelled at the new construction everywhere, cranes lifting heavy material upwards, scaffolding around half erected stone buildings, crowded electric and horse-drawn trams, and streets with no end that she could see. 'She had been sheltered in her peaceful corner of the world,' she thought. The endless streets and tall buildings played tricks with her sense of direction. She realised with considerable trepidation that she did not even know her uncle's address. 'Why didn't he give me his address?'

When the coach came to a halt, giving way to a horse-drawn tram full of passengers, she leaned out the window. "Where exactly are you taking me?"

"I'm taking you to an area known as Once. It will take another 30 minutes."

Once wasn't anything her uncle had mentioned to her she was certain. 'There is no cause for concern. There is nothing unusual about this.' With no further explanation forthcoming, she heard the snap of the reins and the coach rolled forward over the tram's rail tracks under the power of its single horse, controlled by a man she didn't know. She couldn't shake her growing alarm; something was definitely wrong.

"Welcome to Madam Josefina's Social House."

"Why am I here—have I now been kidnapped?"

"Not exactly. You're free to leave at any time—but I don't recommend it." He dislodged her trunk from the driver's box with a forceful kick, sending it sailing downward. Sofia watched with dismay as it lodged itself into a pile of horse manure and other unidentifiable muck, not that she wasn't comfortable with horse manure. She was looking at the sweating gelding and pondering her odds of stealing the coach.

"I wouldn't try it," Machado said. He'd caught the direction of her gaze and evidently read her mind. "Where would you go? Do you know this city? Do you even have any money with you?"

"I'm supposed to be staying with my uncle, the Senator Hugo Montserrat." Sofia had considered the Lieutenant's comment about money. She knew she was in a dire predicament—vulnerable to the whims of the daunting Lieutenant.

"Senator Montserrat doesn't want you staying with him. Apparently, you're some kind of vicious murderer. I find that hard to believe, but who am I to judge? We can't have such a person endangering the life of a senator. You'll have to stay here."

"It's a brothel. Take me to the Spanish Embassy immediately!" She was bluffing and they both knew it.

"I'm going to be honest with you—it's best you completely understand the situation," he said. "The Spanish authorities are about to issue a warrant for your arrest if they haven't already done so. If you make it easy for them and attend their embassy, they'll simply take you into custody and ship you back to Spain—you'll be sentenced to death for your crimes. They use the garrotte I'm told."

"I had nothing to do with their murders. I loved my parents dearly."

"The evidence suggests otherwise—I'm told," he said, showing little desire to argue the point. "There is a room and a bed here for you. As I see it—there's no other place for you to go." He dislodged her trunk from the pile of manure, kicked off the larger chunks, and hoisted it back onto his shoulder. "Follow me," he said, and walked through the grand wooden doors. Sofia looked again at the coach and imagined he was listening for the snort from the horse and snap of the reins. Instead, she followed behind him.

"I'm going to introduce you to Josefina—the Madam. You'll have to discuss your longer-term arrangements with her. She's in charge here."

"I won't be staying long. As soon as I can arrange to get to my Uncle Hugo's house, I will leave."

"Let me be crystal clear to you Miss Montserrat—you've misjudged your uncle. It was he who arranged for me to bring you here. The instructions were very specific—you were not to be brought anywhere except for a brothel. I've done you the favour of bringing you to a clean, reputable one." He transfixed her in a cold, reptilian stare. "Your beloved uncle is not who you think he is. I'll tell you something that you're not to repeat. He is a vicious, violent man—particularly with women—and especially with a belly full of whiskey. You're

106

safer here. So far, you've merely been naïve. Showing up at his door would be stupid—and possibly fatal."

The depth of her Uncle Hugo's betrayal was beginning to dawn on her, and although she was desperately trying to understand why, the sequence of disastrous events clouded her comprehension. It seemed more important to focus on her present circumstances. But the words of the gypsy woman Mirella reverberated in her mind, 'Be careful who you trust—survive at all costs.'

"So, this is Sofia?" asked the buxom, rouged woman with a wig the colour of fire, while looking her over from bottom to top, as if taking stock of a chattel she might bid for.

"I'm Sofia."

"And what have you done to get yourself an escort to my establishment by such a fine officer of the police dearie?"

"I don't know. I came to this country from my home in Spain under the premise that I would stay at my uncle's residence while an investigation into the murder of my parents ran its course. Now I'm told I'm to stay at a brothel!" Her voice had risen despite her best effort not to sound belligerent.

"Your uncle is Senator Hugo Montserrat?" Madam Josefina said.

"Yes, he is."

"Trust me you're better off here dearie," she said, looking at Machado with a knowing glance.

"So, I've just been informed."

"I'm terribly sorry about your parents—I'll have a room set up for you. How long is she staying for Lieutenant?"

"It's going to be a lengthy stay by my reckoning," he said.

The implications of Lieutenant Machado's statement made Sofia want to cry in frustration. She'd become a pawn in a game she didn't understand and over which she had no control. Sofia looked around the courtyard. There were several small round tables and wooden chairs, currently sitting empty. There was a bar under the cover of the overhanging second floor, with two beer taps and several kegs stacked in a corner.

Bottles of spirits were resting on shelves behind the bar. A spindly teenage boy, with an eyepatch and a mop of black hair, was fussing and polishing glasses behind the bar. Looking upwards to the second and third floors, she saw several women in various states of dress, hanging laundry on lines that crossed the blue sky above the courtyard. The smell of bleach hung heavy in the air.

"These women are prostitutes?" Sofia asked, causing Josefina to snort.

"Indeed, they are. They're a sweet bunch—I'm lying—they're crapulous trollops one and all. Don't leave your valuables where they can see them."

"How did they come to be here?" Sofia asked, hoping their circumstances were not similar to her own. Evidently Madam Josefina mistook the look on her face for fear.

"Oh, there's no need to be afraid of them. This isn't some jail for delinquents. No one is going to put a knife in your ribs for that bracelet on your arm—which is very beautiful by the way." Sofia self-consciously pulled her sleeve over the bracelet, a present from her mother.

"You'll get to know them. They all have an unfortunate story, but they're here making an honest living. The men in Buenos Aires are lonely and need a woman's company occasionally," she said. "That's a service that my noble social house provides and I'm damn proud of it—the devil I am but let's just say it pays the bills."

Sofia saw that Lieutenant Machado had levitated to the bar and the one-eyed teenager was serving him mineral water. 'Conveniently leaving me with the Madam who will persuade me to become a prostitute.'

"Now listen to me dearie—there's rules you'll have to follow. This is a registered brothel and it gets inspected every now and then in order to keep the city and the health authorities happy. Don't piss them off—there's a lot of ways they can make trouble for us. The ladies are also registered, and can't be away from the brothel after sundown. If you're wandering around like a little lost sheep after dark, the coppers will pick you up. They'll assume you're one of mine and you'll end up in the lock-up down the street. Then I'll have to pull some strings to get you out—understand?"

Sofia recalled the experience of resting her head, exhausted and tormented, on the straw smelling of urine after she'd been arrested in Jerez. That was enough to convince her she should abide by the rules.

"Tico!" Madam Josefina called over the teenage boy. "This is Señorita Sofia. She is the niece of Senator Montserrat."

Sofia saw a dark expression come over the boy's face. "The Senator is a bad hombre."

"Yes Tico—I've explained all that to the poor child," Madam Josefina said to shut him up. "She needs a room. There's is a small one available on the third floor. See that it's cleaned and prepare the bed."

"Yes, Auntie Jo."

"Tico is your nephew?" Sofia said. She thought it was best to display some gratitude, as she had no plan and nowhere to go.

"Lord no. He's an orphan. He lost both of his parents to yellow fever and lost an eye from a beating at the orphanage. He makes himself useful around here, so I look after the poor boy. Excuse me dearie—I need to speak with the Lieutenant for a moment on a point of business."

Sofia was grateful for a reprieve to collect her thoughts. What had happened? They had intimated that her Uncle Hugo was some kind of vicious sadist towards women. She found that surprisingly easy to believe, and it explained the standoffish attitude towards her during the three weeks they had just spent on the steamship. She'd had no real opportunity to get to know him or have a conversation of any consequence. She still had a jumbled recollection of events; from the minute she had arrived at the estate and was knocked off her horse by the civil guardsman.

She'd been treated roughly during their interrogation, slaps across the cheek while they called her a liar, by young men that she knew personally, and had gone to grade school with. They had relished her discomfort. The stuck up, well-to-do Sofia Montserrat had fallen from grace and was at their mercy, although they hadn't shown any. To them, she was now a despicable, scheming murderer. 'They had not been investigating, they'd merely been spiteful,' she thought.

They had refused to write down her words. There would be no official record of her denials for the magistrate to review. 'Are you covering up for your anarchist friends—your anarchist lovers? Were you there to watch your parents die, or did you just fantasise about it from afar? Did you make love to them afterwards?' They were little men and they'd been cruel. A return to her home in Jerez de la Frontera was not an option she had right now.

Sofia watched Madam Josefina and the Lieutenant speaking in low murmurs at the bar. She could overhear a few words.

"He's a slimy cheating little bastard," she heard the Lieutenant say.

"Some cash from the month's take is unaccounted for as far as I can see," Madam Josefina pointing to a multi-paged ledger.

'It's none of my business,' Sofia thought.

"Tico! Go find Octavio. Tell him I want to talk to him right now," Madam Josefina said, sending the scrawny teenager out the front entrance. Then she sat down with Sofia again.

"Your situation sounds dire Sofia," she said while placing a cigarette into a silver holder. She struck a match and lit it, sending plumes of smoke out of both nostrils like a dragon, then crossed a leg over the other and stared at Sofia.

"I offer these ladies a safe and clean place to conduct their business. All the ladies, you see, also rent a room. It's convenient and cheap and the easiest way for them to save money—it's also city regulations. The house takes a cut from every customer served and I supply the social rooms. The cut has to cover their liquor costs, the lease paid to the venerable Police Commissioner De La Fuente who owns the property, and city licensing. I also require a modest salary of course—we're not bloody communists after all," she said, taking another long drag of the cigarette and blowing smoke rings.

"Some of them send money home—highly admirable of them don't you think? Impoverished relatives that they hold dear somewhere in France, or Poland, or Germany. Most of them come from Europe like yourself—but unlike you they came with the intention to make money as a prostitute. Buenos Aires has a deserving reputation as the land of milk and honey for women in the profession. A few of my ladies came across with their boyfriend or a pimp posing as their husband. After they arrived, they went their separate ways for one reason or another and the ladies found their way here. There's a couple of ladies who work extra hard to put food on the table because their husband's wages merely feed their gambling habits and their drinks at the bars. Their husbands have no idea that they work here," she said with a disgusted snort.

"There's no other jobs available for these women. A woman should be able to make a decent wage don't you think? Money is made quickly here—it's not the pennies they would make washing clothes. If treated right, men will pay well for the attention of their favourite lady."

Madam Josefina sighed heavily. "But I'm not trying to convince you that you should work here—you need not concern yourself for a few days. You'll have shelter and food. But we'll have to speak again if your situation persists. It's the only employment I can offer dearie and it's the only work you'll be able to find in this city." She blew another plume of smoke into the air above Sofia's head. "You'll see and hear some things in the evening you won't be used to. Don't be shocked. It's what pays the bills."

"I'll help you with that," Sofia said to Tico, watching him struggle to lift her trunk.

"Gracias, Señorita Sofia," he said, as he had the front of the trunk in a backhand grip, trying to wrestle it up the winding wooden stairway.

He showed her to her room and scurried back down to the courtyard to get her suitcase. Sofia was grateful for a moment alone. She looked around the room. It was basic, a bed, a small table, and a gas lamp. Tico knocked at the door with her suitcase. "Gracias, Tico."

"De nada."

"Who is Octavio?"

"Octavio is the book keeper. He is a very smart man. He does arithmetic."

"Can't you do arithmetic?"

"I don't know numbers."

"Did you go to school?"

"Nobody like me goes to school." He looked pensive. "At the orphanage, the nuns tried to teach me to read and write—I didn't like it there so I ran away."

"Why?"

"Everyone beat me up."

"How did you come to be here?"

"Lieutenant Machado brought me here. He told me I either stay here and work, go to jail, or go back to the orphanage again."

"Did you believe him?"

"Yes. He is the toughest, meanest cop in Buenos Aires and I almost love him like my father. And everybody knows not to piss him off."

"Or what?"

"He will beat you like a dog and make you disappear. You don't want to see what happens to Octavio. He's been a bad man."

"What does the Lieutenant have to do with that?"

"Oh, you don't know. He's in charge of Auntie Jo. She has to pay him every week."

"Why does she have to pay a police officer?"

"Well, it's his boss that owns this place."

"I see," Sofia said. "He collects the money for his boss?"

"Something like that, Señorita Sofia. He is very angry with Octavio. He knows Octavio is cheating him."

"Will he arrest Octavio?"

"I don't think he will arrest him. He will be lucky if he's only arrested—but I don't think today is his lucky day."

Sofia heard a commotion in the courtyard, tables being knocked over.

"Come here you treacherous little swine!"

Sofia walked to the banister and looked into the courtyard. She saw the Lieutenant catch a short, rotund man with a thick moustache and a bald head. He was holding his hands up, trying to protect himself. Lieutenant Machado dragged him to a wall and pinned his shoulders firmly against it.

"How much have you stolen?"

"I haven't stolen anything Lieutenant let me explain," but he was interrupted by a vicious punch to the solar plexus that made him sink to the ground retching and gasping for breath. She watched as the Lieutenant gave him a minute to recover, while he writhed and wheezed and hacked. The Lieutenant walked around him while lighting a thin cigar.

"I want to know exactly how much you've stolen—you're not going anywhere until you tell me." He picked up Octavio by the lapels of his jacket and pinned him to the wall again. Sofia could see him struggling to catch his breath and say something at the same time. He was begging for mercy, holding one hand up, the other hand went to his chest.

The Lieutenant showed him no mercy. With the suddenness and skill of a practiced boxer, he punched him twice more in the stomach making him rise from the ground with each strike, and kicked him in the face as he was falling, ejecting teeth and spitting blood.

Sofia tried to restrain herself, 'It's none of my business,' but could take no more of this wanton cruelty.

"Stop it!" She yelled firmly at the top of her lungs. "Stop that right now." She found herself running down the stairs with Tico tugging her arm all the way down.

"Señorita Sofia don't be crazy, he'll kill you!" He held Sofia's arm to no avail, until she placed herself in between the man and the Lieutenant, then he tried to make himself inconspicuous behind her.

Sofia was past caring, past fearing, and past explaining. Her parents had been savagely murdered and she stood falsely accused. She had been taunted and abused by the Civil Guard. Her Uncle Hugo, pretending to care for her, had lured her far away to an unknown city and left her destitute at a brothel. She was ready for confrontation. She wasn't going to have any more time for mourning and it was time to fight back. Right now she didn't care against who.

"What kind of police officer beats a man this way? Do you want to kill him? Does he have a wife? A family?" She drew herself square to the Lieutenant, purposely putting herself within his striking distance. 'She stared at him with her chin out, unmoving, and he returned the stare with all the calm and caring of a rattlesnake,' she thought. He exhaled smoke over her head, and she braced herself for the inevitable strike.

It had felt like the standoff had gone on forever when her concentration was interrupted by the groans of the bookkeeper. He struggled to his feet, unbalanced and swaying, his face a bloody mess.

"Tico help that man. See he gets home," Sofia said. She turned around to face the Lieutenant, only this time not so close. "I'll be your book keeper," she heard herself say. "I'm an excellent accountant. I ran all my father's business affairs. I can keep the ledgers for you."

Sofia waited defiantly while Lieutenant Machado seemed to ponder her offer, a far-off look and the cigar clamped in his teeth. Until that point, he and everyone else assumed she was doomed to a life of prostitution, Sofia included. She watched, waiting for a blow. Then he lifted an eyebrow towards Madam Josefina, who had also been contemplating the situation in silence.

"I can't stand the bloody suspense—what do we have to lose Vicente? I don't want that squirmy little shite working here anymore."

Chapter 9
The Revolutionary

"Fourteen years ago—our very first revolution—failed as it did," Major Leon Alvarez said, pensively. "We were the best and the brightest—shiny new faces to the faculty of law, attending every radical lecture we could." A bottle of Buchanan's Scotch whiskey sat on the table, half empty. Gabriel Chavez pondered his companion, who was speaking a little too loudly for Chavez's comfort.

"We were young and stupid—and now? We're middle-aged and still stupid."

"There's no need to be cynical. We're wiser now Leon—at least as far as revolutions go."

"Wiser," Alverez said, sharply. "We listened to the glorious speeches of our leaders, and we fought with the police in La Boca." Alvarez waived a fist in a circle. "On the day of the coup, brave General Campos was mysteriously freed from prison to lead the way—but he did the opposite. He stopped the advance and took up a static position in the Parque d'Artillerie. The General had only one job—to take the central police station and secure the garrison. He was paid off— he betrayed us Gabriel." He looked at Chavez with tearful eyes.

"That's two jobs my friend—and no he wasn't paid off. He didn't advance because the coup had been discovered and the government had mobilised their forces from the provinces. General Campos knew the battle was lost and decided not to throw lives away recklessly. It was futile and would've been more of a bloodbath than it already was. He did what a reasonable man would do. The fact of the matter is that it was all poorly coordinated—and that wasn't his responsibility. But that was 14 years ago Leon—we have to push these doubts from our minds." Chavez loved his friend dearly but didn't want their decision to attempt another coup questioned at this advanced stage.

"I'm just saying we can't trust the generals," Alvarez said, "and we have to be careful."

"I agree Leon—but this time we don't need them. We just need the junior officers. Are your colleagues are still with us?"

"Yes."

"Then it will finally be our time for true democracy Leon," Chavez said, shaking his friend's forearm fondly. "This farcical election will be the last time they can buy the presidency or their seat on the senate. Take that bottle back to the barracks for our friends Leon. Tell them I salute their courage." Chavez saw Leon back safely to the barracks, and made sure he didn't fall into the hands of the cops—again.

Twice now, Chavez had had to pay a bribe to a desk sergeant at the local police station to free his inebriated friend before the military police learned of his condition and reported him to his superiors. He had not wanted him to suffer yet another demotion. And on this occasion, he couldn't afford any loose lips giving away their plans to the cops.

He'd felt badly when Leon had told him that he'd had enough of law school, and that he had enrolled in the military officer's academy. He wanted to change things from within, he'd said. Prior to law school, Leon had enjoyed the time they'd spent as conscripts in the army, more so than Chavez. 'He was a good leader of men, when sober, a true son of Argentina,' Chavez thought. The two of them loved their country.

Like many educated men of their generation, they bemoaned the constant outflow of its capital, used to pay back foreign loans. "They're running a scam Leon. The politicians that give generous incentives to the British to develop the railways and shipping infrastructure, are the very same ones whose ranches benefit from the exports bought by the British. They're the very same ones that agreed to pay their guaranteed profit margins using the country's gold reserves, devaluing our currency. They're the very same ones that have the audacity to buy off the voters with the profits they've made," Chavez had said to his friend, slamming his fist on the table. It was the kind of statement you only made to someone you trusted, because it was sedition.

Now, having safely returned his friend home to his doting wife, he needed to get home to his own. Their two children, both girls, would be long since asleep. She would smell the whiskey on his breath, would be mad he was late, would turn away from him again in frustration. 'It was a marriage going badly,' he thought. His infidelities with an opportunistic lover, a mistress, or an attractive clerk at the Ministry had been discovered one too many times.

'At least, she wouldn't smell perfume on his collar tonight,' he thought. He was smart and idealistic, and truly loved his wife. But he also had striking green eyes, and sharp Latin facial features that women found attractive, that made it easy for him to cheat.

Chavez meandered towards home, unhurried, pondering his precarious position. He was an Argentine national from an established family, the sort of family that approved of the uncontested power that wealthy landowners-come-politicians had enjoyed for decades. One evening over brandy he'd made the mistake of admonishing his family's pandering to the establishment, much to his father's consternation, and received a blunt dose of reality.

"Dear boy—how do you think we got all of this? This house, our savings, our land holdings? How do you think I paid for your law degree and your apartment in Retiro?"

But Gabriel Chavez had no mind for business. He was an idealist, part of the next generation that would bring true representative democracy to a nation known internationally as a haven for dubious political and banking practices. He'd fallen naturally into the field of law and graduated summa cum laude. He'd been hired as a protégé by a similarly minded progressive bureaucrat within the Ministry of the Interior, the likes of which were beginning to manifest themselves within the various ministries.

His superiors took note, impressed with the rigour with which he threw himself at his work. Chavez climbed steadily up the promotional ladder and now found himself appointed to the heady position of Deputy Legal Secretary, of which there were several at the service of the Minister.

For now, he was content. He told himself he had influence over policy, and higher-level decision making. He was privy to briefing reports from the general staff of the military, describing potential encroachment on their borders with Chile or Uruguay, as well as the recommended diplomatic or armed response. He summarised the reports received from the chief of police on the status of the threat posed by increasing numbers of European anarchists now flocking to the city—a cause for which he held little sympathy.

'No government or bourgeoisie? How the devil would things actually work—who would make their decisions?' He drank at bars with like-minded civil servants, disenchanted with electoral embarrassments, and corrupt practices that benefited the few in political power. He'd led a charmed, privileged existence. Nevertheless, the revolutionary flame burned bright in his soul. 'Soon.'

Chavez sat in his small office on the second floor of the ministry building on Avenida de Mayo. The envelope he had received was embossed with the seal of the Spanish embassy and marked confidential. It was addressed to Gabriel Chavez, Legal Secretary, Ministry of the Interior, For Your Eyes Only. It was received from the Office of the Legal Attaché of the Spanish Embassy, he was told.

He wasn't surprised to be addressed personally. He thought it was likely from a Spanish lawyer with whom he'd cultivated a close working relationship, for the purpose of reciprocal favours, as needed. It was common to have such contacts within the various embassies of Buenos Aires. It made for efficient fact finding, discreet working level machinations, communication, and channels of influence when the minister so desired. 'When things got dire and the battleships were lining themselves up for the broadside volley,' the minister liked to say.

Breaking the embossment with a paper knife, he found his intuition had been correct, and he read the note from his friend with piqued concern. 'What the hell is going on?'

A Discreet Matter of Concern

We feel it necessary to inform you that this Embassy has received troubling information. It has come to light that a person described as a senior Argentine police official, identity unknown, recently made contact with known mercenary elements in Barcelona.

Three former soldiers, rumoured to have engaged in contractual murders, were hired for a special mission in the city of Buenos Aires. They have relocated to Argentina recently by way of the steamship Sirio.

The information is unverifiable at present, however, a reliable informer of many years was well-placed to receive information of such an activity, by way of conversations overheard between the concerned parties at a waterfront bar. The informer then arranged to watch departures at the port and witnessed the boarding of the three subjects on the Sirio. The information was reported through channels of the Civil Guard located in Barcelona.

Given the nature of the information the reporting of such information through customary police channels seemed ill-advised. Spanish Ambassador believed it best to pass the information to a trusted colleague within the ministry.

Miguel Alcazar
Office of the Legal Attaché
Embassy of Spain, Argentina

'A senior police official and three mercenaries? It's off the books then—but for what reason? To avoid briefing obligations through the ministry—to avoid tipping off someone like myself? They're investigating our coup d'état. Could they be on to us—me?'

Chavez was unnerved but he'd been careful to insulate himself. 'They would be spies, unknown faces in the bars. Pose as civilian supporters ready to take up arms. Assassins? I would think the police would be quite willing to conduct select assassinations in lieu of another bloody battle with the army on the streets.' He rubbed his temples. He was uncertain they would be assassins but he couldn't take chances. He had to act quickly—had to identify the men, and the senior police official.

Only the investigative division would be involved in such a thing. The ministry kept all the briefing documents forwarded from the police department. He could have his aide review those from the investigative division, identify the signatories and their positions, and create a shortlist. 'Could this be sanctioned by the chief of police himself?' He had a mental picture of the former soldier Colonel Rosando Fraga, another favourite of the ruling political class that had enjoyed a series of patronage appointments from one high bureaucratic position to the next. He had been recently appointed by the President, Manuel Quintana, to replace Chief Beazley. 'A personal friend of the President.'

Chief Fraga might implement such an audacious operation, being new, in an effort to impress everybody. 'It changes nothing.' If Chavez found the men, what would he do? That was a question for later.

"What have you discovered?" He had recruited Nicolas out of the law academy. He met the young man while attending the academy as a guest lecturer. Nicolas had cornered him outside the lecture hall to inquire about employment possibilities at the ministry. He had the right pedigree, Argentine heritage, politically progressive, and Chavez had given him his calling card.

"Come and see me at the ministry when you have your law degree. I'll see what I can do." He'd hired Nicolas last year, and the young lawyer was progressing well. But he had not told his aide everything, certainly not that he was involved in the planned coup d'état. He didn't know if his aide could be trusted with such secrets just yet. 'That conversation could wait for another couple of months,' he thought.

"There's a steamship in port called the Sirio," Nicolas said. "I saw it berthed at the dock and spoke to the port master's office. It will be loading and taking on coal for another two days. It's registered to an Italian shipping line, Navigazione General Italiana. I have the address of their storefront, it's on Rivadavia. Would you like me to go there?"

"No but fine work. I'll stop by this afternoon myself," he said, hiding his concern. "I'd like you to go through the reports originating from the investigative division of the police department—let's say for the last year."

"The anarchists?"

"What about the anarchists?"

"Most of their reports as of late relate to the anarchist threat. The police are quite preoccupied with them."

"Yes of course."

'Why didn't I think of that? It could be an operation against the anarchists. Except that would be a perfectly normal investigation by the police. There would be no need for such secrecy, and to cut out the ministry.' Chavez thought the operation could be used to investigate both groups. His adopted band of revolutionaries, the Civic Union 'radicalissimos,' were noble men wanting to eradicate issues of corruption, governance and voting practices. They were the lawyers, doctors, civil servants, and most critically, lower ranking officers of the military.

They couldn't be more different from the anarchists, who couldn't care less about such things. 'They're a ridiculous bunch really.' He thought it was more likely the operation was targeting his group.

"I would like you to make me a list of their officers. Names and Ranks," and to throw Nicolas off the scent, "we need to build and maintain a list of contacts within the specialised investigative division. This will be helpful."

Chavez left the ministry and walked eastward across the Plaza Mayo and then along Rivadavia until he saw the office. Navigazione General Italiana Steamship Travel and Freight Exportation was stencilled in gilded letters forming a globe on the window. A small, bespectacled man, bow tie and a waistcoat, was calculating numbers on a piece of a paper behind the counter and hadn't noticed him enter.

"Good day, Señor. My name is Gabriel Chavez—I'm with the Ministry of the Interior." He handed the man his calling card in order to impress and to indicate he expected his questions to be answered. "I'm told the steamship Sirio belongs to your company?"

"Indeed, it does, Mr Chavez. Is something wrong?"

"Not at all. Can you tell me if it made a port-of-call in Barcelona prior to its voyage to Buenos Aires?"

"Yes, it's a regular stopover. It starts in Naples and stops in Genoa and Barcelona, amongst other places."

"I see. I wish to locate three men that travelled to Buenos Aires on that ship. They would have embarked at Barcelona."

"I'm not sure I can help you locate them. We don't keep a lot of information here at the office. We only keep records of those that travelled in first and second class for a short time before they're disposed of. Do you have their names?"

"I don't have their names—that's what I hoped you would tell me. How many people boarded at Barcelona?"

"I don't have the exact number—it could have been several hundred. There were at least a thousand people that travelled to Argentina in steerage class alone. You could check with customs. The Captain provided them with a passenger list and every passenger has to declare themselves to customs at the port. They record their age, their occupation, and where they came from."

"Of course," Chavez said. Investigations were not his purview, and he hadn't thought of that. "Is there anything else that you can think of that would help?" 'The man seemed sympathetic,' Chavez thought. He might as well try for more.

"No—but you could check with the ship's Captain. His name is Juan Perez—he's staying at the Hotel Metropol. He'll be sailing in two days."

Chavez walked towards the ministry, pondering his next steps. He decided he would entrust his aide Nicolas with a little more information. He needed many tasks done urgently that he couldn't possibly do all by himself.

He walked down the hallway to his office, the dark wood door adorned with his brass name plate. Through the shutters he discerned movement, and heard shuffling noises. Alarmed that someone was rifling through his files and private notes, he burst in, discovering his aide Nicolas inflagrante delicto, his pants around one ankle and one foot on his desk, mounted upon a pretty clerk from the typist pool.

"Good Christ Nicolas!" Chavez quickly gathered his composure. There was no time for disciplinary distractions. As an afterthought, he closed the door and looked away so that they could dress themselves with some level of dignity. "This isn't a brothel dear boy." Chavez's initial irritation gave way to amusement while his sputtering aide and the young woman scrambled to put on their clothes.

"I'm sorry sir! It's just—we had nowhere else to go."

Chavez held the door open for the young woman who, flushed with embarrassment, made the briefest of eye contact with him, 'A plea for discretion,' he thought, and hastily exited. He thought her highly desirable at that moment. He stopped himself from laughing out loud. Ironically, he'd had used his office for similar libertine activities on occasion, but he didn't want to condone the same behaviour from his aide.

In some respects, he sympathised, young couples discreetly courting had to seize every opportunity away from their prying parents' eyes. On the other hand, he wasn't certain his impertinent aide was courting her at all.

"Next time use the lock. Do you have the police reports I asked for?"

"There were only a few," Nicolas said, adjusting his clothes and retrieving the files from the floor beside the desk. "I've noted the names and ranks of the police officers that signed the documents for one reason or another."

"Leave them right there. I have another job for you—consider it urgent. I want you to retrieve the customs records of all the passengers that disembarked from the Sirio. Then filter out the names of all the men that embarked at Barcelona, ages 25 to 40. I want a list of those names."

"May I ask exactly what you are looking for? It might make it easier."

"I'm looking for three former soldiers. They are here in Buenos Aires—for nefarious reasons that we must identify. This matter has to be kept strictly confidential. Tell no one—understood?"

"Of course, sir."

Chavez looked at the neat pile of reports stacked on his desk and thought Nicolas was extremely competent, despite today's indiscretion. He hung up his jacket and lit a cigarette. He looked at the handwritten list of names and ranks of the involved police officers. Nicolas had arranged them from lowest ranking to highest ranking. There were various Lieutenant's and Captain's that initiated the reports, but always one figure that signed off their approval. 'Commissioner Felipe De La Fuente, Commander Investigative Division.'

Chavez had met him before. He was a large man who walked with a pronounced limp, due to a wound inflicted upon him by the insurrectionary soldiers at the Parque d'Artillerie 14 years ago. Chavez had just graduated from the law academy at the University of Buenos Aires. He was a nobody but had volunteered to help the central figures of the Radical Civic Union keep track of the progress of their coup d'état, running dispatches between their positions. He'd been kept away from the real fighting, a good thing as many of his peers had been killed, or imprisoned.

Over the years, Chavez had time to go through the ministry records, looking for any mention of his name, and had found nothing. He would not be known personally to the investigative division as a revolutionary threat, so he thought he was safe for now.

Commissioner was the highest rank on the briefing note. A commissioner reported directly to the chief of police. They too were typically patronage appointments and would be tied in some way to someone within the reigning cadre of the president and senators. All of them were the long ruling politicians he despised.

The police commissioners would have been intimately involved in the last round of elections, with their men watching at the polls for those who voted for, and those who voted against. They would have intervened wherever they had to, in order to ensure the success of their sponsor. They were part of the state bureaucracy that would fight tooth and nail to preserve the status quo, and they were no friends of his.

'Commissioner De La Fuente—you are the senior police official. Why have you hired three mercenaries? Who are you going to kill?'

He finished his cigarette and pondered the spot on his desk where the young woman's breasts had been pressed. He walked down the stairs and made his way to the area where the women were typing the various documents required of their assigned bureaus. He made eye contact with the young woman he'd interrupted an hour before.

Chavez was fortunate. The clerk manning the front desk of the Hotel Metropol was familiar with Captain Juan Perez. He led him across the grand mosaic floor, by a winding marble staircase, and into the reading room. The

Captain was seated alone, in a regency styled chair, sipping tea, and smoking a cigar. Several newspapers lay on the table beside him.

"Good evening Captain, my name is Gabriel Chavez—I'm with the Ministry of the Interior."

The Captain rose from his chair and shook Chavez's hand. "I've been keeping myself abreast of the politics in your country Señor Chavez. Please have a seat."

Chavez sat. "I'm looking for three men Captain. They embarked on your ship at Barcelona."

"Can you tell me more?"

"They're former soldiers. They've come here to kill someone. That's the extent of what I know. Your office gave me some information, but not enough to identify them. They said I should check with you."

"Do you know what class they travelled in? I don't recall three men travelling together on the upper decks."

"They probably travelled in steerage to remain discreet."

"Well—I will caution you there were several hundred men that boarded in Barcelona, in steerage class. I kept an initial record of every passenger to account for everyone while at sea and I've given the list to the port authorities. But every passenger had to pass through customs when they debarked at the port."

"I'm aware. That's unlikely to help me find the three men I'm after. I don't know their identities, and don't know where they are staying."

"It may not be the three men you're after, but there was an incident on board during passage. The chief steward had to arrest three men and I authorised him to place them in the brig for the remainder of the voyage."

"Can you tell me anything more?"

"They'd taken issue with a young merchant called Joaquin Cuéllar. I understand he owns an export business here in Buenos Aires. He's a proper young man—eager to please and entertain. He was giving Tango lessons in the lounge which some families—wives and children mostly—were quite enjoying. They'd got it in their heads to put on a show for the poor sods in steerage after a bout of rough weather—to raise morale. It seemed like a worthy endeavour, so I allowed it. These men took exception to Cuéllar. God only knows why. Maybe they knew him from somewhere else, but I'm only speculating."

"That's it?"

"There's more. They'd been drinking. Later they ambushed Cuéllar outside of his cabin and beat him senseless. They could only have known his cabin location by bribing one of the crew—not something I'm proud to report."

"I can assure you that your company is not under any investigation by the Ministry of the Interior Captain—such matters are hardly my concern."

"I'm glad to hear it. It's a matter we prefer to handle privately. It was fortunate I'd sent the chief steward to check on Cuéllar's well-being. They got there barely in time to save his life."

"What made you think to check on this fellow Cuéllar?"

"There was an astute young lady that had forewarned me. She had helped Mr Cuéllar arrange the show. She had somehow noticed that the three men were unusually hostile towards Mr Cuéllar. You may wish to speak to her—her name is Sofia Montserrat. She's the niece of Senator Hugo Montserrat. They were travelling together."

"That might be helpful Captain thank you." Chavez deliberately underplayed the Captain's mention of the Senator. He knew Montserrat carried considerable influence with the President, and was deeply involved in committees pertaining to the nation's security. "Did you record the names of the three men? They may not be the men I'm after, but it can't hurt to track them down."

"Their names are in the ship's log. I'll send a note to you with the information when I return to the ship tomorrow. There's one more thing I should mention."

"Yes?"

"As required by law the three men were turned over to the civil authorities at the port—the Police of the Capital. They were given custody to a Lieutenant Machado. My chief steward was bitterly disappointed that the three thugs were immediately unshackled and set free. We couldn't even guess as to why that came about, considering the seriousness of Cuéllar's injuries."

Chavez's heart was pounding so hard he could barely make out the Captain speaking. Lieutenant Vicente Machado was one of the names Nicolas had identified from the briefing notes. 'These are the three mercenaries the Spanish Embassy warned me of!'

"You've been very helpful Captain. I'll look forward to receiving your note tomorrow with their names. I can send my aide to retrieve it and save you some trouble."

"As you wish."

Captain Juan Perez watched Gabriel Chavez leave, and then looked again at his card. 'Senior Legal Aide, Ministry of the Interior.' He felt badly, as he could have mentioned one more thing. He was scheduled to meet his acquaintance, Commissioner De La Fuente, for a drink at the Jockey Club, later that evening. He intended to complain to De La Fuente, about his police department setting the three ruffians free. It wasn't right. 'I'll let De La Fuente know that the ministry's on to his department's shenanigans. It would be the honourable thing to do in return for sponsoring my membership into the Jockey Club—give the man a chance to clean his up his mess. That's the way we prefer it in the shipping business.'

Chapter 10
Broken Chains!

A month had passed since Sofia landed at Madam Josefina's Social House. Sofia had accepted her circumstances, learning the culture of the brothel and immersed herself in the business. Staying busy at all times kept her from thinking about her parents, the ranch in Jerez, and sinking into despair. She knew that her parents would have wanted her to fight to conquer any obstacles put in her way, and that helped her focus on the task at hand. Madam Josefina couldn't complain about having one room less and another person at the table, things had gotten far easier since she'd agreed to have Sofia take over as the brothel's bookkeeper.

Firstly, she'd taught Sofia the basics, and Sofia caught on quickly.

"It's strictly a cash-based business dearie, and by that, I mean cash up front where you can see it—no exceptions. No watches or IOU's—no loaners, and no freebies on the house when they're feeling lovey-dovey for little Mr Brown eyes," Josefina batted her eyes with such a dramatic flourish it made Sofia laugh. She was unlike anyone Sofia had known, and her frank manner led Sofia to believe she was essentially a person that could be taken at her word. Josefina used humour and self-deprecation to communicate in lieu of threats or commands.

"I want you to take the money—don't let the girl lay her grubby hands on it for a second—and it goes straight into the lockbox. This is a strict rule of the house that I've learned the hard way. Otherwise, one or all of the lovely ladies will at some point think it smart to charge more than our fair asking price, and pocket the difference herself before paying the house fee. Our client base will suddenly dry up like an old witch's twat. Word on price gets around quickly in this business I'm afraid. Men that work hard for their money don't like to throw it away—they'll go elsewhere for their pleasure."

"Once you take the fee, you record the transaction under the lady's name. Now listen because this is important. Save yourself some grief. One of the charming lasses will inevitably take it upon herself to accuse you—or God help them, me—of not marking the transaction so as to pocket the fee yourself. It can't be helped—they get desperate for a litany of unexplainable womanly reasons. But the result will be the same—disciplinary action of an unpleasant sort by the inestimable Lieutenant. So, every once in a while—during a busy evening—you corner each lady and remind the poor dear exactly how many clients she's serviced. Makes it harder for them to hit you with a bald faced lie the following day—understand?"

"Yes," Sofia said.

"Good—earnings are paid to the ladies at the end of their day for the same reasons—the next morning at the latest if something causes a delay. You'll see in the books that I pay the rent and a professional services fee to the Lieutenant on a monthly basis. But let's worry what those services are another time."

Madam Josefina was taking note of her suggestions. Sofia had studied the ledgers over the course of the month, and had noticed a few things she thought pertinent to discuss with Josefina.

"The more clients a woman sees in a day, the more money she makes and the more money the social house makes."

"Correct you are," Josefina said, preoccupied with a newspaper.

"Some encounters don't take as long as others."

"That's an incredibly astute insight for a neophyte," Josefina said.

"Are there other impediments to the ladies time?"

"The ebb and flow of the customer's arrivals, the availability of rooms when the house is busy. You've seen how full we get Saturday evenings, and it happens on occasion during the week."

"I'm sure you'll tell me if my comments aren't welcome," Sofia said.

"I'll do more than tell you dearie—what's on your mind?"

"I've also observed that there is unproductive time when the ladies are waiting. They have to stall and maintain their client's interest—I think we have to make better use of the rooms. If one is held for someone who isn't ready, I'll signal for another lady to use the room. This should work fine if the ladies give me a signal when they're ready. Basically, I'll control the use of the social rooms so that there isn't any down time."

"Well, it can't hurt to try. They will have to cooperate of course, but leave that to me."

"In my experience, if someone finds a way to help them make more money, you won't have to tell them twice. If I see there still isn't enough rooms, we can all take turns giving up our personal rooms."

"You're just a bundle of ideas now, aren't you? You must have driven your father crazy," Josefina said.

"He always said I was too focused on my goals—he thought I should slow down enough to get to know people."

"Well, that was good advice by my reckoning. The ladies have to get to know you or they won't trust you. One more thing before I forget."

"Yes?"

"Keep your eyes out for the quarrelsome types. We can't put up with our girls getting beaten up or slapped around. If it happens—there has to be payback I'm afraid. So, if you see something like that happening—or about to—Tell Tico. He'll make a run for our security. You'll see what I mean in due course."

"When you say payback, you mean like Octavio?"

"Oh, he got off easy dearie—I'm worried the Lieutenant is growing soft."

Madam Josefina watched with silent approval as Sofia cleverly put simple ideas into action. She was winning over the working ladies, if somewhat begrudgingly.

"So, who's the new girl that refuses to get her hands dirty? You can't stay a virgin forever—at least not here," one of the more outspoken ones said. Her name was Zoryana and she was from the Ukraine. She had a throated husky voice and a propensity for vulgarity, only to be outdone by Madam Josefina herself.

"This is Sofia. She has brains and knows how to count exceptionally well. Having paid attention at school—unlike you lot of lascivious sluts—she has no need to get her hands dirty. Her chastity is not your concern," Josefina responded to the hoots and shrieks of all within earshot.

"Brainy Sofia kept me waiting for a room twice last night and my customers didn't wait. Cost me two fares, didn't you, little Miss Numbers."

"I did—but that's not going to happen anymore. We're going to implement a new system. There were some rooms not being used while some of you were entertaining gentlemen in the courtyard. From now on, the second-floor rooms will be shared and I will schedule them. If you're preoccupied in the courtyard, the room has to go to someone else that's ready to go. I'll be watching and keeping track," Sofia said.

"Why in the world would we do that?"

"You'll be able to make more money in less time."

"Why didn't you just say so? Keep talking, sugarcakes—I'm starting to like you," Zoryana said. There were chuckles, but no more objections.

Sofia was surprised to be asked for her advice by Madam Josefina, but she kept a neutral attitude so that she wouldn't annoy her. Josefina had taken her by the elbow to a secluded corner where the other ladies couldn't hear.

"I think we could use a musician to keep people entertained and get them in the mood, if for some reason they can't do that themselves. Yesterday it seemed to me that some of the men were bored. They arrived early, as you yourself noted, but didn't want to go to a room right away. I think the blighters wanted attention—they wanted to look around at the wares and flirt. I saw a few walk out. They didn't like what they saw perhaps, or they weren't entertained," Josefina said.

"I used to have a musician come with a guitar and sing. He was Italian and the music was beautiful. But I wasn't sure he was worth the cost. Now I'm concerned we are losing customers to other brothels. I want to preserve our reputation. What do you think dearie? How do we keep this place first among equals?"

"I think it's a good idea. Music is romantic, and can stir up emotions, amongst other things. The men will be more inclined to stay, consume liquor, open their wallets, and make an evening of it."

"I agree—I wanted a second opinion. If the men are inclined to stay for the entertainment, the randy ones may go twice—and we double our take!"

"Tomorrow take this note to the Café Bonita in Constituçion. Follow Jujay down to San Juan. You'll see it on the corner. Talk to any waiter and ask when Tony will be playing—see if you can leave the note with the waiter. Tony will know what it's about."

"Alright," Sofia said, looking forward to escaping the confines of the three-storied colonial style house that served as a brothel. Sofia went up to her room to put the note away, and then decided she would inspect the second-floor private rooms where most of the entertaining occurred. They were cleaned and smelled of bleach. She had to duck under sheets drying on clotheslines.

Most were small rooms, enough room for a bed, a coat tree to hang garments, a nightstand with candles, a gas lamp in the corner with a curious multi-coloured, stain-glass mosaic that further engendered the boudoir setting, washbasins and chamber pots for emergencies, the latrines being located on the main floor.

One of the rooms was bigger than the rest. Madam Josefina had been blunt.

"That one is specially designed for those inclined towards variety, more than one lady—or man—or to perform before an audience to satisfy their exhibitionist impulses, or to merely watch the proceedings themselves," with a flourished wave of her arm. "Oh my—are we not ready for this conversation," Sofia had felt her eyes widen.

"Well I'm glad I can teach you a few things about life while you're here—and better you hear it from me than one of the more plain-speaking ladies. Let's just say some of the ranking officers in the military, and some of their well-placed friends from Barrio Norte up the road—occasionally like to book that room for their exclusive entertainment requirements. Oh, and they pay double per lady, plus a service charge for the extra space."

Sofia looked around the room. There were two large beds, a see-through, basket weaved screen between them. 'Only the illusion of privacy.' There was a high closet with folding wooden doors, designed with spaced shutters for air flow. The closet contained stacks of basic wooden chairs, arranged neatly inside the closet.

'Some men and couples will pay just to watch dearie!'

As Sofia was looking in the high closet, she heard a murmur of voices. 'They were speaking so softly,' she thought. She looked around and couldn't see anyone, couldn't make out where the voices were coming from. 'The closet?' She moved towards the closet, not detecting any noise. But she heard the voices again, whispering. 'Why are they whispering?' Not whispering, just muffled, like they were far away. She looked into the depths of the closet and in its furthest corner, where no light of any form reached, she saw a black iron grill, a vent. Her curiosity aroused, she put her ear to it, and the voices leapt out, clearly and distinctly. She could hear every word spoken from the room below, the one used by Madam Josefina and Lieutenant Machado for private meetings.

'It's Zoryana, the Ukrainian one.' Sofia appreciated Zoryana. She was challenging and defiant, but not sneaky. She was forthright to the point of being crude, but she spoke her mind without looking at her peers for acknowledgment or validation. Zoryana was a tall brunette, who kept her long straight hair tied

130

back in a basic ponytail. She had the brown skin of her ancestors, the feared Mongol invaders, and looked beautiful without make-up. Like many larger women, her bust was full and prominent.

'And Hortense!' Sofia was wary of Hortense, who had propositioned her with a pricing scheme she wanted hidden from Madam Josefina.

"It's easy enough for me to offer extra once I have my man in the room. It's just a small tip for my special services. We can split it, as long as you don't tell Madam Big-pockets. You know as well as I do, she takes too much of a cut."

Sofia thought she knew no such thing. She was not going to do any scheming behind the back of her benefactor, who probably knew every trick in the book herself and would quickly uncover the scam. Hortense had not taken well to Sofia's refusal.

"Don't be a stuck-up bitch! Do you think you're better than the rest of us? You're a greedy whore just like me." But then she had thought better of her outburst. "You're probably right—it's not a good idea. I'm from Pigalle Square, tu vois. I learned you never turn down an opportunity to make a few sou's."

"That must have been difficult."

"Wasn't so bad. I had my man. He thought we could make better money here in Buenos Aires. There was too much competition in Paris. We had an apartment here and were married—but we weren't actually married tu vois. We had an arrangement. He was good company but he didn't like to work, and I didn't mind my job at all. The money was much better here as a matter of fact."

"Why did you come to this brothel?"

"Because my man decided to end our arrangement and the bastard kicked me out. He'd found a younger girl—a real bitch!" And after blowing cigarette smoke in Sofia's face, "Let's keep this discussion to ourselves shall we. Don't say a word to anyone. I'm not afraid to do something fucking nasty to your sweet little ass—tu comprends?" 'She'd put her chin close to Sofia's then turned and marched away like a general on a parade square,' Sofia thought. She knew she had to be careful with Hortense.

Through the grill she could hear Hortense pitching a similar scheme to Zoryana. Hortense was the opposite of Zoryana physically. Shorter, with fair hair and crystal blue eyes that men found alluring. A shapely figure, but petite. And evidently a pit-bull.

"Don't worry about the old cow—I can just talk to Vicente. He listens to me."

"Vicente will slap your silly little French arse back to Pigalle Square if he thinks you're skimming from the house. Do you think he hasn't seen this trick before? You shouldn't forget that Madam Josefina is practically married to his boss De La Fuente—who is the real owner of this place." 'Zoryana was the one making more sense,' Sofia thought.

"I have Vicente under my spell. He gives me presents you know—where do you think I got this dress?"

"You're a silly whore without an ounce of common sense. He slips you money and buys you gifts so that you'll spy for him on the rest of us. Then you tell him a few lies so he keeps buying you things. But once in a while you have to tell him something that's actually true or he'll realise what you're up to."

"It's the game that's played with the cops at home in the Ukraine and probably everywhere else in the world. This is a good brothel to work in. Do you know why? Because Madam Josefina and Vicente run things fairly. I like it that way myself. It keeps everybody happy. Don't think that they don't have their eyes on you. Oh and just leave Sofia alone. She has a kind heart and means well."

Sofia stood back up from her prone position in between the chairs. She'd heard enough and felt badly for spying. But she'd learned two important things. She had made a friend in Zoryana, and that was reassuring. She needed to remain attentive to the relations between the ladies. This wasn't the estate in Jerez de la Frontera, with a lead ranch hand to settle quarrels. Or was it? Had she become Josefina's lead hand?

'Something like that,' she thought, thinking of old Roberto. Why had he been so useful to her family? Because he knew how to ranch, and he garnered respect, trust, and loyalty. For now, that's what she owed Madam Josefina. She had to take a deep, slow breath, remembering her former life at the estate. 'Don't be a foolish, sentimental woman, survive!' Mirella's words.

She had also learned something else she thought could be important. Whoever De La Fuente was, he owned the property, he was Lieutenant Machado's boss, and he was Josefina's lover. A ranking police officer of some kind. 'He's an associate of my Uncle Hugo.' They had rendered her uncle a service by bringing her to the brothel.

Sofia was enjoying the walk to Café Bonita, and decided she wasn't going to walk the straight line south on Jujay as instructed. At Belgrano Avenue, she decided to walk eastward for a few blocks and then continue southward on whatever side street she felt like. This was one of the few times she had strayed away from the social house, and she found herself mesmerised by the bustle on the streets. People, mostly well-dressed men, walked quickly, like they were late for something. She felt out of place in this regard—found herself strolling to make the outing last longer.

Horse-drawn taxis and carts of all sorts predominated on the wide streets, and people scrambled back and forth between them. They were taking their lives into their own hands, but managed to squeak through to the shops on the other side, the butcher, the shoe store, or the grocer. Workers were packed into large horse-drawn trams, going somewhere, the tanneries, the construction site, the foundries, or the docks.

'The working-class men dressed well,' Sofia thought, a sharp contrast to the rags worn by the field workers in Jerez. A suit, albeit frayed and dusty, a trendy gentlemen's hat—a bowler, or a trilby, and tweed flatcaps worn with a jaunty tilt.

She headed south until she came across Independencia and thought she should backtrack west to Jujay. It was now mid-morning and the traffic grew sparser as she approached the café at the intersection of San Juan. She saw the café on the other side with a sign stencilled on the window under a blue awning canopy. There were tables outside, with a few patrons smoking cigarettes and reading newspapers. There was a waiter, as evidenced by a green apron over an otherwise immaculate get-up, a pressed pin-striped shirt with a bowtie around a stiff collar, in the classic pose of waiters everywhere, one foot tucked under a knee while leaning against the stone wall.

He watched her with curiosity, raising an eyebrow as she approached between the tables. Sofia couldn't help herself, having seen the customers reading newspapers, she tried to read their titles. 'Broken Chains!' An anarchist newspaper, and she was seized with a fleeting melancholy that made her forget her purpose for being there, if for a moment.

"Good day, Señor. Can you help me? I'm looking for a musician called Antonio—"

"Tony."

"Tony is not here right now. He'll come to play in the evening."

"I see. Can I leave a note for him?"

"Yes of course. Who should I say it's from?"

"Well, it's from Madam Josefina—Madam Josefina's Social house." Sofia said, with a small degree of hesitancy.

"Ah—of course," he said, tucking the note into his vest pocket.

Sofia looked at him. "I'm not a prostitute."

"No, no," he stammered, "please don't take offence. I didn't mean to imply you were a prostitute—but I wouldn't blame you if you were. This is Buenos Aires."

"Do you have a newspaper I can read?"

"Excuse me?"

"A newspaper—like the one that man's reading, Broken Chains!"

"We have a few newspapers on the counter that were left by the customers. Would you like something less dire? There is a copy of La Naçion, or The Herald."

"Yes—but I would also like that one," pointing at the paper the customer had left behind, "Broken Chains!"

"Of course. Take them—no charge."

Sofia placed them in her bag and gave the waiter a frank stare. "Is it an anarchist newspaper?"

"Yes Señorita. Anarchists, socialists, and unionists read that one. But essentially the publisher is an anarchist."

"Do you know him then?"

The waiter's eyes grew wide and he stood up straight. "I don't know him. Are you asking on behalf of the police?"

"No—I'm sorry if I've been asking strange questions. It's just that I would like to write articles. I've published articles before—in an anarchist newspaper in Spain."

"What kind of articles?"

"The kind that will only be printed by certain newspapers for some reason—although I don't consider myself to be an anarchist."

The waiter hesitated for a moment, but then seemed to make a decision to trust her. "Come back tomorrow—at the same time. I'll see if he will meet with you."

"Thank you." Sofia walked away, and on the way back, used the last of her money to purchase a fountain pen, ink and paper.

Chapter 11
Ambition

De La Fuente leaned back in his studded leather chair behind the ostentatious Victorian desk that took up only a small part of his office. Its gleaming mahogany surface was bare but for the fountain pen, blotting paper, and a box of cigars. There was a bar in the corner, to properly receive guests, or have an early one himself. A bottle of pure malt whiskey sat in its bottom drawer, waiting for the day he was finally appointed as chief of police. Nevertheless, he'd come a long way from the days of the block-wooden desks used by duty sergeants.

His office formed part of the new baroque headquarters building that had been built on Moreno, a couple of blocks south and east of the Palacio Del Congresso. The building was white with a gold facade, a spectacular forged-iron awning covered the front entrance and there were ornately decorated interior patios, all indications of the prominence the institution played in the stability of successive governments.

The department claimed to be at the forefront of criminal detection, and its anthropometric section had embraced European methods of identifying criminals through an intricate series of facial measurements. It was also experimenting with the newest technique of bertillonage, using fingerprints as a unique identifier of recidivous criminals. 'I suppose I'm going to have to familiarise myself with this bloody foolishness.' But he was sceptical. If anything, he considered the scientists working in the section to be prima donnas that challenged the traditional power wielded by his detectives.

De La Fuente had the heel of his bad leg resting on a corner of his desk when Vicente knocked loudly on the wooden doors and entered.

"Boss," Vicente said, nodding and removing his bowler.

De La Fuente was pleased to see him. Vicente was like a younger brother to him, and their fortunes were irreversibly intertwined. Vicente only ever called him 'boss' when they were alone. A subtle show of respect. It was likely the only form of affection Vicente would ever show for him. 'Other than risking his life carting his 240-pound body away from the gunfire of the insurrectionary soldiers all those years ago.' De La Fuente supposed that was enough.

"It's time for a cigar my boy. Come on." He rose from his seat, took two larrãnega's from the cigar box, clipped the ends, and limped towards the open window shutters.

"How are the coffers at the Social House?"

"We've had a lean period—but the lease to yourself is covered and it's still in the black. We won't match last year's profits though."

Vicente had told him just enough to keep him from complaining. He had a unique way of conveying information using the least words possible.

"Tell me honestly lad—has it ever appealed to you to strike out on your own? Purchase a property? I can keep my eyes and ears open for something suitable. Word of mouth is everything in real estate. You need to start adding more income to your lieutenant's salary."

"No. I've got enough to do as it is."

He's too dedicated to me, De La Fuente thought with a small amount of guilt.

"I've kept the operation with our clandestine agents a secret. Neither the chief nor the other commissioners have been briefed—we'll continue to keep it between the two of us. I've had some doubts as to the wisdom of setting them loose—but I've made up my mind to go ahead as originally planned."

"We must take advantage of them as long as possible. We'll need to keep them motivated by giving them just enough money to entertain themselves, but not so much to make them stand out. Enough to have a regular at a brothel—not mine—and wet their whistles should do it. They have low standards—I found them in a dockside bar in Barcelona after all."

"We'll want them well-established amongst the anarchists prior to International Worker's Day—May 1st." Vicente nodded in comprehension. May 1st had been utterly riotous for at least three years running.

Unions rife with socialist and anarchist elements competed with each other for dominance, raised the stakes and recklessly charged at the police lines to garner the admiration and loyalty of the workers. But for this they had paid a bloody price. The previous year, the police had opened fire with rifles into the mob, killing and wounding several people.

"These riots are of minor interest to our endeavour. Up until now our country has managed to escape the scourge of assassinations and bombings. But it's only a matter of time—and the critical mass of zealous European anarchists now present in Buenos Aires tells me that our time is coming soon."

"We've paid a lot of money to our informers—there's been no such information."

"That's true—but our target group knows how we work. They know who our informers are—suspect anyway—and feed them only what they want us to know. They're clever enough to throw in some legitimate scraps for good measure—and take out their competition at the same time. I know for a fact that in the past we've played the part of useful idiots to the clever ones—we underestimate them."

"The three men can continue to live in the heart of things, in my tenement in Barracas. They can take jobs, get hired, get fired—move on to something else. If I've gauged them right, they'll do this naturally. I want them prying their way into the tightest circles of the hardcore idealists. They'll be our eyes and ears— not only passive spies—but instigators of doubt and dissension. We need to cast a wide net—capture any rumour, scheme, or threat, and then use it to our advantage. Who are they planning to kill—what weapon will they use? They can do whatever is necessary to secure the confidence of the anarchists," De La Fuente had raised an eyebrow and was speaking matter-of-factly.

"Do you understand lad?"

"Yes."

"I simply can't have anyone of importance killed on my watch. I have the Senator backing me—speaking directly to the President. I will be the next chief of police—there is no one else left in the department for them to pick once there's a change of presidency—they need loyalty, and that's been my trademark. Revealing this operation at the opportune time will dispel any doubts of my worthiness of the position."

He caught Vicente's eyes—as always, they were those of a serpent— calculating and emotionless. "I would place you in my position lad—if you're wondering—commander of the investigative division. How would you like that?"

"I haven't thought about it much."

"Now you need to. These aren't the brightest men lad—keep them on a tight leash. They're disposable if need be. The minute they become a liability—no one's going to miss them."

Vicente gave a faintly discernible nod, taking a steady draw on his dwindling cigar.

"Watch your fieldcraft—meet with them discreetly."

"Just another day in Buenos Aires Boss."

"Indeed."

At 3 pm, De La Fuente had Machado take him to the Jockey Club in his coach. He was meeting with Senator Montserrat, whom he hadn't spoken to since their voyage to Spain. He recalled with vivid clarity the urgent telegram he'd received from the Senator, after the steamship had berthed overnight in Montevideo. The tone had been cryptic, wary of gossipy telegraph operators. '—willing and able to earn her keep,' in other words she was a prostitute. He had acceded to the request. Combined with the information he'd received from Colonel Gimenez, he was aware of every duplicitous move the Senator had made during his trip to Spain.

The deed had been done, Vicente had taken Sofia to a brothel, and now it was time to claim his due. The ground had shifted considerably. While he'd been at the conference in Madrid, President Quintana had appointed Colonel Fraga as the chief of police, to replace Beazley, who had resigned as expected. The resignation had sparked a brief but futile race between the commissioners. This round the President had wanted an outsider, a military man. De La Fuente needed to know why, in order to position himself for the next round. The Senator was key to influencing Alcorta, who as the Vice President, would soon replace the dying President Quintana.

He thought of his clandestine operation. He needed at least another year to produce tangible results. But there was some hope if the Senator could pull the right strings. De La Fuente had covered up his vicious murder of a young prostitute two years ago, and was now collaborating in the cover up of his despicable crimes in Spain. The Senator owed him and he intended to collect.

Vicente brought the horse to a halt in front of the Jockey Club, on Florida, in the south fringe of Recoletta. De La Fuente found the Senator seated in a salon, ensconced in the horse racing section of La Naçion.

"Felipe—sit down before you fall down you lame old bastard. Whiskey soda?"

"Too early for anything else."

Montserrat signalled at the waiter. "I'm pleased that you asked to meet at this location. It's important that you be seen here regularly. You have to shake hands and rub shoulders with the other senators, that's the main thing. Are you sure you can't make a donation?"

De La Fuente knew he was being baited, and reminded of his station. The Jockey Club was the social dwelling for wealthy businessmen. The club's chairman was the President himself, and significant donations were a mark of pride for members of the establishment. For De La Fuente, however, this posed a problem. He owned a couple of old houses, one of which had been converted to a profitable tenement in Barracas, the other a brothel. He also drew a senior bureaucrat's salary.

But none of this was enough to put him in the league of the Senator with his massive land holdings, ranches, sinecures, and paid memberships on influential boards. A significant donation that would catch the eye of the wealthy President was not feasible in his case, and the Senator knew it.

"How is my niece doing? Have you been keeping track of her? Imagine my shock to learn she was a prostitute and involved in the killing of my dearest brother and his wife. Nevertheless she's a Montserrat—I won't allow the spectacle of her being led to the garrotte."

"You have my condolences for the tragedy that befell your family Senator. The scourge of anarchism impacts us all and threatens our way of life. I've made arrangements for your niece, as you requested. You're more compassionate than I could have been in your position."

"You have my gratitude. It may come to pass I will need one of your officers to provide a deposition—to the fact that she is a practicing prostitute now in Buenos Aires. This will help with inheritance matters. I refuse to allow her any claim to the Montserrat Estate at this point. Can you blame me?"

"Certainly not Senator. The deposition won't be a problem."

"Good."

"I'll get to my immediate concern. I'd like to know the details around President Quintana's decision to appoint Colonel Fraga. Quite simply why? The man has absolutely no relevant experience that I can see."

"It's bad news Felipe—and the appointment is a grave mistake if you ask me. The President is convinced that an experienced soldier is required—a steady hand at the helm to quell the rioting. Someone that can think with military tactics and strategy—and has close ties to the generals in order to spy on them. The President remains concerned with their loyalties. So for now it's Colonel Rosenda Fraga, from the Ministry of War. A highly decorated infantry officer apparently. You know him I believe?"

"Yes I know him."

"Be sure to offer him your congratulations Felipe—stay on his good side. I know exactly what you want from me, and I intend to deliver. Fraga is ambitious—he'll want an appointment as a Minister soon enough. I've already told you—Quintana is very sick. I'm certain he will die soon. Alcorta will become the President—and it's him that I have to convince of your suitability."

"I'll be sure to congratulate Colonel Fraga."

"He doesn't have your feel for the pulse of this city. He will not be well received by the press. Your time will come."

'That's what you would say in order to retain your influence over me—because I know all of your filthy secrets.'

"But of course, Senator—to your good health." He held up his glass and toasted the Senator with a smile on his face.

De La Fuente descended the stairs of the club deep in thought. 'It's still within my grasp. Unleashing the mercenaries within the ranks of the anarchists will be my master stroke one way or another.' His mind then turned to another matter. He needed to ensure the Senator wasn't arrested by the Spanish authorities. That would be a disaster. There needs to be a deposition stating that Sofia Montserrat was engaged as a prostitute? Would the Spanish authorities fall for it? Perhaps if it was reinforced with a fake confession to one of the other prostitutes at Madam Josefina's. That could be done if necessary, but all this to ingratiate himself to a man he despised? Did he really want this so badly? 'Yes he did and such is life,' he thought.

In the privacy of his office, he finished his conversation with Vicente.

"Keep them on task, no side adventures, no surprises. They do nothing without you knowing about it in advance." Vicente nodded.

"Test their information. Cross check it with the information received from your informers. I don't want them to think they can just make things up."

"I suppose that's happened once or twice," Machado said.

"I mentioned they're not exactly high philosophers—but they'll have to learn the anarchist vernacular—and be ready to follow through with any low-level buffoonery thought up in their circles. This will ingratiate them enough for our purposes. They can't write a thesis, but they can distribute one easy enough—drop off bundles of their revolutionary newspapers, distribute red scarves, paint slogans on buildings—all more or less harmless."

He had to put his bad leg up on the desk again. It was throbbing. Putting the leg helped him calm himself and think. He needed affirmation that Vicente was fully committed. "It's entirely possible my play with the Senator will not succeed, at which point they'll have to take out a former soldier. How do you feel about that?"

Vicente raised one razor-thin eyebrow. He wasn't normally asked about his feelings. "I've no love for soldiers."

"Nor I lad—nor I. First things first, get them into the anarchists."

"Understood."

"Another thing. My good friend Captain Juan Perez—the one who threw our men into the brig of his ship—received a visit from the Ministry of the Interior. A senior legal aide, one Gabriel Chavez."

"I've never heard of him."

"I have. He's one of their high-minded lawyers—an eternal discontent. He'll have taken part in the 1890 coup d'état in some way—he's of that age—and he'll have fallen in with Irigoyan over the last election. The ministries are riddled with them—products of the university law school. We owe them nothing. They were shooting at us from the windows—backing up the rebel troops—and killed our men. We know Irigoyan's plotting something again. Keep this in mind if Chavez gets too close."

"It's getting hard to keep a secret."

"I should have known. The bar in Barcelona was undoubtedly riddled with informers—Colonel Gimenez warned me of such."

"Does it change anything?"

"Not a single thing." De La Fuente was silent for a moment, thinking about Sofia Montserrat. "This woman—the Senator's niece—keep her where she is for now. The Senator has asked me to deal with her for him—it's a deal that I'll have to keep."

Chapter 12
A Free Woman

Sofia and Madam Josefina sat on stools at the bar, fanning the humidity away from their faces. The bar was placed under the second-floor overhang to protect it from the weather, on this day the sun burned fiercely onto the tables and chairs resting on the cobblestone patio of the courtyard.

"I'm no farther ahead in balancing the ledger. I've gone back 6 months, there are unexplainable discrepancies. I don't want to cause any more trouble for Octavio—but the stated earnings are consistently short. It's amateurish accounting."

"What do you mean the stated earnings are consistently short?"

"The ledgers report the earnings of 15 prostitutes each month, including the month I took over. It under reports the actual earnings. There are 22 prostitutes working here right now, and I assume that was the case in previous months."

"Oh my—you're a bright girl Sofia. Too bright for this job—but it's the only one I have for you right now. It's time I introduced you to the reality of running a brothel." Sofia had no idea what was coming next.

"There are two sets of ledgers."

"Two sets of ledgers? That's probably illegal."

"Listen to me dearie—there are two sets of ledgers. The one that you're working on right now is the official ledger—it's the one that we provide to the city inspectors. Our registration fees and taxes are based on those figures."

"I see."

"I didn't think it would take you long. 15 prostitutes is the maximum we're allowed by the city's regulations. The venal buggers thought they were being smart by setting a limit—they thought it would result in more brothels paying fees into their coffers. But I have decreed they can officially go fuck themselves. There's no honour amongst thieves."

Madam Josefina's demeanour endeared her to Sofia. She wondered if they could actually be friends, or if Josefina would betray her at some point as well. What would happen once another accountant came along?

"However, if one of those little pricks makes his way in here and starts counting—we'll need to act quickly. Some of my ladies will need to make themselves scarce—or they'll have to swear up and down that they've limited themselves to a single client and are otherwise employed as waitresses. In other words, we'll tell them a pack of bald-faced fucking lies. Understand?"

"Yes."

"Now—if one of the blubbering maggots gets smart and figures it out—tells us he'll turn the other cheek in exchange for monetary dispensation," Josefina had started to shout but then calmed down, looking around to see if she'd been heard, "—then the bribe shall be paid—but this is what's known as a fucking last resort dearie."

"Alright."

"The next secret is exactly that—a secret—and something that is told to one of these gossiping slags is precisely the opposite. Understand?"

"Yes."

"The second ledger is the unofficial ledger. Ironically—it reflects the absolute truth so help me God—insofar as earnings are tallied. This one is for the Lieutenant. He has insisted—emphatically—that it shall be this way and I dare not bear false witness to him. Ever. Understand."

"Yes."

"Take the bad with the good. Our Lieutenant knows all there is to know about this business. There hasn't been a book keeper yet that has managed to fool him—and they've tried dearie—oh how they've tried. It's never ended well. Cost them each a finger—in one case two. Understand?" Josefina held up a hand with the forefinger tucked into the palm.

"Yes." Sofia believed Lieutenant Machado was quite capable of such an atrocity.

"That said—he's been able to keep the city officials away. But always best to be prepared. Understand?"

"Yes."

"Good girl. Now tell me something, what do you notice about this month?"

"It's been slower than last month—considerably."

"In your humble estimation, is that good or bad?"

143

"It's bad."

"Correct—and something smells foul to me. Sudden drops in attendance shouldn't happen all things being equal—if men could just turn it on and off like a faucet where would we be? Talk with Tony the musician and see what you can learn. In his trade, he gets around to the other brothels. But he keeps his opinions to himself unless he's asked—so let's ask. I want you to see how the other brothels are doing and figure out what's going on. Now I'll be needing my nap love."

Tony wouldn't be around until six that evening, and Sofia finally had a few minutes to herself. She went to her room and read the newspaper she'd collected at the Cafe Bonita. Broken Chains! She looked at the front page and an article caught her eye.

Why are you disenfranchised? You arrived in this land to provide much needed labour, to work long hours six days a week, often for less than fair wages. Your labour is turned into profit by the Argentine export machine, and the taxes you pay fill the coffers of a government for whom you cannot vote for. Taxation without representation equals oppression! Your path to citizenship and the right to vote is blocked by mandatory conscription into the army—oppression!

The article only referred to men. She thought she would gladly serve in the army if it meant she could vote. The headline to the next article read:

A Truncheon to the Head for Workers. The police are now tasked to serve the wealthy business elite. What else can explain the consistent overreaction to the strikes which are a right of workers simply asking for a fair wage? Yet the truncheons rain on our heads and our colleagues are marched to the jails en masse. They claim the communists and anarchists work together seditiously against the state, and use the Residency Act to arbitrarily deport our brothers without so much as advising their families. Honourable men have disappeared, placed forcibly on a ship's steerage, bound for Europe. We hold the chief of police responsible for these high crimes against our brotherhood.

She leafed through the newspaper from front to back. There were no articles on women's suffrage. She saw her opportunity if the publisher was interested. On the other hand, maybe he had no interest at all in women's issues. There was only one way to find out. She returned to the Café Bonita for news from the waiter. The waiter gave her the address and directions on a napkin and got back to serving, it was too busy for him to talk for long.

20 minutes later, she found herself on Independencia, facing an imposing set of high wooden double doors attached to a neoclassical facade. 'Nobody would hear her knock,' she thought. There were windows high above the doors, but they were closed. There were stairs surrounded by a wrought iron fence that led downwards, so she went down to look inside the windows.

They were dirty and the bright sun caused a clear reflection of her own image. She used her hands to shield the glare and pressed her face close. She could hear some shouts and she could see a large cast iron machine, all wheels and levers, of what could only be a printing press.

Encouraged, she knocked, and then hammered on the door with the palm of her hand, trying to be loud. The noise died down from inside, and a moment later the door was opened tentatively. A wizened man of 60, with spectacles and wispy black hair, peered out.

"Who are you?"

"My name is Sofia Montserrat."

"Are you affiliated with the police?"

"No."

"Well you had us concerned. Such knocks are sometimes followed by the police bursting through the doors with sledgehammers."

"I assure you I have nothing to do with the police."

"Why are you here?"

"Because I read your newspaper," she said, pulling out her copy of last week's Broken Chains!

He stepped further out, and went up a couple of stairs to look out to the street. Apparently satisfied, he ushered Sofia inside. "Can I please ask you to be careful about showing our newspaper so near to our office? Are you the woman from the Café Bonita?"

"Yes."

"I was expecting you a few days ago."

"I couldn't come then."

"Why couldn't you come then?" He asked, evidently suspicious that she'd gone to the police.

"I had to work."

145

"Are you a prostitute?"

Sofia realised now that in Buenos Aires that was a legitimate question. "I'm a bookkeeper at a brothel, Madam Josefina's Social House. I have no other employment options at this time."

He nodded. "I was told you had written some articles for the anarchists in Spain."

"Yes. I've handwritten one for you. I don't own a typewriter."

He took the folded sheet from her hand and read it quickly. "This was printed in Spain?"

"In Jerez de la Frontera."

"We've never included articles related to women's rights before—to our shame. I'll have to discuss it with my colleagues though. Is this how you would like to your name published, a Free Woman?"

The question gave Sofia a flashback of everything she had left behind, of her first lover Francisco and their discussions, her grandfather's counsel, the ranch, the day she'd left for the market to negotiate with the union for the field workers—and never saw her parents alive again. She was seized with an oppressive melancholy. 'A Free Woman, don't I wish.'

"Yes."

The walk back to the brothel helped clear her mind. The great influences in her life—her mother and father, her grandfather, Mirella the gypsy woman, would not approve of her falling into a morass of self-pity. 'This is my life now—and there's work to be done.' She arrived in the late afternoon, and it was still quiet. Men normally started to trickle in at this time, with a rush about seven in the evening. But for the last few weeks nobody had arrived until 6 pm and it wasn't getting any better. She remembered the task given to her by Madam Josefina. 'Tony.'

She cornered him the minute he clamoured through the doors, laden with his guitar case and a bandonéon. Although, Tony claimed to be a master of the public trams and knew every way possible to get to Madam Josefina's, there was always an inevitable walk of about 200 metres, so he claimed, unless he was willing to pay for a coach, which he wasn't. He was a large man on a wide-set frame. He was always breathing hard and sweating profusely upon arrival, using his instrument cases to push through the doors.

Sofia took the guitar from his hands and led him through the metal, bistro-style tables arranged neatly in the courtyard to one sitting in the shade.

"I have some questions I need to ask you."

"Yes of course—but first I'm very thirsty Sofia," he said using a handkerchief to wipe his brow.

"Tico! Fetch Tony a pint of beer please."

"What is it Sofia," Tony asked, wiping froth from his lips with his jacket sleeve, having gulped down half the pint.

"Are you playing music at other brothels?"

"That's how I make my living."

"Have you noticed that we're not as busy as we used to be? The customers are fewer and the ladies are waiting and wasting their time. It's concerning."

"Perhaps you should pay me to come more often."

"Do you think you'll attract more customers?"

"It's not just me that you need—I'm only the music. It's the dance. Tango is catching on. The men have discovered something else besides football and gambling. Now they dance Tango and are getting competitive about it—so they need music. That's why you need me here more often."

"Yes, I've seen it performed before. It's a mysterious dance, and romantic I would say." She was thinking of the unusually close embrace of the couple, unlike traditional European dances. "But we're not a dance hall, the ladies have to work. They can't waste their time," Sofia said.

"Listen to me," Tony pleaded, with mock Italian sincerity. "I don't want to see Madam Josefina's Social House go broke. I like playing music here. But the brothels that are doing well have prostitutes that dance Tango. The men can dance with them for a few songs, or more, before they go to a room. I see men practicing everywhere—they want to show off their skills. So that's where they spend their money."

Sofia looked at the empty tables with their unlit candles, and when she looked upwards at the interior balconies, she saw some of the prostitutes dressed for business, waiting for customers to show, and others had not even dressed yet. They were getting listless, and Sofia thought that some might leave the social house for another brothel if business didn't pick up. "I have never seen any of these women dance Tango, or anything else for that matter," she said. "This doesn't leave me much hope."

"I know someone who can help. He can give them lessons and teach them the basics. This is what a few of the brothels have done."

"I would have to convince Madam Josefina, but I don't think it will work. We can barely afford to pay you. I doubt we will be able to pay him."

"The lessons won't cost you anything. I can ask him to do it for free—let's just say he owes me a few favours."

"Why would he agree to do this," Sofia said. She was sceptical that anyone would do such a thing for free.

Tony opened the hard-shell case housing the bandonéan and sat it up on his knee. He played a few random notes, his eyes resting vacantly on Sofia while so doing. "He'll do it. I'll tell him to come here Monday at noon. Your job will be to have students ready."

"Monday at noon." Sofia said. She was distracted by Lieutenant Machado's tall figure entering the courtyard in his habitual deliberate manner. She watched him disappear around a corner, towards the room in which she had overheard Zoryana and Hortense talking about her. Then she felt her heart stop and she froze. She was looking into the face of the largest of the three thugs that had assaulted Joaquin Cuéllar on the steamship.

He looked at her briefly in the eyes, gave her a lascivious once over, and kept walking. He hadn't recognised her. Why would he? She hadn't interacted with them directly on the Sirio, nevertheless, she looked down and turned to walk to the bar so the other two did not see her face. 'There was no sense pushing her luck,' she thought.

She watched them walk around the corner towards the room as well. She caught Tico's attention and gave him an inquisitive gesture with her hand. He shrugged and held his hands with the palms upward. He didn't know what was going on. Sofia was overcome with curiosity, so she walked to the corner and stopped to listen. Not hearing anything, she peered around the corner and saw that the door to the room was closed. She ventured forward into the shadow of the hallway and then heard voices speaking, the sound escaping from the space between the door and the floor.

She walked closer to the door, place both hands on the wall for support, and knelt until she could hear the voices more distinctly.

"Listen to me very clearly gentlemen," she heard Lieutenant Machado say in a menacing tone. "You're not the police—don't identify yourself as such—ever.

That will ruin your ability to act as our spies and I'll have you on the first ship back to Spain. You have to remain clandestine or you're of no use."

"That's a bitter disappointment—we thought you were going to pin shiny badges on us and have us arrest all your subversive commies," to a round of anonymous laughter, "—at least that's what the police commissioner seemed to indicate." To which, again, she heard some insouciant snickering. "What exactly will we be spying on then Lieutenant—to earn all this money you're going to pay us?" Sofia knew the voice, it was the jabbery one talking. She also knew that the Lieutenant was a serious man, in fact she had never seen him laugh. He wouldn't be impressed by their irreverence.

"Your mission is to infiltrate the anarchists. We don't want this European nonsense to take hold here. I'm putting it to you in simple terms because you're simple men. I want you to identify the ones who plan to murder our citizens. Names, addresses, and what was said. That's it. Nothing else unless I say so."

Sofia momentarily lost her balance and brushed the door slightly with her hand as she caught herself from falling over from her awkward squatting position. She sprung up as silently as she could and spun around to exit the hallway area—running headlong into Tico, who had snuck up behind her and was also listening to the conversation.

She sent him scurrying and heard the door open behind her. She caught the eye of the skinny, jabbery one peering out just as she rounded the corner at an unsuspicious walk, trying her best to look nonchalant. She continued toward the bar, giving Tico the harshest glare she could summon, but his single eye refused to meet her stare.

Although, she was dreading being found out, nothing happened, but no one came out. They had not been concerned. But she was. 'Infiltrate the anarchists— they were spies.' She needed to be careful with Lieutenant Machado. He couldn't learn of her articles. Now that she thought about it, it was the first time she had learned what the nature of his official police duties were. Apparently, part of it was to spy on the anarchists. She had not told anyone in the brothel about her article, including Madam Josefina, but where had she left the anarchist newspaper Broken Chains! Had she left it out somewhere in plain sight for anyone to read? She decided she had better check her room and make sure it was still in her bag.

She walked briskly up the stairs to the third floor, resisting the urge to run. As she turned down the hallway, she almost collided with Hortense, who was semi-dressed, and had a sheepish look to her.

"Why the bustle Sofia? There doesn't seem to be anyone arriving yet."

"What are you doing out here?"

"Just wandering around visiting—is that such a crime now? Why so touchy?"

"It's just I've never seen you on this side."

"Well now you have ma cherie."

Sofia walked slowly to her room. The door was unlocked but that is how she had left it. She looked around, everything seemed to be in its place. Except her bag, which had somehow made its way to the chair. 'Didn't I leave it on the bed?' Peering inside, she saw the newspaper, and breathed a sigh of relief. Tomorrow she would bring it to a trash container down the street. She felt curiously alive and clearheaded at that moment, as if she had just made an important decision, and was relieved of the contradictory voices in her mind. She was going to play this game under Lieutenant Machado's nose.

He would not stop her. Advocating for social change was her raison d'être. She went back to work and thought about how she would get the ladies to attend the Tango lessons on Monday.

Chapter 13
Tango

Tony took the tram eastward along Rivadavia towards the port, four contiguous docks that received ships carrying migrants and industrial equipment and sent them away laden with beef, wool, and agricultural goods to the hungry mouths of Europe and the United States. With the docks in sight, he used his guitar case to pry his way through the crowded tram and debark his heavy frame with a thud—leaving behind several aggrieved passengers cursing at him. He walked southward along the western edge of Parque Cristobal Colon and turned eastward to reach the boardwalks where he had a clear view of all the ship loading activities.

He put his guitar case down and sat on its upturned edge. There was a steamship tied in, and he saw the hatches were open, as there were men gathered on the deck shouting and fastening ropes. His two older brothers were stevedores. Having finally moved out of their parent's house, they had taken up residence amongst the tenements in Barracas, closer to their workplace.

His brothers described their work at the dinner table and he thought they would be near the ship's hatch, preparing the net sling that cradled a draft of goods, and swinging the loaded boom over the dock where it could be lowered. Both brothers were tough, hearty men that were good at physical work. Despite their differences, they were a close Italian family, and still gathered for Sunday dinner at their parent's home. His brothers bragged about the brawls they got into, always over work issues, and it seemed like they were falling into extreme, and potentially violent, ideological battles. He worried about them.

As of late, he had taken to bringing Tico, the orphan teenager, to the Sunday dinner, thinking it would do the boy good to eat a hearty Italian meal, and get away from the brothel. He could certainly stand to put on some weight.

Surprisingly his brothers had taken a shine to the spindly teenager, vowing to get him onto their crew once he filled out.

"You make sure he's taken care of until he's big and strong little brother, then we'll take charge of him."

"The new accountant is teaching him arithmetic and how to read. She's told me he's a good student, and could go to university," Tony said, thinking Tico would not fare well amongst the pugnacious stevedores. He knew they had big hearts through all their bluster, but Tico was not destined to be large, nor tough.

"Well if she doesn't come through for the little guy, let us know."

Last Sunday dinner, they'd said something that concerned him. He didn't want to betray them, but he was conflicted. He was going to pay an early visit to his friend Joaquin Cuéllar at his warehouse and warn him, but wouldn't tell him where he learned the information. He got up and trudged along the dock, weaving through the stevedores and a line of passengers exiting from the customs shack.

He made his way southward along the boardwalk until he could see the warehouse, its two massive doors rolled open to expose its innards of heavy timber framing and storage areas. He could see Joaquin's employees offloading heavy sacks from a horse-drawn cart.

Some of them had a malevolent looking tool hanging from their belts, a metal hook with a wooden handle that stevedores used skilfully to tip, pull, and push sacks and containers. The men's sleeves were rolled up, and sweat formed patches on their shirts under their suspenders, along their spines and under their arm pits. Most of them ignored Tony, but others eyed his guitar case, and looked forward to hearing music played at a cafe, a worker's hall, or a brothel later that evening.

It was Saturday, when he and Joaquin spent the evening composing and choreographing their show. They used the warehouse after the workers had finished their shifts, as it had the space they required. He looked at the stairs that led upwards to Joaquin's office, not fancy, just a practical wooden desk and cabinet that he could lock valuables, contracts, ledgers and documents inside. At the top, he passed Pablo's cramped little space, and he tipped his derby at the wiry little firebrand. Tony respected anyone that took their business seriously, as Pablo did.

"Tony—you're a little early—I'm afraid I still have some work to do."

"Yes—no problem," Tony said. He remained where he was, looking at Joaquin quizzically.

"I can clearly see there's a problem. What is it?"

"I need to tell you something."

"And what is that something?"

"I can't tell you where I got it from—but I have to tell you something. It comes from my brothers."

"You have absolutely no idea how to keep a secret my dear friend."

"You can't get them into trouble okay."

"I would never get your brothers into trouble. They're no bother to me."

"Last Sunday they said something at the table that made me very concerned for your safety."

"Go on."

"They said that there are anarchists working here in your warehouse—if they're provoked they'll resort to violence."

"Who are they?" Joaquin was somewhat alarmed. This was the second person to tell him this. He looked out his window and saw Diego at the receiving end of a line of men, piling heavy sacks of grain. Diego looked up and caught him looking at him, then looked away. 'He's always on the lookout for something.'

"He's the leader," Tony said.

"Thanks for the warning. I don't see what I can do about their personal convictions, but I'll keep it in mind. You can leave that guitar here for later if you'd like."

"I will, thanks." Tony decided not to bring up his conversation with Sofia just yet. He would save that for after their rehearsal.

Joaquin watched his friend descend the steep stairway. He was agile despite his heavy frame. Joaquin had seen him demonstrate a surprising degree of athleticism, when he would demonstrate some piece of Tango choreography he had in mind. Joaquin recalled the afternoon he'd been walking with Tony on a crowded street, and an orphan teenager had seen fit to snatch Tony's violin case from his hand.

The youngster had sprinted away, yelling triumphantly. But he had badly miscalculated the situation, as Tony's 50-metre sprint could put a rugby halfback to shame. With his powerful legs churning him forward on his toes, he would've put a rugby halfback to shame. He easily caught the boy. However, Tony didn't have a cruel bone in his body and let the scruffy orphan off with a knuckle rub to the scalp.

Joaquin's mind wandered back to his Tango play. He couldn't decide how many acts just yet, and continued to agonise over the storyline. He had come up with the idea of composing their own songs, he would write the lyrics, and Tony would arrange the music. Tony wanted to play their songs at his cafe gigs, and Joaquin had agreed. They were meant to be shared, after all. Then a year ago, following an outing to the opera, he had thought of the idea of a full play, opera style, with acts, and actors dancing.

They wouldn't burden the actors with singing, this would be Tony's job. He would sing a series of songs that connected to tell a story, with a proper beginning, middle, and end, 'at least three acts,' and an audience living the story through dance. But he'd faltered with the complexity of all the components. He'd had several false starts with story ideas that he'd subsequently discarded. 'Too bland—no passion—too soppy—too pollyanish—too philosophical—too political 'nobody wanted that!' The list went on.

What would it take to inspire him? An idea that was so appealing the story wrote itself? He had no idea. For now, he would keep trying, and wait for whatever moment would lead to his creative breakthrough. 'And what will it take to get this shipment loaded into the warehouse.' He looked down at the warehouse floor. The men were taking a break. He estimated there were 50 more sacks to bring in from the trolley. Hauling sacks was hard on a stevedore, and they worked in teams to lessen the strain and injuries. Two men helped another get the sack shouldered at the cart, and two men helped take it off the shoulders of those playing the part of mule. He could see that one of the stevedores, an older man in his 40s, wasn't getting up from his perch on an upturned sack. Diego the foreman was giving him a tongue lashing.

"You have to do your share of the work like everybody else you lazy old bastard—get to it! We don't want to be here all night."

Joaquin thought he would go lend a hand. Were his ribs up to it? He was about to find out. He descended the stairs, rolling up his sleeves.

"Let him rest Diego! I'll take his spot. He'll be fine come Monday. All right men. Let's finish this up and get you on your way," he said, receiving a begrudging nod of respect from Diego.

Joaquin was content. He was content that all three volunteers were coming, when less dedicated women and men may not have. He felt kinship with his cohorts, and was excited for the evening's work ahead.

154

He left the great sliding doors to the warehouse open far enough for one person to fit through, and serendipity provided a sliver of incandescent moon to illuminate the boardwalk, while the gas streetlights glowed yellow. First to appear through the doors was Costanza the waitress, and she'd gone to great lengths to look her best. She had dressed simply enough with a practical, pleated walking skirt, and a scarlet Garibaldi blouse with long sleeves and frills at their ends. But it was her new shoes that stood out. Edwardian style—a pointed toe, a medium height heel, and two tones of leather that were laced halfway to the shin. Costanza held her skirt up to her knees to show them off.

"My husband doesn't know and I'm sure as hell not going to tell him. I've never had such fancy shoes before."

"They look absolutely marvellous dear Costanza," Joaquin said, knowing the occasion required a compliment. "But I suggest you do tell him, in fact, I suggest you wear them to bed tonight with nothing else. Your man will not be thinking how much you paid for them, I assure you." She smiled, evidently considering his suggestion.

She smiled. "Yes that will probably work."

He made small talk with her, inquiring about work at the cafe. She'd been his second Tango instructor and brought him to a good level. Where had she learned the dance? From a former lover, she had said wistfully. How had she developed her style? I was a prostitute and danced a lot, without further elaboration. It didn't behove Joaquin to pry any further.

"I'm curious about the heel—let's try out these new shoes of yours." He led her through some easier, then more difficult figures.

"How do they feel?"

"Absolutely divine."

Next, Ennio came bounding through the door. The troupe's latest addition, Ennio was a happy-go-lucky Argentine national from a moderately wealthy family. He was attending the university and was studying accounting, but he needed to do something to make him more interesting to the ladies. 'I want them to see my dangerous side!' This evening, however, he had foregone the dangerous look in favour of a dandyish one Joaquin thought.

Arriving through the doors with a leap worthy of the Russian ballet, he landed perfectly upright on one foot and skidded to a halt, assuming a heroic pose with both hands atop a walking cane.

"Fear not—for Ennio has arrived!" Neither Joaquin nor Costanza could resist laughing. Despite his braggadacio, Joaquin liked his attitude. Ennio thought that if something was worth doing, it was worth over doing. This evening that appeared to be his costume. Joaquin looked him over, starting with his boots, which were a glossy patent leather around the bottom.

"I had a bootblack buff them up just before I got here. I told him one drop of polish on the satin finish and I would cane his skinny rump!"

Indeed, the upper boot was made of adorned paisley satin vesting. Next came grey pinstriped trousers, a paisley silk waistcoat that almost matched his boots, a poke collared shirt, and a crimson tie knotted four-in-hand. 'He must have consulted a men's fashion magazine.' The young man and his costume were shrouded in a cutaway morning jacket, and the ostentatious ensemble was topped off by a straw showboater.

"You've set the bar high this evening Ennio, that tail would make a penguin jealous," Joaquin said.

Finally, Tony squeezed his way through the opening, having to push the door open another foot in order to fit. He held a hand and led in the veritable Countess Martina La Rochefoucauld, 'la Comtesse,' formerly of the Ukraine, now the widow of a French aristocrat, who'd made a small fortune manufacturing small arms in the town of St Etienne.

Having died of heart failure in the throngs of passion with Martina, 'He wouldn't have had it any other way,' she moved to Paris, established herself as a high society regular, and whenever she'd had enough of its gauchiste snobbery, she found a different cosmopolitan centre to spend a year or two. She'd placed a mischievous add in a newspaper, 'actress and dancer for hire', and had received a note from Tony in due course. Discovering she was neither; Joaquin and Tony were nevertheless encouraged by her enthusiasm. They decided there was nothing to lose, and welcomed la Comtesse to their troupe.

This evening, she glowed underneath a hat with an artificial garden blooming on top of it. She wore a button-down frock coat that hung past her ankles suspiciously, and Joaquin held his breath for what was about to come next.

"We shall spend a splendid evening together my darlings," she pronounced through a toothy smile. At age 49 if a day, she was the oldest of them, but she kept herself in shape, and radiated youthful energy. She liked to put her figure on public display as often as possible, 'Let's get to work, shall we? I'm not getting any younger darlings!' and with a flourish she flung off her coat to show off her latest acquisition from her tailor on Corrientes.

A moment of sombre silence hung in the air while la Comtesse turned from side to side, red-gloved hands on her hips, letting them bask in her beauty. Joaquin stared expressionless, withholding judgement. He had never seen a dress like it. The main colour was black, but it was adorned with scarlet frills that hung from the lower hemline as well as a faux hemline that crossed her bust, and sleeves that stopped at the elbows. A wide red sash was tightened high at the waist, serving as a corset.

There was an audacious slit in the hem at the front that served to display a shapely leg as she walked. The hemline hung below her knees at the back. Black net stockings covered her exposed legs, and black lace ankle boots completed the boudoir ensemble. Looking at her colleagues, she became unnerved.

"Is it too much darlings?"

Joaquin circled around her, taking in its libertine style, imagining its effect on the Tango choreography, and the audience. "It's perfect."

Later, after their three intrepid volunteers had left, Joaquin sat on a wooden crate beside Tony, reflecting on the evening's rehearsal. "That was our best— your playing was inspiring."

Tony grunted. "I have a personal request."

"Anything at all my friend."

"I would like you to provide some Tango instruction to some—ladies—at Madam Josefina's Social House."

"Absolutely not."

"Just like that you refuse? What happened to 'anything at all'?"

"You can't be serious Tony. Madam Josefina's Social House is a brothel correct?"

"Yes."

"And by ladies you mean prostitutes correct?"

"Yes."

"Exactly what I was afraid of—why are you asking this of me?"

"I made them a promise."

"Good Lord Tony—what sort of promise?"

"Free Tango lessons."

"I think you may have lost your mind. Wait—I'm going to look for it—is that it over there?"

"Joaquin please be serious. Listen. I make a very modest living. Josefina hires me to play regularly, so I don't want her to go out of business. Over the last month, they've had fewer and fewer customers, and I can tell you exactly why. There is no Tango at Madam Josefina's. The other brothels hire musicians and their prostitutes dance with the men."

He paused to let Joaquin ponder the idea that Tango was developing organically in the brothels. "The more people learn this dance, including prostitutes, the more people will be drawn to our shows."

"I don't dispute your logic."

"Then you'll do it?"

"No."

Tony let out a dejected sigh and slumped in defeat.

"I simply can't Tony. I've never been to a brothel, and I worry that my family would learn of such indiscretions. Father Devechio has me under constant surveillance and employs spies to tell him if I as much as fart in the wrong direction. I would never get away with it."

Tony decided to try another tact. "How is your Tango play coming along?"

"It's coming along—I have some ideas I'm exploring," Joaquin said, weakly.

"We both know it isn't. Listen to me—how can you write about Tango if you don't see how the people that you describe in your stories live?"

With no response from Joaquin, he decided to play what he thought was his trump card. "There's a woman there that you should meet. Her name is Sofia. She's the bookkeeper and practically manages the brothel for Madam Josefina. She's smart—and quite feisty I must say, and Spanish like yourself. I made a promise to her. She'll have the ladies ready on Monday at noon. It will make her—and I—look bad if you don't show up."

"Ouch. You just made me think of the woman I met on the voyage back to Buenos Aires. I was quite taken with her—but then I blew my chances with my usual mule-headed behaviour. I need to forget about her," Joaquin said. "You're right—I need to experience the brothel setting at least once—for the sake of our music of course. I'll explain it to Father Devechio that way when he finds out—as well as my parents God help me."

"This means a lot to me," Tony said. "And remember what I told you about Diego."

As he made the trek to Madam Josefina's Social House, Joaquin grew nervous. 'Why on earth would I be nervous about standing in front of a bunch of prostitutes? It doesn't mean they're sex fanatics.'

Following Tony's directions from his warehouse, he'd taken the tram westward along Avenida Rivadavia, to Plaza Once, having slapped away the hands of two young pickpockets, he walked north to Gallo and turned left onto Valentin Gomez. Looking for the building Tony had described, he stepped squarely into a pile of malodorous green horse dung, and let out a long breath of frustration.

'This must be it. Do I knock or just barge in? I'll knock. Loudly or softly? Good Lord—only a fool would knock on the doors of a brothel.'

Pushing one of the two large doors open, he came face to face with a startled teenager, who'd been asleep on a small bench inside the entrance.

"Buenos dias, young man—I'm the Tango instructor. They're expecting me."

"My name is Tico. I'm in charge," he said, with all seriousness. "Sofia asked me to bring you in."

"Sofia you say," he said, clearing the dry lump in his throat. "Remind me what Sofia's last name is."

'It would be wise to at least check.'

"Montserrat—do you know the Senator? She's his niece."

The teenager's offhand statement brought Joaquin's world to a momentary halt. He felt his face flush and redden. He wasn't sure if it was anger, embarrassment, excitement, or something else. Had she not told him she was staying with her Uncle Hugo the Senator, or had he made an assumption? He had no answers and it didn't matter. He entered the courtyard and their eyes met as she descended the stairs.

She was leading a mob of unruly women in various states of undress. Joaquin took off his bowler, watching her direct her flock to the open courtyard area, tables piled on top of each other to make room. She glanced at him, then walked over at a business-like pace.

"Señor Cuellar—what a pleasant surprise. I had no idea Tony was sending you," she said, with uncertainty. "But I should have guessed when he said the lessons were free. I recall that you have a good heart—and these ladies desperately need your attention."

"They will most certainly have it," he said, still in disbelief of his turn of fortune, trying to suppress the urge to embrace her. "I have some questions for you—perhaps at a better time," he said, and then more loudly, "I'm at your disposal."

"These are your students—I'm sure you'll find them most willing," she said, a little too loudly to be natural.

Joaquin watched her walk towards a sturdy, buxom woman whom he thought must be Madam Josefina. 'My dear Sofia, I will do whatever you ask of me, no matter what you've done to land yourself here.' Then he realised there were 224 predatory gazes observing him watch Sofia, so he wrenched his eyes away and walked to the open area. Before he could say anything, he was confronted by a pretty woman with curly hair, her chemise pulled high, waggling a bare set of breasts at him.

"Yes Sofia, I'm sure he will find us all most willing," she said, causing shrieks of laughter.

Joaquin laughed as well.

"That was an amusing distraction—but you only have me for two hours, so I suggest we get started. As there are more of you than I expected I will have you form two rows and make sure you can see me if you're in the back row."

"Oh, you don't have to worry about that, we'll make sure we can see you!" again to licentious cackles that Joaquin ignored.

"Tango basic to start. One line will play the male partner and then you'll switch. Do your best to master this, then I'll show you some other figures that I believe you'll find appealing."

Sofia walked towards the bar, knowing Madam Josefina was watching her intently. She told her herself to play this right, as Josefina was hyper-vigilante in detecting scams within the confines of her brothel. It was not a question of enforcing ethical conduct, but rather of missing opportunities for profit. Sofia's instinct was to keep their relationship a secret for now, not wanting to discuss events on the Sirio, or the notion of being romantically involved, which they most certainly were not. But it had been such a relief to see him walking through the grand doors.

"Sofia, come over here dearie—you seem familiar with this young man."

"No, it's the first time I've met him."

"Is that a fact? Well unless I'm mistaken, I just saw Cupid's arrows pierce both of your young hearts. He seems to be a nice gentleman. With manners like that—he's certainly not our regular type."

"I suppose not. But he would fit in with some of our special closed events—the ones for the politicians and army officers." Sofia was now desperate to dispel any notion of a relationship between herself and Joaquin, she just had too much to worry about. Besides, there really wasn't one, was there? Hadn't she decided he was too full of himself to be her type? In any case, she certainly didn't want Lieutenant Machado knowing about their acquaintance. The less he knew the better.

"Has he been here before?" She still seemed unsatisfied.

"Not that I remember. Tony knew of him and arranged for him to come and teach Tango."

"He's got a momentous task in front of him if you ask me. Most of these fensucked giglets appear to have two left feet. Lord Christ save me from the vagaries of this business. Just how many times do you expect this young man will grace us with his presence without charge?"

"He said he would come five days in a row—he said five lessons would give them a good start."

"Since you're so disinterested we have to demonstrate our gratitude in some way. Which of these flirtgills do you think would suit him? I'll be extremely disappointed if he can't be enticed into one of their lairs."

"Maybe Hortense, the French strumpet," Sofia said, turning Madam Josefina's Shakespearean weaponry against her. "He's already seen her top half and seemed quite impressed."

Sofia's back was turned to the group, while Josefina was seated facing them. Joaquin had now asked one line of ladies to pair up with the other, take a dance hold, and repeat the figure. His eyes had flickered to Sofia. "No dearie—it's you he's interested in."

For five consecutive days, Joaquin endured the congested tram along Avenida Rivadavia, guarding his pockets from the orphan thieves that stared at him hungrily, and avoiding the fresh piles of horse manure that decorated the street, inviting him to sink a virgin shoe into them once again.

For five days, Joaquin exchanged enthusiastic greetings with his new pal Tico, who was stood to like a palatial guard whenever he entered the grand wooden doors. For five days, Joaquin tried to steal any snippet of conversation from Sofia, attempting to figure out why she was now employed at a brothel, before prying eyes compelled her to limit their interactions.

For five days, he instructed 224 half-clad women on the black art of Tango, interrupted periodically by Hortense flashing her breasts—every freckle and mole of this wondrous display now emblazoned in his memory.

Each day, he experienced a sense of urgency to return to Josefina's Social House, like a horse increasing its pace when returning to its stable. He needed to enjoy the presence, if nothing else, of Sofia, now certain she was the woman of his heart and soul, only to leave with yet more incertitude, more questions, and more confusion. Each day he managed to hold her gaze for a few moments, conveying what he could with his eyes, joy and anticipation for the most part, and every day he found a way to touch her hand lightly and discretely, to let her know his heart was open. But as he lay in bed gazing upwards he was troubled by her responses, 'It was reluctance,' he thought, and so he tried to convince himself that he was not in love with a woman who gave every indication of attempting the same foolish act of insanity.

He couldn't guess why Sofia remained distant, but he knew he had to do something bold, and so, by day four, he had a plan. On entry the following day, he would pass Tico a letter, and ask him to pass it secretly to Sofia. Could he trust the teenager? Of course, not. He didn't know his circumstances, but it was all he could think of. He would ask Sofia to write him a letter, and he provided the address of his warehouse. She could find a way to get him a letter, if she wanted to, and then they could arrange to meet at a private location.

On the Friday, Tico took the letter willingly, shoving it into a frayed pocket.

"Of course, Señor Cuéllar. You and Sofia are a match made in heaven—I could never stand in the way of true love," Tico cried, to a forceful shush from Joaquin.

He brought his 22 students, some more able than others, to an acceptable degree of proficiency, and today he'd planned a special surprise, Tony would come and play Tango music for them, all of the songs that he played in the evenings, so that they could practice properly. He wanted to see them experience the magic of combining dance with music. 'He would dance with each of them for a short period as well, give each one some final advice, and then he would be finished, all obligations satisfied,' he thought.

He avoided looking at Sofia, as always seated at the bar with Madam Josefina, and succeeded in so doing until finishing. Then he allowed himself one desperate glance, making unfortunate eye contact with Madam Josefina, 'Damn her watchfulness,' and then to Sofia, who's eyes had gone wide and were locked on the entrance. Following her gaze, he felt a rush of adrenaline and fear.

Overcoming his shock through sheer force of will, he turned away and drew his derby over his brow. Fortunately, the three men were preoccupied with the sight of the prostitutes dancing together in close contact. They stared lewdly at the women, while Joaquin angled himself so that they saw only the side or back of him. Then he made eye contact with Sofia, who understood his precarious position but could only let the moment play itself out. They finally walked to the hallway towards their meeting room.

A moment later, while hastily bidding his students farewell, he caught sight of the tall, foreboding policeman he had seen with his three tormentors at the dock. He walked through the courtyard and disappeared into the same hallway. The policeman had looked him up and down with a pair of reptilian black eyes without so much as breaking his deliberate stride.

Tico had given Sofia the letter, which she hid it in her room to read later, and it weighed in her mind. Customers arriving that evening passed an announcement chalked onto a sandwich board, placed in the entranceway so that it couldn't be missed.

Welcome to Josefina's Social House. Now featuring Tango in the courtyard.

Men had taken their tables. They were approached and asked to dance by one of the prostitutes, and several of them accepted the invitation. Madam Josefina, however, had been shrewd about the change.

'I've still got a business to run. Remember your time is valuable. Nothing changes in terms of time. If you spent 15 minutes chatting and flirting before, now you can make it 5 minutes of flirting and 10 minutes of Tango. Then you focus on our core business. We'll see if this lures the ruttish miscreants from the horse track in Palermo, the underground gambling houses, or wherever they're hiding their feckless clot poles! Cheers!'

Sofia noticed that the women had readily adapted. Now only time would tell if it would bring back customers and revive the brothel. It took her past midnight to balance the two ledgers, and pay the ladies their wages. The remainder of the evening's take was placed in burlap sacks of bills and coins and given to Madam

Josefina to place in the safe. She said good night to those that were still around and retired to her modest room, grateful for privacy. She opened Joaquin's letter. He had elegant handwriting.

My Dear Sofia. Imagine my surprise just a few short days ago to find you employed at Madam Josefina's Social House. I had imagined you would be staying with your uncle the Senator. I have clearly misunderstood your situation, however I cast no judgement. A woman's means of earning wages is far more limited than those of men. It is my sincere hope that we can see each other again soon. I included the address of my warehouse where I keep an office. Please send me a response. I hope you will consider this soonest. Yours truly, Joaquin.

He was everything that was right for her, handsome, motivated in his pursuits, stable, and amusing. She'd had to turn away several times while he goofed off with the ladies, so that Josefina wouldn't see her laugh. She had felt her spirits brighten each morning when he'd arrived bounding through their doors. Having won over the ladies on the first lesson with his warmth and enthusiasm, he nevertheless saved his best smile for her, and made her feel special.

Then she felt her posture slump, and the dark melancholy returned. She couldn't pursue a romance with Joaquin, such a well-intended, responsible man. It was certain heartbreak for him, and her. She could be apprehended and put in jail, or worse, at any moment. According to Lieutenant Machado she was wanted by the authorities of Spain for murders she didn't commit, and facing a death sentence. She had regrettably complicated things by resuming articles for the anarchist newspaper Broken Chains! as a Free Woman. Lieutenant Machado could decide to arrest her himself, just for that it seemed. Or he would threaten to kill Joaquin just to control her. There were too many dire possibilities, she couldn't stand the thought of it, and wouldn't have it on her conscience. She would have to break his heart right now, as well as her own. The single tear on her cheek led to a stream, and then a river, and she held a blanket to her mouth to muffle her uncontrollable sobs.

"Tico why is the letter opened?"

"I'm sorry Señor Cuéllor. I know it was supposed to be a private letter. Hortense surprised me outside of the doors as I left. She made me open it—she'll tell Lieutenant Machado."

"She read it?"

"No, she made me read it. She can't read."

164

"And you can read? I'm pleasantly surprised."

"Sofia has been teaching me how to read and mathematics. I'm smart she says—a quick learner."

"Indeed, you are Tico. Who exactly is Lieutenant Machado?"

"He's the tall police officer that protects the brothel. Madam Josefina pays him a big portion of the earnings. The Lieutenant is very tough. He beats up anyone that gets drunk and misbehaves, or hits a woman. My job is to fetch him when something bad is happening."

"I see."

"This letter is bad news. I'm sorry."

Señor Cuéllar. We are most grateful for your time spent assisting our ladies with their Tango. It was a special week with more levity than we are used to. Unfortunately, I must decline your offer to meet. I have no wish to pursue a future relationship with you. My present circumstances simply don't allow for it, and those circumstances will remain private. It is best that you forget me, and move on with your life. I wish you the best with your future endeavours. Sofia.

"Thank you, for your assistance Tico. Good lad. I think you'd best return."

"She isn't what you think, Señor. Did you know she murdered her own parents in Spain?"

"Excuse me?"

"Lieutenant Machado told me so. That's why she has to hide at the brothel with us."

Chapter 14
Confessional

On a sweltering Sunday morning, Hugo Montserrat felt sweat dripping down his spine and beginning to stain the underarms of his shirt. He was dressed in his best suit that morning, despite all indications of a hot day ahead. It was an important day for Hugo, a day of atonement. It would not serve him to be half-hearted about today's confessions, he needed to bare his soul and face the judgment of God almighty. Nothing less would do. His sins were many, significant, and unconfessed—God had taken note. Of this he was zealously certain, for how else to explain the run of misfortunes he had endured this last month?

It had started with a fortuitous wager at the hippodrome in Palermo. He had a practiced eye for spotting an outsider horse with long odds. He liked the trot of Rio Grande whom the handicapper had given less weight, and he hid a surge of excitement—recognising a bet that could give a large return. He went big and won big, gloating to himself while nods of respect were proffered by those who recognised his win was the result of shrewd calculation.

Later that afternoon, having consumed two whiskeys neat in rapid succession, he used his winnings to buy into an exclusive high-stakes poker game organised in a back room of the Jockey Club, with a few of his wealthy cohorts. As always, his judgement was diminished in direct relation to the amount of spirits he consumed.

He let himself be goaded into throwing all his chips in, by Senator Da Rosa, who'd been watching him closely, and had paid the waiter extra to keep Hugo's glass of whiskey full. 'Go on Hugo old man, use a few of those pesos you won at the tracks!' Hugo had railed at his condescending laugh while looking his tormentor in the eyes, thinking he was bluffing.

Having been relieved of his morning's winnings, common sense almost ruled the day, as he got up from his chair to leave.

"Leaving so soon Hugo? It was bad luck—happens to the best of us. You're normally a heartier soul."

He couldn't stand the implication he'd lost his nerve at the best of times, let alone while under the influence. "And what if I decide to stay?"

"We know you're good for it, old man. I'll front you the chips against that ranch you have near Bahia Blanca. Since you got it for a whisper, it shouldn't be all that dear to you anyway."

He looked around the table. They were men that he knew, and he hated the idea of losing face. They were silent, all eyes upon him. The offer against his first ranching property was too tempting to refuse, as he again failed to notice the waiter refilling his glass.

The following morning, his head had hurt so much he'd been unable to rise from bed. He recalled being dragged from the club and into a coach by Lieutenant Machado and one of his burly detectives, then into his entranceway in Barrio Norte. He knew he had lost one of his most profitable ranches the evening before, and prayed he'd had the good sense to keep the slaughterhouse and meatpacking plant off the table. 'I can jack the service prices up for the rotten bastard!' He remembered his adversary Da Rosa at the table claiming justice had been served, 'That's for Luis Pedro old man! May god rest his soul.'

Two weeks later, he received notice from the British railway company that serviced his former ranch. They declined to renew his tenure on their Board of Directors, and thanked him for his many productive years of service to their company. Of course, his salary would be terminated forthwith. It was to be redirected to the newest board member Senator Da Rosa, who'd humbly agreed to take on the extra responsibilities, despite also being heavily burdened with decisions of the state. 'I will see the bastard's face in the sights of my revolver!'

The following week, he took stock of his diminished empire. His other two ranches were of high property value, and generated sufficient liquidity to maintain his nominal salary. But he was now more vulnerable to strike actions by the anarchist-controlled unions dominating the export distribution lines—the railway mechanics, the slaughterhouses, the stevedores and port workers. He would have to keep a close eye on that situation, and his allies in the police department would damn well help. His senatorial salary assisted, but no self-respecting Senator of Argentina would settle for a single salary, when they had so much bank credit to take advantage of. And there remained the problem of his incessant gambling, the losses from which continued to mount. Next, he read the letter he'd received from his lawyer in Cadiz, Adelmo Vega.

Dear Sir,

Please be advised this firm has received official notice from the Chief Legal Counsel attached to the Spanish embassy located in Buenos Aires, Argentina. Counsel for the Montserrat Estate, Jerez de la Frontera, challenged the assertion that Sofia Montserrat, sole surviving daughter of Antonio and Maria Montserrat, deceased, was serving as a common prostitute in the city of Buenos Aires and had requested evidence thereof, as several witnesses at the estate claim it to be contrary to her true character.

The Spanish Embassy saw fit to send an agent to the registered brothel known as Madam Josefina's Social House, and confirm that Miss Sofia Montserrat was offering services as a prostitute. This agent attended the social house for three consecutive evenings and observed the proceedings. Miss Montserrat was observed working behind the bar, handing out chits to women that were employed as prostitutes, and tending ledgers.

The agent made an attempt each evening to employ Miss Montserrat as a prostitute, and was refused each time. Furthermore, he was finally advised that she was not registered as a prostitute, but rather as the bookkeeper for the aforementioned premise. This account was confirmed by three independent witnesses to the clandestine agent, including a teenage boy named Tico, last name unknown, a prostitute called Zoryana, and Madam Josefina herself.

Truth be told, he hadn't even thought about the young woman since he'd last seen her on the steamship. All of his fine work—dispatching his brother Antonio and his wife Maria, pinning the blame on local anarchists, manipulating the Civil Guard into considering her a suspect, tricking her into travelling to Argentina, forcing her to take refuge at a brothel—was now in jeopardy because she'd been clever and had avoided a fate as a prostitute.

Yes, God was clearly displeased with him and today he needed to atone. He crossed the Plaza de Mayo towards the Metropolitan Cathedral, mingling with the masses of the city's faithful. The regulars were in attendance, as well as the city's elite, senators and congressmen, the bankers and lawyers, and the hard-crusted businessmen like himself, tipping their hats to their colleagues and flirting with their wives.

Today he ignored them. His eyes were locked onto the triangular pediment of the portico. Its carved facade depicted a scene from the Bible's Book of Genesis. 'Joseph reunited with his father Jacob in Egypt, after his jealous brothers connived to sell him into slavery,'—as I was sold into slavery at the ranch of Luis Pedro. 'Joseph persisted with hard work and rose to become an advisor to the pharaoh,' as I have risen to become a senator, and advisor to the President. Yes—my path was as righteous as if it had been written in the bible!' The similarity he imagined between the biblical story and his own struggle convinced him he was on the righteous path. He continued into the church, eager to relieve the burden of his sins. He was going to seek out Father Devechio to hear his confession. Afterwards, following a sizeable cash contribution during the offertory, he would be at peace accepting the body and blood of Christ during the eucharist. Then he expected his fortunes would turn for the better.

Why did he sense he could trust Father Devechio with the burden of his sins, however vile and despicable? Father Devechio was at least a decade older than himself, and that seemed important. He couldn't stand the thought of a sanctimonious youngster casting judgement. He'd had a conversation with the priest outside of the confessional booth many months ago, testing the waters.

"Tell me Father—have you taken many confessionals from men like myself? Pioneers from the plains—doing what had to be done to see this country settled?"

"I have heard the confessions of many of our statesmen. Politicians of the highest order, generals of the army, and businessmen like yourself have graced my confessional Senator. There isn't much a priest my age hasn't heard."

"Have you been in Argentina for many years, Father?"

"All of my life, my son."

"I suppose you have heard confessions from true men of war then?"

"Indeed, I have. There are many military officers who were duty bound to slay the enemy—but it weighed on their souls nevertheless. In these cases, the killing of the enemy is justified in that it protects the peace. There is debate amongst us priests that killing on the battlefields is not done with deliberate consent—and is therefore not a mortal sin. But this is a theological technicality—and shouldn't distract one from attending the confessional. Unless these sins are confessed, one's soul descends straight to hell, and confessing your sins will bring you back into God's grace."

That discussion had taken place a few days after he'd killed the beautiful young prostitute at Josefina's Social House. She had reminded him of his brother's wife Maria, and he'd butchered her while acting out in a drunken, jealous rage. He hadn't been able to admit he was at fault for the crime to himself, let alone a priest. He told himself he had no control of his actions due to his rage, and since he then lacked full knowledge of his actions, it couldn't be a mortal sin.

But even if it wasn't, his latest orgy of violence at the Montserrat family home certainly was. He had to place his faith in God, a merciful father who wants to forgive him. There was no more delaying his confession. Walking determinedly toward the confessional, he stopped abruptly at the door, paused, and entered reluctantly. Father Devechio watched him curiously through the screen.

"Why do you hesitate, Senator Montserrat?"

"Forgive me Father, I fear there will be retribution for my sins and I'm conflicted."

"The retribution you must truly fear is the fiery depths of hell my son."

Hugo dropped his eyes. There was an agonising imagery playing in his mind—a casket lid sealing him in without escape, and the casket being placed in the beautiful marble tomb he had purchased in the Recoletta cemetery. His soul then leaving that peaceful place behind, descending into the fire, burning and screaming in pain for eternity. He entered the confessional.

"Bless me father for I have sinned. My last confession was years ago. My sins are many and grave father," he said softly through the screen wooden grill to the shadow leaning close.

"Continue, my son."

"I don't know where to start."

"Are they venial sins or mortal sins?"

"Both."

"Have you taken another god?"

"No."

"Have you worshipped false idols?"

"No."

"Have you taken the Lord's name in vain?"

"No."

"You are here every Sunday it seems, and have respected the Sabbath?"

"Yes."

"And you have honoured your mother and your father?"

"In my way, I have done so yes."

"Have you killed someone my son?"

"I've killed many people father." He choked and sobbed for a minute, but then recomposed himself.

"You are in pain my son. Like many others that participated in the Conquest of the Desert, you were executing God's will by protecting the settlements and bringing Christianity to the hostile pagan Indians. Their murderous raids and resistance to these efforts necessitated regrettable actions. I have heard this many times from the soldiers who served this country and the church. Do you come to confession as a penitent, truly sorry for your sins and with a grim resolve not to sin again?"

"There is more than my participation in those battles father. As a young man I experienced greed—and that greed made me marry a young woman that I did not love. I grew to despise her. I married her because I coveted her parent's prosperous ranch. Their standing with the provincial bank allowed me to obtain a loan with which I purchased my own ranch, where we took up residence. It was in an area populated with hostile Indians. I patrolled my lands myself. Whenever I came across their women and children, I shot them, otherwise they would tell their warriors where my cattle and horses were—to be stolen later."

"A month later I received a dispatch by horse rider from the army garrison at Bahia Blanca—a warning that I should evacuate with my wife immediately. A council of chiefs had pronounced that I was to be killed, and a war party was being formed for that evening. But running away was not my style. I didn't say anything about it to my wife, and I rode to a nearby hill to hide with my rifles. That evening, from a distance, I spotted the raiding party heading for our farmhouse. I got closer and watched from behind a crop of rock as they set fire to it. My wife ran out of the front door on fire—screaming. I heard their war cries—and laughs. They tamped out the fire on her clothes and hair and stripped her naked. While crying in agony from her burns, they raped her, and then beat her to death."

"Do you mean to say that you didn't have the courage to intervene and save her?"

"No. I'm in fact a brave man. Greed and hate drove my decision not to act."

171

"This is a grave sin, Hugo, and it's complicated but God will forgive you. This must have occurred many years ago."

"Yes—before the Conquest of the Desert. After she died, I became like a son to her parents. She was an only child, they had no-one else. My greed made me take advantage of their good will, and I obtained loans that were leveraged against their land. As my own land acquisitions grew, so did the ranching operations and I hired more ranch hands and gauchos. We conducted raids to quell the thievery and rustling. Indian men, women and children—were all treated the same and died by our bullets or under our hooves."

"God will forgive you, my son. It was an endeavour to bring peace. Is there anything else you wish to confess?"

"Yes. There is more father. I have experienced lust and anger, and it forced me to abuse a young woman—a prostitute."

"How did you abuse the young woman?"

"I was drinking and became lustful and then angry. When the woman was naked and waiting for me to embrace her, she reminded me of my brother's wife, whom I had loved, and who pushed me aside to marry my brother. The young woman resembled her. I was consumed with rage. I smashed the end of a whiskey bottle—I stabbed her in the face and the throat and severed an artery. There was blood spurting and when I realised what I'd done I tried to save her—I tried to stop the bleeding." Is that what he'd done? It must have been. But why did he continue to dream that he then strangled her?

The priest had taken a deep breath, and was silent for a few moments before he managed to speak. "God will forgive you, my son."

'Has my faith ever been so tested? How can God possibly forgive such heinous crimes?'

"There is more father. During my trip to Jerez de la Frontera I experienced pride and greed and it caused me to kill my brother and his wife. Then I was forced to kill their maid, who had witnessed my crime. It left their daughter destitute—and I tricked her into coming to Argentina and delivered her to a brothel here in the city."

"You have committed many mortal sins my son. Your penance must reflect the gravity of these sins if you ever wish to feel God's grace within you again. Pray and repeat after me, my God, I am deeply remorseful for having offended thee. I loathe my mortal sins because of thy punishment, which I deserve, but most importantly because they offend thee my God, who art all good and who righteously deserve my unquestioning love and devotion. I solemnly intend with thy help to sin no more and to avoid these circumstances that lead to sin."

"Did I hear you say that you acquired valuable properties while committing these sins?"

"Yes father. I could donate some very valuable land that I have acquired—upon which a church could be built to serve the citizens of Bahia Blanca."

"To return to the path of righteousness you must donate this land, and you must read your bible Isaiah 57:15. Joel 2:13 says, 'and tear your heart and not merely your garments.' Now return to the LORD your God, For He is gracious and compassionate, slow to anger, abounding in mercy and relenting of catastrophe. Follow this path my son."

Father Devechio waited in the confessional until he heard Hugo Montserrat leave. Tears were falling from his cheeks and he felt dizzy. He stood up from his bench while bracing himself on the wall. He walked slowly to the washroom and felt himself heaving, until he wretched putrid green vomit. 'I have met Satan himself.'

Chapter 15
Spies

January 1905. For Gabriel Chavez, the new year brought hope. The elections of February the previous year had once again been catastrophic. The man he had practically worshipped for a span of 15 years, Hipolito Irigoyan, had declared that no members of the Radical Civic Union, the grassroots political party Irigoyan led, would participate, for fear of legitimising a corrupt election. Chavez had been bitterly disappointed. Irigoyan's strategy was to let the Argentine people observe the 1904 election for the sham it was, as only politicians from the established Autonomist party would win, and grow popular support for a coup d'état soon after. The coup was to occur last October, when the newly elected President Manuel Quintana began his term, but their supporters amongst the military's officer ranks had not been ready.

His association with Irigoyan went back to 1889. As a student at the Faculty of Law of the University of Buenos Aires, Chavez, and his friend Leon Alvarez, had been enthralled when a group of 3000 elites—doctors, lawyers, engineers and university students—formed the Civic Union to oppose the entrenched oligarchy. Chavez came to the attention of Irigoyan, a previous student of the Faculty of Law, and the two became friends.

They discussed their vision of Argentina's future, citizens voting freely for their candidate of choice, and elected city officials. Irigoyan grew to trust Chavez completely and eventually asked him to help draft a manifesto—to be read during the government coup being planned in collaboration with dissatisfied military officers.

'The manifesto would prove to be a seminal work,' he thought. It identified the primary themes of the patriot's struggles—electoral corruption, pandering to British banking and rail interests, and irresponsible monetary policies that were easily manipulated by politicians and businessmen. His personal touch to the manifesto, his streak of genius became their slogan, return the country to its people.

'But the coup had not succeeded and 15 years changes many things,' he thought. Surely the greater Argentine people had had enough of the endless cycle of corruption, and those politicians that advanced their own business interests before those of the country's. Argentina was meant to be better than that, and the corruption had to end.

From October to December, Chavez had delayed his inquiries into the mystery of the three mercenaries working clandestinely for Commissioner De La Fuente. He'd had to solidify planning around the public announcement of his new manifesto, borrowing much from the old one, and pass messages to the limited numbers of military officers that were supporting their coup.

The blatant bribery of voters by wealthy contenders had shaken the beliefs and dedication of many junior officers, and their support for the coup was critical. He wanted the officers to have an opportunity to provide input and be aware of the contents of the manifesto, in order to ensure that they remained committed after the coup. After several meetings with his friend Major Leon Alverez, he felt reassured. He was on track with the manifesto and was in the process of putting the final touches to it. The new year would bring monumental change, and he felt the thrill of being on the cusp of a great victory. One or two months at the most and they would be ready to give the signal to unleash their revolution. This time they would get it right.

Yet he was uneasy with the unfinished business of the three mercenaries, to the point he was losing sleep. It was an unacceptable risk as it presently stood. 'They could very well be targeting him specifically,' he thought, 'or would they have bigger fish to fry? Irigoyan? Or the military officers perhaps?' He couldn't risk that either.

So, he'd had his assistant Nicolas find the address of Joaquin Cuéllar's export business amongst the registries in order to continue his investigation discreetly. Cuéllar had managed to raise their ire on the steamship for some unexplained reason, and he needed to find out what that reason was. Cuéllar would know something.

"Got it sir. Cuéllar's Export Import Madrid, established 1894 Buenos Aires. Address number 10, Azopardo, it's across from dock 1."

Chavez exited the ministry building on Avenida de Mayo and had the coachman take him right to the large bay doors of the warehouse, Cuéllar's

Export Import Madrid painted in large red letters above the massive doors. One of the doors was wide open and he walked in. It was exactly as he'd imagined, burly, sweaty men in the January heat, loading large burlap sacks, 'Good God those bags must weigh 100 lbs easily,' onto a horse-drawn trolley. They stared at him suspiciously. From his tailored suit, boots polished to a spit-shine, and derby, they knew he wasn't there to lend them a hand.

Chavez lifted his chin and straightened his shoulders fighting a bout of insecurity. He was far from the waxed hardwood floors of the university, and the Ministry building where he normally dwelt. There was a set of steep stairs he could see that led to a landing and a closed office with dirty windows.

He climbed the stairs and from his vantage point saw a closed area on the other side of the warehouse that was evidently refrigerated. He could see frost on the heavy plastic flaps sealing the room while allowing a pulley assembly with giant meat hooks to transfer lamb and beef carcasses into the cold storage area.

A man emerged from the office, approximately the same height and weight as Chavez, but a few years younger. His trousers and vest matched and were of good quality, his shirt sleeves were rolled up, 'Not afraid of manual work,' and beads of perspiration dotted his brow. The neutral expression on his face was only slightly more friendly than the overt hostility emanating from the stevedores below.

"Señor Joaquin Cuéllar, I presume?"

"Indeed."

"My name is Gabriel Chavez, I'm with the Ministry of the Interior." He handed Joaquin a small business card with an official looking inlay, 'Senior Legal Counsel.'

"How can I possibly be of help to the Ministry of the Interior?"

"I'm here to ask you about an incident you had with three men on the Sirio—during your voyage to Buenos Aires. The ship's Captain gave me your name."

"Finally! I thought the matter would eventually be looked into. Those bastards ambushed me in front of my cabin in the late evening. I didn't even see them coming. They broke one of my ribs. It was very painful—it took me weeks to recover."

"Why is it they attacked you specifically?"

"Don't get the wrong impression. I had never seen the bastards—I mean gentlemen—in my life before this incident. I was performing with a group of

176

volunteer Tango dancers on the lower bridge. As far as I know, I upset their precious sensibilities. I gave them a tongue-lashing I suppose. I assume that's still not a crime. That's all I know of them and that's all I care to know of them."

'Chavez was already annoyed with Cuéllar, a man playing innocent,' he thought. "You're telling me that this is a case of you being the wrong man in the wrong place at the wrong time? That's a common excuse for those that won't accept responsibility for something they've instigated—for reasons of fear most often."

"You've just managed to call me a liar and a coward in one short sentence! Now tell me—why should I put up with any more of your questions. As far as I'm concerned the men appear to be connected to the police—with whom I assume your ministry is very familiar."

Chavez chided himself. It was never a good technique to insult someone from whom information was required. "I apologise—I misspoke. Is there anything at all that you can tell me about them?"

"Yes. I've unfortunately seen them again—a couple of months ago. Miraculously, they didn't recognise me. It was in a brothel—Madam Josefina's Social House. I agreed to teach Tango to the ladies of the establishment as a favour to my musical collaborator Tony—and also for Sofia. She is their bookkeeper. I met her on the Sirio as well."

"That's useful but something doesn't make sense—she reported them to the ship's Captain, but is now socializing with them. What am I missing?"

"I don't know. I saw them meeting with a tall police officer when they were escorted from the ship. Then they appeared at the brothel, and disappeared in the back. Now that I think of it, the tall police officer attended the brothel at the same time. I learned later that he was Lieutenant Machado."

"Are you romantically involved with Miss Montserrat," Chavez asked, on the lookout for any means to persuade, threaten, or blackmail should it be required. 'He hadn't gotten much further,' he thought.

"I'm afraid not."

"Why not—don't you like women?"

"I inquired," he sighed. "She wasn't interested. She's recovering from the tragic loss of her parents. They were murdered in Jerez de la Frontera. She came to Buenos Aires to convalesce."

It had seemed that Cuellar had intended to say more, but then didn't. He's hiding something. Her parents had been murdered—the Senator's relatives in

Spain. "I see." 'I must find them—mercenaries connected to the head of the investigative division of the Police of the Capital, and to Senator Montserrat, a confidante of the President! They are certainly engaged in surveillance of Irigoyan and revolutionaries like myself—they're killers planning assassinations.' It was a good theory, but then he couldn't make sense of why the woman had been cast off to work at a brothel. There were still too many unanswered questions, he would need to visit his colleague at the Spanish Embassy, and inquire what they knew about the murders of her parents.

The coach was waiting for him outside the warehouse, and he took it directly back to the ministry. He walked down the hall to his office and paused at the door, listening for signs that his amorous aide was using the topside of his desk for another conquest from the basement. Not finding Nicolas inside, he descended the stairs and continued to the typist pool, where he saw him chatting to the pretty woman that had now shared both of their physical affections.

"Nicolas," he called, snapping his fingers in rapid succession. "Follow me." He led his young aide to his office and closed the door. "I'll need you to set watch on a brothel. It's called Madam Josefina's Social House."

"On Valentin Gomez."

"You've been there before?"

"No—of course, not!"

"There's no need to be embarrassed. Will you be recognised?"

"I went there once—or twice—while I was in university. I think it's been a long enough time that I won't be remembered."

"Scallywag! No matter. Listen now—I need information—whatever you can find out. There's a woman called Sofia Montserrat. She's the bookkeeper apparently. I want you to attend the brothel, set eyes upon her, so that you can recognize her later. There are also three men that I am searching for, that might be there. I can't describe them myself as I've never seen them before. Their names are Matias, Javier, and Emilio. Don't approach them if you somehow identify them. They're dangerous mercenaries and won't hesitate to harm you. Do whatever you have to in order to fit in as a client."

"Yes sir—anything for God, country, and the ministry!"

"Good attitude. Then I want you to disguise yourself and take watch from the exterior. If the woman leaves, follow her and see where she goes. If you see the three men, follow them. I want to know where they live, drink, and use the latrines—but I especially need to know who they meet with." 'Will I get the young man killed? It must be done.'

Nicolas could barely contain his excitement. What an unusual task! What exactly was his boss up to? Had he detected a hint of panic in Chavez's tone? This was not in keeping with his character. 'Whatever his reasons, I'm sure they are important for the ministry.' He thought he would enter the brothel at about six in the evening, once the heat had died down, and stay for at least a couple of hours.

'Why would one hurry from a brothel? That would surely seem suspicious to the Madam and this Sofia woman.' He would cavort with one of the prostitutes—the prettiest one! Not like his experience with his drunken university pals, taking the first one that latched on to him.

He entered through the grand wooden doors and walked into the open courtyard. A different atmosphere than he expected greeted him. A stocky musician was playing a haunting melody on a bandonéon, and singing in Italian. There were four couples dancing in the middle of the tables lining the walls of the courtyard, under glowing lanterns that weren't yet casting their light. He found himself transfixed by the seductive scene, so he took a seat at a table and watched.

"Would you like to dance, Monsieur?" A pretty woman with curly hair tied in an unruly bun said huskily into his ear. She was close enough that he could smell her breath—enticing him, and her perfume.

"They're dancing rather—closely," he said, torn between the erotic spectacle of the dancing, and that of the scarlet bodice showing under a loose blouse.

"It's Tango Monsieur. It's how it's danced," she said, taking his hand. "You can hold your hand high like this, and put the other on my back—further," she said, adjusting his right hand so that it encircled her back and landed on the side of her rib cage, tantalisingly close to her breast. She leaned forward until some of her weight was pressing into him, nuzzled her head into his cheek, and threw one bare arm over his shoulder languorously. He could smell the fragrance of her hair, and he felt her heart beating against his own chest. "Are you alright?" She asked with a whisper.

"Yes."

"Have you ever danced Tango?"

"No."

"Then let's walk. Push me backwards gently. What's your name Monsieur?"

"Nicolas." Concentrating on his dancing, holding one hand gently, keeping the other on her back ribcage, and walking in time with the somnolent musical tempo, he forgot his plan to give an alias, and most other parts of his task as well.

"My name is Hortense. Je viens de Paris. Do you speak French?"

"No. That's a beautiful French name."

"Thank you, I'm from Paris," she said.

"You're a good dancer Hortense."

"You're a good dancer as well Nicolas. Would you like to go to a room?"

"Yes."

"You'll have to pay Sofia at the bar. Come on—I'll take you to her."

Afterwards, Nicolas sat propped up against the brass headboard in a mild state of wonder. He'd been astonished by Hortense's use of her mouth and exploratory fingers, in turns throwing his head back in ecstasy and then watching the process in fascination. 'It's called fellatio Monsieur Nicolas.'

Then he remembered his task. He thought he should ask her some questions. His boss Chavez hadn't specified to do such a thing, urging caution instead. But he'd said nothing about bedding one of the prostitutes either. It went without saying that if you're sent inside a brothel to spy, you'll have to act as any of its customers would. He watched her disappear behind a screen to wash herself, and then towel her shapely, tanned legs dry. He decided to try.

"Tell me—Hortense of Paris—how long have you worked here," he asked, trying to be charming.

"None of your business, Monsieur Nicolas," she said. "Would you like to become one of my regulars? I've still got a few Parisienne tricks—but only for my regulars."

"I might." He thought that giving her hope would make her more willing to talk, and less willing to betray him. He was desperate enough to please Chavez that he decided to push further. "What do you know of three men that come here—Matias, Javier, and Emilio?"

"I don't know anything about them. Why do you ask such questions?"

"I'm looking for them. I was told they came here." She was being too inquisitive for his liking.

"Well you're free to look around but I don't know who you're talking about. Can you get dressed now? Others will need this room."

"Are you certain you don't know them? They're Spaniards I'm told." She had aroused his suspicion.

"No—it doesn't sound like anyone I know."

"Alright Hortense of Paris. I'll come by again. You can keep watch for me. I would like to experience these other tricks." He exited the room and descended the stairs that led to the courtyard. He looked towards the bar and saw Sofia, the young women he had paid for the attentions of Hortense, speaking with a large buxom woman he knew instantly must be Madam Josefina. She was looking directly at him, and he tipped his hat to her while continuing towards the doors.

The following day, Nicolas stationed himself at the intersection of Valentin Gomez and Gallo. He was 100 feet from the doors or so and could see people go in and out of Madam Josefina's Social House. Earlier that morning he had tracked down a bootblack and purchased his battered shoe shine valet with some brushes and polish. 'Alright, I'll pay your price but you'll have to throw in your cap as well!'

Now with the cap pulled down low, an old tweed suit, and some boot polish on his face and hands, he put his back against the stone facade corner, and set about avoiding eye contact with any potential customer.

After only a couple of hours, just when he was beginning to feel paranoid about looking out of place, Sofia emerged and headed in the opposite direction, westward on Valentin Gomez, then south on Avenida Bulnes. Nicolas stuffed his valet and brushes into a sack, threw it over his shoulder and followed at a distance.

He followed Sofia until she reached Independencia, where she turned westward, and then disappeared down some stairs. When he walked by the stairwell, he looked into the window, but couldn't see anything due to the glare. He walked a further 50 feet and then removed the shoe shine valet from the sack and set up his station. About an hour later, Sofia emerged from the stairwell along with an older man wearing spectacles, who was perspiring profusely. 'I'll be damned—the little vixen is cavorting as a prostitute behind the back of Madam Josefina,' he thought.

When she left in the direction she had arrived, he passed by the stairwell. The door was wide open, and he glimpsed familiar machinery, and heard men speaking. 'An underground press!' Evidently his boss was on to something nefarious, and he couldn't wait to report his findings. 'It would be one of the many anarchist publishers that plagued the city,' he thought.

On the second day, he set up his observation post in the same spot, and watched triumphantly as Sofia emerged from the entrance of Madam Josefina's Social House and walked away in the same direction. He once again followed her at a distance, and once again observed that she spent approximately one hour in the basement of the clandestine publisher.

On the third day, he again watched Sofia leave the Social House, about the same time. As he packed up his shoe shine valet, to follow, he took off the bootblack's flatcap and wiped his brow with a red handkerchief, an exaggerated gesture, before again following from a distance. The signal. Nicolas again observed her disappearing into the stairwell on Independencia, but this time he set up his makeshift shoeshine station on Avenida Buedo, the route she normally took to return to Madam Josefina's Social House. An hour later he saw her emerge, speaking with the same elderly gentleman, and turn North onto Buedo. He removed his flatcap and wiped his brow with a red handkerchief.

"Sofia Montserrat, I presume?"

She was startled by the man half concealed in the shadow of a doorway, but quickly regained her composure. "To whom do I have the pleasure of speaking?" She took a quick measure of the well-dressed middle age gentleman, with emerald green eyes, who stepped towards her.

"My name is Gabriel Chavez. I'm with the Ministry of the Interior. I hope I didn't frighten you."

"Not at all—what can I do for you?" She managed to keep a calm appearance, but her heart was racing. A scenario flashed through her mind of being placed under arrest and given to the Spanish authorities. She did not wish to spend another night in the custody of the brutish young men of the Spanish Civil Guard.

"I'm conducting an inquiry into a sensitive matter of security. I have reason to believe you're in a position to assist. But tell me, is there any reason you would not see fit to cooperate?"

'He had deliberately trapped her with his question,' she thought. Does he know of her predicament with the Spanish authorities? "No, of course, not."

"Excellent. I need your help. There are three men that are the focus of my investigation. They are former Spanish soldiers and their presence in Buenos Aires is of concern to me. Do you know of whom I'm speaking?"

"I may."

"Good. It is my belief that they attend Madam Josefina's Social House on occasion.

That's your place of work?"

"Yes."

"What can you tell me about them?"

"They meet with Lieutenant Vicente Machado. He works for the Policia de la Capitale. Are you acquainted with him?"

"I'm asking the questions thank you. Why are they meeting with Lieutenant Machado?"

'He knows the Lieutenant,' she thought, and she knew she needed to be careful what she told him. "I have to return to the social house, Señor Chavez."

"Let's walk there together while you answer my questions then. Why does the Lieutenant meet with these men? What does he want them to do?"

"I don't know—it's none of my business. He doesn't include me in their conversations."

"I want you to find a way to be a part of those conversations." He stood in her way. "This is of the utmost importance for this country. These three men are scoundrels and are up to something treasonous. The Lieutenant is part of their nefarious business as well—he's telling them exactly what to do."

"With the utmost respect, I don't work for the Ministry of the Interior. Why should I do that for you? It would put me in danger."

"If you refuse, I may have to advise the Spanish Embassy of your whereabouts. Did you know they are seeking your extradition?"

"No."

'He knows about me—and the Civil Guard is going to arrest me!'

"But I'm sympathetic to you staying in Buenos Aires. This is where immigrants come for a new beginning. Why should you be any different?"

'I'm cornered—I have to do this.'

"Alright."

"Take this address. It's an apartment I keep for secret business. On Monday, when you leave the brothel to work at the anarchist newspaper around the street, go there instead. I'll be waiting."

'He also knows about Broken Chains!—he's been watching me.'

"It's all I ask in return for turning a blind eye to the demands of the Spanish Embassy—," then he softened his attitude. "—actually, I've decided I'll even help you. I'll tell them that you left Buenos Aires—that you took refuge in one of the western provinces, unknown which one. I'll throw them completely off your track if you do this for me. Would that do you a service?"

"Yes."

"Excellent—we have a deal."

"What exactly do you want to know about them?" Better to know what Chavez was after before giving up information freely. She wasn't certain that she would tell him anything just yet.

"I'm interested in any information you hear about them a coup d'état, Irigoyan and the Civic Union, whom they're spying on, and what they're going to do. I believe they're planning assassinations, and that's not how we work in this country."

'As far as I know they're spying on anarchists—who would never attempt a coup d'état. What are you up to I wonder?'

The three Spaniards arrived on the Friday afternoon, later than their usual time. Sofia was serving drinks, and giving out chits to the prostitutes each time she received a payment and they took a client to a room. 'This is the worst possible time for them to arrive. What am I supposed to do? I just told Zoryana to use the one room that I need to be in.' Then she saw Lieutenant Machado enter, cross the courtyard where two couples were already dancing Tango, and turn the corner towards the room that the three men had gone. She had to take a chance. 'I have to go now!' Gabriel Chavez believes they're planning to assassinate people. She would find out if that was true.

She walked unhurriedly to the stairs, then bounded upwards two at a time once she was out of sight of the occupants of the courtyard. She looked around the corner down the second-floor hallway, seeing the door to the room was open. She ran on her toes, holding her skirt up, and peered in. Empty. She walked briskly to the closet, crawled underneath the wooden chairs piled three high, and manoeuvred the closet doors shut, looking out their venting slats.

Sunlight was making its way in through the window shutters and cast horizontal lines throughout the room. She held her breath and her hair, and crawled forward. She placed her ear directly over the vent, which acted as a sound trap, and let her breath out slowly, calming herself. Nobody was speaking yet below.

Her life had once again taken an unwelcome turn with the appearance of Gabriel Chavez. She had begun to feel secure, and her articles were published

184

weekly. Although constrained at the brothel, with opportunities to research non-existent, she found that conversing with the prostitutes produced abundant fodder, particularly in the form of discrimination towards women. Girls were not held to the educational standard of boys, if they'd attended elementary school at all, and many of the Argentine prostitutes were utterly illiterate. A few had been seamstresses and dressmakers, making a third of the wages a man would make, insufficient for subsistence on their own. A few had been domestic servants, working long days for a pittance. Others had abandoned abusive husbands, gambling and drinking precious wages away. 'Although women's suffrage was dear to her, the bread and butter issues were more immediate, and that was just fine for now,' Sofia thought.

Tutoring Tico had also been instructive. In the orphanage, he'd met children whose parents were lost to yellow fever or tuberculosis, or whose mother had died in childbirth, and were abandoned by their despairing fathers. He was small, he'd said the nuns had tried their best, but there weren't enough of them to control the bullying. It tore at her heart strings, and she thought it would be gratifying to see Tico move into a proper profession. But he only had one eye. A school teacher? She'd reminded the newspaper's readers to remember the orphanages and the poor funds. It was ironic that these issues weren't particularly radical, yet she could only be published in an anarchistic newspaper. She supposed she should be grateful for it, and for allowing her to write anonymously.

Two things occurred simultaneously, jarring her back to the present, and making her acutely aware of her precarious position. She heard Lieutenant Machado's familiar growl through the vent.

"What's your situation and what information do you have?"

"Matias and Emilio have taken on jobs as cart drivers, and I've been hired in the stables."

Sofia recognised the voice of the skinny, talkative one, and made note of the names.

"There's talk of a strike, the port workers and ship stokers. They figure if they strike together, they will be stronger and they will be given what they want this time. Emilio learned that from a businessman who hired his cart. Isn't that right, Em?"

"What do they want now," Lieutenant Machado asked. She thought he didn't seem particularly concerned.

She was distracted from the conversation by the room door creaking open. She heard Zoryana's husky voice ushering a man inside, which promptly gave way to the unmistakeable signs of a lustful first volley, moans, and the mashing of lips and tongues. Sofia lifted her head enough to peer through the slats of the closet door, and saw a shirtless man with his face smothered in Zoryana's bare cleavage. Zoryana had thrust her head back and was pulling the man into her buxom, encouraging him. She took his hands and placed them over her breasts with a squeezing motion. Sofia was shocked by the hedonistic display, absent of tenderness, then reminded herself it was Zoryana's profession. Sex without love. Although Sofia had now worked at the brothel for months, she had not imagined the transaction occurring in such a manner. A matter of sating physical desire only.

She slowly pressed her ear to the vent again, hoping she hadn't missed anything.

"We've been to two meetings where strike actions were discussed. They said that complementing sectors need to strike at the same time in order to shut down the shipping. They are asking the stevedore's union to join the strike as well. They like it when the stevedore's join in because they're the most willing to fight." The skinny one was still doing the talking.

"Do you have their names?" Lieutenant Machado asked.

"Javier—give him the notes." That was the big one that spoke. She also thought his tone had the ring of a command.

"Forget what you've been tasked with in Spain. Has there been any talk of bombs or assassinations?" Lieutenant Machado again, irritated.

Sofia then heard a soft knocking at the door of the room. She lifted her head just enough to put an eye to the open slats of the closet door again. She watched Zoryana unmount from a position on top of her man, his cock glistening and rigid, and walk to the door. Sofia thought she was a handsome woman that looked good naked. She was tall and heavy, 'regal', and her breasts swayed as she walked. Zoryana opened the door slightly, checking who was there, and then let in Hortense and another man.

"Did Sofia see you come up?" Zoryana asked.

"No. She snuck off somewhere," Hortense said. Sofia was momentarily confused, but then understood. Hortense had come up with a scheme to use one bedroom but two prostitutes at a time. Madam Josefina only made the percentage of one prostitute, and the two of them could split the fare of the second customer.

Sofia could imagine Madam Josefina's reaction if she found out, 'Does the randy slut have any sense of decency whatsoever?' The question was answered when Hortense abandoned her client near the door and set her attentions upon the man waiting patiently on the bed, still sporting an erection.

"I like a man that knows what makes me happy," Hortense said. She grabbing the man's cock with both hands and pushed her mouth down on it, until it disappeared from Sofia's line of sight. Then her head began to bob.

'Good Lord!' Sofia didn't understand how Hortense did not choke. She had never thought about using her mouth so physically during sex. She had heard of felatio and assumed it involved licking. Nobody had told her it involved practically swallowing a man's cock, but then again, she'd never asked. She had never had time to learn about men, always busy with other interests: keeping the Jerez estate profitable, mastering flamenco, or critiquing her latest chosen ill of society. There had simply been no time to chase boys, and she wasn't one to gossip with other girls about men. Hortense was now unknowingly giving her a masterclass in the French technique, in addition to cheating the brothel's coffers. Zoryana had cornered the second man against the door and expertly unfastened the buttons of his pants. It was her turn to surprise Sofia. Demonstrating unlikely agility and balance for a woman her size, she squatted on high heels, the only items of clothing she wore, with a wondrously straight back worthy of any trained flamenco dancer, and fellated the man in unison with Hortense.

To her annoyance, Sofia had once again been completely distracted. Why am I so interested? Because if I know nothing about sex, how will I ever please a man? She froze. Someone was scraping at the vent. She held her breath, detecting his presence mere inches from her face. She could smell his breath, rank and sour. She felt her eyes widen, her heart pounding like a drum in her skull, and she fought down her panic. The presence was so close she heard the cackle of tobacco burning, and a plume of cigarette smoke snaked its way upward through the iron grill, making her suppress a cough.

Then Zoryana spoke loudly, telling her client to move to the bed, where the other couple were copulating with such force the bed pegs were scraping back and forth on the floor.

"It's just your whores hard at work Lieutenant," the skinny one said, practically into her ear, and she heard him step down from his position at the ceiling vent.

187

Sofia felt tears of relief welling. She told herself to control her breathing, in slowly through the nose, out slowly through the mouth. *Listen to the men,* she told herself, *that was the more important of the events unfolding before her.*

"This information isn't useful—we have many informants telling us about this sort of thing. This isn't why we hired you. Identify the extreme elements— the crazy ones zealous enough to kill politicians or other people. You're all former soldiers. Talk about those you've killed in war. The zealots will be attracted to you—they'll want your advice. When they do, find out if there are weapons being hidden, and bombs being made. If someone mentions killing, make them your focus. Befriend them and offer your help," he said. "Don't stop on the way out. I don't want anyone asking you questions."

Lieutenant Machado had said the final word and she heard them leave. Now she needed to get back to her post at the bar. She'd been gone for too long. She peered through the slats of the closet door and saw the four still on the bed, intertwined. Both of the men were now thrusting in a lustful frenzy, encouraged by the women, until breathy growls marked their climax.

"If I didn't know you better, I'd say you just got laid," Madame Josefina said. "You have that flush to your cheeks. But then I remembered that you're immune to the sins of the flesh. Where've you been dearie? I've been slinging drinks like a 20-year-old—when in fact I'm a fat brothel keeper. I can't keep up anymore."

She had sat on a stool and was rubbing her calves. "I'm glad to see you're back. I thought that you might have stowed away on a steamer and sailed back to the Spanish hills from whence you came. Should I be concerned?"

"There is nothing to be concerned about. I'll give you plenty of notice before I stow away on a steamer. It would be the least I could do." Sofia liked Madam Josefina. She had been kind to Sofia in a time of need, she supposed. Whatever Sofia decided to report to Gabriel Chavez, she would ensure it did not bring any harm to Madam Josefina or the brothel.

Chapter 16
Safe House

Sofia sat in her room, pondering what to tell Chavez. She hadn't heard anything about a coup d'état. There had only been instructions to spy on the anarchists, in particular anarchists that planned on killing someone, and it seemed to her this was something the police should be doing. But she had to tell Chavez something. He had told her that the Spanish authorities wanted to extradite her. She was sceptical, but she couldn't risk it.

She had hoped that the Civil Guard had advanced their investigation, found the actual murderers of her parents, and proven her innocence. She longed for news, but had no means to acquire it without going to the Spanish embassy and risking arrest. If she was deported, she would be brought to Jerez, where they had executed anarchists using the garrotte. She had witnessed the brutal executions as a teenager. She recalled the bloodlust of the crowd that had formed in the public square, in front of a raised platform with four sinister looking chairs. They were of sturdy wooden construction, a seat attached to a solid post with an iron collar affixed to it at neck height. An iron bolt, with a handle on one end and a series of razor-sharp blades on the other, passed through the post just above the collar.

As the executioner rotated the handle, the bolt was screwed steadily forward into the back of the prisoner's neck, driving the blades through the skin and sinew, and slowly into the spine. If it worked as designed, the rotating blades eventually severed the spine and drove it upwards through the brain, causing instant death. But sometimes it didn't work as designed, and the blades pushed to either side of the spine. In this case, the executioner had to extract the bolt somewhat, adjust the prisoner's head in the collar and try again. In either case, the process caused a slow, agonising death for the baying crowd to relish.

The four wretched prisoners were marched onto the platform by the Civil Guard then seated, and the iron collars were clasped around their necks, their heads secured in place. Last rights were given by the priests, and then the four executioners began turning the bolts from their positions behind the chair. The touch of the rotating steel blades to the back of the neck made the prisoners flinch and they pushed their heads forward into the iron collar, but it was futile. The screams were quickly muted as the larynx was crushed against the collar, and their deaths were marked by a mask of morbidity, bulging eyes and an open mouth.

The four condemned prisoners had been anarchists, convicted of murdering two citizens they deemed to be bourgeoisie enemies. Evidence of guilt had been supplied by an informant, and subsequent confessions were obtained under torture. It was flimsy evidence, but that's all that had been required to be sentenced to death by the presiding judge. Spanish justice had spoken, possibly unjustly, and could easily do so again. She pictured herself being marched up the stairs of the raised platform, a priest awaiting, and the executioner beckoning her forward to the cheers of the crowd.

Then came a bout of self-doubt. Had she somehow contributed to her parent's deaths? Had her negotiations for the field workers that morning enraged the anarchists to the point that they had wanted to teach her a cruel lesson? Was she the real target and they had found her parents at the ranch instead of her? What had her Uncle Hugo seen? He hadn't told her how he'd survived and escaped. Did he hide like a coward, too ashamed to admit it? She wanted desperately to confront him. But these thoughts were not useful to her right now. If she wanted to avoid her appointment with the executioner, she had to provide Chavez some information.

His instructions had been simple. She only needed to place a note, with her initials and the time, into the mail box marked #7 at his clandestine apartment on Talcahuano. The gate into the courtyard would be open for an hour at noon. That would be the only time she could place a note into his mailbox. The mailbox was checked daily at 2 pm.

She walked north to Avenida Corrientes and took a horse-drawn tram eastward to Talcahuano. Approaching noon, Corrientes was bustling with pedestrians walking to its cafes and restaurants. Turning onto Talcahuano, she walked a short distance northward until she found the address. The gate was unlocked, as he'd said it would be, and the mailboxes were on the left in neat rows. The shiny brass of #7 beckoned and she placed her note in its slot. She couldn't help herself and walked on the stone path to a doorway. Through the glass, she saw a wood floor shined to a gloss. In the middle of the lobby, a black iron structure of posts and screens reached upwards and disappeared through the ceiling. It had an accordion style door with a stairway to the left. She saw movement in the iron structure and stared in wonder as the elevator descended, the door was pushed open and two men stepped out. She hurried back out the gates onto Talcahuano and walked calmly towards Corrientes to lose herself amongst the other people.

She returned two hours later, as her note had indicated, and tried the gates. They were open. She walked through and found Chavez smoking by the doorway. He nodded without saying anything and motioned her to follow him inside.

"Were you followed?"

"No—who would follow me?"

"A lot of people if they knew what you were up to," he said. "I had you followed for example."

The elevator stopped at the third floor and Chavez opened the door. "Come on."

She followed him into a hallway with two rooms. He used a metal skeleton key to open the door and stepped aside to let her in.

"This is your secret apartment?"

"Yes."

"Do you live here?" It was small and sparsely decorated. Only the basics; a sofa, a few wooden chairs around a table, fountain pens, ink and paper, and a typewriter. The walls were bare except for a round clock in a wooden frame. There was a small bar with bottles of liquor and glasses.

"I stay here on occasion. I meet with people here when I need to be discreet."

"What kind of people?"

"People that can't be seen at the ministry building—like yourself."

He had taken off his fedora and Sofia noticed for the first time that he was a particularly handsome man—black hair, sharp Latino features, and swarthy skin that contrasted the remarkable emerald colour of his eyes. 'If someone described this man, they would start with those eyes,' she thought.

"I wondered if you would come."

"Even a woman like myself is capable of following simple instructions."

"There's no need to be sarcastic,' he said, an amused look on his face. "Even some of my colleagues don't manage to respect procedures. And you're hardly a simple woman Sofia. I had Nicolas find some past editions of the newspaper you've written articles for—Broken Chains! I assume your alias is A Free Woman?" He didn't let her answer. "There's no need to deny it—it's hardly a concern of mine at the moment. I actually think it's admirable. Would you like some sherry from Jerez?"

Sofia hadn't consumed anything alcoholic since the steamship voyage from Spain to Argentina. She rarely drank, but found herself wanting to taste the familiar spirit distilled in mass quantities near her home.

"A small glass, thank you."

"What time do you need to return to the brothel?"

"By 5 pm at the latest."

"Then we better get started. What do you have to tell me?"

"I was able to listen to their conversation. There were some details that I couldn't hear—there were loud distractions," she said, recalling the image of Zoryana on top of her client, facing his feet, with her face close to that of Hortense, who was also on top of her client. Hortense was holding the back of Zoryana's head, looking into her eyes, sharing an unrestrained moment of erotic pleasure.

"The Lieutenant told the men to infiltrate a group, I don't know who." She said, unwilling to divulge their mission with the anarchists just yet. "They're supposed to focus on an inner core of fanatics—find out if they have weapons, like rifles and bombs. That's what I heard. Their names are Matias, Emilio, and Javier."

"I need more information than that—when will you hear more?"

"Whenever they meet at the Social House."

"Are you sure there isn't anything you haven't told me Sofia?"

'He was too skilled not to test her story,' she thought. But she wasn't going to let him bluff her and held his gaze. "I'm certain. I'll tell you when I learn more."

Had she felt something else stirring while she'd been in the presence of Gabriel Chavez? The sherry had warmed her stomach and allowed her to relax. The erotic spectacle she'd witnessed from the closet persisted in her memory. He had a masculine presence that she found attractive; a confident gaze, and his voice had a pleasant timbre. In the elevator, they had been physically close, and she smelled the tobacco on his breath and the brilliantine in his hair. 'She was missing out on a part of life,' she thought, an utterly reckless romance, and to hell with everything else. She could be imprisoned and dead within a month— executed in front of her peers and the field workers she'd hired to sow their crops. They would jeer her, and then drink themselves to sleep without so much as a single thought of her innocence. She would die without experiencing the unbridled passion that occurred every night behind closed doors in the brothel. The next time they met, if Gabriel Chavez tried to seduce her, as she believed he intended to do, she would let him.

The following Friday things were less chaotic. The three men, Matias, Emilio, and Javier, arrived earlier in the afternoon and there weren't any customers in the brothel. Sofia slipped away to her listening post, in the closet of the second-floor bedroom.

"Javier, tell him about the newspaper man."

"It was a little confusing Lieutenant. I thought we were listening to one of the usual anarchist speechmakers—government is corrupt, oppresses the working class, that sort of thing. But then he went down a different track and people became confused. They started to argue with him. They didn't like his idea."

"Which was what," Lieutenant Machado said.

"He started talking about a coup d'état—as in overthrowing the government. He said the anarchists should support the Radicals, some kind of political party. He said they had the support of the army and that they were going to overthrow the government by force."

"What's his name?"

"His name is Alberto Ghiraldo. He's the owner of La Protesta, a newspaper."

"Did he mention any names of the Radicals?"

"He said that the leader is Hipo Irigoyan."

"That's the Radical Civic Union. They tried to overthrow the government a long time ago. How many men was Ghiraldo speaking to?"

"There was about 20 of us in the hall."

"What was their decision."

"They said no—it's none of their business. They're all immigrant workers and don't want anything to do with a revolution against the government, only to form another one. Some of them got angry with him for even suggesting it."

"Did Ghiraldo give the date that this revolution would happen?"

"Next month."

"Keep to my instructions—focus on the anarchists."

That sombre remark ended their conversation, and Sofia heard their chairs scrape against the floor. Sofia waited for them to leave before extricating herself from the closet. She crossed to the door quickly and exited the room.

"Sofia?"

Sofia was startled but hid it. Hortense had been in the hallway for some reason.

"Hello Hortense."

"What are you doing in that room?"

"I was checking to make sure it had been cleaned and prepared. I do this for every room." Sofia was surprised how easily the lie came to her.

"You do a lot of things I don't know about it seems—why isn't Tico doing that."

"I have him doing some homework right now." Sofia was surprised how easily the lie came to her. "You shouldn't concern yourself with what I do. I'm helping the woman make the most money that they can—and be organised about it—that's all."

"You seem to have your fingers in everything. I'm beginning to wonder if Madam Josefina should be worried that you'll take her place and she'll find herself out of her job."

"That's ridiculous. Madam Josefina will be here long after I'm gone. I won't be here forever."

"We'll see about that."

The following morning, Sofia left early. She needed to attend the basement suite that housed her adopted newspaper, Broken Chains! 'You could never mistake an anarchist publication,' she thought, their titles rife with symbolism. She hadn't had any time to draft a new article or even think about it. She thought she would recycle one of her old articles if Bernhardt would agree to it. He was always searching for articles with fresh perspectives to keep the newspaper interesting in order to increase its subscriber base. She knew it was not profitable and Bernie was probably subsidising it himself. She had come to know and trust him, and he had confided in her.

He was a lawyer, he told her, when he needed to be anyway. This morning he took it upon himself to take Sofia upstairs to meet his wife Gertrude. Mendelson was their last name, they were German Jewish emigrés, and had taken up Argentine citizenship 30 years ago. It was apparent to Sofia that they were still hopelessly in love, holding each other's hands and looking deeply into each other's eyes. 'What charming, mad, old fools—I adore them!' 'Her parents had been like that,' she thought.

Why had they decided to leave their Germanic homeland thirty years ago? When she asked the question, they had looked at each other conspiratorially. 'We needed to lie low for a while. Then we had children and just decided not to return.' A cryptic way of saying they were being sought by the authorities. Sofia was quickly learning there was a preponderance of such types in Buenos Aires, including herself, ironically. But it was still not the time to be advertising her travails to people she had just met, and she kept her story to herself.

"Sofia, at some point you must consider leaving the brothel. It's not the place for you. You're a talented woman and can do many other things. Gertrude and I have talked. I can offer you a small wage to work on the newspaper. You can stay here until you find a proper apartment."

Sofia was almost overwhelmed by the unsolicited kindness. They didn't know of her purported crimes, of course. For now, she needed to stay at Madam Josefina's Social House in order to continue to spy for Chavez, until such time as she met her end of the bargain with him. "That is a truly generous offer—I'm grateful. May I take some time to think about it?"

"Of course, my dear." It was the first time she'd heard Gertrude speak. She had the voice of an angel, a voice of strength and certainty.

'The information she had for Chavez was valuable,' she thought. She had the names of two revolutionaries, Alberto Ghiraldo and Hipo Irigoyan. Additionally, the three Spanish thugs had reported to the Lieutenant that the anarchists had refused to join with Ghiraldo and Irigoyan, who were planning to overthrow the government. That was important information—would it be enough? Would he advise the Spanish embassy that she had fled Buenos Aires to parts unknown? Could they agree that the conditions of their arrangement had been fulfilled and just go their separate ways? No. So she wasn't going to tell Chavez that the three mercenaries were instructed to focus on infiltrating the anarchists. That might negate her usefulness to Chavez, who seemed interested only in those planning a coup d'état, clearly not the anarchists.

If she hadn't satisfied his conditions yet, she would probably hear more at the brothel, or could string him along if absolutely necessary. Was she capable of making up information to keep her value to Chavez? She wasn't prepared to go that far. 'But she would eventually have to be assertive about his promise,' she thought, and reminded herself that he should not be trusted.

At Avenida Corrientes, she stepped onto the running board of the horse-drawn tram. She took a seat on a bench facing forward near the front, and enjoyed the spectacle of people bustling about along the sidewalks and ducking out of the way of the tram on the street. A Clydesdale with a black mane and white feet pulled it along easily under the gentle nudge of the coachman.

A block before she reached Talcahuano, she got off and wandered onto the sidewalk. She caught sight of her reflection in a large window and stopped. She preened her hair, which was long now. It hadn't been cut in months, but until this moment it hadn't bothered her.

'What do I want?' She asked herself, wondering about the sudden concern for her appearance. 'I don't want a companion. I don't need his sympathy, and I don't need the burden of his ambitions. There is no possibility I could love a man who blackmails so readily.'

It was past noon and the gate was open. She placed her note into the slot of the #7 mailbox and turned and walked back into the street, almost colliding with a tall gentleman walking hurriedly in the opposite direction. She had an hour to wait and decided to explore the neighbourhood. She admired the architecture. It was even more European than the architecture of Jerez. 'So new.'

Yes, that's what it was. A new city rising, yet anchored down with the familiar paternalism of Spain. But she didn't want to entertain any such deep thoughts right now. Her time outside the brothel was limited and too valuable for philosophical musings. She could reflect on such things all evening to her heart's desire. Not right now.

It was time, but she hesitated, trying to make a decision about something that she wouldn't consciously acknowledge. Outside of the gate she looked upwards to the third-floor window and he was there looking at her, quizzically with his emerald eyes. She met his stare, sensing his desire, sensing her own, and made up her mind. In the elevator, she continued to meet his gaze. 'What do I want from him?'

There was no time to be coy and no time to play childish games. Through the doorway there were no impediments, no other guests, and no reason to stop. She felt her passion rise and moved close to him, and he accepted her invitation and pressed his lips open into hers. 'I want to forget—I need to forget everything for a while.' She surrendered to her desire.

Vicente didn't like surprises, not one little bit. That's why he paid Hortense a small stipend, to keep her eyes and ears open. He knew Sofia left the brothel some mornings, but hadn't really cared up to this point. 'So, what Hortense?'

All the women needed to leave the brothel occasionally. He wondered if Hortense was leading him on to justify the little payments she received from him, like she usually did. But then she said something that caught his attention. A man that had never been to the brothel had been asking questions about the three former Spanish soldiers, like he was a detective.

'The stranger was undoubtedly looking for Matias, Javier, and Emilio, and had somehow become aware that they frequented the brothel,' Vicente thought. He was well-dressed, she'd said, and spoke like a gentleman. Educated then, a lawyer perhaps, most certainly a government official. He didn't have any detectives like that. But he supposed it could be one of the lawyers that worked in the bureau of the chief of police, someone outside of his sphere of influence.

Then he remembered what Commissioner De La Fuente had told him. The Captain of the Sirio had been questioned by an official with the Ministry of the Interior, Gabriel Chavez. He had inquired specifically about the three Spaniards. So, it was the Ministry and they had found out the men were attending Madam Josefina's Social House. 'But why would they care about three foreigners spying on the anarchists?'

The question bothered him. It floated aimlessly in his brain like the wisp of smoke coming from the glowing embers on the tip of his cheroot. Sofia had also been on the ship with the three men, but he'd been told that was merely a coincidence. To this date, even Senator Montserrat had not been briefed on the operation. But Chavez would have found a way to question Sofia, he thought—and she would have told him where the three men could be found. She had no reason to hide this from anyone and would think little of it.

The next time the three men came to the brothel to report their activities to him, he would use them as bait to draw out his foe. He would watch their arrival and departure to see if someone was following them.

And so, as they left, he lit a cigarette, and tended his mare harnessed to his coach. Nobody watching him would have known that his eyes, shadowed by his bowler hat, had done a 360-degree survey of the street in front of the brothel, registered every possible doorway shadow to conceal oneself, and every bench to sit and read a newspaper.

As the men rounded the corner and disappeared from view, he clambered into the seat and had the mare bring the coach about at an unhurried pace. Still nothing. This was as far back from the men that anyone would be following them, and no viable suspects could be discerned. They were not being followed.

His mind then turned to Sofia, he would follow her. It was always a good idea to know what brothel employees did while they were away from it. Months ago, he'd told Sofia that the Spanish authorities would be looking for her, without actually knowing if it was true or not. He'd assumed, rightly, that this would keep Sofia motivated to remain at the brothel. She would be out of sight tending their books and other things that were difficult, if not downright impossible, to find an otherwise qualified person to do. And her services came cheaply, which he liked most of all.

With his coach parked to the side of the road a distance away from the brothel, and standing behind the horse, he saw Sofia emerge. He fell in behind her, keeping pace easily while keeping her in view. His height was an advantage, able to see over the odd group of people that traversed or milled between them. Walking southward on Avenida Buedo, he regretted not using his coach and thought about turning back. But on Independencia, Sofia turned and then disappeared down some stairs. Vicente walked up to the stairwell and peered down, just as the door opened. Sofia emerged, talking with an older man with wire spectacles. Vicente heard the unmistakeable sound of a press churning out copy.

He whistled down a bellowing street hawker and bought himself a newspaper, La Naçion. He backed into a shaded doorway to shield himself from the heat of the late morning sun. Sofia emerged from the stairwell an hour later. She walked North on Buedo all the way to Corrientes, and he closed the distance between them, anticipating difficulty keeping her in sight on the busier avenue.

She was paying a conductor the fare for a westbound tram and he fell in line several people behind her, then took possession of the outside corner of the last bench, ready for a quick exit. He stayed on his bench with his newspaper spread wide when she got off, then as she approached a sidewalk, he jumped off the slow-moving tram on its furthest side. He saw her turn north onto Talcahuano and again closed the distance. He saw her turn into a doorway, hesitating. 'Why isn't she going in—is she at the wrong place?'

But he couldn't watch any longer without being noticed himself. There were significantly less people on Talcahuano, and if she re-emerged from a doorway suddenly, he would be caught out. He decided to wait on Corrientes and walk back and forth across Talcahuano to peer down it. He made a critical error when he avoided a crowd, and got too close to the building at the corner, and almost ran headlong into Sofia. He skipped out of the way and continued unabated, walking away with his back to her.

Following her for the next hour had been tricky as well. Had she not been a complete amateur, it would have been impossible. But then his patience paid off. She had stopped and was looking upward; at the building she had gone into just before. He saw a man looking down at her from the third-floor windows. 'Good for her, she's taken a lover.' 'He was wearing a bespoke suit, oiled hair—he comes from money,' Vicente thought. Gabriel Chavez?

That evening, Vicente returned to the apartment with another detective. No lights were on in the window where he'd seen the man. The detective picked the lock of the gate in a second and they took the stairs to the third floor. #7 appeared to be the room in question. Vicente nodded at the door and the experienced hands of the detective worked his lock pick tools again quickly, and they entered the room. He crossed the room in the darkness, drew the heavy curtains, and then turned on the electric light. 'Strange—not much to search.' He looked around at the sparse decor.

'Bottles of liquor, a table and chairs. It was more of a meeting room than a place to live,' he thought, and even less of an apartment to receive a lover. There was only one bedroom and the bed was unmade. 'Spoke too soon—they're lovers.' About to leave, he looked at the desk in the bedroom. It had a locked drawer. He snapped his fingers at the detective and pointed at it. The detective opened the simple lock with ease, and then let out a soft, low whistle, looking at something in the drawer.

The blued steel of the Colt revolver changed everything. The bullet tips of the loaded rounds showed in the open slots of the cylinder when he picked it up. 'You have now piqued my interest, Señor Gabriel Chavez—and you have seduced my cherished bookkeeper. Why would you do such a thing?'

Then he saw the corner of something further in the drawer, and he knew it held the answer. He peered in, careful not to disturb it, until he understood how it was held in position against the underside of the desk. 'Twine around a screw.' He unwound the twine which wrapped around two pieces of paper folded together to hang them in their hiding place. He brought the papers underneath the yellow glow of the electric light and unfolded them. He read through the note with enough of a frown forming on his face to alarm the detective.

"What is it Lieutenant?"

"It's a manifesto. The apartment is a meeting place for revolutionaries, and this gentleman is planning to overthrow our government. Unfortunately for them, this government pays our wages. It's dated February 4th—two weeks' time." Vicente folded the papers exactly as he had found them, wound the twine around them, and hung them from the small hook under the desktop in the drawer. His eyes were drawn again to the revolver. He took hold of it by the wooden handle, broke open the cylinder, dumped the rounds into his hand, clicked the cylinder closed, and placed it back in the drawer, as he had found it. He walked around the room and studied the gun from all angles. Could someone see it was no longer loaded? He thought not.

Vicente followed Sofia again the following week. She left in the morning and followed the same itinerary. Firstly, to the residence on Independencia that hid a known anarchist's publishing equipment in its basement suite, and then all the way to the centre of Buenos Aires, to the third-floor apartment on Talcahuano, presumably to meet her lover, and secret revolutionary Gabriel Chavez. Did she know his plans? Probably not, he mused. Chavez wouldn't involve a woman unnecessarily, certainly not a lover, until the deed had been done, if even then.

He'd had a detective from the political section post a watch on the residence on Independencia, and he'd come away with a copy of the publication Broken Chains! The detective had seen only one woman come and go from the basement suite, one Sofia Montserrat, occupation bookkeeper, Madam Josefina's Social House, his report read. The detective opened the copy of the newspaper while showing it to Lieutenant Machado. He tapped a gnarled forefinger on an article on its first page, identifying its author as A Free Woman. "That would be Sofia Montserrat," the detective said.

Vicente took a deep breath and expelled it noisily between closed lips. "Can't a woman enjoy time away from work without cavorting with two of our country's enemies—on the same day?" Vicente had been incongruously animated, and they both laughed heartily.

Chapter 17
Coup d'État

February, 1905. De La Fuente sat amongst the small group of men assembled in President Quintana's office at la Casa Rosada. Ecstatic to have been asked to attend a meeting of the highest level, he would nevertheless remain silent until requested for information, as he'd been instructed by Senator Montserrat. The President appeared unimpressed with the events he'd been advised were about to unfold. At 70 years old, he still had a mop of curly hair, white as it was, and a full beard trimmed to a point. But his illness was evident. De La Fuente took note of those present. General Carlos Smith, Chief of the Army General Staff, a veteran of three prior attempts to overthrow the government, and two military campaigns, was a man who didn't shy away from difficult circumstances. De La Fuente and he had fought the rebels together in 15 years ago, and gave each other a respectful nod.

Colonel Rosendo Fraga, was recently appointed as Chief of the Police of the Capital and also an experienced military veteran. De La Fuente had offered his sincerest congratulations on assuming the post, which Fraga had acknowledged with indifference. Senator Montserrat was the only politician present, apart from the President. His presence assured the President of the loyalty of the senate. As its senior serving member, he chaired the powerful Committee of Justice and Security, amongst others, giving him complete access to the sensitive information collected by De La Fuente's detectives of the investigative division. He had requested to have Commissioner De La Fuente present, to provide details relevant to their meeting, without consulting Colonel Fraga. Evidently he didn't want Fraga to think he had a choice.

The President had wanted a final discussion with the principals required to manage the imminent crisis, and had kept the numbers small, for the sake of his sanity De La Fuente presumed.

"General Smith—what is the military's position?"

"Everything is under control Mr President. My senior officers in command of forces within the city of Buenos Aires have an excellent grasp on the breadth of disloyalty within the junior officer ranks. Those involved in the sedition have been moved to less sensitive posts. The city armoury is secure in case of attack, a practical certainty, and a defence plan is in place. The senior generals commanding forces in the provinces report similar facts. There will be a smattering of sedition amongst their junior officers, and they have been identified and isolated."

"Very good. Colonel Fraga—the police interests at play."

"I'm pleased to say the loyalty of the Police of the Capital is without question—to a man, the commissioners tell me Mr President. The fact is that police officers are not natural allies of this seditious lot. Very few of my men attended the universities and haven't fallen for the revolutionary sentiment fostered in the law and medical faculties. To the contrary, they've made bitter enemies of such progressive minded individuals through the course of their duties. For a full intelligence brief, I'll defer to Commissioner De La Fuente, who's had his detectives on the ground watching every move they've made."

"Thank you, Chief," De La Fuente said. "Firstly, I've confirmed that it is the usual suspects, the Radical Civic Union Party, more or less the same individuals encountered in the uprisings of 90 and 93. Irigoyan is their leader, and we all know he's clever enough strategically speaking. He wants the coup d'état to be led by civilian factions, or at least appear to be, even if it is being pushed hard by some of the officer cadre of our military."

"For political legitimacy, he will want any major actions to be taken by his civilian followers in order to establish a de facto government that will be recognised by Argentinians, and reported as such to the leaders of other countries. Their actions will have to reflect their manifesto, of which we have seen a draft, and it is very much being touted as a people's revolt."

"They're a ragtag bunch of university students and educated professionals with little experience in either battle tactics or getting punched in the jaw for that matter. I have also confirmed that the hardliners in the anarchist and socialist circles have turned down requests for their support—they don't want anything to do with it. There will be no complications from that end—thanks to the superior work of my detectives." He hesitated for a moment. It had felt good to be advising the President. This is exactly where I belong. He looked at Colonel Fraga, who remained silent, giving nothing away.

"Excellent—we'll only be fighting on one front then," the President said.

"Mr President if I may," Senator Montserrat said, interrupting. "Now would be a good time for us all to agree on a point of strategy. Although, it appears the threat of a coup d'état comes only from one front as you say—the Radicals—it would nevertheless be advantageous for the security of our country to treat the situation as if the threat actually comes from two fronts."

"Go on, Senator."

"Although, the situation appears to be well in hand, I recommend that you declare a state of siege—authorised under Section 23 of our constitution—which as you know will suspend its guaranteed freedoms. Of particular interest to us is the freedom of the press. I am told there are literally dozens," he looked at De La Fuente for confirmation of his number and received a nod, "dozens of anarchist presses churning out pro-union propaganda that, if allowed to continue, will lead to the demise of our business interests. With International Workers Day, May 1, fast approaching, a general strike, or at minimum, a coordinated series of smaller strikes, will be top of the anarchist's minds. On the heels of an attempted coup d'état, they'll smell blood and want to test our political fortitude to resist their demands. We need to head this crisis off right now."

As he spoke, Montserrat surveyed the faces of the men in attendance. De La Fuente saw they were listening intently to the Senator, nodding their agreement. Perhaps he shouldn't doubt the Senator's ability to persuade the President that he should be nominated as the next chief of police.

The Senator continued. "Most of the anarchist presses are run by immigrants, be they Spaniards, Italians, or Polish, they've all brought their despicable European ideas to our shores. I propose to all of you here, that now is the time to put full use to law 4144, otherwise known as the Residence Law. Although, it's been around for a couple of years now, we haven't really applied this law with— let's say alacrity. Colonel Fraga, do you agree?"

'He surprised the Colonel with his question,' De La Fuente thought.

"I wholeheartedly agree Senator. I'm not completely familiar with the law just yet, however, it should be used to full effect—as you suggest," Fraga said.

"Good. Then it will fall to your department, with the resources under Commissioner De La Fuente's command—who are familiar with the law—to rid us of these presses once and for all, and the immigrant troublemakers that run them. The law provides executive power to deport any threat to national security or public order within a three day span, and to hold such persons in custody until such time as we see them marched onto the lower decks of a steamship. The state of siege will allow Colonel Fraga's men to disrupt gatherings of syndicates contemplating strike action and perhaps—for the first time in years—we'll see a peaceful spring where our businesses can prosper to their full potential!"

De La Fuente saw that the President was nodding his head in agreement, and thought the Senator's speech had hit its mark.

"Mr President—what say you to this proposal?"

"Agreed Senator. I'll declare a state of siege during this treacherous act by Irigoyan—for the greater good of the country."

Vicente liked his revolver shiny and dust-free, especially when he was likely to use it. He snapped open the cylinder, inspected the rounds, and looked into the barrel for obstructions. Over the last two weeks, he had observed exactly what he'd expected, allowing him to exercise some means of control over the situation.

'Sofia Montserrat had stuck to her routine the Friday morning, walked to the location of the Broken Chains! newspaper, something he should put an end to,' he thought. She then proceeded to the third-floor apartment on Talcahuano, where she met with her lover Gabriel Chavez, whom he now knew was a lawyer within the Ministry of the Interior.

He had assigned two detectives to follow Chavez and find out everything they could. It hadn't taken the detectives long to confirm his identity, having followed him to his home address, and then to the Ministry. A knock at the door of his residence after he had left the following morning produced definitive results. It was answered by the woman of the house, who willingly answered all questions put forth by a municipal census official updating their records for the neighbourhood. It also hadn't taken them long to identify the military officer Chavez was seen drinking with in a quiet corner of a brasserie, having followed that officer to his home and then to his garrison inside the city. There had been a follow-up briefing with General Carlos Smith to ensure he was aware of Major Leon Alvarez, Chavez's fellow conspirator.

General Smith had confirmed their suspicions. He'd been warned of Alvarez through his own intelligence networks. Alvarez was one of many that had been overlooked or denied promotions, not having demonstrated the requisite support for the government to be considered. This seemed to be the prime motivator for the sedition fomenting within the officer ranks of the military. However, a deeper dive into his personal files revealed he'd attended the same law school as Chavez for a period of time.

Vicente didn't know exactly when the coup d'état would be initiated, but he knew it would be soon, as the manifesto had been forward dated February 4. He therefore needed to get this personal business done now, as he'd agreed with De La Fuente. Gabriel Chavez had been inquiring about the three clandestine agents, whom had been infiltrating the innermost ranks of the anarchists with a great deal of success as of late.

After months of attending the meetings in the worker's halls while professing kinship with the most vocal and pugnacious, they'd finally gained a level of acceptance. Information was suddenly flowing like a river from the normally cautious, tightly-knit circles. First names of any hotheads that might commit a vicious act of murder, of the kind so prominent now in Europe, were eventually fleshed out with a patronymic and a nationality, and the list was growing daily. De La Fuente had proclaimed that this work could not be put at risk, and therefore Vicente would make it so.

He'd waited as long as he could. It was Friday, February 3, 1905, and therefore Sofia Montserrat's day to make her rounds. He expected her to confer first with her cohorts at the newspaper Broken Chains! and then meet with her lover at their preferred location. His plan was to wait until she entered the apartment, thereby confirming Chavez's presence inside. They would wait 15 minutes for them to settle down, or settle into the bed, and then make a surprise entry. This offered the least opportunity for Chavez, and whoever else might be in there, to barricade themselves inside. That was a situation that he most decidedly wanted to avoid, as it would pose unnecessary danger to himself and his colleagues, and give Chavez the chance to bargain his way out of the encounter.

15 minutes to the second, according to his gold timepiece, after watching Sofia enter the open gates to the courtyard of the apartment, Vicente gave the signal. A squad of two plainclothes detectives and two uniform police constables gathered at the gate with their Colt revolvers, Mauser rifles, a shotgun and a sledgehammer. A detective picked the lock expertly and they moved swiftly up the stairs to apartment #7 on the 3rd floor. Vicente nodded to the uniform, and the sledgehammer arced and struck the door handle. The handle shattered, but a

rickety metal rod stubbornly held fast, keeping the door from opening to Vicente's alarm. He put his oversized boot to the door near the handle, causing the door to burst open and they charged in. The hallway was empty, as was the living room, so Vicente ran towards the bedroom door, launched a swift, forward kick at the handle, and crashed through the door.

Vicente saw Gabriel Chavez, naked but recovering quickly from his confusion, spring from the embrace of an equally naked Sofia, and run towards the desk. Chavez clawed desperately at the drawer and, getting it open, managed to grasp the handle of the revolver sitting inside where he'd left it. A thunderous bang and simultaneous strike to his left ribcage, like that of a weighted cane or cricket bat, spun him violently away from the desk, and Sofia screamed in horror. Chavez somehow managed to retain the revolver in his hand and bring it level to Vicente's heart. He pulled the trigger weakly, causing its cylinder to rotate, a smile of triumph forming at his lips. But when the hammer dropped there was merely a sickening, empty click, and then another, and another.

A thunderous bang marked Vicente's second shot, from close range. It struck Chavez squarely between his startled emerald green eyes, blowing a hole the size of a cricket ball out of the back of his skull, spattering the wall, and the dresser near Sofia, with pieces of skull, blood, and brains.

Vicente quickly adjusted his aim to Sofia. She was holding out her empty hands, looking at him defiantly. Only the slightest quiver of her lips and trembling hands gave away her fear.

"I'm not armed," she said, holding her shaking hands in front of her.

Vicente looked at the detective and gestured at him to lower his shotgun. He grabbed the blanket and threw it at Sofia. He walked over to Chavez's prostrate naked body and lifted the revolver from his hand. "He forgot to load his weapon—a foolish mistake," he said, bringing a grin from the detective.

Vicente then put his hand under the drawer and withdrew the folded papers held in place by twine. "Did your lover tell you he was planning to overthrow the government?"

"No."

"That's what I thought," Vicente said. "Well—he was," he waived the paper at Sofia. "This is a manifesto. Do you know what that is? Of course, you do—you're an anarchist—they're always writing such things."

"I'm not an anarchist." Sofia said.

Vicente looked at her and pondered her statement. "Chavez was no anarchist either—just a spoiled lawyer with a big house who couldn't leave well enough alone. You won't be able to publish anything else. My officers are shutting down their presses. We know their locations, including the one where you've been publishing."

Another detective entered the bedroom and stared at Sofia with contempt. He murmured something to Vicente that she couldn't hear. Vicente nodded at the detective and he exited.

"I've just received some bad news. The old man, Mendelson, attacked the police officers that raided his basement. He's been shot dead."

'Survive at all costs,' Mirella had said, 'find your way through the fog.' It was Lieutenant Machado's casual recounting of the death of Mendelson that finally gave rise to tears of shock and sorrow. But for some odd reason she couldn't stand the idea of appearing weak in front of him and his detectives. She dressed herself quickly, allowing herself brief glances of Chavez's naked corpse splayed on the floor with his arms wide and his skin already developing a pale blueish tinge. His eyes stared upward at the ceiling, never to see the fruits of his revolution. Should she feel sad for him? He was a human being, worthy of respect, and they had shared moments of physical love. But he had lied to her, and callously manipulated her into spying for him. He had put her in danger by making her come to the apartment, where he had been planning the coup d'état all along. He had chosen the path of violence, to overthrow the government, and revolutions always resulted in the deaths of innocent people. 'What was he going to do with that gun he'd hidden in the drawer?' He would have killed anyone that resisted, she supposed. He gambled with lives and lost his own. Then she realized she was now freed from his blackmail.

Her thoughts turned to Bernhardt and Gertrude Mendelson. Their reward for working towards a better world, and kindness to a stranger in need? Death at the hands of the police for him. And for her, loneliness and despair. They had not deserved this. They were the victims today, not her.

Chapter 18
Five Acts

March 1905. "Gentlemen—think of all of your clients in London and Chicago. If the rail workers, cart drivers, meatpackers, and stevedores decide to launch coordinated strikes—it will effectively shut down the export industry on which we all depend." Senator Hugo Montserrat surveyed the expressionless faces of the men he had summoned to his meeting room.

"My fellow senators and congressmen, it is in the best interests of your provinces and districts that the flow of goods and capital remain unimpeded. Remember that Argentina's success, requires that foreign businesses continue to buy our beef, wool, and grain. And remember that they will only continue to do so if we guarantee that they will actually receive the goods for which they have paid. If they lose confidence in our determination to see these deals through to their end, they will stop investing, our access to capital will dry up, and our goods will wither on the vine and rot in the fields. So, the question is not 'will we retain the confidence of our clients and investors?' No! The question is only how?' One way is to continue to entertain their demands."

"But conceding their demands never results in contentment. The unions don't say to their members 'they gave us a raise so let's get back to work.' Oh no," he said, wagging a finger dramatically at his enraptured audience. "They will say, 'They conceded! They are weak! Now is the time to press for more demands!'"

There were agreeable murmurs from the group. Hugo sat still, only his eyes shifting between the men, looking for signs of disinterest. None that he could find. He continued. "As you all know, I have the ear of the President, and was called to offer my advice through this difficult period. Treason! We didn't know there were so many traitors amongst us. There were many bureaucrats who had thrown in their lot with the Radicals." Another pause for dramatic effect. "We can't afford to be complacent gentlemen. We have to root out those that threaten our livelihoods."

He stopped again. He sensed the men were sufficiently concerned and waiting for the solution, which he so happened to have. He continued in a sombre tone.

"These last few months I have been keeping long hours with our chief of police Colonel Fraga. Making sure that our police force is on top of things, and they have done a fine job once again. We owe the department our thanks. Today I have invited Commissioner De La Fuente," he said, allowing De La Fuente a moment to nod, "to answer questions you may have, although some of the details are best kept confidential. Commissioner De La Fuente is in charge of the detective division, who courageously detected and subverted the plot to overthrow our President. Commissioner—briefly—what can you tell us about the aggressive measures your department undertook to thwart this treachery?"

De La Fuente took his cue. He had been instructed by Senator Montserrat on exactly what to say to this particular group of men. "Thank you, Senator. What I can say is that for several months now, I've had clandestine resources in place to inform our department of any seditious plots, both within the officer ranks of the army, and within the ranks of the Radical Civic Union. We have learned from the mistakes of the past," he said, tapping his crippled leg with his cane, "that these affairs are to be taken seriously. This time we made no mistakes."

"Well done, Commissioner!"

"Hear, Hear!" There was a hearty round of applause, with leather-soled shoes and walking sticks clacking the polished wooden floor. There was now a growing spirit of fraternity amongst the group, many of whom had helped themselves to the decanters of whiskey at the bar Hugo had wisely set out for the occasion. They liked what they were hearing. Hugo sensed it was the moment to try for the first concession he wanted from them. "Gentlemen, these occasions serve to remind us, that we shouldn't think of ourselves as enemies. There's been some bad blood as of late. I myself have experienced some things that were not— collegial." '*Had he been clear enough?*'

Senator Da Rosa stood up and hushed the men with his hands. "Hugo, don't let it be said that I will let a careless wager cause friction amongst this fine group of men. I'm well aware of everything you've done to get this country through this crisis. In good conscience, I cannot witness a patriot like yourself suffer while your colleagues and I profit. If you've got a trick up your sleeve that will see us through the spring, I'll see to it you get your ranch back for half its value!" Da Rosa looked around at the men, waiting for signs of support for his seemingly generous offer.

"You got that ranch for free on a drunken bet Da Rosa. You can do better than that!"

Senator Montserrat could barely hide his glee.

"All right then. A quarter of fair value and another glass of your Dewars Scotch and we'll call it even."

That brought shouts of laughter and encouragement, and more banging of canes on wood. "Well done Da Rosa!"

Hugo gave Da Rosa his warmest smile. 'I'll still see you in the sights of my revolver one day!'

"I accept your generous proposition Senator Da Rosa. Gentlemen—there's more to this than you think. The Radicals are no longer our concern—our real concern are the anarchists. They've infiltrated our work force and it would be a mistake to underestimate their ability to unite the unions. I have made recommendations to the President, and he has agreed to extend the state of siege for the full 90 days. That is enough time for us to take full advantage of the suspension of freedoms to rid ourselves of our enemies once and for all."

"And how exactly do we take advantage of this situation, Senator Montserrat?"

"Gentlemen, those clandestine agents our colleague Commissioner De La Fuente spoke of, have been working side by side with the anarchists, advising us of their names, their meeting places, their leaders—the ones that get them organised and agitated—and the location of their newspaper offices. The state of siege allows our police officers to put any agitators caught out past curfew in jail."

"If they are not citizens of this country—and most of them aren't—we ship them back to Europe where they came from. Furthermore, the state of siege gives the police the powers to shut down their presses without cause. Raids will be conducted, presses given the sledge, and their journalists—who are often also their organisers—will be deported. Commissioner De La Fuente, tell the men honestly, am I exaggerating the situation your officers find themselves in?"

"Not at all, Senator. The powers of the state of siege combined with the powers of the Residency Act provide a once in a generation opportunity to cleanse this country of the anarchist malaise. My officers will act with all due haste."

This was the moment for his shocker. "Gentlemen—then we will force a strike."

There was scoffing and muttering of disbelief. "How can that possibly be a good strategy?"

Hugo smiled. "We lock them out—no wages! We have identified enough non-union men and dissenters that will work through a strike—and our goods will continue to be shipped. From a unique position of strength—which won't happen again in our time—they will have to accept the offer of lower wages. Gentlemen we will incur profits the likes of which we haven't seen in years!"

He'd sold it, they were all in. But now he needed to convince the business owners, who weren't politicians, that the effort was worth the aggravation. They would all have to agree to announcing a uniform low wage to force the strike. But they couldn't know of his strategy to use the state of siege to deport agitators, and they would be reticent to make such a commitment. Some businesses were doing better than others and would balk at the extreme measure, when they could afford to pay more and avoid trouble. He would have to find a way to threaten them.

He was also able to offer them the services of men not belonging to a union, or willing to report to work against its directives. His employment agents had formulated lists of men willing to work no matter what. Almost to a man, with wives and children, they had hungry mouths to feed and couldn't afford to strike. It was going to be an acrimonious summer, however he held a strong hand of cards, and they had to be played now.

June 1905. "Joaquin—a gentleman is downstairs asking to speak with the owner—that's if you can refer to a politician as a gentleman. He's a senator I believe," Pablo said leaning through the window of his small warehouse office.

"Senator? That's unusual, I'll be right out." Joaquin gave himself a quick look in the mirror, slicked some stray hairs on the sides back behind his ears, and went down the stairs to meet his surprise visitor. "I'm Joaquin Cuéllar, I'm the owner. How can I help you today Senator?" he said, recognizing Sofia's uncle.

"Joaquin Cuéllar you say. Hugo Montserrat. Your name sounds familiar. Have we met before?"

"Most certainly not—I would remember having met someone such as yourself before," Joaquin lied, wondering if he should mention Sofia, then decided against it.

"Let's go talk in your office. Your men are looking at me like they want to roast me on the spit." The Senator walked up the stairs with heavy thumps, while Joaquin gave Pablo a questioning look. Joaquin saw that Diego was watching the Senator with a look of absolute hatred. 'This day may not go so well,' he thought, and followed the Senator up the stairs.

"You've got a real bunch of bastards working for you here."

"They may not be to your liking—but they come to work on time and put in an honest day's work." Joaquin watched with dismay as the Senator clipped the end of a Cuban cigar and lit it, spewing smoke into the confined space of his little office. Then he took a blast of smoke in his face, but he wasn't going to give the Senator the satisfaction of showing his irritation. "What possible concern are my employees to a state representative?"

"When I held my meeting with the independent export import companies last week, I had my assistants taking attendance. A few of the companies didn't bother to send anyone—yours for instance."

"You shouldn't take offence—I have other things I like to do in my spare time."

"Ah—I see. Well I'm happy to hear it was just a case of you not understanding what your priorities are."

Joaquin received another blast of smoke to the face. "Perhaps you should explain yourself. How is it that I don't know what my priorities are?"

"Had you known, you would have attended. Tell me Señor Cuéllar—are your creditors local?" The Senator asked, and continued without waiting for Joaquin to answer. "Yes, they are. I have a lot of sway with the banks. If your stevedores join in another strike, you'll have to find another way to keep your stock moving. Isn't that so? Otherwise your goods will sit in the fields, or the trains, or your warehouse undelivered—and if you can't invoice your clients, how many weeks will you have before your creditors demand payment or else?"

"Or else what?"

"Don't play stupid Cuéllar—or else they foreclose."

"I've got a long-standing relationship with my creditors Senator. They've never balked at extending credit through such situations before, so I don't see why they would now."

"You're being naive. Let me spell it out for you. I've spoken with the banks. They uncomfortable when we settle negotiations, only to return to yet another unstable situation asking for more credit. They're over extended as it stands. One good bank run—which we've seen many times before—and they'll have to close their doors. So, we've come to an understanding that this fall, a firm stance will be taken by all business owners in this port—should there be a strike. And in order to ensure their wishes are taken to heart, they've agreed that only a small amount of credit will be offered."

"Well—I've done my part Senator to avoid a strike." Joaquin was starting to let his agitation show. "I've invested in equipment that makes it easier on the backs of my stevedores—and I provide higher wages than similar businesses."

"Yes—that is precisely the problem. My plan will only work if everybody plays by the same rules—an agreed upon lower wage in order to force a strike."

"And suppose I refuse to play your game?"

"You'll eventually see things my way. You just need a little time to contemplate the future of your little family business. Cuéllar—from Madrid is it? I met your father at church."

He was suddenly face to face with Joaquin. "Listen to me! This spring I'm going to force the unions to accept a uniform wage decrease. If not—they get locked out. I have men ready to replace them the day after. With thousands of stevedores working on these docks, the replacements will go to the large publicly traded companies first—as well as the small businesses that cooperate with me." He was looking down towards the warehouse floor. "I'll give you a month. If I don't hear that you've modified your wages by then—," he opened both hands towards Joaquin, "—then you're on your own."

The Senator had a gloating look of triumph on his face, then looked down to the main floor. "I don't think that son-of-a bitch is happy to see me here."

Joaquin felt the perspiration dripping from his nose. Since when did he sweat during meetings? He looked out the office window down to the main level. His lead stevedore Diego was looking upward with the particular brand of hatred only he could summon. He had been right—it wasn't going to be a good day. "He doesn't appear to be happy at all."

"You're going to fire that bastard."

"I'm still dwelling on your first proposition Senator. My hiring practices are of no concern to you or your scheme."

The Senator hit Joaquin in the face with one final blast of smoke. "Good day, Señor Cuéllar."

"Something bothering you?" Tony said.

"I suppose my mind isn't where it should be."

"Where is it then?"

"A couple of weeks ago I had the strangest visit. It doesn't bode well for my business—but I'm not sure there's anything I can do about it. Senator Montserrat came to the warehouse. I might as well have been visited by the devil himself."

"The Senator that abandoned his niece to work in a brothel," Tony asked.

"What do you know about that?"

"Only what Sofia tells me. She's a determined worker that one. I doubt Madam Josefina could run the place without her now. She's accused of murdering her parents in Spain. The Senator brought her here to hide her—but then he decided she was too dangerous to have in his house. She's trapped. Lieutenant Machado keeps her around as the bookkeeper—and to help manage things when Josefina is suffering from gout. Machado has threatened to hand her over to the Spanish embassy if she tries to leave."

"Tico told me as much—but she's not capable of such a thing."

"The authorities believe that she assisted anarchists—who were bent on killing rich landowners. They think she became involved in the anarchist's plan because she wrote articles for their newspapers. That's all she said to me—you should ask her about it yourself."

"I can't—she refuses to see me. Is she seeing someone?"

"No."

Joaquin thought, 'Tony was probably lying to save his feelings.' They fell into silent contemplation for a few moments, but eventually Tony's curiosity overcame him. "What did the Senator want?"

"He wants me to lower the wages I pay my stevedores—to par with those of the larger businesses. He wants to force a strike. The saving grace is that this didn't occur in January during the harvest. That's my busiest time when I need them working. I have a little room to breathe—until August when the wool starts arriving."

"Remember I warned you that some of your workers are hotheads. They could sabotage your goods, or break your equipment, or worse. My brothers say the cops are making life a living hell for the anarchists. They've broken up

214

meetings in the halls, raided the presses, and the leaders are being jailed and deported. They are going to push back—there's bound to be trouble."

"I'm still considering the alternatives. I don't want to become the enemy to my men if I can avoid it."

"You're a good-hearted man—but you've got some hard decisions to make." Tony changed the topic. "Let's discuss this week's performances."

"Good idea—remind me how we're going to manage your ambitious schedule."

"Tuesday, we perform at a dancehall in Barracas—down near the river— during a dance held by the black community. They're good dancers and have their own favourites, but nothing like the Tango."

"What do they dance then?"

"The candombe for one. It's a rhythmic dance to drumming—lively—with seductive hip gyrations by the women and the men shimmy the shoulders and chest." Tony did maudlin demonstrations while he said this, making Joaquin laugh.

"Sounds interesting—anything else?"

"Milonga as well. It's a partner dance like the Tango—but happier. The tempo is quicker, but the musical beat is the same."

"How did you come to know all these dances?"

"I'm a musician. I play wherever I can and whatever music they want."

"I noticed the beats were more pronounced this evening."

"It's called marcato."

"Yes—marcato, I approve—it makes our style more unique. I'm rewriting our Tango play again by the way—it was too cheerful. I don't want it mistaken for Milonga as you say. The Tango is longing—I'm not going to try for anything else."

"I agree."

"What performance is next?"

"Next is the I Bonita, where you had your first lesson. We'll be asked to perform there regularly."

"Excellent—a most deserving venue. Where's the last performance?"

"I need to discuss it with you. It's in a hall—a hall of the people. It will be part of several things going on—classes, speeches, and other theatrical performances. What I'm trying to say is that it's an anarchist event."

"So? Is there something that concerns you about it?"

"With a state of siege declared—any anarchist event could be raided by the police. We might have to make a run for it—and I would worry about Costanza and la Comtesse."

"I suppose we should forewarn our ladies and see if they're willing to face the risks."

"Let me get this straight, darlings," la Comtesse said in her breathy voice, "you think that me being carried off into the dark night by a handsome— probably young—police officer is some sort of risk? That would be the best thing that happened to me in years!" Joaquin and Tony laughed.

"Costanza—what do you think?"

"The people in the halls are my people. It's my opportunity to dance for them, and stand in solidarity against this madness the government has launched against its workers. You won't talk me out of this performance."

"Ennio—what about you?"

"The advantage of having rich parents is that we can afford lawyers. I'm the last person anyone needs to worry about."

"You're truly wonderful companions—bravo. Let's do the show then—as Costanza says—as an act of solidarity with the people."

Vicente had needed to check on the motivation and morale of the three men. As of late, he'd preferred to speak to Matias, who'd been their leader in all things, and who he could see had an outsized influence on the other two. Life was good, Matias had assured him. They'd seen the nest egg building up in their bank accounts, no need to return to Spain anytime soon. He'd given Matias enough cash to bring the other two to a brothel, not Madam Josefina's Social House, to blow off some steam, once they'd done their work, a final reconnaissance of the target.

A couple of weeks ago, talkative Javier got them into trouble at a meeting with an anarchist group calling themselves Bakhunin's Shock Brigade. They had received an invitation through Javier's insistent efforts with their general secretary, 'I thought they meant business with a fucking name like that!' The meeting went badly. Firstly, not one of them understood anything about the tenets of socialism, anarchism, communism or anything else bandied about by the studious group claiming to be the newest vanguard of the movement, and they'd had their pedigree challenged.

Secondly, although the intellectually inclined circle seemed intent on living up to their name, but they couldn't agree on any legitimate plan of action. Javier had picked up on their use of the term propaganda by deed, an act of violence against any factory or business owner, or best of all, the government. While bragging of their non-existent revolutionary accomplishments, Javier went too far, arousing the group's suspicion. 'Tell us one thing you've done that we can actually verify!'

They'd emerged from the scathing dressing down with bruised egos and tempers flaring. Matias had told Vicente honestly that he'd barely suppressed an urge to punch one of them, or Javier, in the face. More practically, it was apparent that they had to commit an act of so-called propaganda by deed in order to re-establish any semblance of credibility. So Matias had hatched a plan, for discussion.

"We need to conduct an attack on something that they hate—the police."

Although Vicente had given the hulking man a cold stare until he'd wilted, he'd in fact been pondering the suggestion.

"Continue."

"I've walked by the small police station in San Telmo during the evening several times. When there are cops inside the lights in the window are on. It's always closed by 2 am. We'll write a slogan across the building's stone foundation using red paint, and then firebomb the wooden doors. Nobody dies," Matias said.

"How does this help your credibility?"

"We'll tell them that we're going to commit an attack that evening. The newspapers will report it the following day. They'll want to claim responsibility—it gives them bragging rights to the other groups. And then we're in."

Vicente watched the three men approach the station from the shadow of a doorway at the end of the block. They didn't know he was watching, but he knew better than to leave things to them. He had shanghaied Tico, who was sitting at his legs, drowsing. When he gave Tico the signal, which now would have to be a kick in the ass, he would run to the closest hotel, and tell them to call the fire brigade. There was one relatively close and they had a steam powered pumper pulled by horses. They would easily stop the fire from spreading and killing anyone.

At midnight, he saw the lights go out and a cop emerged from the door, easily discerned in the distinctive tunic and cap, resembling an English bobby's hat. The station was empty. An hour and a half later, he saw the men arrive and take watch on the station. Eventually, talkative Javier approached the building with a bucket of paint.

To Vicente's irritation he took a long time, painting large letters that were four feet high, Revenge for the Persecuted. It was supposed to include Anarchists as Vicente recalled, but evidently Javier ran out of paint. There had been the odd passer-by, who'd been coaxed along by a string of invective from Matias. Now he saw them pulling bottles from a bag. Matias had said they would be filled half with kerosene and the other half with the more explosive gasoline now being used for cars. A fuse, with matches at either end, was held against the bottle with elastic bands, which they were now lighting. 'It was time,' Vicente thought, and kicked Tico.

Normally, the young cop would have been at home in bed. However, on this particular night that was not to be. The quiet shift he and his partner had hoped for failed to materialize. The three drunkards that were finally settled down and snoring inside the holding cell had resisted and fought with them. Not surprising, given they'd insisted on picking a fight with any unfortunate wretch they'd come across in the street. They'd beaten up an old man, who'd berated them for beating up a younger man, who'd intervened in their bullying of a young bootblack, who'd tried to pick one of their pockets. There'd been too many assaults to just send them away, or drop them off in another neighbourhood.

So, they'd dealt with them firmly, after a drawn-out street battle in which the two good-natured cops received more bruises than they'd given. They'd handcuffed them and brought them to the station in the back of the wagon to sober up in the cell. At 9 pm, the three drunks were still belligerent and the two cops realised they couldn't be freed until they'd slept it off. It was too late to bring them to the central prison, and they reckoned it wasn't worth the fight to get them in handcuffs again anyway.

They drew straws, and he'd selected the short straw, realising later he should have confirmed the straws held by his wily partner weren't both short. So, he had to stay, sleep in the cot and guard the three drunks in their jail cell, as per departmental regulations that defied all common sense. But the rules were the rules, and if the duty sergeant learned they'd had the temerity to break said rules, there'd be hell to pay.

He'd cursed loudly on losing the draw, thinking of his rugby game the following day. He was the star halfback of the local team and would be sluggish. He trained hard and needed his sleep. His widowed mother would be worried when he didn't come home, as she always waited up late for him. 'Damn it all,' he thought, and having seen his partner out the door, locked it and kicked open the folding cot, its ragged canvass hanging pathetically from the metal frame. 'Is this the best they can do?' He unbuttoned his police tunic to use as a blanket and tried to get comfortable.

Awaking in a tortured state of half slumber, he rolled over to ease a cramping shoulder and neck, and heard glass smash against something outside, shards tinkling down upon the cobblestones, and an odd thump followed. He dismissed it as his imagination. A few seconds later he again heard glass smashing and the unusual thump, but in his torpid state he still didn't recognise the danger.

His survival instinct finally kicked in when he opened an eye and saw the flickering of fire, and smelling the acrid smoke seeping in through the upper edges of the heavy door. He staggered to the door, which fortunately still had the heavy skeleton key inserted in the lock. Wrenching the door open, he saw a short, squat figure running away, through a circle of flames. He instinctively gave chase, leaping through the gasoline fuelled flames, rapidly gaining on the little bastard that had now raised his ire, forgetting about the three drunks snoring in the cell. At striking distance, he went low into the tackle, scooping the fleeing figure's legs together at the knees, and bringing him down hard.

He thought the arrest was going to be easy, but he punched the man hard in the jaw for good measure. To his surprise, the punch merely seemed to activate the little man, who he now saw was stout and muscular. The man fought back, punching with tightly closed, experienced fists. A strike caught the young cop in the temple, stunning him momentarily.

But his training and youthful spirit would overpower this fucking hooligan firebug, except that now there was a long, flickering shadow cast over him from behind. He looked back and was relieved to see a familiar face, until the weighted end of the Lieutenant's cane, swung with the force of a cricket bat, hit his temple and crushed his skull inwards.

Vicente listened to De La Fuente rant about the killing of the young cop in San Telmo. He decided, on this occasion, it was better not to tell him anything about the venture.

"I knew the bloody anarchists were going to be trouble Vicente! Now I've got to go console the young officer's mother—a widow to boot. He was a good lad. The beat cops will be looking for payback on the anarchists no doubt—we'll have to keep an eye on that situation. Tensions are already running high."

"But—this plays into my hands perfectly. Public opinion is onside. Our raids have been validated—the press be-damned. As for the families of the poor buggers that were burned up in the jail cell—they'll have to come and see me if they want an explanation. Their arrests were their own damn fault according to the desk sergeant. I'll let the widow know we are fully committed to driving this scourge back to Europe from whence it came. We've got to get moving so that we can see her before the bloody reporters get to her—leave her with some subtle messages for them—if you understand my meaning."

"We," Vicente asked.

"I'll need you to bring me there. We can talk about our strategy—and you can help me break the news to the poor dear. You need to develop your empathetic side."

"Tony! Good news—I rewrote the lyrics again."

"Oh no," Tony said. "I just memorised your last version."

"Don't worry, it's just the final verse—act five."

"The ending?"

"Of course—act five is always the ending."

"You've re-written act five—the so-called ending—six times now. Last week you fiddled with act three. The week before that—I forget, but I know you changed something!"

Tony's voice had risen in exasperation. Joaquin mimed a hurt puppy dog's face, making Tony laugh. He sighed in defeat. "Bring me through the acts that will jog my memory."

"Act one, departure for an opportunity in a faraway land—"

"Right." 'I came of age in an unfortunate time, I was loved by my mother and father but my aspirations were not forthcoming, my father said to me I must go to Argentina, far away across the sea—' Tony sang while Joaquin mimicked a conductor, much closer to Tony's face than he needed to be while mouthing the words as well. "Yes—you have it. Let's do act two."

The performance at Café Bonita was encouraging. There had been too many people at the brasserie style restaurant to do it inside, so they had cordoned off a square outside and placed the tables around it, with standing room behind the tables. As the Tango play had progressed, passers-by stopped to see what the commotion was about, swelling the size of the audience.

Tony had been in fine form—he summoned tears when a young man left his family to work in a far off land, he laughed when the young man realised his talent for carpentry, he gave an exasperated sigh when the young man fell in love with a married woman that didn't love him back, he cried tears again over a broken heart, and he marvelled at love found where he hadn't been looking.

The others danced—Joaquin and Costanza to start, a local favourite for the crowd who called her by name, playing the grieving parents of a lost son. Ennio alone to dazzle, a young man confronting the challenges of a new life. Ennio and la Comtesse in a forbidden liaison, she a wandering spouse bored with domestic life. Joaquin and la Comtesse, revealing her coup de grace—the black and scarlet dress with the slit at the front revealing provocative net stockings up to mid-thigh. The husband had put a stop to the philandering. Ennio and Costanza, playing the couple in love for eternity. The troupe held hands in a line and bowed, marking the dénouement, to a subdued but warm reception. 'It was a hit,' he thought, 'for the working-class neighbourhood in need of a distraction.'

"A lesson will go over well—don't you think Tony?"

Next, they went to the dance hall in the far southern quadrant of the Barracas neighbourhood, by the Riachuelo River, where the black citizens had congregated through the years. They were received by the owner Tomas, a tall, debonair, black man, sporting a bowler hat and cane with a pommel shaped like a bull's head. Tomas payed special attention to la Comtesse. His eyes ravaged her shapely legs as she stepped down from the coach. He kissed her hand and payed her a suggestive compliment. He let out a booming laugh when he received a lascivious flirtation in return.

Unexpectedly, the theme of the immigrant story stirred resentment amongst a smattering of men in attendance. After some hollering, Tomas seized a particularly belligerent drunk by the back of his collar and his belt and ejected the man headlong through the doors, casting a mild pall over the performance.

But the awkward moment of silence ended with polite applause. The attendees were anxious to get back to dancing and Tomas took the opportunity to dance with la Comtesse, after providing generously portioned glasses of champagne to the Tango troupe and reassuring them their performance had been appreciated.

La Comtesse, soon after, sprained her ankle. Fortunately, Tomas was quite prepared to see her home in his personal carriage, and she was quite prepared to accept his offer.

"Do you think she really sprained her ankle," young Ennio asked Joaquin, during the return back in their coach.

"Why would you think otherwise?" Joaquin said, his eyes averted.

"What did she say Tony?"

"Maybe you should ask her yourself."

Joaquin felt his mouth go dry and his heart beat faster when the Sofia emerged through the door of the warehouse. He found himself at a momentary loss for words. Here she was in front of him, and he felt everything in his complicated world had just become simple again. He could handle the pushy Senator, and he could handle the acrimony he would face from his crew of stevedore's, if he had to lower their wages. He could handle his creditors, if there was a strike and they refused to extend credit. There was always a way forward and these somehow became lesser matters with Sofia standing before him.

"Cat got your tongue," she said.

"It most certainly does."

He clapped his hands together and smiled. "Since I apparently have no words, shall I show you your figures?"

"Tony it's not like you to fret," Joaquin said.

"I have a feeling that something's going to go wrong. The People's Hall, on a large sign above the doorway, tells the cops exactly what goes on here. Look— some of the men are wearing red armbands, their symbol. That's like waving a cape in front of a raging bull. Normally I don't have to worry about these sorts of things. To make matters worse, my brothers are around somewhere as well."

"Your brothers will be proud of you when they watch our show. There's no need to worry—and look at all the women and children. The cops aren't going to raid this place. Trust me—it'll be alright."

"I hope you're right."

The carriage they had been waiting for pulled up to the front of the hall. Ennio had volunteered to retrieve the two ladies, Costanza and Sofia. Joaquin held each of their hands to steady them as they stepped down. He didn't want any more twisted ankles.

"The order has changed. We are the last show. There's a play and a lecture before we take the stage. We're moving up in the world—we have an actual stage and we can go wait in a dressing room."

Joaquin took note of Sofia's appearance, exotic and seductive. She had a black silk blouse with red trim and a plunging neckline, and a red full-length skirt that hugged the hips and was high on the waist, but flared outwards at the thighs. She had tied back her long dark hair in an ornate side ponytail with a red bow.

"Is the makeup too much? I borrowed some from Zoryana, one of the prostitutes that fell in love with you," Sofia said.

"Ah yes—I know the one," Joaquin said, teasing. "You're always beautiful—the audience will adore you," he said. The smile she gave him warmed his heart.

"I would wear this skirt for flamenco performances, it's all I have I'm afraid."

"It's perfect."

They walked near the walls of the giant hall to reach the dressing room. It was dark and they had to walk through a gauntlet of men standing at the back. A packed audience was watching a play. A man was swinging a large hammer at an anvil, and another man, a foreman, was telling him to swing faster and harder, or they would take longer than 16 hours to finish the work day. Then the foreman left the imaginary foundry to speak to its owner, in an imaginary office separated from the foundry by a large canvass. The owner told the foreman to keep the labourers working for 16 hours a day, 7 days a week, but was reminded the anarchists had negotiated a 6-day work week.

Joaquin watched for a few moments to analyse the audience. It was mixed with families and single men, much like the composition of Buenos Aires. He thought they would appreciate a break from the barrage of anarchist propaganda omnipresent in the city, mostly in the immigrant, working-class areas and the tenements.

"I have high hopes the audience will appreciate some levity after that sombre play, and we're going to provide it for them," Joaquin said, while joining the others in the dressing room.

While they waited patiently for the play to end, Joaquin played mother hen, going over the order of songs and dances, and any peccadilloes they'd remedied from their previous performances. Finally, an organiser signalled for them to take the stage. The sun had set and it was completely dark in the hall, except for the stage which was lit, resulting in Joaquin not being able to see into the audience. Why should that bother him, he thought? He just hadn't experienced it before, he supposed, dismissing the thought. He watched Tony take the stage with his stool, and gave him time to sit and steady himself with his guitar and bandonéon close by. Then he would take the stage himself to give a spoken introduction, before Ennio and Costanza danced in during act one. Yet he was unexplainably troubled by a hulking figure in the shadows, did he know him? This was no time to lose his concentration. He walked onto the stage.

The close out dance of Joaquin and Sofia in the final act brought a hush, this was an audience that cherished its theatre performances, and the Tango play was a first for it. They were left to guess if the play was a tragedy or would have a happy ending. Alas, just as it seemed to be the latter, the couple was torn apart forever. Tony's heart and soul were laid bare for the audience to see, finishing the music with the haunting, lonesome sound of the beautiful bandonéon, and Sofia's tears were real. The lights faded and all was dark. The audience didn't know whether to clap or wait, hoping it wasn't over. The stage lights came on and the performers were holding hands in a line.

Joaquin was elated. Several bows were required of the group until the clapping finally died down, and all the lights for the hall were turned on. As people stood to leave, Joaquin scanned the audience, remembering the mysterious figure in the shadows. Something in the back of his mind was telling him it was important to figure out why. Then he remembered. He felt the panic rising in his chest and fought to suppress it. They would have recognised him. He needed to keep everyone safe.

"Quickly—everyone to the dressing room!"

"What is it Joaquin?" Sofia asked, alarmed.

"It's the three men from the ship. They're here—I saw them before we started but didn't realise it was them until now. They'll be planning something I'm certain. Where's Tony?"

"He walked into the hall when the lights were turned on." Ennio said.

"Damn it! Alright listen all of you. I want to get you all into a coach and get you out of here. It's not safe."

"What about you Joaquin," Sofia asked.

"I'll join you later. I'll only make all of you targets as well. It's me they'll be after. I'll go see if the coach is waiting right now while there are still people around. If anything, that will make them hesitant to try anything stupid."

Joaquin walked into the hall, where several people were loitering. As he walked, men shook his hand and women mimed clapping to signal their appreciation for his performance. He nodded gratefully. There was no sign of the three men. Did I imagine the whole thing? He walked out into the street and saw coaches waiting in the alley. There was no sign of the three men. Encouraged, he began walking toward the coaches. As he traversed the entrance to the alley, he held up his hand to signal the first coachman.

"Leaving so soon?"

Joaquin spun around. It was the skinny, talkative one that had spoken. They had been waiting for him in the shadows of a doorway, knowing he would need a coach. A trap.

"It is time I left—yes indeed." It was stupid, but it was all he could think of to say. He knew he was in trouble. He could be killed by the thugs. They were more than capable of such an atrocity.

"Where's your fat friend—the guitar player?"

Evidently, they were concerned about Tony. "I'm afraid he had to leave— but I'll let him know how impressed you were with his performance." Again, stupid. He wanted to keep the others out of it. It was the least he could do for his colleagues, and Sofia.

"We've got some unfinished business," the talkative one said, and lunged at him. But Joaquin was sinewy and lithe, and his father had made him take boxing lessons in his youth. He feinted to his right and punched Javier in the jaw hard with a tightly closed fist, buckling his knees and making him drop onto the cobblestone, chin first.

The big one laughed. "Nicely done. I wish I'd done that to him myself. But now it's my turn." He was quick, and caught Joaquin by the lapel. He jerked Joaquin towards him and head-butted him on the bridge of the nose, breaking it. Joaquin was stunned and blood streamed from his nose down his lips and chin. He staggered and fell over Javier, who was struggling to his knees behind

Joaquin.

"This is none of your business. Stay out of it," Matias said to the coachman, who had been watching.

"Do you want me to stay out of it as well?" Tony had arrived silently, in time to see Matias strike Joaquin with his head-butt.

"I'll handle him," Emilio said, both eyes still blackened from the punches of the now deceased police officer. But Emilio had barely uttered the words and was struck on the side of the head with a heavy bandoneon in its case, breaking his jaw, and swung with such ferocity it rendered him unconscious. Tony turned to Matias.

Although, he was large, Tony outweighed him by 50 pounds. He was also mad. With a bellow he closed on Matias, putting his head into Matias' chest, knocking him off his feet, several paces from where he'd been standing. He landed on Matias, knocking the wind from his lungs forcefully. He was about to strike Matias in the head, but a man the same size as Tony caught his fist.

"Careful little brother. You need that hand to make a living. We'll handle these men. They're bigwig anarchists and can cause trouble for everyone. Take your friend to the hospital."

"Damn it! They did it to me again." Joaquin was seated beside Sofia in the waiting room of the hospital, his nose heavily bandaged.

"You're a very brave man Joaquin." Sofia held a hand softly to Joaquin's jawline, looking into his eyes. Her touch and her words made the pain bearable, and the promise of love gave him strength. "Thinking of us, you stupidly put yourself in danger, as you always seem to do." They tenderly touched lips until Joaquin winced from the discomfort of the pain in his nose.

"It's late Sofia. It may be difficult but I will find for a coach to take you back to Madam Josefina's."

"I'll return in the morning. Tonight, I'm staying with you."

The evening passed into the morning, while they shared their physical passion through laughter and tears. Laughter for their joy and love, a deep love, and for the relief of finding it. Tears for Sofia's tragic circumstances, and the burden of her unanswered questions—the false accusations that left her stranded at a brothel, surviving through determination and the business acumen she had acquired in her youth, now complicated by something she had desperately tried to avoid—love.

Chapter 19
A Tragic Accident

January 1907. Senator Hugo Montserrat needed a few quiet moments to contemplate his predicament. He sat in the worn leather chair in his office, staring at the toe of the boot he had lodged on his desk. Even with the overhead fan the heat and humidity were stifling, so he took his whiskey on the rocks. In ritual fashion, he placed the drink to his right, then his hand fell on his humidor made of Spanish cedar. He could always think better with a cigar, and he needed to think.

He could put some of his worries into a compartment far in the back of his mind, as they were of the spiritual sort. That morning, he'd returned a second time to confession with Father Devechio, asking penance for a fresh round of transgressions. He hadn't killed anyone lately or, God help him, committed blasphemy. In fact, after leaving church, he forgot why he'd been spiritually troubled in the first place. But there was a bigger issue.

"Forgive me Father for I have sinned."

"Are these grave sins?"

"You'll have to tell me Father."

"Describe your sins Senator."

"I've been underhanded in my dealings with others."

"You're a politician and politics are meant to be adversarial. You can't tell your political opponents your true intentions—that would be foolish."

"I'm glad to hear that Father."

"Is there anything else you need to confess?"

"Yes—work on the church I'm building in Bahia Blanca is stopped. I've had to concentrate my funding on other things."

"What other things could be more important than constructing a church for those in need, and forgiveness for your mortal sins of the past? What could be more important than eternal damnation to the fiery depths of hell?"

"I was afraid you would see it that way."

He was going to have to get it finished. That was his penance for the heinous crimes he'd committed, and then he could call it even. He thought he could probably secure another loan for its construction if he threatened the bank, he would think of something. The banks were right, he'd secured too much debt against his assets, primarily his last ranch in the province of La Pampas.

Thank God he had this ranch. Like everything else in the country, it was reaping profits from the sale of beef to Europe and the United States, and the lands were producing sizeable crops for export as well. He'd even managed to provide himself a sizeable salary from its earnings. Nonetheless he'd missed two large payments to creditors, for reasons he declined to explain to Father Devechio. He'd fallen into drinking and gambling extravagantly, again.

He had a brief vision of beheading Senator De Rosa as he used a double blade guillotine cutter to clip the cigar. He struck a match and held it to the end, rolling it over the flame for an even burn. The oak scent of its smoke calmed him and narrowed his concentration. De Rosa had reneged on their deal to return the ranch he'd lost in the bet. However, he hadn't delivered on his end of the bargain either. The deal had been to break the unions, in particular those that exercised control of workers in the port, and lower their wages. That had been the agreement, but how could he have known that the country's general prosperity through that year meant labour was even more in demand than years past, putting them in the strongest position ever to strike for better deals?

The damned stevedore's union was the problem, he thought bitterly. They held strong on the picket lines and didn't give in. His blackleg labour had been too intimidated to show up for work, and the embattled cops had been wary of escorting anyone across the picket lines. The export-import merchants had capitulated and again agreed to higher wages, the opposite of what he'd wanted to accomplish. He'd lost his credibility with the merchants when he hadn't been able to follow up on his threats. He'd given up, admitting to himself his plan had failed.

At least he'd been recognized by his fellow Senators for ridding the country of copious amounts of troublemakers. During the state of siege he'd convinced President Quintana to declare during the attempted coup d'état of February 1905, there had been more anarchists deported than any prior period. And the increased volumes of deportations under had continued long after the state of siege expired.

'You called it right Hugo—that was the way to go! Whiskey glasses clinked while he was presented with a plaque at the Jockey Club. For exceptional services rendered during the country's time of need, and so forth. He'd promptly thrown it in the garbage.

His thoughts returned to the half built church, as he blew smoke that curled around the toe of his boot, still resting on his desk. He'd had the nightmare again, causing him to awaken violently in a puddle of sweat. Drifting from his peaceful resting place in the Recoletta cemetery and descending into a blazing fire. 'You're losing your mind to the devil—think!' He took another pull on the cigar and exhaled slowly. It was the ranch in Jerez that held the solution to his cash liquidity, more precisely his lack thereof. But it was also the problem. It had considerable value. Despite being in the family for—centuries? He didn't know and didn't care. His father's sentimental stories of the family lineage had bored him. It's only worth to him was monetary. Acquiring sole ownership would allow him to leverage its value or sell it. Either choice would allow him to refinance construction of the church, receive forgiveness for his mortal sins, and sleep well again.

For that, he needed De La Fuente. Unfortunately for the Commissioner there'd been mild cause for concern that summer, when President Quintana narrowly escaped assassination by a lone anarchist, who had shot wildly at the horse-drawn carriage the President and his wife were travelling in. The insolent bugger was now serving a life sentence in the national penitentiary. A Pole, yet more European trash in his opinion.

Following Quintana's death by natural causes in 1906, Vice President Jose Alcorta had assumed the presidency. Alcorta didn't wish to die violently at the hands of anarchists, and like his predecessor, decided that appointing yet another military officer as the chief of police was the safest choice. The outgoing incumbent Colonel Fraga was duly replaced by one Colonel Ramon Falcon, a man who preferred riding his horse into rioting crowds with sabres drawn, to unseen detective work.

'De La Fuente let us all down Hugo. Quintana was almost shot. Where were his acclaimed detectives—enjoying their siesta? Better to have a steady military hand again.'

The Senator had told the new President that that the would-be assassin was a lone wolf, and couldn't have been detected by De La Fuente or anyone else for that matter. But he didn't budge.

'He'll have to prove himself to me Hugo. Maybe next time—if he's as good as you say he is.'

There was still hope then. Hugo could use that as fruit of temptation in order to retain De La Fuente's loyalty. The cunning bastard will sink me the minute he thinks I can't fulfil my promise.

He decided a motivational talk with De La Fuente was in order. The new President, at the very least, knew of the accomplishments of his detective division in reducing the threat posed to the country's economy by the anarchists. He just needed to see prolonged consistency in their operations to suppress them. De La Fuente would be encouraged and would agree to stay the course, what other choice did he have?

Then he would cash in his quid pro quo. Sofia needed to die—by natural causes of course. The Spanish authorities and their lawyers couldn't argue with a death certificate, the issue of ownership would be resolved, and the estate in Jerez de la Frontera would be all his.

Vicente wasn't happy. He didn't like his marching orders from Commissioner De La Fuente one little bit. Their conversation had been terse.

"She has to go," De La Fuente said, drawing a finger across his neck to make sure there was no misunderstanding. "It was only a matter of time Vicente."

It wasn't that Vicente had grown sentimental or fond of Sofia, it was practical. Over the last two years she had taken over the accounting, and then gradually assumed a large part of Madam Josefina's duties as well, due to her struggles with gout. Sofia had a knack for spreading out clients amongst the prostitutes more equitably, diminishing the amount of time he'd had to mete out discipline to squelch the bickering and cat-fights. With the addition of Tango dancing, better profit margins were being shown to the municipal authorities, keeping the tax collectors happy, and double the profits were showing in the second set of books, augmenting his Lieutenant's salary considerably. She had a head for numbers, she came cheap, and there was far less for him to do. He would have to find another such bookkeeper before she died. That was his first big problem.

Natural causes? How the hell would he do that? Shooting, knifing, or an axe to the head would be absurd for any coroner to specify natural causes on the death certificate, even those that owed him absolute loyalty. Drowning? Maybe.

He'd had her followed by the three Spaniards, now growing lazy and making easy wages. He was tiring of them. But it was what they'd been hired for, and they needed to be kept busy for a while longer.

"Tell me everything she does."

They'd followed her movements for two weeks, setting up watch on the exterior of the brothel entrance, paying off black boots and street urchins to cover the gaps. "Four times we followed her to a warehouse at the docks, Madrid Export Import Company. It's the business of Joaquin Cuéllar, the Tango dancer. They're in love—they embrace and kiss when she arrives at the warehouse. Then they play Tango music and dance. On two occasions, we followed Sofia and Cuéllar to his apartment. She stayed overnight and returned to the brothel in the morning."

Vicente raised an eyebrow. He liked where this was going.

"Having seen what we've seen, I've got an idea," Matias said. "In the evening while they're preoccupied, we'll bar the doors from the outside, and then light it on fire with gasoline. It's built of wood and has large, dry, wooden beams. It will burn to the ground and leave no evidence. A tragic accident."

"Indeed," Vicente said.

January was Joaquin's busiest month. The wheat harvest was ending in a mad crescendo, and this year had been his best ever. As the railroads penetrated further and further into the fertile lands of the provinces outside of Buenos Aires, the farms grew. Ever-increasing volumes of sacks of grain were off-loaded from the trains at their stockyards, loaded onto horse-drawn carts, and brought to the warehouses at the docks. Nothing that the Senator had threatened him with had come to pass. To the contrary, the stevedores' union had been successful in its demands for lighter sacks, eight-hour weekdays, and higher wages.

Joaquin had had to hire more stevedores and offer even more competitive wages if he wanted reliable workers, in direct opposition to what the Senator had demanded of him. It hadn't hurt his business at all, he mused. The growing export volumes meant better profit margins, and if he wanted to benefit from the good economic times at hand, he simply had to hire more workers and pay them more.

As did his competitors, so it all seemed fair. Nevertheless, the warehouse was busting at the seams, with diminishing available square footage the sacks were being piled higher, which made the crew complain. Joaquin took a deep breath, and let it explode outward noisily through his lips.

"What's up boss?" Pedro asked.

"I just had another encounter with Diego. He was really worked up. And then just when I thought things would come to blows, he just turned around and huffed off. He's a very difficult man."

"I never understood your decision to promote him in the first place."

"He has the respect of the men, and they listen to his orders. We always manage to get our goods to the ships with him around."

"If it's any consolation, I think he's just putting on a show when he argues with you. He would never actually hit you—he simply has too much to lose— best foreman's wages in the port."

"That's what I'm counting on—I don't need my nose broken again."

Joaquin had a good run this last year. The family business was booming, and he'd been able to share this exciting news with his parents in Madrid. They were less excited when he described the success of his Tango show.

He had not told his parents about the happiest part of his life, Sofia. It had been hard not to; it would give his mother hope for grandchildren. But now was not the time for such announcements. He himself was ready—ready to propose, ready to be a husband, ready to provide her with shelter and protection, a new life. Sofia, on the other hand, was not ready, for she had tumultuous concerns that required resolution before she could move on with her life. How could he help her? She did not want him making inquiries at the Spanish embassy, did not want to risk alerting them to her presence in Buenos Aires, her residence and employment at Madam Josefina's. But how else could they acquire some news of the investigation of the murder of her parents. Was it still going, was she formally accused by the courts, and were there warrants issued for her arrest? All questions that held her in a vacuum, bereft of the information that she desperately needed to get on with things.

For now, he had to let things be, but he was content. Twice a week she came to him, they danced, they laughed, they held each other in their arms and they were happy. Once a week she slept at his apartment, their love desperate and deeply emotional, as if each time could be the last. Then she left, as independent as the moment she'd arrived. But he thought that she needed his love just as he needed hers, and their worlds were better for having the other in it. And this was just how things needed to stay for now.

Hugo decided he should stay sober, but the temptation of a post celebratory libation was too much for him. He poured a generous portion of Dewars into a crystal tumbler—both of which were perks present in all of the Senator's offices in the recently finished Palacio del Congreso. He'd been tipped off by De La Fuente that it would be tonight, he could count on it. But Hugo didn't like to count on others, not with things of such importance.

Downing the first glass of whiskey, he poured himself a second, to sip patiently, as he brooded. His knuckle touched the box of cigars beside it, and his fingers fumbled for a cigar. Empty? A premonition that things would not go according to plan that evening. He would never admit it to Father Devechio, but he was highly superstitious. Bad luck. 'False idols.' He'd had enough to confess already; this would have to wait for later.

De La Fuente had been vague. If his Lieutenant was using men who weren't detectives, who were they? He decided he'd better watch things as they happened, and make sure the job was done right. He hadn't gotten to his position as Senator by blindly trusting his supposed allies. Now wasn't the time either.

He pulled open his desk drawer and looked at the two firearms. He withdrew the.45 calibre Colt revolver, his preferred weapon. The other, the C96, should have been disposed of long ago. It could have been used as evidence against him. But he couldn't bring himself to get rid of it, 'It was a memento of the best day of his life,' he thought, and he'd risked bringing it back from Spain. He left it in the drawer. Peeking into the cylinder of the Colt, he noted it was empty. He cracked it open, and gave it a spin. There were loose.45 rounds in the drawer, and he took them out, examining each one before inserting them into the cylinder's six chambers. He closed the cylinder with a satisfying click. Holding the finely engineered killing instrument made him feel powerful, 'invincible!' He put on the shoulder holster and loosened a strap which constrained his shoulder and chest.

The sun was down and he checked his watch, 8:30 pm. The men would only wait until they were preoccupied inside the warehouse, so he needed to get there soon. He slid the revolver into its holster, nestled under his armpit reassuringly, donned his suit jacket, and walked out into the night, its crepuscular darkness concealing the bulge under his arm.

Arriving in full darkness, he checked his pocket watch. 9 pm. It would happen soon. Sure enough, several minutes later, he saw three figures approach the warehouse with a nonchalant gait. They walked to the large sliding doors at the front, and produced something. A chain? Yes, that's what it was, and managed to silently wrap the chain around the two door handles, holding them closed. Good. Then they jammed a piece of lumber between the front man-door handle and the boardwalk. Nobody could possibly exit from either entrance now. Good.

Two of them broke away, disappearing from his view then re-emerging, each carrying a jerry can. He heard the sloshing, feint from the distance, as the two men poured gasoline on the base and walls of the warehouse. 'Don't forget the back—there's a refrigeration room at the back that will have a door. For God's sake—!' But they didn't do anything at the back. That meant that anyone inside would simply escape from the refrigeration room. A match was truck and the flames crept quickly and stealthily up the exterior walls. And then he saw them run away.

'Cretins!' He walked quickly towards the warehouse, looking for bystanders, but not finding any. He ran the rest of the way as the flames rose up the walls on two sides of the warehouse. He stopped at the chained sliding doors. He needed to get inside, needed to make sure the whore that stood between him and his parent's ranch died this night. 'No fucking mistakes.'

He used his jacket to unwind the hot chain and heaved the large door open by a crack. The flames had penetrated to the interior and some of the large wooden support beams were on fire. The smoke had descended to waist level, obscuring his view inside. He drew the revolver from his shoulder holster and entered.

Sofia's weeknight venture to Joaquin's warehouse had brought stability, nurturing her love for Joaquin, and hope for the future. Her work at Madam Josefina's Social House kept her preoccupied most days, and as she was tutored by Josefina through the Machiavellian ways of a brothel madam, she took on more and more of her responsibilities. The working prostitutes had come to appreciate her business acumen, providing an intriguing atmosphere that included the latest trends of Buenos Aires and the experiences that led to steady, if not increasing attendance.

Sofia had developed expertise in the Tango herself, providing lessons to the ladies and even having Joaquin and Tony's show on occasion. It was now a professional show, and the brothel had to pay for the performance through part of the evening's take. This might have upset the prostitutes, as their wages essentially payed for the performance. However, Sofia patiently demonstrated how much business increased on the evening of the performance, with the added latent effect of the show turning newcomers into regulars as well, something they admitted begrudgingly.

She was polite and professional to Lieutenant Machado, but otherwise distant. 'He still controlled her, and she had to tread carefully with him,' she thought. The threat of advising the Spanish authorities at the embassy of her whereabouts if she left the brothel crept into their conversation from time to time, so she stayed where she was. She refused his offer to increase her meagre wages, however, knowing they would come from Madam Josefina's share, which would foster resentment between them. She needed Josefina on her side. She'd been kind to Sofia, defending her from transgressions by the ladies, and convincing Vicente of her value. Sofia, in return, covered for her when she was suffering from the pain of gout, and other mysterious ailments, and couldn't bring herself to get out of bed.

But Vicente had asked her a pointed question recently, leaving her ill at ease. 'Josefina may not be long for this world now. And if you were able to leave, who could I get to replace you?'

'I could train Zoryana, she has a head for numbers and knows basic math. But she brings in a lot of money as a prostitute.' Sofia had wanted to appear helpful. It was best not to anger Vicente. She had witnessed him execute her treacherous lover Gabriel Chavez without a qualm, not to mention beating several men severely, after they'd mistreated a prostitute.

Although, she loved Joaquin, she still feared their relationship would result in disastrous consequences for him. He had hinted at marriage, and she had dared to ponder it—a wondrous existence with a ranch and a business and children. He was delightfully quick-witted, handsome in the Spanish way, and a good dancer! She had missed her flamenco, but now she danced Tango, and it was a fine dance. They laughed like children when they were together, and they were a good match. She was grateful for his persistence now, and with him and the Tango shows she thought less of the death of her parents and her home in Jerez. She had an agreement with Madam Josefina that one night a week she would be absent for a few hours, and another night she would just be absent, spending a joyous evening in the arms of Joaquin. They had been lovers now for a year and a half, it had passed quickly.

This evening as she walked along the boardwalk to Joaquin's warehouse, she had an uneasy feeling, el duende, which she had not experienced for a long time. Mirella the gypsy woman spoke of it often. She said spirits drew near whenever flamenco is performed, that they are dark spirits, spirits of death. As she walked, the feeling stayed with her. Was she being silly? On seeing Joaquin, she embraced and kissed him, and it stayed with her then.

Tony played the guitar, while they danced, and it stayed with her then as well. It finally made sense when thick, black smoke billowed down from the ceiling at an alarming rate. She saw the licks of fire come through the upper seams and spread quickly along the beams. Joaquin saw it at the same time.

"Fire—Good Lord, it's taken hold, bring me water Tony!"

"Water's no use, Joaquin! We have to get out!" But the doors wouldn't budge.

"To the man door everyone," Joaquin yelled, now beginning to panic. "It shouldn't have been this difficult to open the doors." But the man door refused to open, even when Tony threw his considerable weight against it.

"Damn it—into the freezer room—run now!" Joaquin held her hand tightly. He pushed Tony through the door to the room, then turned. "The doors are opening—someone has saved us!" Sofia ran beside him, momentarily relieved of her panic. But then she saw her Uncle Hugo and felt her relief transform into confusion and panic again, all in the space of a millisecond, as he was aiming a gun at them.

"Joaquin, look out—he has a gun!"

She felt herself pushed aside suddenly, and heard the sharp retort of gunfire at the same time. Joaquin had shoved her behind a large wooden beam. She heard him grunt and scream in pain and knew he had been hit. It was getting hard to see now, with the rapidly descending black smoke. She knelt low to the ground, holding Joaquin's head.

"He hit my thigh," Joaquin said, panting from the pain, his face covered in sweat from the searing heat of the fire all around them. Too much was happening.

"You're going to die tonight you little whore and the ranch will be mine— I'm going to kill you like I killed your whimpering parents!"

Sofia heard him, and the fog in her mind surrounding her parent's murder finally cleared. Of course, it had been him. She knew what she had to do. She felt for it using her hand, by patting upwards on the large wooden support column. She had seen it before the smoke lowered, now she grasped it, the wooden handle of the stevedore's hook. She held it firmly in her hand, knowing her uncle was coming towards them, trying to see through the thick smoke. She got low to the ground by Joaquin's head, and saw his feet approaching under the smoke.

Steadying her nerves, she stood up and swung the hook at the place where his head would be. She felt it strike and pierce something soft like jelly, an eyeball, she screamed in fury and pulled it hard with both hands, feeling it plunge deep into the socket. A high-pitched shriek escaped from her uncle's mouth. The handle of the stevedore's hook was jerked free from her hand as her uncle's body twisted and spasmed, and he ran blindly into the inviting, outstretched licks of the blazing fire.

A big hand grabbed her arm. Tony had Joaquin's arm around his shoulder, and they ran together through the open warehouse doors into the crisp, clean air of the night.

Vicente stood with both hands atop his walking cane. His eyes squinted with concentration, as he studied the smouldering wreck of the warehouse, in the peaceful dawn light. The weary firefighters put away their hoses and let the compression hiss out of the steam powered pumper. They had gotten the anonymous call towards 11 pm. By the time they had arrived at the burning warehouse an hour later, they were met with billowing, black smoke and a warehouse engulfed in flames.

The warehouse couldn't be saved, but the fire had to be controlled so it didn't spread to other buildings through the wooden dock structures and boardwalk. A single wall stood precariously, but the firefighters hacked at it with their axes until it fell.

He walked down to speak to a man giving orders. "Lieutenant Vicente Machado, detective division."

"Juan Hernandez." The man replied.

"Captain?"

"You could also call me that." He eyed Vicente suspiciously. "What brings the detective division here today? We normally deal with the uniforms."

"Did you see anything suspicious about the fire?"

"Hard to tell. It's burned to the ground. That includes any indication of what caused the fire."

"Who called it in?"

"Someone called Tony."

From Vicente's vantage point, all had been going as planned, until he'd seen the Senator running towards the sliding doors, an interesting development. He'd heard one gunshot, and then a squeal he would remember for a while. Then out came Sofia, Cuéllar, and the Tango musician. Cuéllar would be going to the hospital, he had a bloody leg and couldn't walk. What happened to the Senator? He had watched until he knew no-one else was coming out alive. "If your men are finished, I'll go look around."

"Be my guest."

Vicente walked over to a young uniformed officer.

"How long have you been here?"

"I arrived before the firemen—a few minutes before midnight."

"What did you see?"

"All I saw was fire to be honest. The entire warehouse was ablaze when I got here. There was no chance of saving anything."

"Did you see anyone?"

"No-one."

"Go home. I'll look after things."

Vicente circled around the structure looking outwards for vantage points, and as he identified the obvious ones, he looked around for any signs of the gasoline the men had used. He found nothing. 'They're getting better, at least there's that.' He walked a little further away to a final vantage point, thinking it was a little too far away for them to have gathered their supplies there, but best be certain. He frowned as his eye caught something that reflected the rising sun and sparkled. He picked it up and examined the unique inlays of the cane. 'So, you watched things unfold from here.' That wouldn't go into the report. He threw the cane into the junk pile of a neighbouring warehouse.

He walked to the edge of the soused embers, sombre grey ashes now, and studied the position of hefty iron hooks and pulleys that were intact amongst the ruin. He judged where the large doors would have stood, and gingerly picked his way in. It had been a large warehouse, but now it was razed to the ground. Anything that was constructed of steel or iron was left charred and covered in ash, forming ghostlike figures. A pulley, wheels for the conveyor belt. He was looking for a corpse, knowing it wouldn't be a pretty sight. He mulled over the possibilities as he took a few steps in, stopped and looked around in a circle, poking underneath the ashes with a stick, then repeated the exercise again. The corpse might be stiff, with the joints bent from the muscles contracting, as the water they contained evaporated from the intense heat.

There might be some small piece of identifying evidence, a pocket watch with an inscription perhaps. He had to know one way or the other, before the coroner arrived. He might also just be looking for skeletal fragments if all the sinew and cartilage had been burned away. 'It was probably the latter,' he thought, judging from the damage.

And suddenly there it was, as he'd thought, a bone protruding from the ash. He stepped toward it gingerly and squatted beside it. A forearm? Maybe, he didn't know.

He patted under the ashes with his hand. A skull. But not just a skull, a skull with a steel hook through an eye socket, its point lodged through its underside. He had no doubt, that if he searched the ashes thoroughly, he'd find a gun as well. But what was the point? 'The butcher's bill was paid, Commissioner—just by the wrong person.' He held the skull through the free socket and hammered the hook on an unidentifiable iron protuberance until it freed. A stevedore's hook with the wooden handle burned away.

He then placed the skull exactly as he'd found it. A tragic accident.

Chapter 20
Assassination

"This is an entirely different situation Vicente. I hadn't considered that the Senator would lose his mind and get himself killed. The young woman lives—good on her for outfoxing the cunning bastard. He overplayed his hand—something he was famous for apparently—given the debts he racked up. Good riddance—he was bloody tiresome. Always insisting we hound some union leader or other, labelling them as an anarchist and a threat to the country—my arse lad, my bloody arse," De La Fuente said. "What am I telling Chief Falcon?"

"Accidental fire. He'd been drinking heavily—the whiskey decanter in his office was three quarters empty and the lid was off. No sign of his revolver." Vicente didn't mention the other firearm he'd found, an automatic pistol with 7.63 calibre ammunition.

"He brought it to the warehouse?"

"I heard a shot."

"I'll take that as a yes. He went there to finish the job—didn't trust the men."

De La Fuente paused and waved a loose finger in the air, trying to decide something. "Chief Falcon doesn't need to know about the revolver. What else?"

"He passed out, and his cigar lit up the stock and the timber framing. The fire spread quickly. The Senator was there for personal reasons—he frequently visited the businessmen at the docks—cajoling, bribing, or threatening—probably in that order. That's common knowledge."

"Witnesses? I don't want any surprises from the press."

"Sofia—I'll handle her."

'She's always in the middle of things.'

"The owner was there as well, Joaquin Cuéllar. He's the passenger that our three agents beat up on the ship. He's not saying anything either."

"Lovers?"

"Yes."

De La Fuente raised an inquisitive eyebrow. "The men must be frustrated. Cuéllar seems to elude their wrath at every juncture. What has the coroner determined?"

"Accidental death by fire."

"The men are clear then?"

"Yes."

They were standing at the commissioner's favourite spot to talk, in front of the two tall windows of his office on the third floor, looking outwards over Moreno, but back enough into the room so that their voices didn't carry out into the street. "We've expanded our intelligence gathering, haven't we?"

"Yes."

"We now have informants both within the senior ranks of the Socialist General Union of Workers and the Anarchist Regional Workers Federation—correct?"

"Yes."

"We even have reporting from within the League Against Rents and Taxes."

"Yes, we do."

"The time will never be better to use them as I originally intended then. We both know it's worth the gamble."

Vicente nodded in agreement.

"Do you understand what I'm telling you to do?"

"Yes."

"While he's perched on his horse."

Vicente walked northward from the police headquarters towards Avenida de Mayo and the Plaza Lorea, a large rectangular park area that stretched westward from the Palacio del Congreso for several blocks. He looked left and right, wondering if there had ever been a peaceful Mayday in that damned park. In the years he'd been a uniformed cop, he'd celebrated the day by lining up with the other cops, tightening their hat straps under their chins, holding their clubs wide across the hips, and waiting for the inevitable command to charge.

Vicente had revelled in those moments, doling out club strikes, punches and kicks in as equitable a fashion as he could. He pulled his fingers away from the scar on his temple, where a pugnacious stevedore had unexpectedly wrestled the club from his hands and bashed him with it. He had suffered a cracked skull and a concussion, and had problems with his balance for weeks.

'When did it start?' He couldn't say for sure, but for several years now, International Worker's Day in Buenos Aires had become one of mayhem and death. 'Since De La Fuente made me a detective.' They started off peaceably, with speeches on soapboxes, red flags fluttering, and the singing of nonsensical revolutionary songs.

But then the hard men would push forward towards the police lines, itching to fight. They would have iron pipes or chains hidden in their sleeves. Eventually, some of them, drunk, tested the patience of the police line, all too happy to respond, and then things would explode.

As the size of the crowds grew year over year, they would plan for both a police line on foot, and mounted police officers ready to charge. Those that took pride in their horsemanship looked forward to this day. The great beasts bearing down on a rampageous crowd made it separate, people falling over themselves trying to escape, dropping their weapons and trampling their unfortunate companions, or those foolhardy women with their children that refused to leave their men. As of late, if the cavalry charge didn't work, the rifles came out and on command were fired into the crowd. Although, the rifle bearers did their best to pick a deserving target, the less deserving also fell, wounded or dead. He didn't miss the fray. He preferred the predictability of the raids in the aftermath, planned investigative work with much better odds.

The chaos provided the perfect camouflage for an assassination. He was a lousy shot with a rifle, but he'd received training on the Mauser model 1891 as a conscript and as a uniform cop. Its 7.65-millimetre round could easily traverse the park. He paced the longest possible trajectory across the park lengthwise and estimated 450 metres. 'Too long. He'll be trotting back and forth, a moving target.'

Width-wise was the better option. He sat down on a bench for a few moments, ostensibly relaxing, but looking for watchers. He then stood and paced the width of the park. He estimated 120 metres, 'A shot anywhere between 40 to 80 metres then.' There were no suitable buildings on the south side, presenting opportunities to fire a rifle while remaining relatively hidden. He ran his eyes along the buildings to the north. 'The tenements.'

He walked to the easternmost part of the park, in front of the Palacio, where the police would gather and form ranks. Then he faced northward, and selected the building where they would hide. Although, the intended target would be perched on horseback, they would still need to fire from a high enough point to have a clear shot over the crowd. He thought it unwise to go inside and wander the hallways of the building. He would stick out like a sore thumb. As he walked toward the building, he saw that most of the windows were open, and cloths and linen were strewn on lines suspended inside. He took note of the building address. 'Leave the rifle. Egress northward through the buildings—plan the escape route in advance. Exit onto Bartolomé Mitre, a busy road, blend into the crowd and disappear.'

Walking back into the park, he snapped his fingers at a bootblack.

"Shine them up boy."

"Si Señor!" 'The boy was sharp,' Vicente thought. He set his box down under Vicente's boot and began scraping the residue dung that had collected around the heel.

"Who lives on the second floor of that building?"

The boy looked to where Vicente was pointing. "I don't know."

Vicente flicked him a 20-centavo coin with his thumb, which the boy snatched confidently from the air. "How would you like to make yourself another?"

The boy, wily beyond his years, looked at him with suspicion. "What do I have to do?"

"Go up to the second floor—make your way to the window of the room in the middle. Wave at me—if you have the right room, I'll give you the okay. Then you tell me the number of the room—nothing to it," Vicente said, giving him a vulpine smile, he thought was friendly.

"That's worth 50."

"50 it is boy."

The bootblack looked up at the building, his wrinkled brow revealing his concern. But he couldn't resist the temptation of another 50 centavos. He left his shoeshine kit with Vicente and walked into the building. Vicente concentrated his gaze into the open windows, then heard commotion and a woman cursing in Italian. He made out the movement of the woman and saw her swinging a cooking pot. Then the boy arrived at an unsteady trot, holding the back of his head.

"Did you get the room number boy?"

"22."

Vicente flicked him a 50-centavo coin. "Finish the boots."

Sofia found herself brooding, which was not like her, she preferred to manage bouts of melancholy by keeping busy. Sitting on a stool behind the bar counter, she slouched and held her face in her hands, then caught herself and straightened up. She missed Joaquin, longed to melt into his arms where she felt safe.

Too late, she was startled by Josefina. "A man got you down dearie? Oh, don't even answer that—I know how to read the mood of my ladies."

"Perhaps—yes," she said.

"Anyone I know? The charmer that taught these lovelies the Tango? Yes? And what has he done—run off somewhere? He hasn't been fucking that French slut Hortense, has he? I saw she had her eye on him."

"He had to return to Spain to discuss his family business with his father."

"Spain? I see. Will he be returning?"

"Yes—soon enough, I think. There was a fire at his warehouse. It burned to the ground. My uncle, the Senator, was behind it. He died in the fire." She felt a macabre sense of relief each time she re-lived the moment she stuck the stevedore's hook through his eye. 'My parents have been avenged.' She wondered if that made her a horrible person, but she didn't dwell on the question for long.

"The son of a bitch got what he deserved, and I mean no offence to your grandmother."

"What do you mean?"

"He killed one of our girls. Right up there in the room you're staying in. It was a horrible, bloody mess. That's why none of the other girls would take it."

"Why wasn't he in jail—was he charged with this murder?"

'Maybe my parents would still be alive.'

"My goodness no. He was a senator after all—a friend of the president and all the other miscreants that hold high political office. They're more chummy than a pack of whores—pardon the irony. Vicente, and my beloved Felipe— Police Commissioner De La Fuente should you ever come across him—and something tells me you will—were part of his inner circle. They did his dirty work—and there was plenty of it. Your uncle had a lot of influence in this city. So, they covered up the murder—in spectacular fashion I might add. Not a word in the newspapers about it."

244

"I see," Sofia said, now thinking that Lieutenant Machado had been involved in the fire as well. But why when he obviously needed her at the brothel? Because his boss Commissioner De La Fuente told him to, for her uncle. She realised she could still be in danger, even though her uncle was dead. She needed more information.

"Speak of the devil," Madam Josefina said.

Sofia watched the three men cross the open space of the courtyard and walk towards the hallway that led to their usual meeting. She knew he would soon make his way through the front entrance as well. "I'd like to lie down for an hour."

"By all means dearie. If I need you, I'll send Tico up to fetch you."

She made her way to the room, entering with deliberation, no sense looking sneaky if she was caught, but the room was empty. She slithered underneath the tangle of chair legs in the closet and eased its shuttered doors closed. She could hear Vicente talking in the room below now, and with the deadly stealth of a lioness hunting for her pack, she lowered her ear over the floor vent.

"Gentlemen—your final task—then you'll have to return to Spain."

"But we were just starting to like it here Lieutenant—we've got lady friends now I'm afraid," Javier said, disrespectfully, Sofia thought.

"Our lady friends are whores you stupid bastard. Listen to the Lieutenant when he talks." That was the big one, Matias, reining in a recalcitrant private.

"You must have wondered why we went to the trouble of bringing experienced soldiers to do the jobs we've asked of you. Now you're going to find out. There will be a bonus—a large one."

"What exactly do you want us to do?" Javier again.

"You're going to take somebody out—like the good anarchists you are—an important public figure—Police Chief Ramon Falcon."

"Lieutenant—with all due respect to yourself and the good Commissioner— the anarchist that shot the American president was immediately captured and fried on the electric chair. They talk about the fool's heroism all the time." Javier again.

"The American president was killed by an amateur at a close distance. He had no escape plan. Your professional soldiers—you're going to use your rifle skills from a distance—from an elevated position in the shadows where you won't be seen. He'll be on horseback presenting an easy target."

"Why do you want the police chief killed," Matias said, suspicious.

"I won't fill your heads with foolish notions of patriotism. The simple fact is the Commissioner is next in line to succeed him—and he wants this process hastened along."

"We like simple facts Lieutenant—they're more trustworthy. We'll do it— go on." Matias said.

"Two of you will go to Bahia Blanca. Take the train—the Great Southern. Don't discuss this business with anyone. You'll purchase a rifle there. Nothing fancy—but good quality. If anyone asks, you've been hired as security at a ranch, nothing more. Get plenty of ammunition and find a place to do target practice. Make sure it's sighted for accuracy at 60 metres."

"Emilio is a damn good shot." Matias said.

"Emilio it is then. Javier take this address. The room is on the second floor. There's at least one woman living there. Your job is to get the three of you access to the room. That's where Emilio will shoot from."

"I have a way with women left home alone." Javier said.

"Plan your egress from the room once the shot is fired. Go northwards, through the building to Avenida Bartolomé Mitre—don't exit from the west or east side—you could be spotted by police officers running to the sound of gunfire. You have plenty of time to do this while Matias and Emilio are away. Your second job will be to recognise Police Chief Falcon to see him—well enough to point him out to Emilio in a crowd."

As the men left, Sofia extracted herself from her cramped position under the chairs, and opened the closet doors with a free hand. 'What will I say if someone walks in? I lost an earring and was looking for it.' But nobody walked in. It had been an hour at least since she'd told Madam Josefina, she needed a rest. 'Too long!' She walked briskly down the hallway and stairs. To her dismay, the brothel was bustling.

Tony had arrived and was playing his guitar and singing a Tango, five prostitutes were dancing with prospective clients, and three more were hounding a flustered Madam Josefina for a room key before their men lost interest.

"Sofia! Where've you been—never mind I don't need to know—just get these ladies some rooms so they can get to work."

Sofia knew exactly which rooms to assign, and diffused the crisis in short order.

"I'll check that the other rooms are properly prepared," Sofia said, hoping to escape Josefina's glare for a few minutes, in order to think about what she'd heard.

"Just a second dearie. Tico told me you weren't in your room resting. Is there something you want to tell me? Are you having a sordid lesbian affair with one of these idle-headed harpies?"

Tico had overheard and was looking at Sofia curiously.

"Nothing so naughty or dramatic. I found a more comfortable bed to sleep in. I was dead to the world."

"Well—you don't exactly look rested. All right, get the rooms sorted out and come right back."

Sofia nimbly dashed back up the staircase with a handful of keys, trying to recall every bit of information from the conversation. 'A rifle, a room on the second floor, Police Chief Falcon, plenty of time.' My God—they'd planned the cold-blooded murder of a public official! Why? Because Commissioner De La Fuente wants his job. Can I sit by idly while such a thing happens? I'd be as bad as my uncle, answering her own question. But how to stop it? Could she trust anyone in the police department with this information? She imagined herself going straight to the Chief himself, the intended victim. What would he do? Confront the Lieutenant and Commissioner De La Fuente? They would easily discredit her story. Then they would kill her, and go ahead and kill him anyway.

Sofia pondered her dilemma throughout the evening. 'When?' She remembered Vicente also saying the target would be on horseback. This was a riddle she needed to solve.

About 11 pm, a group of four junior army officers arrived and took a table. 'They were young and handsome,' Sofia thought. Their uniform shirts were clean with precisely pressed creases, and they smoked and listened intently to the music. There were often military groups that attended, the non-commissioned ranks stuck together and always drank to excess. Junior officers would arrive together as well, but wouldn't stay if there were non-commissioned soldiers around. Occasionally, there would be a group of senior officers, who made prior arrangements, early afternoon to early evening, before anyone else was allowed in. They were older, distinguished by greying hair, full beards trimmed to a point, subdued in their conversation, and respectful to the prostitutes. Some allowed themselves to be convinced to go to a room—some didn't. Those that did paid well, motivation for the ladies to nab a regular, although it was a rarity. They arrived early and they left early to attend more reputable establishments, the Jockey Club, or Circulo de Armas.

Impressively Madam Josefina knew them all by rank and last name, although after a few drinks she called them by their first names, followed by her favoured term of endearment dearie. Sofia thought of the leather holsters that hung from their cross belts, polished to a mahogany gloss. The solution was in front of her. One of the senior military officers could surely investigate and arrest Lieutenant Machado, Commissioner De La Fuente, and their three mercenaries. She just needed to choose the right General or Colonel, someone she could trust. There was a reservation for a party of senior military officers the following week. She would need to choose one then.

As she waited for the group of high ranking military officers to arrive, Sofia pressed Madam Josefina gently for information, to avoid piquing her curiosity.

"Who exactly are these senior military officers that need the entire brothel to themselves anyway?"

"Under their uniforms they're just men like all the others," Josefina said, and then added, "most of them are serving the country at Godforsaken garrisons out in the provinces somewhere. Whenever they congregate for a meeting in Buenos Aires, General Camarillo butters them up by bringing them here to start their evening and remind them what a woman looks like. They're old and wise enough to be first in line dearie if you know what I mean. Then he wines and dines them elsewhere."

"Am I to take it that General Camarillo resides locally then?"

"Yes—that's how you're to take it. What's going on in that devious little mind of yours—and don't you dare shrug and tell me it's nothing."

Sofia should have known she couldn't fool Madam Josefina. She had to trust her, at least partially. "I've been hoping to speak to a senior military official about an urgent matter."

"That sounds dire—what exactly is the urgent matter dearie?"

"One of their officers is going to be shot—by an anarchist," Sofia said, a small lie. "Someone confided this to me."

"I thought you'd given up on that lot. Why don't you tell Vicente? That sort of thing is his bailiwick—he'll have it sorted out in short order."

"I would rather he didn't know that I've been associating with anarchists. He wouldn't take it well."

"You're right—he'll skin you alive. Best leave him out of this. All right here's what we'll do. I'll slip the General a note and ask him to read it later. I don't want to spoil the evening for him. I'll ask if you can meet with him tomorrow to report the threat to one of his men. Will that do?"

"Yes."

"He's a darling so go easy on him. His first name is Angel." 'She said this like she knew him intimately,' Sofia thought.

The next day, Sofia made her way through Once and rode the horse-drawn tram eastward on Rivadavia. The route to the military headquarters buildings on Defensa was one she knew well, as it was only a few blocks away from Joaquin's former warehouse. Her arrival at the front gate caused a great deal of angst for the Sergeant on duty, who wasn't satisfied with her responses as to why she needed to see the General.

"The matter is confidential. He's expecting me."

A fresh-faced 19-year-old corporal was finally dispatched to General Camarillo's bureau to see if he would receive her. The General's executive orderly, a young lieutenant, admonished the corporal both for keeping Sofia waiting and for wasting the General's precious time.

"Don't you realise he's got a schedule to respect? Escort the woman here immediately."

Sofia was thus encouraged that her plan had worked this far; and she was now in the office of the cherubic-faced General that coincided with his first name, a majestic white moustache, and eyes that bounced erratically, one minute friendly, the next, they were the eyes of a madman. Sofia had not noticed this trait the previous evening, and it left her unsettled. But time was of the essence, and she had to follow through with her plan. The orderly remained in the office standing formally at ease; his legs apart and his hands behind his back, waiting to be dismissed by the General. The order did not come.

"Last night my beloved Josefina slipped me a note. Imagine my concern when I read that one of my officers is in danger. So—what is it that you have to tell me?"

"It's worse than you think. I didn't tell Josefina the exact truth for fear that she might inform the wrong people. I've overheard plans to assassinate the chief of police Ramon Falcon." There was no discernible change of expression from the General, although his eyes continued to bounce madly.

"My dear—such matters are best reported to the police department. They are well-equipped to investigate and intervene if it's necessary."

"I had considered that. The problem is that the men responsible for the plan are high-ranking officers within the police department and if I were to report it to them my own life would be in danger."

"What exactly did you overhear?"

"I heard an officer giving instructions to three men—mercenaries—former Spanish soldiers. Two of them were to travel on the train somewhere and purchase a rifle. The other was to occupy himself with gaining access to a second-floor room of a building—to shoot from. There is a woman living in the room and I believe she's in danger as well."

"Who exactly is this officer?" And in response to Sofia's hesitation, "Are you silent because you're afraid to tell me his name—or is it because you're lying to me?"

'How dare he!'

"Sir—I wouldn't travel all this way, and endanger my life, to lie to a general. I'm a Montserrat and my parents raised me to tell the truth!" She met his gaze defiantly now, having made up her mind to see her intentions through, to stop the vile murder of a public official. "His name is Lieutenant Vicente Machado. He said Commissioner De La Fuente had given the order."

The expression of the General changed dramatically, his eyes now still, and he exchanged a concerned glance with the young Lieutenant standing at the door.

"I know him." He tapped his fingers on the desk, looking out the window now, and his tone had changed. "Where is the building?"

"I don't know," Sofia said, her mood sunk to despair, realising nothing could be done without this critical information. But then the riddle came to her, now obvious. "It will happen on International Worker's Day, May 1. He will be on horse-back Lieutenant Machado said. Police Chief Falcon will be on horseback in his uniform, and he said that they would have to recognise him in a crowd." Sofia saw the appraising look come across the General's face.

"Were there any witnesses to this conversation other than yourself?"

"No."

"You've placed me in a very difficult position Miss Montserrat. My army has had a black stain upon it since the attempted coup d'état two years ago. Many of our officer cadre committed treason—the worst possible offence against the government. We're in no position to simply arrest senior police officers—they

250

can easily characterise it as yet another insurrection. Your word against theirs is a precarious position. As you say—your life would be in danger." He was looking at his orderly. "Going to Chief Falcon with it will produce the same result. On the other hand, my honour dictates that we must do something."

"I have a suggestion General." It was the first indication the young Lieutenant had been listening.

"What is it?"

"Myself, Sergeant Castillo, and Corporal Santos will dress in plainclothes that day.

The building in question must be on the north side, and must be more or less adjacent to the mounted police lines for them to make such a shot. We'll position ourselves to watch the windows and intervene when we see them."

"I suppose it's all that we can do Lieutenant. Don't let yourselves get caught up in any sort of police investigation if you're required to intervene. Stop them from shooting Chief Falcon and then disappear. At that point—the mission is over."

And to Sofia, "You have your wish—is there anything else?"

"There is one thing you've overlooked."

"What is that," The General asked, his irritation at being questioned evident.

"I have to accompany Lieutenant Ramirez as well."

"Good Lord—I absolutely forbid it! What good could that possibly do?"

"I'm the only one that will recognise the three mercenaries tasked with the assassination."

"Good day, Señorita. I hope you'll excuse the interruption, but I was told you provide an excellent laundry service. I've moved into a room nearby and was hoping to find someone to wash my clothes. I'm getting desperate," and then the kicker, "I can pay you well."

While she looked him up and down, he decided he liked what he saw. Early 40s, smooth olive skin on a bare shoulder showing where her blouse had slipped, the swell of a breast holding his eye, and an earthy beauty that her ragged clothes couldn't hide. Just as he thought, she was in no position to refuse such an offer.

"Good. I'll bring a bag of clothes tonight—wait. I forgot to ask you something. Is there a husband or man of the house that would object to you taking my clothes at that time?"

"My husband is working in the countryside. I haven't seen him in months."

'There was a curious twinkle of mischief in her eyes when she said this,' Javier thought. That evening he brought his clothes, and tested her receptiveness. "If I was your husband, I would never leave a beautiful woman like yourself alone in the evening."

She brushed her hair back, self-consciously, then looked away. "Thank you, for saying that. I don't think my husband is concerned about such things."

"Then he's a fool. When does he return from the countryside with his wages to buy you a new dress?"

"Our money can't be used for such things I'm afraid," she said while smoothing the impossible wrinkles of the tattered skirt. "We send the money home, to Spain. Our families are even poorer than we are."

The following evening, giving her spare change three times the amount she was used to charging, he produced a flask of sherry, the sweet fortified wine from Jerez, guessing that she was familiar with the spirit. "I keep this handy for the occasions I need to celebrate. Tonight, I want to celebrate your beauty. Would you care for a small glass?" Her defences came down, and the desolation and loneliness of her existence receded to the back of her mind.

"Yes, I would."

Later, after having made love to her in as sweet and gentle a manner as he could stand, he took advantage of her arousal, and satisfied his lust in his customary fashion, punishing her with hard thrusts from behind while pulling her hair, taunting her with a hand around her throat. He reminded himself she needed to remain alive, for now. "Just in case your husband arrives, is there a back way out to Bartolemé Mitre?"

Advising the Lieutenant that the room and escape had been secured, his next task was to lay eyes on Chief Falcon, and memorise his features and his movements. The Lieutenant had posted him nearby to the main police headquarters, waiting for an opportunity to point out the Chief to him, but that had been unfruitful to the Lieutenant's frustration, and he could only have so many shoe shines before he became suspicious.

"How do you know the Chief will even be on his horse that day Lieutenant, if you don't mind my asking?"

"It's being passed around the department like a venereal disease, the Chief is bragging that he'll personally quell the riots on horseback. He's brought in a few of his colleagues from the army as mounted reinforcements. Although, he's the police chief he still prefers to be called Colonel—a military man through and through. If he says he's going to be on horseback—he'll be on horseback."

"Well then—he loves his horses. Can't stand them myself—went straight for the infantry. If you don't mind me saying—won't they be off training somewhere on those horses?"

The following morning, equipped with an old pair of binoculars, they surveyed the field beyond the stables of the police academy near Flores. "That's the Chief riding the black thoroughbred, the rear legs are solid white below the hock. Take a look."

"A black thoroughbred you say Lieutenant—I don't know my horses very well—but if that's him with the waxed moustache curled at the tips on the black horse, I'd say he'll be hard to miss," Javier said, peering through the binoculars. "That's him—curly black moustache, officer's cap, black horse with white below the hock of the hind legs."

In similar fashion to the International Worker's Day protests of recent, the marches, solidarity chants, red flags, and revolutionary speeches along Avenida de Mayo and in the Plaza Lorea facing the Palacio del Congreso became harbingers of an inevitable descent into chaos. This was the day when tens of thousands of workers—bakers to blacksmiths and every craftsman's vocation in between, celebrated their struggle for humane working conditions—a living wage, reasonable hours, and a weekly day of rest.

Within the labour movement, a clash of ideals, anarchism versus socialism. For some, this was splitting hairs, for others it became the essence of their very being and they would die for it. Others didn't care for such high-minded ideas; they just wanted a better life. On this day, all intersected, primed to explode with concentrated energy on the hated tool of the state, a fidgety line of uniform cops that stood between the crowd and the congress building.

The latter's senior officer cadre were all too familiar with the scenario, and kept most of its troops in reserve, saving their precious energy. The police line would thicken in commensurate proportion to the throbbing, heaving mass of angry humanity before it, the apex of which usually occurred late in the afternoon. Those in command of the baying police line, based their decisions on the expectations of their paymasters, such as when they'd had enough of the mischievous antics of instigators in the crowd.

The union leaders were generally a responsible sort. They discouraged their members from bringing weapons. Especially firearms, as this gave the police reason to fire indiscriminately into the crowds, as had occurred on the last International Worker's Day. However, in every union existed a core of men who revelled in combative environments, intent on one upping their comrades with displays of bravado. They were having none of this peaceful protest foolishness, ineffective in their opinions, leaving that for the do-gooders they openly despised. This was their day as well, and the spark that would set them off, was held in the whiskey flasks in their pockets. As the police well knew, this tended to happen late in the afternoon. It was now, more or less, late afternoon.

She passed by Lieutenant Ramirez and made eye contact. Sofia had tied her back, her most discernible feature, and covered it with a scarf, like most other women in the crowd. Her plain dress and blouse were dull and tattered from three years of constant use and washing. She saw the sergeant and corporal, loitering a few yards away from their officer. The three were also dressed like most other workers in the crowd, with frayed suits and flatcaps. Lieutenant Ramirez had told her he was most concerned with the block of buildings that stood between Entre Rios and Solís, and thought they should focus on them. There were many open windows on the second floor, with lines of laundry and shadows obscuring the view inside.

Sofia felt a mixture of trepidation and despair. It was her responsibility, she had to recognise them, spot the room they were in, and point Lieutenant Ramirez towards it. Then she would have done her job, with nothing further to do but wait out the ensuing events. If she didn't spot them, the Lieutenant could do nothing, and the sooner she saw them, the more time the Lieutenant would have to save Chief Falcon. It was all up to her.

The men closest to the police line were growing boisterous, and several men at the front were yelling randomly at the police officers closest to them, taunting them and waving their fists. She could almost sense the thoughts of the police officers with their hat-straps cinched under their chins, only the shadows of their eyes showing, wanting to break out of the line and lash out at their tormentors. To her dismay, a single file of horse mounted police officers emerged from behind the Palacio del Congreso, and trotted into a position behind the police line. 'Chief Falcon is there!'

There were many high-ranking officers amongst them, as evidenced by the regalia of their uniforms. Some had displays of medals received from military campaigns of past, all had sabres waiting to be drawn from the long scabbards hanging from their saddles. They barked orders towards the police line in front of them, as streams of police officers on foot now reinforced the front line.

Sofia tore her eyes back to the second floor of the buildings in front of her, looking desperately for any sign of the three mercenaries. And then suddenly, as clearly as she could see her face in a mirror, worry lines creasing her brow, a hanging shirt was brushed aside with an arm, and for a single second she saw Matias's broad face, before it receded into the shadows of the interior. 'That's them!' She almost jumped for joy, she knew exactly where they were, except now she had lost sight of the Lieutenant and men. 'Where are they?!'

She pushed her way through the men looking away towards the police lines, who drowned out her shouts with their own. She caught sight of the Lieutenant, and saw him making his way towards her, trying to follow the direction of her gaze.

"I saw them—follow me!" She ran towards the doors of the building, pointing to the window she had seen Matias momentarily. "They're in that one."

Matias was at the window again, and saw her point. He ducked back in.

"They saw us," she shouted as loudly as she could, and watched Lieutenant Ramirez run through the doors and up the stairs, followed by the sergeant and corporal. She ran after them, uncertain the Lieutenant would recognize them up close.

Then, the loud crack of a rifle shot pierced the din of the crowd as easily as a locomotive's whistle pierces the still quiet of a town station, and Sofia realized it was too late. There was a stunned silence for a few seconds, and then she heard a volley of shots come from outside.

Vicente was observing events from across the square, opposite the building he had selected for them to use. Normally he would have preferred a closer position in case something went wrong, but today that would do more harm than good. It was best not to be seen close to the building when the shot was fired.

He observed a shift in the demeanour of the people in the square. Collegial songs of solidarity had given way to angry shouting. There was now pugnacious to and fro between the crowd and the cops in their line in front of the congress building. He saw they had been reinforced significantly and were readying themselves for a fight. The mounted officers positioned their horses into a line behind the men, and he looked for Chief Falcon. He spotted him atop his black thoroughbred, easy to recognise with that ridiculous moustache, although it had thickened out somewhat, which was odd. But then he saw a different mounted officer, with a finer moustache but with the same rolled tips, also on a black thoroughbred. That was Chief Falcon, wasn't it? He wasn't close enough to confirm. Which one had he pointed out to Javier? The one with white below the hocks, which he wouldn't see. 'Damn it to hell!'

He began pushing his way through the crowd, to get close enough to see the hind legs of the horses. Had he pointed out the right man to Javier? It was far too late to correct the error if he had. Javier wasn't the thinking type; he wouldn't wait to see the horse's legs. He was going to see two identical men and point out one to Emilio, with a 50 percent chance of getting it right. Good gambling odds, and Javier liked to gamble. That's exactly what they would do, and it might still work out. Except that now there was a third, and a fourth officer on horseback with similar moustaches, all on black thoroughbreds.

He was inextricably stuck in the thick of the angry mob closest to the police line when the rifle shot rang out. Then he was bowled over by a rush of people, panicked and trying to escape the danger area. Vicente fought to get back on his feet before he was trampled to death, which he managed to do, punching anyone who pushed into him. His eyes grew wide seeing police officers in the line raise their rifles at the command of—Chief Falcon—and he fought to get to the ground again, where there was better odds of surviving.

At the end of the hallway, three men burst out from a room, running at full steam. From behind the corporal, she saw Javier was in the lead.

"Stop right there," the Lieutenant shouted, his pistol raised, causing a momentary stand-off in the hallway. Then they charged.

"That's them!" Sofia warned.

A loud pistol shot followed and a deep crimson splatter of blood and skull hit the whitewashed wall. Two more shots in quick succession followed, and she saw Matias's large body fall forward with the momentum of his charge. The one she knew as Javier had been running in the lead and managed to veer off into another hallway towards the back of the building before Lieutenant Ramirez had opened fire. She saw the Lieutenant aim down the hallway and fire at him once, then chase him with his men.

Sofia decided she had done everything she could to help. She looked down at Matias, he had stopped breathing. A few metres down the hall, Emilio was crumpled like a pretzel, and his eyes were wide open with shock. Sofia looked at the bloody mess on the wall a metre away, and then turned his head, the back of which was missing. They were dead. The door to room 22 was wide open. She had to check on the woman they had spoken of. Was she alive?

"Hello?" The room wasn't big. The woman, whoever she was, was lying naked in the corner. Her skin was waxy with blotches of blue and her legs and arms were stiff with rigor mortis, the room smelled of death. Sofia felt a pang of guilt. She'd been too late. Too late to save the chief of police, and too late to save this woman. She felt the tears well in her eyes, and was startled by the sudden appearance of Lieutenant Ramirez.

"She's dead. As are the two in the hall. The third got away—but I hit him as he ran through the door. There was blood on it." He walked to the table in the middle of the room. "There's your rifle—you were right." Seeing Sofia was not moving, he added,

"Our job is done. We have to get out of here—out the back."

Vicente walked toward the building, where he could see uniform cops bent over, gathering their courage to charge up the stairs just beyond the door. He drew his revolver from the shoulder holster. "Let me through!"

The uniform cops looked at the tall Lieutenant and parted. They all knew exactly who he was, knew him by his reputation, a man to be feared. They watched dumbfounded as he walked up the stairs with his revolver extended, ready to shoot. "They're dead—so stop quivering in your boots."

'Matias and Emilio—dead—where's Javier?' He remained expressionless, watching a pair of youthful uniformed cops staring aghast at the dead bodies in the hallway. "Anarchists," Vicente said.

A stocky police sergeant emerged at the stairs.

"Did they manage to shoot anyone," Vicente asked.

"They got Captain Suarez atop his horse—shot him right between the eyes."

"A mounted officer—they wanted to make it count. I know who these men are—we've had our eye on them. Look after this crime scene—get the coroner here and tell him I'll identify the men for him at the morgue later."

"Can't you stay here to meet him sir? I've got men posted around the body of the two Captain as well and it's bloody chaos out there."

"Don't question me—there's a third man in the wind Sergeant—and he's dangerous. He shot his two comrades. Obviously, they were witnesses to the murders and could betray him. He may be ready to shoot others."

Vicente walked down the corridor leading northwards and through the door, noting the blood smear. He stepped on something and picked it up, a shell casing, 7.63 mm. He meandered through a hall that zig zagged endlessly until coming to stairs that led to an exit onto Bartolomé Mitre. '—and off you ran into the crowd—pursued closely by a soldier.' He thought he'd better forewarn Commissioner De La Fuente the plan had taken a disastrous turn, so he walked briskly to the police headquarters. As he approached the front entrance, a skinny teenager in the shadow of a doorway across the street waived for his attention. 'Tico!'

He crossed the street to the doorway, making sure no-one was watching him. "What's going on?"

"Your spy Javier is at Madam Josefina's Social House—and he's been shot—high in the back—there's a lot of blood."

"Get back there and make sure he stays put. Place him in a room if he's not already. Everyone is to leave him be."

"Yes sir. Are you coming?"

"Yes, I'm coming." He watched Tico bound away at a full sprint, noting he had grown and was beginning to thicken. A soft brush of youthful whiskers had formed on his chin and jawline. 'Your spy?'

After retrieving his coach, he retrieved another item, for what he had to do next, something he'd retrieved from the Senator's office, a Mauser C96 pistol, along with its 7.63 mm ammunition. He pulled a razor-sharp knife out from the rim of his boot and cut the tip off a cigar. He lit it, clearing his thoughts and calming his mind. He snapped the reins and coaxed the mare into a steady trot towards the brothel. He was at his best at moments like this, exalting in uncertainty, confident he would ascertain the best outcome possible in the circumstances. He always did.

Arriving at a leisurely pace, he made his way through the entrance. No hurry. At the bar, Josefina looked at him and said nothing, Sofia at her side also looking at him inquisitively.

"Tico!"

"Yes Lieutenant?"

"Bring me to him."

He followed Tico into the room and shut the door. "Guard the door."

"Yes Lieutenant."

He walked to the bed, where Javier was lying. He was holding his chest near the shoulder, pale and panting, fear showing in his face. "Lieutenant—I need a doctor!"

"Who shot you?"

"I don't know, there were three men. They had pistols, army pistols."

"Like this?" He drew the pistol from his jacket pocket.

"Yes."

Vicente took aim at Tico's heart and pulled the trigger. Tico didn't have time to scream or move or hide. He only had the slightest fraction of a moment to lament the tragedy of his un-lived life, and his death, as the bullet pierced his young heart, blasting pieces of it out through the exit wound onto the door behind him. Vicente was leaning over Tico's slumping corpse in a second, then he turned and aimed his revolver at Javier's head. Javier's eyes went wide, for once he had no words, before the crack of a second gunshot marked the end of his life.

In the late evening hours at police headquarters, Commissionaire De La Fuente reassured Chief Falcon that it had been just another Mayday, nothing much different from others of recent past. There was one dead mounted police officer, a total of 12 dead anarchists, and, as always seems the case, two innocent bystanders. Nine of the anarchists had died from the volley of return fire given on the orders of the Chief himself.

"It was the right call," De La Fuente said, reassuring the circumspect man.

Two more had been shot by their comrade while trying to escape from the apartment following their cowardly assassinations of the police officers.

The third culprit had been located hiding at a brothel, following some of the finest detective work in the history of the department, from his Lieutenant. Unfortunately, the man opened fire when the Lieutenant confronted him, and killed a street urchin standing nearby. It was yet another tragic murder—adding to the toll of senseless killings. Needless to say—the Lieutenant shot the scoundrel.

But all in all—things could have been worse. Tomorrow is business as usual.

Chapter 21
Matador

Joaquin was sweating from the physical effort of limping and keeping pace with his father Salvador. He hadn't expected it to be so hot, unusual for April in Madrid. He had a cane for when the pain struck, and the hamstring of his right leg felt like it was ready to snap. He was cautiously optimistic now about regaining full use of the leg. His first week in the hospital in Buenos Aires had been agonising. With Father Devechio at his side, he'd prayed that gangrene wouldn't set in, and he would keep his leg. He hadn't prayed, confessed, or even attended church in a long while. In fact, he wasn't certain of his faith anymore. However, on this occasion, he decided it wouldn't hurt to ask God to spare him his leg, and it apparently worked.

By the end of the second week, his wound had healed sufficiently to return to his apartment, although walking had been difficult. His maid cleaned and cooked for him, and he welcomed anyone that had time to see him, Sofia in particular. She had sat beside him at the hospital every day, holding his hand. She felt she had brought the disaster upon him, but he'd convinced her he needed her in his life, with all the consequences that brought. In the first days after the fire, Joaquin had been feverish, and wondered if he had dreamed the events of the burning warehouse. But finally, his head had cleared and they discussed the bizarre event.

"I killed a man—a flesh and blood human being. There's no going back. I know I had no choice, but I feel like I'm a different person. He spoke so cruelly about killing my parents. I should have known—I was naive."

Joaquin squeezed her hand. He had no words, but he was happy to be alive.

"I didn't know what to expect from Lieutenant Machado. I thought I would be arrested, but he seemed more concerned about the brothel. He told me to continue working—away from the eyes of the Spanish authorities. He said that they're still looking for me. He needs me there. Madam Josefina is not well, and some evenings her gout is so painful she can't attend to her duties. For now, this is the only choice I have, but I can't trust him."

"You can stay here with me Sofia; I can protect you." But they both knew that had been a ridiculous statement considering what had happened at his warehouse. However, over the ensuing weeks they had discussed Sofia's situation and decided something had to be done, waiting was only exacerbating her circumstances.

Then he'd had a difficult conversation with his accountant, Pablo, who'd taken the business in hand while Joaquin was in the hospital. They'd lost everything—their stock, their ledgers, most capital assets including the warehouse, the gear and tools—all lost to the fire. Pablo had taken it upon himself to write letters to the clients overseas, cancelling pending shipments, and of course, laying off the workers. It hadn't been easy.

Diego Salvador, the foreman, acted up and threatened both Pablo and Joaquin. "I know what the two of you are up to—this is a fraud—you lit the warehouse on fire for insurance. I found a jerrycan smelling of gasoline nearby in a garbage—you're just trying to screw us from our wages!"

The jerrycan made sense, with the Senator showing up to kill Sofia. That part wasn't something Joaquin wished to explain to the fire department or anyone else for that matter, certainly not his employees. Sadly, they would be bitter, and would have to look for work as day labour on the docks until he got his business started again, if he got it started again.

When he'd recovered sufficiently, he had returned to Spain. He needed to speak to his father in person to discuss the viability of continuing the business, explain the fire, and the situation with their creditors in Buenos Aires. It had taken him most of March and part of April, to travel by steamship to Lisbon, and then by train to Madrid. Despite the dire circumstances, he was overjoyed to see his parents.

He had missed the bullfights. Now walking into the Plaza de Toros in Madrid's west quadrant Carretara de Aragon where he'd come after church during his youth, he felt a mixture of melancholy and excitement. '10 years already!' They passed through the front entrance, a keyhole shaped portal, notched out of a magnificent facade. They took their seats with thousands of others for whom the bullfighting tradition was entrenched in their soul.

"It's not surprising how the death of Senator Montserrat has suddenly resulted in a more welcoming attitude from the banks," his father Salvador said. "We have plenty of assets to leverage our borrowing against, so it was questionable banking practices to refuse our credit requests or give such ridiculous conditions. I don't understand why he chose our warehouse in particular to set on fire and then enter with his guns blazing like a damn madman!"

Joaquin stayed silent. Their attention was directed to the procession entering the bullring, waved in by the young King Alfredo XIII, who was in the royal box overlooking the arena. The matadors with their respective teams of mounted picadors and banderilleros paraded around the arena waving at the audience. The matadors stood out, recognisable from their wide shouldered jackets resplendent in gold brocade, their faces impassive, that of men who faced death for a living. The King's mounted bailiffs in black suits and cocked hats filled out the procession, a ceremonious addition to convey the orders of the King.

"Father there's a woman—"

"Of course, there's a woman. When something doesn't make sense, there's a woman involved. I've been patiently waiting for you to tell me about her."

"How did you know—Father Devechio?"

"I've received letters from him—yes."

"You've got to stop spying on me," Joaquin said.

"That was the deal I made with your mother."

"What did he say?" Joaquin asked.

"He said she was enterprising. He approved—but she's been the victim of something tragic. He didn't elaborate. So? Tell me about her."

Joaquin hesitated. The first match had started and the bull had charged into the ring, trotting now, looking for someone or something to vent his anger upon.

"The picadors are nervous," Joaquin said.

"It's big. They'll have to use the horses skilfully for protection." Just as his father said it, the bull charged at the horse, putting its head down and then lifting with his mighty neck and razor-sharp horns. The bull received a firmly planted jab to the neck from the lance of the picador, but its right horn pierced the belly of the horse as it lifted it off the ground. The picador fell forwards, rolling lithely as he hit the ground, and the matador entered and waved his cape to distract the bull.

"What about this woman?"

"Her name is Sofia Montserrat—she's from Jerez de la Frontera." He knew this would pique his father's interest, although his father didn't flinch.

"Jerez you say—sherry? Or ranches?"

They had dispatched the disembowelled horse and were hauling it away on a cart pulled by donkeys.

"Her family owns a large ranch about 10 Kilometres east of Jerez she tells me. The Senator was her uncle. Her parents were murdered by anarchists three years ago—or so say the Civil Guard."

The picador had re-appeared in the arena with a new horse, and the other picador was circling the bull. The first strike to his neck hadn't had the intended effect of damaging the muscles, and the bull still held its head high. It was now charging the second picador with its head down, horns aimed again at the underside of the horse's belly.

His father reluctantly tore his eyes away from the spectacle. "Why did the Senator try to kill you—protecting her honour perhaps?"

"Sofia and I had been standing close together. He shot at her but hit me instead. He screamed that he was going to kill her—just as he'd killed her parents. He'd gone mad."

"I see." There was applause from the crowd, pleased with the second picador's skilled strike to the bull's neck. He had managed to remain on his mount, despite the horse receiving a goring to the belly. The horse collapsed in a heap, but the bull's head was now lower to the ground. "So, he killed her parents, and was trying to kill her?"

"Yes—his motive being the inheritance of the ranch."

The banderillos, small spears with a harpoon tip, were stuck in the rump of the bull's neck in order to weaken the massive brute, and the blood was flowing. Then the matador took over the centre stage from his team, strutting directly toward the bull. His father locked his eyes on Joaquin, who knew a tough question was coming, his father being an incisive man. "Why exactly is she in Buenos Aires?"

"She stands accused by the Civil Guard. The investigating officer claimed she had provided anarchists with the information they needed to commit the murders. She was forced to flee to Argentina, tricked by her uncle, the Senator. I met her on the steamship."

With the movement of his cape, the matador had lured the bull into several passes, the horns missing his legs by a whisker, drawing cheers from some and whistles from others. He now took the killing sword from its handler.

"Do you love this woman?"

"Yes."

The crowd held its breath as the matador lunged with acrobatic grace, the moment of truth. The sword plunged clean and true between the shoulder blades of the swaying bull who, despite its wounds, was intent on one last try to gut the hated matador with its horns. Instead, it dropped onto its front knees and died. The crowd applauded. The matador had put on a good show, which the crowd knew was due to the courageous nature of the bull.

"Then you must go to Jerez."

It was now approaching 9 pm and they were riding back towards their residence in a carriage.

"There will have been a hearing and witnesses will have been called by the investigating magistrate—likely anyone who worked at the ranch who may have seen or heard something. You can ride out to the ranch and ask around—see if anyone is there. You can still ride a horse?"

Joaquin noted the sarcasm. "It'll do me good to ride again."

"The Montserrat's will have a family lawyer representing the estate in regards to the inheritance. Find out who it is and talk to him. He can tell you if trials went ahead and what happened if it did."

"I've never known you to give excellent advice like this before," Joaquin said overly seriously. They both laughed and settled into a period of silence, where Joaquin was content to listen to the creaks of the carriage and the trot of the mare on the cobblestone. His father sighed, the kind of sigh that demanded attention.

"What is it?"

"Bad news I'm afraid. I happen to know the judge in Jerez. He's a distant relation of our own lawyer—I've spoken to the man twice. They were not conversations one would easily forget."

"Why is that bad news?"

"He's the same judge that sentenced the anarchists to death following the Jerez rebellion in 1892. It was a mistake—an overreaction. They died horribly— by the garrotte."

Joaquin let out a loud breath constrained between his lips. "Should I speak with him?"

"He's an opinionated old curmudgeon—a real bastard—but yes. To get the best account of the situation you would do well to speak with him. I'll arrange it."

'His father had been right,' Joaquin thought. The judge was a curmudgeon— he was also antagonistic, mule-headed, and reeked of garlic. He had Joaquin transfixed in a hostile stare.

"Tell me young man—what interests the mighty Cuéllar family of Madrid in a criminal matter of Andalucia?"

The judge's voice dripped with arrogance, and it irritated Joaquin. He had worked out an explanation with his father for such questioning, which was only slightly false. "We run an import business. I've recently had a fire at my warehouse at the port of Buenos Aires. We've had to notify our clients that their orders had been destroyed. We're exploring another beef supply—closer to home."

"How does that involve the young woman Sofia Montserrat?"

Joaquin had not mentioned her, only inquiring if the anarchists had been prosecuted for the murders on the estate.

"So, let me see. You have a business in Buenos Aires, where I'm told Sofia Montserrat is hiding out. If I were cynical, I might say that you're actually here making inquiries on her behalf."

Unfortunately for Joaquin, he had never inherited his father's penchant for poker, and his expressions were revealing.

"Ah—so that is the case. You've been bewitched, is that it? She was highly adept at the flamenco—I've seen her perform on stage. A real beauty—and smart apparently. Now you listen to me. The Civil Guard haven't produced hide nor hair of the anarchists that massacred that family. But they have a record that Sofia Montserrat had been seduced by the anarchist that published their newspaper. Without any further information, I can only deduce she was part of the plot. She advanced the cause of the anarchists and set herself up for a sizeable inheritance—that's called motive."

"But surely you recognise it's completely out of character. She was a loving and loyal daughter. What did your witnesses say about that?"

The judge raised his voice. "That's a matter for her defence lawyer to raise during the trial."

Joaquin tried a different tack, part of the plan he had formulated with his father. "Were you aware that her uncle, the Argentine Senator Hugo Montserrat, was at the ranch when the murder's occurred?"

"Ah—I suppose you're inferring that he killed the Montserrat's—and their young servant—and painted all the propaganda in their house. It's not very plausible. Captain Dominguez was the investigating officer. Do you think him a fool as well? Let me give you some advice. It's best that the woman returns to Jerez and we get on with the trial. It's within my power to conduct it in her absence, and I'm losing my patience. In that case, she won't have a good representation of her defence."

Joaquin saw no point in hiding the truth. "I will advise her of this sir, I'm sure she will pay it her utmost heed," he said, in as respectful a tone as he could muster. 'Muleheaded curmudgeon indeed.' The judge's comments did not bode well for Sofia, he thought.

The next day he rode to the Montserrat Estate, having haggled a price to use a saddled mare for the day, leaving his pocket watch as collateral. 'They will have questioned all of the servants and hired hands—see what they told the Civil Guard.' Having kept a good pace for an hour, he reined in to a trot before a well-tended fence line and passed under a varnished sign that announced 'Montserrat.' A man, with a mop of grey, unkempt hair and skin like leather, stood at the stables, watching Joaquin approach.

"My name is Joaquin Cuéllar. Who do I have the honour of speaking to?"

"They call me old Roberto."

"Do they? Clearly, they're mistaken—you don't seem old at all," Joaquin said, to a stone-faced silence. "Have you worked here for long?"

"Many years, as have my wife and sons."

"You knew Sofia then?"

The man's eyes hardened. "I knew her well Señor. What is she to you?"

"We are very good friends. I see her often—in Buenos Aires where I live," and getting no reaction from Roberto, "we dance together."

"My wife can make us some coffee," Roberto said.

They discussed the hearing held by the judge around a beaten table.

"Captain Dominguez was very antagonistic—he didn't believe me. But I didn't see the anarchists that committed this horrific crime." He choked, and tears welled in his eyes. "I failed them."

"Was the Senator Hugo Montserrat at the ranch when it happened?"

"Yes. I didn't speak to him after the murders, but I'd picked him up at the train station and brought him here. My two sons were the coachmen, and he wanted me to sit with him and talk."

"What did he say?"

"He offered my sons jobs on his estates in Argentina, which was very kind. But he said something I later found to be unusual."

"Go on."

"He said he'd been warned by the Civil Guard—he was close friends with Captain Dominguez growing up—that there were anarchists in the area that wanted to kill landowners."

"What did you find unusual?"

"Nobody knew anything about this—nobody else had been warned. It was never spoken of at the hearing, and the judge didn't ask me about it. My sons didn't know about it—and they knew all the coming and goings in the area— from their friends and the peasant girls. And Captain Dominguez didn't say anything about this either. The Senator was the only one who knew about this, and he warned me. As it stands, it's still a mystery where that information came from."

"I see."

'The bastard was setting up the murders to be blamed on the anarchists— he'd planned it very carefully beforehand.'

Did he dare follow through with meeting with Captain Rafael Dominguez? Joaquin found himself depressed with the idea of confirming their suspicions. 'You must meet with the Civil Guard officer that conducted the field investigation—get a measure of the man. Is he an honourable and open-minded individual that will accept evidence as presented? Or is he an obstinate fool, fearing for his reputation—that his original theory be proven wrong, much to his embarrassment?' This is something you must know and may be the single most important factor. The investigator will have a long-established relationship with the judge, and will be able to sway the judge's thinking one way or the other.'

A young man in uniform, two lines of shiny buttons curved upwards and outwards on the black tunic, and a dusty tricorn hat, stood blocking the door of the outpost.

"I would like to speak with Captain Dominguez."

"Who should I say is calling?"

"Joaquin Cuéllar of Madrid—about the Montserrat Estate. He's expecting me." The young man indicated for Joaquin to follow him in. The office smelled of sweat, dust, and hay, and the remnants of the previous night's drunkards. There was only one office door and the guard rapped on it.

"Come in."

"Joaquin Cuéllar of Madrid for you sir," the young guard announced. The Captain waived Joaquin in with his two middle fingers and—turning his hand over—shooed the young guard away with a similar motion. He did this without removing his riding boot from the corner of the desk, or changing the placid expression on a dark shadowed face that had needed a shave since the day before.

"You have questions about the massacre at the Montserrat ranch, I'm told."

"I do yes."

"It's been three years." A long pause, tempting Joaquin to reply, to no avail. "What are your questions?"

'The Captain wasn't going to give anything up voluntarily,' Joaquin thought. "Have you given any thought to an alternative theory about the murders?"

"You're a friend of the young woman, Sofia Montserrat?"

"Yes."

"And you're from Madrid—but actually you're from Buenos Aires?"

"Yes."

"You're her lover." A statement.

"Yes."

"Your theory is that Hugo Montserrat committed the crime and made it look like the anarchists, according to the judge."

"Yes."

"We were advised that Hugo Montserrat is dead—in a fire accident."

"It can hardly be described as an accident, but that seems to be the position of the police."

"You're claiming it wasn't an accident?"

"It was my warehouse that burned down. He entered while it was on fire and tried to kill Sofia. I was in the way. I had a bullet extracted from my leg to prove it," Joaquin said, tapping his leg with his walking cane. "He had the protection of the police."

"Why would he try to kill Sofia?"

"For the same reason, he killed the Montserrats—the inheritance. Rumour has it he was a reckless gambler—lost an entire ranch during a poker match. This sort of profligate betting is common in Buenos Aires."

A long pause during which the Captain's expression didn't change. "He was my friend—from childhood—we went to school together. Did you know this?"

"No." Joaquin's hopes sank.

"Right from grade school. We endured many canings from the teacher together. We got into endless sorts of trouble. As teenagers we drank together. He was a violent drunk. Liquor made him lose his Christian charity—he was bigger and bullied me and anyone else nearby. He beat me up often—but I was loyal to him."

He finally removed his boot from the desk and looked at Joaquin. "His brother Antonio—Sofia's father—was even tougher than Hugo. He loved Hugo—but he wasn't afraid to punch him out. Hugo hated him."

This had taken a strange but encouraging turn, Joaquin thought.

"I also hated Antonio. One day, not long before his death, I had the temerity to suggest to Antonio that Sofia and my son were a good match—and he laughed in my face." He locked eyes with Joaquin. "But my son is happily married now, with children of his own. As is my daughter."

Another long pause ensued, in which Joaquin gave up on guessing what Captain Dominguez was going to decide. "Things become clearer with time. Apart from the scene, there was never any evidence found that anarchists were even near the Montserrat ranch when the murders occurred. I find that strange."

"So you'll consider Hugo Montserrat as a viable suspect?"

"Yes—but that doesn't change anything for Sofia. She will have to return for a hearing, and I can't tell you what the judge will find. The only evidence was at the house. All of the local anarchists were arrested, including her former lover, Francisco. That man couldn't hurt a fly. He didn't hold up well during the interview. None of them did. So, the questions remain—was Sofia Montserrat involved with other anarchists besides the local ones? Or was it a plot by Hugo? He's dead Señor Cuéllar—he's taken his secrets to the grave."

The Captain wrapped his fingers on the desk while he looked at Joaquin pensively. "You know—he was a very religious man. We'd served as altar boys together at the cathedral. He took it very seriously. I thought it was strange how such a son of a bitch could be such a God-fearing man. He would confess every single detail of our transgressions—and when I didn't give the priest the same story, I was beaten."

His conversation with the Montserrat family lawyer had been fruitful. The lawyer had fought tooth and nail on Sofia's behalf, at a hearing meant to declare that she had turned to prostitution for a living, at a brothel in Buenos Aires. He'd known it was nonsense. He'd produced affidavits by staff of the Spanish Embassy in Buenos Aires that she was working as a bookkeeper.

"It was a preposterous notion—the girl was as bright as the sun—she practically ran the estate for Antonio. Now that his rogue of a brother is dead—she's become the sole heir to the estate. Unfortunately, that doesn't change the accusations against her—preposterous as well—they were one of the closest families I've ever worked for. But she'll have to convince the judge of that—another matter indeed."

Later that evening, after Joaquin had pried out of the Montserrat family lawyer that the estate had been maintained through a family trust fund held at his firm, Joaquin pondered his conversation with Captain Dominguez. It too had gone well enough, and he'd come away with a considerable amount of news for her.

But of all the things the Captain had said, the fact that the Senator had been a highly religious person gnawed at him. He recalled now that he'd seen the Senator at the cathedral in Buenos Aires, on one of the few occasions he'd forced himself to attend. It was probably nothing, he decided, and he dismissed it from his thoughts. It was time he returned to Buenos Aires.

Chapter 22
Tosca

Joaquin looked down into the holding area of his new warehouse. With a settlement from the insurance company, and a loan from their bank, Joaquin had rebuilt a facility that took advantage of the improvements at the docks. The booms, pulleys and netting were sturdy and appreciated by the crew of stevedore's they'd hired, some of which had worked at his old warehouse. It had a larger refrigeration room to accommodate the expanding volume of beef destined for Britain and the United States, a covered receiving area where the horse-drawn carts hauling goods from the train could be unloaded and sent away without having to turn around. His father had been explicit, 'Move more goods in less time, Joaquin.'

He had hunted down his old accountant Pablo and lured him back with the promise of a bonus and a better salary. Although, the accounts and ledgers had been destroyed in the fire, Pablo had nevertheless managed to re-establish several old contracts by memory. Many former clients were persuaded to return to Joaquin's export business through an initial discount offer, losses to be absorbed by the bank loan. Under pressure, he worked long days and evenings, and time had passed quickly.

His leg had recovered as much as it was ever going to. He felt it when he assisted loading the heavy goods, filling in when a crew was short or a man was injured. He also felt it at times when he danced certain movements in Tango, but he'd learned to compensate.

He had returned from Spain to find Sofia introspective and distant. When she finally told him, what had happened to Tico, he held her tightly, through the night, into the early morning hours. 'My God—what a courageous woman!'

Through Tico's formative years she'd converted him from an illiterate street urchin to a capable bookkeeper, who could read and write, who had a future.

'Joaquin, do you think I could get him into a university?' Her intervention into the attempted assassination of Chief Falcon had ended in an orgy of blood and death, and the heavy burden of guilt weighed upon her. 'An innocent teenager *and woman, atwo* police officers, and several protestors payed the price.' Had it been worth it? 'Only God knew, and the price of doing nothing could have resulted in far worse,' he thought. And she was still trapped in Argentina, unable to move on with her life.

Then, a glimmer of hope. Feeling unusually troubled, he had sought out Father Devechio at the Metropolitan Cathedral and spoken of Sofia during his confession. His relationship was lustful, but he desperately wanted it to be love, a marriage with children. But she came with seemingly insurmountable complications. When he had described Sofia's tragic loss of her parents, Father Devechio had exclaimed 'My Lord forgive me, she is the niece of Senator Montserrat!'

Joaquin realised the Senator might have described his crimes in detail to his confessor, Father Devechio—and had asked him to do something which he could not. 'God will decide Sofia's fate, Joaquin. I cannot, nor can any priest, disclose a confession. That would be an offence to the church and I would be excommunicated—but more importantly, it would be an insult to God.'

There it was. He had never known a more principled person than Sofia, yet every institution seemed determined to betray her—the cantankerous judge in Jerez, the intransigent Captain of the Civil Guard, the police department, and now, even the church. He'd told her of his findings in Jerez, and cautioned her.

'The judge is a spiteful old man—he'd use flimsy evidence to order her execution.' So, she remained stuck in her purgatory, condemned to serve Lieutenant Machado, a man she despised, her future an impressionist haze of uncertainty.

But he wouldn't abandon her, as he loved her with all his heart. So, whatever her reasons were for refusing to marry him, 'Now is not the time,' he would be content with the way things were. What was it the strange gypsy woman had said? He'd taken his dinner on a flowered terrace in Jerez. There'd been a flamenco show, the dancing was spectacular from the beginning to its culmination, a blinding crescendo of tapping, clapping and chanting. The music had been hypnotic and foreboding. The dead crying out for justice, they say. He hadn't seen her approach, but all of a sudden she was there beside him, her gaze penetrating.

"I've heard Hugo Montserrat is dead."

"Yes," he said, somewhat disconcerted. "Did you know him?"

"Is she safe?"

Joaquin assumed she had been referring to Sofia. "Not entirely."

"Soon the fog will lift, and she will return."

Damned gypsy woman made no sense. Prophecies. Nothing he would mention to Sofia.

Sofia found herself as angry as the prostitutes over the announcement. Their monthly rent was increasing by 20 percent, Madam Josefina tentatively announced to the unruly assembly in the courtyard. Lieutenant Machado sat at a nearby table, seemingly disinterested with his legs crossed and boots on a table, but his presence very much part of the plan to prevent the protest getting riotous.

"I'm sorry, dearies—but you can't blame me. It's the city that raised its taxes and caused all this nonsense. Isn't that right, Lieutenant?" Josefina said.

"That's right," he said, not getting pulled into explanations.

"We have to increase our rates then—the customers will have to pay up," Hortense said.

"We can't do that," Sofia said. "We'll only make it worse for them. They're paying the rent increases as well—it's up 40 percent in some of the tenements. They won't be able to pay for our increase on top of that. They'll go elsewhere or not come at all."

A howl of laughter from the gaggle of prostitutes at the unintended pun caused Sofia's cheeks to redden, but she remained stoic.

"You've all got one thing on your minds don't you—you canker blossomed skuts," Madam Josefina said, coming to Sofia's defence. "What you can do is work a little harder to make things go quicker. Stop enjoying yourselves so much! I want 10 minutes back per customer from all of you. Play it right and they'll never notice." Josefina's voice had trailed off, giving away a lack of conviction.

"I really don't blame them. They're like everyone else living in the conventillos, the tenements—their hard-earned pay needed to go into savings and instead they landed in the landlord's pockets," Sofia said, while she and Josefina watched the others leave, grumbling away in conspiratorial groups.

"Now don't go down that road again dearie—there's nothing but trouble at the end of it."

"I'm beyond caring about my troubles now—I have to say something. I'm not an anarchist—it's just they're the only ones courageous enough to speak the truth plainly in their newspapers."

"Is there anything I can say to change your mind about this?"

"I have to—I've got to speak my mind." Sofia contemplated Madam Josefina's frustration. "Can you keep this from Lieutenant Machado?"

"Dearie I will do anything you want at this juncture. But maintain discipline and watch the ladies closely—they'll be tempted to double charge. The putrid spirit of mutiny reeks heavily at the moment—and I've no wish to be cut loose at sea like Captain Bligh."

Sofia's first article, targeting the burgeoning rent hikes implemented half way through the calendar year, appeared on page three of a daily called the Worker's Rebellion. It was a newspaper that was known, even amongst the anarchists, as being unnecessarily pugnacious towards the authorities and therefore likely to attract their attention. If Sofia had been one to question her decisions, she would have attributed it, in this case, to anger and frustration. But she was not one to question her decisions, and her point had been well-made that high rents impacted all worker's families and required a united response from the socialist and anarchist unions alike.

Her second article went a step further, with the assertion that the municipality only cared about collecting taxes, encouraging the landlords to stuff as many human beings into as few rooms as possible, and prioritising profit to the extent it endangered the health of its citizens. She went on to suggest that disease would spread amongst the children of the working class, 'consumption, yellow fever and a range of intestinal inflictions suffered by living so closely together', and that, as always, it was the role of women to manage the consequences, specifically to bear more children and lead shorter lives.

The article had appeared on the second page, its publisher pleased with what he'd read. Noting an increase in subscriptions amongst the unions, he decided her next article was deserving of the cherished front page. And Sofia did not disappoint. An appeal to their consciences, she'd decided, but she landed on calling the complacency of Argentina's ruling class for what it was—cruel indifference.

As long as the money fattened their bank accounts, they cared not. Her timing had been impeccable, her third article coinciding with the largest scale rent strike the country had known, with over 100,000 people withholding their rent. The police, intent on evicting the recalcitrant occupants, were turned back in droves by women swinging brooms or pouring scalding water on them from heights above. The newspaper's owner, Piero Ricci, was ebullient.

"Keep the articles coming—sales are up and I'm enjoying your castigation of the smug bourgeoise elites!"

"I've got another coming."

He looked at her contemplatively through eyes so dark she could not distinguish his pupils. They gave him a manic appearance. "I've noted that you have a disgust—or is it anger?—about the current state of affairs. Why did you choose this pseudonym, the Enraged Prostitute? You're not a prostitute at all—are you?"

"No—but I don't pretend to be any better. I make a living from their avails. I've come to know them—they're just human beings trying to eke out a living. The regulations placed on women make it impossible to do much else to make a decent wage. The laundress in a one room tenement, with six children and a husband that drinks his wages away—needs money for rent and food. The same for an unfortunate daughter who runs away from the squalor of her parent's home."

"A pimp convinces a woman that he will make her rich. The laws in this country discourage women from seeking education, and discourage employers from hiring them. They are funnelled into prostitution as a profession, and eventually say, 'Why not?' I understand that the world is not a fair place, but here, the authorities are at war with the less fortunate. The business of brothels and prostitutes—it's like any other. I'll be their voice over the rents—and I won't be passive about it because now I'm angry!" Sofia was surprised by the intensity of her own emotion. It wasn't like her, but so be it.

"You're the one."

"Pardon me?"

"You're angry, you're a woman, and you're the one. I've been in this business for 30 years. I publish disgust, outrage, injustice and everything else in between. But it hasn't made a gnat's difference. My life's ambitions have been for naught. I used to be a pacifist—but now I know that Johann Most was right. Change will only come about through revolutionary acts—acts of extreme, indiscriminate violence on the bourgeoisie class."

"There is a small group of us—three men—and we need a woman. Someone ready to lash out on behalf of the oppressed women of Buenos Aires. My newspaper is so popular right now, I can afford to do something I couldn't before—fund our instrument of change—propaganda by deed."

He hesitated, apparently reticent to explain his curious statement further. "Do you truly want to make a difference?"

"What do you want me to do?"

What else would she have said? 'Damn it to hell—not again!' Her association with anarchists was an endless fount of trouble. But out loud, "Of course, I'll help—I'll do whatever you ask, my love," Joaquin said. Exactly how he would help her, wasn't clear to him just yet. He had the uncomfortable sensation of being drawn towards something supernaturally evil. Sofia had described the meeting of Pierro Ricci's group, Ricci had done all the talking.

"From now on, codenames only—if we are caught, their symbolism will resonate with the masses. Myself—publisher, Diego—stevedore, Rocco—foundryman, Sofia—prostitute. You're to meet with the bombmaker—he's insisted on a woman alone. The Teatro Colon on its opening night, during the most fitting opera we could ever imagine—Tosca."

Then she'd gone to meet the bomb maker who'd said he trusted her; he'd read her articles. She'd told him the specifications, publisher, wanted sufficient lethality to kill 50 people in close proximity. Foundryman, was installing ironworks inside the theatre, he would hide it inside, to be retrieved during the show.

"I'll build you something similar to an Orsini bomb, but my own improved design. Have foundryman give you his lunchbox and bring it to me. I'll install it inside the lunchbox. It will need to be thrown—and land on a hard surface. The orchestra landing during the second break, just as they've cleared away. It will kill those closest—in the front rows."

'It was madness,' Joaquin thought. Her hand was on his face, her eyes searching his. "I'm sorry to bring you into this, Joaquin. I love you very much. I don't want you to get hurt, but if we do nothing, many good people will die."

"Let's think this through then. We have to be certain—why can't we report this to the police?"

"The investigation would fall to Lieutenant Machado. He will try to exploit this for his personal agenda or that of his boss. They tried to assassinate the chief of police in order to further their ambitions and failed. It would be naive to believe they would suddenly become altruistic, and protect citizens like they're supposed to."

"I don't trust them. He would force me to become their agent-provocateur within the group—furthering the plot—putting me at their mercy. If they don't stop the bombing, I'll have helped Ricci's group of criminals commit a massacre of innocent people."

"I understand the dilemma," Joaquin said. "What about the General? The one that had his men intervene with my favourite three thugs—God rest their souls."

"He will tell me to report it to the police, or he'll report it to the police himself. He was very clear about his limitations as a military officer. In that case, nothing would change. Lieutenant Machado would be placed in charge."

Joaquin saw that she was being patient and had thought this through completely. "I wish you'd told me sooner—perhaps before you met with an insane bomb maker."

"I had no choice—Ricci instructed me to, and I needed to confirm it was a serious plot. Otherwise, I may not have needed to involve anyone at all. If I refused to participate, they would carry it out with someone else. At least now, I'm in a position to sabotage their plan—somehow." She was silent for a moment. "There's a complication—you're not going to like it."

Joaquin dreaded what she was about to say. Sofia never exaggerated and never created unnecessary drama. "What is it?"

"I've been followed. I noticed him when I left the bombmaker's mechanical shop on Australia—a detective."

Joaquin nodded. He was pacing with his hand on his chin. He was good at resolving practical problems and was determined to come through for her, and those citizens whose lives were at stake. He thought of the danger they faced, but the danger didn't outweigh the alternative. He realized it really hadn't been a choice for either of them.

"I'll need you to do something for me, and I'll need Tony's help."

Vicente stood beside Commissioner De La Fuente, who was smoking a cigar, contemplating the view outside of his tall office windows.

"The Enraged Prostitute has garnered quite a following amongst the leagues of tenants—entirely logical as most of their leadership are women who concern themselves with paying rent. The articles are perceptive."

"I can handle her."

"I hope you're right. It was wise of us to stay out of the fray on the rent strikes. The uniforms really caught it from the ladies—they know how to handle their brooms," he said, chuckling.

"Chief Falcon is using our work to impress the President and the Senate Committee on Internal Security. It's doubly annoying to me, since he cut my budget in order to increase the size of the public order contingent—several detectives had to transfer back into regular policing duties. We're a shadow of our former selves. Unfortunately, he's in a position to claim all the glory, as Senator Montserrat is no longer around to sing my praises. I'm as far from the Chief's position as I've ever been."

"Following Sofia has turned up something of interest."

"How so?" De La Fuente's face was implacable through a cloud of cigar smoke.

"Piero Ricci—he's the publisher of the Worker's Rebellion, the one that publishes her articles. A detective pegged him as an extremist. His colleagues bet against it—the detective cashed in."

"I'm not following."

"She met with Giovanni Randazzo."

"The names are all starting to run together I'm afraid my boy." De La Fuente exhaled smoke slowly. "What's so special about him?"

"He's the railroad engineer—their explosives expert. He blew himself up—partially—while assembling Orsini bombs for the rebels in Rosario in the 1893 rebellion. He's easily recognised—one side of his face is mangled. She met with him at his mechanical shop after meeting with Ricci." Vicente waited patiently, until De La Fuente nodded with a wry smile.

"Ricci and Randazzo are connected?"

"A detective pulled up the customs record for Ricci. He arrived on a steamer that had departed from Genoa, Italy, October 18, 1880. The customs ledger shows Randazzo was on the same ship. It's not definitive. However, when the detective examined the court records, he found a notation where to find Randazzo following his release from prison. He was convalescing from his facial injuries at a residence here in Buenos Aires. The detective then proceeded to watch the residence and saw Ricci going in and out. Municipal records confirm it's Ricci's house."

"All this from following the Montserrat woman?"

"Yes."

"Why is she doing this?"

"She's become enraged like her alias suggests—that's my guess."

"Their target?"

"Remains to be seen. Randazzo was seen exiting his shop with a suitcase. A detective followed him to the train station and lost him in the crowd. He hasn't returned yet. If our theory is correct, he's gone somewhere to obtain explosives. He knows where to get them."

"Damned fine police work. I suppose we'll keep watching in order to identify everyone that's involved—the question being when to arrest them."

"If we decide to arrest them," Vicente said.

De La Fuente held him in his gaze for a moment. "I see," he said, looking back out his window. "A very astute point lad. The shoe is now on the other foot, so to speak. A bomb that killed innocent civilians would completely discredit Chief Falcon in light of his drastic cuts to the detective division. He's been bragging to senate and congressional committees alike that he's single-handedly brought the anarchist threat to its knees. You know—there's a sentiment within these committees that he's actually come down too hard on the anarchists—and that's likely to produce unwanted results, such as what you've just described. A force majeure such as this could change everything. I won't apprise the Chief just yet. Let's keep it to ourselves for now—keep our options open."

"As you wish."

Joaquin and Tony strolled at a leisurely pace along Australia, allowing themselves a discreet look at the entrance to the mechanical shop. There was a train yard taking up the north side of the street for several square blocks, and industrial shops faced out onto the street. Smoke belched out of chimneys poking skyward from corrugated metal roofs, and coal and soot covered the faces of the men at work. A cacophony of metal clanging and train whistles threatened to pierce their eardrums. Sofia's description of the street and shop had been uncanny.

"Where does she get her memory from Tony?"

"Promise me that if we get out of this alive, you'll marry her and take her back to Spain. My nerves are completely shot. Look—my hands are trembling— a musician's hands can't tremble! I need you both gone from my life—however, I'll gladly play at the wedding."

Tony's camaraderie cheered him up. "Thank you, for helping, I couldn't do this alone. I promise it will be a big wedding and there will be Tango! I'll hire an orchestra to play with you and you can conduct them. Look my friend!" Joaquin pointed to a cafe on a street corner. A young couple were dancing Tango in front of the tables while an older gentleman coaxed a mournful melody from a violin. "The youngsters have taken up the Tango now—it's broken free of the brothels."

"My dear friend—for your information it's already broken free of Argentina and is apparently the rage in Paris. Our good friend Martina, la Comptesse, left the country with a young lover. He's now making a living teaching Tango in the Parisian salons."

"Can we claim credit for this?"

"Let's stay humble for now—and remain alive. If we're successful at those two endeavours—then we'll claim our due."

Once they'd passed a good distance from the entranceway, they looked back. It was a busy street with enough pedestrian traffic that they didn't stand out. Horse-drawn carts, heavily laden with equipment for the shops, traversed the street without regard for right of way, or concern for pedestrians, in a hurry to their destinations.

Joaquin concentrated, trying to discern any conceivable form of traffic convention within the pandemonium before him.

"You're nodding to yourself like a village idiot," Tony said. "And you're standing in manure."

Joaquin looked downward and found his friend wasn't joking. He shook his left boot distractedly to dislodge some stubborn remnants, and suddenly, his thoughts crystallised. "I know what to do!"

It was Monday, May 18, exactly one week prior to the grand opening of the Teatro Colon—and although Sofia's outward demeanour never showed it, she was racked with doubt.

'I can't let anyone die. If I have to, I'll drop the bomb myself in a safe place.' She thought of Joaquin's reassuring words, 'You have to trust me Sofia—this will work. I swear to you!' He was always overconfident—only to have his plans go awry. But it was part of his charm that he could adapt readily and laugh about it. He would say anything to reassure her, and would risk his own life to help her if he had to—but she didn't want him hurt again. So, she had listened to his plan intently, identified all assumptions from the weak to the strong, subjected them to a merciless inquisition, and found herself convinced it had a reasonable chance of success. It was all she could ask for in the circumstances.

'—assume you were followed by detectives—then they saw you enter the bombmaker's mechanical shop. Assume they know who the bomb maker is and what he does. It stands to reason that they believe you're part of a bomb plot, having met with such an individual. In this case, their first opportunity to arrest you will be when you're carrying an item, presumably the bomb, away from the shop. That gives them evidence that you and he have contrived to commit a mass murder—and they've put a stop to it.'

'They must be watching the bombmaker's shop. If they don't arrest you at that point—then assume that they want to see where you bring the bomb to identify what your target is and if others are involved—that would also be a good time to put a stop to things. If nothing happens once you have taken the bomb away and it has been brought to the Teatro Colon, then your intuition was right—they're up to something nefarious, perhaps even letting the incident follow its course. Obviously, none of these scenarios suit our purposes.'

The day before, she'd received the note signed publisher. The package was ready to be picked up. The note also said that foundryman, had only two days of work left on site. 'He would be stalling, polishing the decorative ironworks he'd helped install,' she thought. His opportunities to hide the bomb in an accessible location at the theatre were rapidly dissipating and she had no choice, for the plan to work it had to be now. Her mind wandered to the memory of her brutal arrest all those years ago in Jerez—knocked from her horse and interrogated for hours. She tried to think of something else, 'Focus, Sofia!' But the thought made her stomach churn, and the nausea now remained.

She had a lot of walking to do, choosing to wear her sturdy boots. She was meeting Diego, stevedore, at the Plaza Herrera at the east end of Australia near the shop. From there, she would proceed alone so as not to be seen disobeying the bomb maker's strict instructions. She would only have to carry the heavy lunch box to where Diego was waiting, then he would take it, she assumed.

From there, they had a long walk northward, traversing Avenida de Mayo and continuing a block further to the tenement where Rocco, foundryman, resided. Rocco would take it into the theatre and hide it in the ladies washroom on the fifth floor, where the less affluent watched from, standing tickets only.

"The furthest cubicle from the door—I'll place it behind the toilet within the sitting box. You would have to be on your knees and look directly in to see it—and nobody will want to do that," Rocco had said.

Sofia had almost laughed out loud, thinking she would have to use it beforehand. That day was one week from today, and if it came to it, it meant Lieutenant Machado was letting the bomb attack play itself out. She welcomed the idea that she'd be intercepted by detectives when she left the bombmaker's mechanical shop, a long distance from the theatre, and that the police would take possession of the bomb and arrest all the conspirators. It would be over and everyone would be safe. But in her heart, she knew it wouldn't happen.

Plaza Herrera was small, and she saw Diego as she approached from the north along Herrera. He was tall with rugged, handsome features, but he was always angry. He was pacing back and forth, fidgety, and it made him stand out. She wondered if she was going to have to reassure him.

"I thought you changed your mind and weren't coming!"

"The time for second thoughts was long ago. Are you alright?"

"What? Yes, of course, I'm alright. What are you implying?"

"You're acting nervous. It would be best if you looked like everyone else loafing around."

"And I suppose you're not nervous at all—is that it?"

"Wait here. Don't come any closer in case he decides to look around before giving me the bomb. Once I have it, I'll bring it here and give it to you. Then we'll walk back together to give it to foundryman."

Diego nodded, shoved his hands deep into his pockets, and leaned against a bench.

"Get going then," he said.

Sofia took a breath, straightened her skirt, looked westward down Australia and walked towards the shop.

Sofia forced herself to remain implacable as she returned from the mechanical shop toward Diego. He was in the same position, hands in his pockets, one foot tucked behind his thigh, leaning against the cement garden wall in the shade of jacaranda trees. As she continued her return eastward along Australia, she caught a furtive movement in a darkened doorway near the intersection with Universidad. A tall man in an incongruent suit with a familiar cane had emerged for a fraction of a second before melting back into the shadow. Lieutenant Machado's profile could never be mistaken. She wouldn't have noticed him had she not been scanning potential hiding spots. She had learned how their surveillance worked.

He stayed where he was as she crossed the intersection and continued towards Diego. She wondered if this was the moment she would be arrested. Would he wait until she was with Diego? Or when she handed him the lunch box? Part of her still longed for this to occur, the police acting in the interests of the community. It would have been reassuring in that sense at least. But she knew to a certainty it wouldn't happen, making it easier to put on a facade of confidence.

"How heavy is it?" Diego asked.

"My arms are falling off," she said. For the last 50 metres, she'd had to hold the lunch box with two hands. The handle was biting into the flesh of her palms.

"Why is it soldered shut?" Diego asked, his voice rising. He was examining the latches.

"The bomb maker insisted—otherwise we'd open it and blow ourselves up. A face like his is very convincing talking about such things."

"I suppose. What's this mark," he asked, pointing at a very small circle, with an upside down 'A' figure stencilled inside of it.

Sofia looked at him. "That's his signature—like a painting."

They set off on the long trek north through the city. Sofia never once looked back, for fear of causing Diego to become more paranoid than he already was. She would lose control if Diego saw that they were being followed. She needed to follow through to the end. And there was Joaquin, 'My love,'—and Tony to think of. She had to report the plot somehow, and get her role in the matter into an official record. On the other hand, the minute Lieutenant Machado and De La Fuente learned that she had reported their deliberate failure to intervene, they would have to kill her to silence her, as well as any witnesses.

With the torrent of possibilities to think through, she hadn't noticed the time pass.

But as she and Diego traversed Avenida de Mayo, she knew what she had to do. She would send a message that couldn't be ignored. *'It will give me a chance at least.'*

Chapter 23
Magnum Opus

"The Teatro Colon—that's the target," Vicente said. "The official opening is May 25, this Monday."

"Is it now," De La Fuente said. "An impressive setting for wanton killing—impressive indeed. How exactly do you know this?"

"Ricci has street urchins delivering his notes. I paid the little buggers off. Despite being married, he maintains three mistresses—all of whom are prostitutes. I've learned more about manipulating women from him than from a decade tending to your brothel," Vicente said, making De La Fuente chuckle. "But there were notes to other intellectuals of his stripe. He ridiculed them for their lack of action—and implied he's on the cusp of something momentous."

"The notes were delivered to their intended recipients following your examination?"

"Of course—including one to Sofia Montserrat. It said the package was ready. He signed it 'publisher,' a codename—implying a secret plan, and foundryman—to whom the package was delivered."

"The package is a bomb?"

"Most certainly. I followed her—she picked it up at Randazzo's workshop—it's hidden in a worker's lunchbox. She met Diego Salvador nearby and gave it to him."

"Just yourself?"

"Yes—no other detectives know that there's a bomb in play."

"Good. Did you intercept any notes between him and Randazzo?"

"No."

"A shame—that would have been stronger evidence against Ricci. Diego Salvador—where have I heard that name before?"

"He's been identified in police reports. He's well known to us—a stevedore. One of their most vicious—always at the front of the strike lines—fighting with our men. I owe him a debt myself—it's been a decade." Vicente was pointing to the scar on his temple.

"How convenient."

"The bomb was then handed to someone I encountered at the brothel. He brought it directly to the theatre."

"—and who was that."

"Foundryman. I don't know his actual name yet—but I do know he's the type that enjoys inflicting pain. I was called by Madam Josefina. He'd taken liberties, slapping Hortense's ass—in the exact same spot repeatedly—until she couldn't stand it any longer and screamed. He had a particular expression when I winded him with the butt of my club and beat him—as if he enjoyed that as well." Vicente contemplated this. "The three of them plotting this act of murder makes perfect sense." He had said this almost to himself.

De La Fuente was only half-listening. "I've got nothing to lose and everything to gain. I've made my decision. Let this run its course." Then he looked directly at Vicente. "Be ready to intervene after the explosion—an immediate round up of the suspects, detailed confessions, will make for quick trials. We'll impress our political masters and the newspapers with the ensuing investigation. Nevertheless, the hounds will be baying for blood, and only Chief Falcon's head will satisfy their thirst. The anarchists get their glory—I get my overdue appointment. Shite my boy—everyone's happy!"

Monday, 25 May. Vicente read the article on the front page of a copy of the Worker's Rebellion brought to him by a bootblack.

'J'accuse! As the French high military command illegally conspired against the Jewish officer Dreyfuss—one of their own brothers—falsely condemning him of treason—so to the insidious stench of fratricide has infected the Police of the Capital. Senior officers contrived to assassinate their leader Colonel Falcon! This occurred in front of us all, during International Worker's Day celebrations last year, when a mounted officer resembling Falcon was shot. This caused Colonel Falcon to order the poorly informed rank and file police officers to fire into the crowd and kill several innocent people.

'Information has been suppressed by the President and the blame for the slaughter has been cast on a rogue cell of anarchists. But it was no rogue cell of anarchists—it was a rogue cell of clandestine police agents! This can no longer be swept under the rug for the sake of President Alcorta's political fortunes. There are eye witnesses now willing to come forward—'

'Damn her!' It was two days old. How had she known and who were the witnesses? It was a problem that he'd have to address later. He had followed Sofia from the brothel to the park facing the front west entrance of the theatre, Plaza Lavalle, where she met Diego Salvador. He watched them from a distance. Vicente had little experience with explosives and was using what he would describe as informed guesswork. If they went into the theatre, he assumed it was to deploy the infernal device themselves, either by lighting fuse caps on dynamite held in the lunch box or by throwing an infamous Orsini bomb, as had been done on numerous occasions in Europe, producing an impact that would set it off. Neither seemed all that wise, but who was he to judge. Perhaps people around them would intervene and stop them—no, they wouldn't be able to hold Diego. 'He's an intemperate brute—he'll fight like a wounded bull!'

He was going to stay outside and observe. Sofia would be impossible to pick out of a thick crowd of panicked people exiting, but he wasn't concerned about her. Diego was an exceptionally large man and would be much easier to spot, so he would concentrate on him. He was looking forward to it, rubbing the scar on his temple. 'Long overdue.'

For a disappointing moment, it appeared that Diego was losing his nerve. But then Sofia, 'Always Sofia,' said something to Salvador which caused him to turn sharply, and they proceeded through the entrance, along with a few thousand unsuspecting opera goers in tailored suits and bowlers, fancy dresses and ostentatious feather hats. A cheerful crowd for a cheerful occasion about to experience the most unpleasant surprise of their privileged lives. 'Like sheep to the abattoir.'

He thought of himself as a wolf. Unlike his more altruistic predecessors, who had executed the responsibilities of the position as a shepherd, protecting the citizens of the city. He had no such compunction. He was prepared to do whatever he must. He owed everything to the Commissioner and didn't want it to end. He would rather die than do yeoman's work. 'A baker? A blacksmith?

How about a stevedore hauling sacks all day—no.' When De La Fuente became the Chief, he would promote Vicente again.

All the way from the street gangs of Pigalle Square. 'Imagine that,' he thought.

He begrudgingly admired Sofia's pluckiness in the same way. Four years ago, when he'd first brought her to Madam Josefina's, and a few times since, he'd thought she was a dead woman. Yet here she was. 'I underestimate her,' he thought. Did she have something to do with the unknown men that had shot the three Spaniards, on the day they had tried to kill Chief Falcon?

If so, how did she know about it, and who were these witnesses now willing to come forward? The intervention by armed men remained a mystery to him, as he'd killed Javier and Tico, both of whom had known too much to leave alive. He pondered this riddle to the point of annoyance. That was a year ago. Why is she choosing to make public allegations now? No matter, she was now too dangerous with her latest article. Her time had come.

But he was uneasy about something, and he wasn't normally one to worry. He'd settled in at a vantage point where he could see both the front entrance where most people would escape and the side of the building where others would escape from smaller doors. If they exited from the other side, he was out of luck. His thoughts returned to Sofia. There was something wrong, three true miscreants—and her. You're either a killer or you're not.

But it was too late for further rumination, as doors burst open, and hysterical masses of people in their evening frippery spilled out. He was taken unawares, as he hadn't heard the explosion. 'Christ look at them all—pathetic bleating sheep!' He strode through them in the opposite direction—brutally knocking anyone in his path out of the way or onto the ground. 'Where is he, God damn it—there!'

He saw the burly stevedore running westward along Tucoman across Cerito, away from the crowd. Diego looked back furtively for pursuers, the sign of a guilty man. Vicente broke into a sprint, approaching him from an angle so as to flank him. Diego would not expect it, did not expect it, until his movement drew Diego's attention and he ran into an alley—which turned into a dead end.

Vicente stopped his pursuit and watched the hefty stevedore turn around with his hands up. They were trembling.

"Oh look—a copper. You all alone? Think you're going to bring me in, do you? You don't have the guts to try—what are you doing—"

Vicente had drawn his .45 Colt revolver from its shoulder holster and pointed it at Diego's heart. For a moment their eyes met. But Vicente couldn't stand people begging for their lives—he just didn't have the patience for it, even if the vengeful delight of the moment demanded savouring. The large bullet leaving the barrel caused a thunderous crack, and thump. As it traversed the breadth of Diego Salvador's chest, its kinetic energy unimpeded, it blew a good part of his heart, lungs, and other contents out through the exit cavity it left in his back. This caused another round of shrieking amongst the panicked crowd, desperately seeking sanctuary from the chaos.

Vicente stood over Salvador, as if to make sure he wasn't going to rise again, then turned and strode double-time to the theatre. Horrified onlookers created an unobstructed path for him, as if he'd just parted the Red Sea. He ran through the front door, taking the carpeted steps upward three at a time.

Vicente continued into the grand hall and stopped. It was completely void of people, alive or dead, to his growing consternation. He walked a little further, taking in its transcendental magnificence, so beautiful, and unexpectedly unmarred. 'It's heaven—a place I'm not supposed to see.'

Sofia took no chances. Early in the second act she retrieved the lunchbox from the stall in the women's washroom early, in case of line-ups, and returned with it awkwardly, under her shawl. She drew some curious looks when she handed it to Diego, but for the most part people were absorbed in the performance. The fifth floor was standing only, and the dress in the section was far more sensible, 'Working class.'

'But societal distinctions melted away in face of theatrical performance,' she thought. These beautiful people were as thrilled with the singing, costumes, and story, as those watching from other levels and the front seats. Their evening was about to be ruined, but she'd done all she could. As the second act finished and the orchestra cleared away, she looked at Diego, who was watching closely for her signal with a fanatical glimmer in his eyes. She nodded and walked away. She heard indignant muttering, 'Watch out,' 'what are you doing?' That quickly transformed to a din of shouts and screams, "It's a bomb!" Then she ran managing to get to the side doors before most—and as the heavy rush of a panicked crowd closed in on her, she exited amongst them.

She hastened toward Paraguay, where Joaquin was waiting with a coach. It was the same coach she had seen a few days ago, with Tony at the reins, and

Joaquin arranging crates nearby, when she'd looked down Australia, as she had approached the bombmaker's mechanical shop. It had reassured her to see them there, and fortified her resolve.

The explosion and the shrapnel will kill 50 people within its proximity, the bomb maker had said in the shop, as publisher had wanted. "It requires a significant shock—throw it from the fifth level onto the orchestral landing, after the musicians have cleared away. But don't drop it—you'd be tempting fate."

Exiting the mechanical shop, she had glanced towards Joaquin, ran her hand through her hair, the confirmation that she had the bomb, and started her return towards Diego along Australia. As she approached the intersection with Vieytes, the coach had passed in front of her slowly and turned south, blocking her momentarily from Diego's watchful gaze, and she had handed the bomb to Joaquin, who was leaning out the window closest to her. He handed her the duplicate lunchbox, with the latches soldered shut. They'd added a small inscription, a circle around an upside down 'A,' a small measure of safety to ensure they never mistook one lunchbox for the other. He had teetered uncertainly for a moment, which would have been comical in any other circumstances, and she thought her heart had stopped. But no explosion ensued, and she had continued towards Diego, seeing Lieutenant Machado in the shadows of the doorway soon after. She had put her faith in Joaquin's idea and it had worked. The rest was up to her.

The theatre was completely void of people, alive or dead, to Vicente's growing consternation. His eyes were drawn to the layers of seating stretching upwards, to the grand arches demarcating the fifth and final floor. He scanned downwards towards the orchestral platform, where a single shiny object stood offensively upright, centred near the front row of seats, mocking him. A lunch box. What has she done?

Approaching the coach, Sofia threw herself into Joaquin's arms and for a moment they clung desperately to each other. It had worked. When they arrived at his warehouse to regroup, she told him she had to return to Madam Josefina's Social House. They'd kept the innocent patrons of the Teatro Colon safe, but for how long she wasn't sure.

"It's too dangerous for you to return to the brothel—you don't know how Lieutenant Machado will react. He could be irrational!"

"Listen to me, Joaquin. You're a good man. I don't know how you did what you did—I had visions of all of us dying horribly as you struggled with the bomb." They laughed with relief, recalling Joaquin's ill-timed clumsiness. Joaquin would do anything to protect her. But she didn't want it to end like last time, a madman hunting them down in a burning warehouse trying to kill them all. "Your plan worked. Now you have to trust me."

She remained steadfast. She longed to stay with Joaquin, but she'd be quickly found out when Lieutenant Machado came looking for her. As it stood, Lieutenant Machado believed her to be fully complicit in the attack. He would either think the bomb had been faulty, or more likely, that she had sabotaged the plot and found a way to render the bomb inert. 'In either case, he could arrest her, or just simply make her disappear,' she thought. She needed the intended audience of her article to find her, quickly. On Saturday, three long days ago, she'd convinced Ricci to publish one last article, the accusal, and he'd been more than willing. With it, she had sent a message, to attract attention at the highest political level, the President, and make them come to her. But she had to return to Madam Josefina's Social House. 'How else will they find me?'

She recognised the man they had sent, Gabriel Chavez's assistant, and he was speaking to her with youthful arrogance and official letter in hand. He told her that they knew it was her making the outrageous allegations. Who 'they' were, he left a mystery. 'Consider this an official summons. 25 Avenida de Mayo. It's the building with the giant clock above the door.'

She watched him strut towards the exit, apparently quite pleased with himself, and then she opened the note:

Señora Sofia Montserrat

Your attendance required Wednesday, 27 May, 1 pm, for clarification and conceivably investigation of allegations submitted against unspecified senior officers of the Police of the Capital. This ministry requires your personal attestation to the veracity of your public statements prior to further action. I look forward to your cooperation in this important matter.

Señor Ernesto Torrente—Attorney

Senior Legal Counsel to the Minister of the Interior

Wednesday, 27 May. "This is an unexpected twist, my boy," De La Fuente said.

The early morning sun was shining directly through the open windows, making Vicente squint. He'd only gotten a couple of hours sleep, and less than that the night before. His head throbbed. "It depends how you look at it."

"It was a rhetorical question," De La Fuente said, irritably.

"As I see it—everything remains the same, only there aren't any dead citizens."

"I was rather looking forward to the pompous asses receiving their just deserts. But go ahead—explain."

"Yesterday we detained a typesetter. We followed him leaving the building where Ricci publishes the Worker's Rebellion. We twisted his arm a little. This unfortunate fellow told us that there was a manifesto set to print on yesterday's front page, Ricci insisted it had to go in the night before—Monday evening."

"Oh my."

"It claims responsibility for the bombing of the theatre."

"—which seals Ricci as part of the conspiracy," De La Fuente said, perking up.

"Indeed—so I ordered a raid on the press. 10 of his workers are now under detention—being written up for the minister's review. They'll be deported."

"Good work lad—continue." The irritable edge had disappeared from De La Fuente's voice.

"The manifesto confirms the lunch box contains an unexploded bomb. It's not a hoax, as the headlines are saying." Vicente pointed at the morning editions of La Prenza—The Press and La Nación sitting on De La Fuente's desk. Both newspapers carried front page stories speculating on the intent of the metal lunch box thrown so recklessly into the orchestra pit on the opening night of the Teatro Colon. Both articles implied gross incompetency by the police department in two respects; failing to prevent the hoax, and then grossly over-reacting with the summary execution of the culprit, a stevedore, who was probably just drunk.

"They'll have to eat their words," De La Fuente said. "I'm going to frame the articles on my wall—I'll gloat whenever I have one of the bloodsuckers in here. What about the bomb maker?"

"Randazzo was arrested a couple of hours ago. He'll be interrogated once the search of his workshop is complete. He had a schematic drawing of an Orsini bomb—his own variation. Dynamite is the primary explosive—several sticks are resting on fragile tubes of nitroglycerin. Concussive shock will drive the dynamite into the tubes and will blow anyone nearby straight to hell. It's conceived to be particularly deadly—by scattering metal shrapnel at high velocity—like bullets."

"And where exactly is this infernal device right now?"

"In my office."

De La Fuente snorted, coughing smoke. "Has it been examined?"

"The latches are soldered shut."

"For what purpose?"

"That's the first thing I intend to ask Randazzo."

They were interrupted by insistent knocking. When Vicente finally relented and opened the door, they were met by the frazzled executive secretary from Chief Falcon's office.

"Good Lord—what is it already?" De La Fuente asked.

"Commissioner—the Chief wishes to see you right now."

"Be a good fellow and tell him I'm a little busy resolving the most heinous attempt of mass murder this city has ever seen."

"I'm afraid he's quite insistent, Commissioner. It has to be now."

"What could he possibly need at this very instant?"

"Have you been living under a rock? There's been a public allegation against unspecified senior officers of the police department. An anarchist mischief-maker, writing under the pseudonym of the Enraged Prostitute, claims there was a conspiracy to assassinate the Chief himself." Reacting to the bewildered expression on De La Fuente's haggard face, he added, "Last year—during the Mayday riot."

Vicente watched Commissioner De La Fuente limp away to face the Chief, with the secretary at his heels. He hadn't had a moment to tell De La Fuente about her latest article. 'How did she know? Damn her!' Hortense had told him Sofia was up to something, sneaking around in rooms on the second floor where she had no business. He had dismissed it as Hortense trying to cause trouble for Sofia, who she didn't like. But he had seen Sofia come down the stairs, after his meeting with Matias, Emilio and Javier. 'The vent!' 'She is a clever hag,' he thought.

Hortense had sent him a message the day before by way of their newly adopted street urchin. 'She's back.' But he'd been too preoccupied with arrests of Ricci and all the men working at his press location. Today's priority had been

Randazzo, the bomb maker, the only person who could tell him why the bomb failed to explode.

He hadn't decided exactly what to do with Sofia yet anyway. She could've been arrested with the rest of them—but it seems he'd dodged a bullet by leaving her for last. He couldn't risk taking her into custody. 'Too many detectives would have access to the woman.' She had to die, somewhere away from prying eyes. He would intercept her himself the next time he had an opportunity, as she left the brothel.

But first Randazzo and his dud of a bomb. He walked with his usual deliberate stride to the holding area in the basement where they kept prisoners for interrogation. A detective had placed Randazzo in the small interview room, manacled to a bloodstained wooden desk. Randazzo was seated in a chair with his legs splayed, his swarthy skin made all the darker by soot and grease. They were both sweating profusely. Vicente sat in the chair opposite Randazzo and studied his face, deeply scarred on the left side, a beaten, compliant gaze.

"Tell me about the bomb."

"I've already told him everything," Randazzo said, looking with trepidation at the calloused hands of the large detective behind Vicente.

"Tell me again."

"It's a variation on the Orsini, an explosive device that uses concussive force to detonate. They wanted assurances of lethality for the closest 50 people. The old design wouldn't do. So instead, I used dynamite with tubes of nitroglycerin pressed underneath it. It was placed in a forged iron shell, packed with metal pellets, and bolted together. Sufficient downward impact would cause the tubes to shatter—the nitroglycerin would explode and set off the dynamite."

"And all this was placed in the lunch box?"

"Yes."

"Dear maestro—your magnum opus didn't work worth a damn—it didn't explode."

"Then why am I getting beaten up?"

The thunderclap of Vicente's slap rocked the prisoner's head. Randazzo was groaning, panicked, sobbing, even the burly detective had winced.

"Be careful Lieutenant—he won't be able to talk anymore."

"I've done this before."

Vicente squeezed the scarred face with a large, bony hand. "Why didn't it explode?"

"My bomb will explode."

"Your bomb was thrown from the 5th floor balcony onto the orchestra landing and it didn't explode."

"Then it wasn't my bomb."

Vicente froze imperceptibly, still holding his face, sensing he was on the verge of solving a childish riddle. He just needed a few quiet minutes to sit and think it through.

But now somebody was hammering on the door. The burly detective opened it. "What?"

"There are two men here from the Ministry of the Interior—they've asked to see the bomb and Lieutenant Machado. They're going to his office. The old fellow's really worked up about something—he's carrying a sledgehammer!"

Chapter 24
Five Days of May

Wednesday, 27 May. When the stenographer, an elderly but spry woman with her hair in a tight bun and small spectacles perched on her nose, had settled into her corner, and Sofia Montserrat in hers, Ernesto closed the door and shuffled towards his own. 'This last week had been a test of his fortitude,' he thought, 'one thing after another.' Saturday—the accusatory article that set off all the fuss, Sunday—summoned front and centre before the Minister, Monday—his evening ruined by the strange hoax at the Teatro Colon, Tuesday—arranging the attendance of the woman now before him, and Wednesday?

He'd just been informed that she was in possession of an Orsini bomb. He'd been rattled by her statement, but something about Sofia Montserrat compelled him to continue with the interview, despite having stepped well outside the bounds of his inquiry.

He looked at the questions he had prepared, sighed, and set the writing pad aside. "Perhaps you should explain yourself," he said.

"The bomb was intended for the opening night of the Teatro Colon. It's disguised as a lunchbox. I switched it for a look-alike."

Ernesto found himself rendered speechless.

"I wish to get my personal involvement on the public record, otherwise I expect to be killed, or charged, or both."

Ernesto's mind had engaged in two activities, and his thought process slowed, as if bogged down in mud. He could only half listen as Sofia Montserrat spoke, as the other half of his mind insisted on reliving select memories, some cherished, others not so much. The first was recent and vivid, an everyday worker's lunchbox, landing with a tinny thump, skidding to a halt on the orchestral landing, in front of him and his granddaughter. 'Had she said it was meant to be a bomb?'

He heard her speak again, and the furious scratching of the stenographer taking her shorthand notes.

"There are two distinct incidents, both of which involve serious criminal acts by senior officials of the police department, Lieutenant Vicente Machado, with whom I'm very familiar, and Commissioner De La Fuente, whom I've never met."

Ernesto recalled the sight of Lieutenant Machado running up the front stairs of the theatre, as he had been exiting, clutching his granddaughter in his arms.

"Go on," he said, in someone else's voice.

"—My employment at Madam Josefina's Social House—three former soldiers from Spain had been hired to conduct certain clandestine activities—I managed to eavesdrop on directions given to them by Lieutenant Machado—they were to shoot Chief Falcon while he was on horseback—International Worker's Day 1907—"

But his mind was overworked, churning too much information around, and he could only process snippets of her statement. Then something else encroached on his thoughts, and pried its way in. Memories grown vague, rising to the surface in bits and pieces.

A quarter of a century ago, a spry 35-year-old version of himself—hearing the news.

"They're going to build an opera house!" Dashing into the formal dining room of their modest townhouse located in the heart of the city, to hold hands with his children and his wife, and dance like mad fools in a circle.

A 40-year-old version of himself pulling strings to secure the humble position of vice chair of the project committee, soliciting design proposals from prestigious architects, a task falling well outside of his normal duties. A favour called in through his wife's influential father, who never liked him or his vocation—and wasn't afraid to say it—closed the deal. His glee, listening to the great Italian architect Francesco Tamburini, describe initial concept designs.

1890—A bitter version of himself sobbing into his wife's arms. The country's financial crash had sunk all hope of its construction. Hours of gloomy dismay, listening to heated debates in the congress on the proposals submitted by the senate finance committee. The project's detractors scoring jarring body blows to the inordinately expensive construction boondoggle, compounded by the impecunious state of the nation's finances.

A 46-year-old version of himself growing cynical, gazing forlornly at the skeletal structure resting on an immense concrete foundation sitting still and silent, the construction frozen. Hope diminishing again three years later, when civic-minded groups began demanding the abandonment and demolition of the eye sore at the centre of the city.

The 52-year-old version of himself, a once dark beard gone grey, hearing the President issue a second decree to continue the project with its original terms, offered hope yet again. Although, the youthful enthusiasm once manifested by dancing and glorious, celebratory love making with his beloved wife—once children were put to bed—had given way to a more sober and fatalistic rendition.

"Here's hoping my darling," a clink of their wine glasses with a brief, but satisfying, kiss on the lips.

Yet progress was made and he occasionally allowed himself to dream, a necessary distraction from a job growing dull from three decades of practice. He barely managed to retain his involvement in the project when the federal funding schemes were turned over to the municipality. His ministry was reduced to overseeing the account with the national bank, but for Ernesto, it was enough.

His most bittersweet memory, turn of the century and convinced the project finally had unstoppable momentum, returning home to share his thoughts with his cherished wife of thirty-five years, only to meet the family doctor and the tears of his grown children as they hugged him. It was a heart attack, they said. They had only just become grandparents to their infinite joy. Devoid of her love, he survived the loneliness of the following years through an endless deluge of grandchildren. He revelled in the role of a recalcitrant grandfather fostering the bad habits he and his wife had been unable to expunge from their own children. 'She would have approved,' he thought.

As a widower, he became more patient with the vicissitudes of the hard luck project, barely evincing a scoff when news of the horrific murder of the project's chief architect made the headlines in 1904. Details emerged of a salacious love triangle, in which the architect barged in on his wife and her lover inflagrante delicto, and he was fatally shot. He died with revised plans for the Teatro Colon in his head. As could only be expected, the ensuing architect found that the theatre's electrical design would burn it to the ground if not changed. Its redesign would delay the completion by yet another two years, which Of course, meant four.

But at last the moment was here. Opening night, Monday, 25 May 1908, and what could possibly go wrong? His favourite grandchild, not by coincidence the oldest, was showing promise with her classical singing lessons at the ripe age of eight. She had taken a keen interest in the opera, and was accompanying Ernesto on his weekly forage to the early showing of the operatic theatres on Corrientes.

The fragmented thoughts were now accelerating, swirling like a thunderous tornado in his head. Clearer memories finally emerged, owing to their recency. His outing with his favourite granddaughter to the Teatro Colon and the wondrous magic of it all—opening night! Passing under the fine green iron canopy draped over the entrance way facing Libertad. He walked with his granddaughter up the marble steps, admonishing her to stay on the red carpet, while pointing out the frescos on the soaring ceilings. On entry to the ground floor level, continuing toward their expensive orchestral seats at the front, the magnificent ceiling chandelier caught her attention, to his immense pleasure. He remembered its cost. He guided her to her seat amongst the throngs of men in their formal attire and uniforms, and the ladies in their gala dresses.

The orchestra struck the first chords of the overture and the curtain was drawn to reveal the church setting. Ernesto's spirit soared watching the fine young men and women of Buenos Aires, the children of established Argentine families and European immigrants that had flourished during its unprecedented growth, playing the violin and sundry other wind instruments while Angelotti, the escaped political prisoner, sang recitative verse, adorned in ragged, bloodied clothes. The first act introduced Ernesto's entranced granddaughter to the jealous Tosca and her well-intentioned lover Cavaradosso, and the plot had bewitched them all by the time of the first intermission.

"—Pierro wanted it to be thrown once a portion of the opera was done—when the audience was completely drawn into the drama—a brutal, murderous shock to the enemy. He chose the second intermission—," Ernesto heard her speaking, feint in the background, but his mind refused to let the memory go.

They'd been happy to sit through the first break while his jabbering granddaughter peppered him with questions of every scene they'd just enjoyed. The second act just as suspenseful as the first, the sinister police chief Scarpia threatening to execute Cavaradosso if she didn't do his bidding and betray her handsome lover.

As the second intermission was signalled by the curtain closing, he was thinking about walking the halls and perhaps treating himself to a weak, 'Hell make it strong,' alcoholic beverage, but perhaps not, thinking of the bother of a line-up while keeping an eye on his rambunctious granddaughter.

"—he wanted it to kill at least 50 people—"

The young men and women of the orchestra, and the odd middle-aged one as well, shuffled the musical scores on their stands and cleared away from the raised landing for their break. Ernesto and others looked upwards because of an unseemly commotion in an upper balcony, where working-class people would have purchased standing tickets. He saw flickers of light reflecting off of a metallic object that had been lobbed from the very same balcony with breath-taking finesse.

It rotated gracefully as it fell through its arc of motion, landed with a sharp thud on the closest edge of the orchestral platform, and skidded to a halt directly in front of him and his granddaughter. He'd shielded her as it had arced towards them, and was relieved to see it come up short. 'A lunchbox?' Some damn philistine had thrown a metal lunchbox onto the orchestral landing. He stared at it, just a few short meters away, fixating on a bizarre inscription, a small circle surrounding an upside down 'A'. A few disgusted curses ensued, until a woman screamed that it was a bomb.

That brief second of quiet disbelief then transformed into terror-fuelled chaos. Shrieks reverberated around the acoustically perfect, horseshoe design of the auditorium. Men and women tripped in their haste to rise from their seats and distance themselves from the stage, causing an infuriating pile-up of squirming people blocking his path. Ernesto forced his aging body to move—'do something!'

He pushed his granddaughter forward, looking for some means of escape through the writhing pile of clumsy fools, clawing and scratching in their panic to extract themselves. Unable to make headway he did the only thing he could think of, and wrapped himself in a protective embrace around the girl, with his back towards the bomb, the infernal machine, the lunch box, whatever it was, and waited for the deadly blast. Nothing. Tears welled in his eyes for the un-lived life of his granddaughter. Nothing.

'Run, you old fool!' Scooping up the crying, startled girl in his arms, he ran up the aisle that had suddenly cleared of retreating bodies. Nothing. Too soon, 'get further away,' to feel any relief. But he made it through the doors at the back of the auditorium with his granddaughter in his arms and thought they were safe. They were alive, his terror subsuming into relief.

He considered them his enemy. Ernesto and his granddaughter—were the enemy.

It was utter madness.

"—his manifesto would read—Last night we struck. The flames, fury, death and disfigurement at Teatro Colon will not be the last—"

Her words were triggering his emotions, astonishment to disgust, then to anger, which smouldered and made him fight his way back to the present.

"Where are the three former soldiers to be found?"

"They're dead," she said.

"Your article mentioned witnesses that are now willing to come forward."

"I can't give you their names—I made a promise to them."

"I see." 'The assassination attempt of Chief Falcon will be easily refuted,' he thought. The accuser works in a brothel, she'd eavesdropped on a conversation, with no further supporting evidence. That would be the clincher for the minister and the President to deny her allegation. It was the most politically expedient solution. "—and you now believe yourself to be unsafe?"

"I've made powerful enemies, Señor Torrente. If I'm arrested for being part of a bomb plot, Lieutenant Machado will kill me—I'm certain of that. He may not even bother arresting me. He has to kill me, he knows I'm his public accuser."

Ernesto saw it all, the Lieutenant following her from Ricci's newspaper location to the mechanical shop on Australia, then delivering the lunchbox into the hands of foundryman, who then secured it within the Teatro Colon. On the evening of, conveniently waiting outside of the theatre to chase down Diego Salvador. His knowledge was also easily refuted.

'I only saw them carrying a lunch box—had no idea it was supposed to be a bomb!' But he believed Sofia Montserrat's deposition completely. The irrefutable evidence that the Lieutenant had shot the stevedore, 'Because he believed he had thrown the bomb.'

"I suppose it was naive of me to think that somebody would just arrest Lieutenant Machado and Commissioner De La Fuente," she said.

He knew that they wouldn't. Yet he owed her an unrepayable debt. He was looking at the lunchbox again, with his granddaughter. The woman had risked her life for them, all of them, a courageous act of decency for strangers. He had to do something for her, the minister be damned.

As Ernesto led Sofia out of the interview room, he was surprised to see several women had gathered outside, and were standing along the wall in the hallway. There were whispers and pointing. Finally, one of them began clapping tentatively, until the others followed suit, for the woman they knew as the Enraged Prostitute. 'She deserves an ovation,' he thought. 'They have no idea.'

Ernesto Torrente was intercepted returning to his office by Nicolas Morente, fashionable as always, checkered trousers, matching waistcoat, ascot tied four-in-hand.

"Señor Torrente—thank God. I thought you'd gone home after your interview. I've just received word the police are holding 10 anarchists, caught red-handed yesterday at the printing press of the Worker's Rebellion. The detective told me that there was a lengthy manifesto going into yesterday's edition."

"Funny enough—the manifesto was in reference to some kind of bomb going off at the Teatro Colon on Monday night. Imagine that. Do you think it's implying that the lunch box that was thrown was supposed to be a bomb? It's ridiculous. You were there sir—I mean—you saw the whole debacle with your own two eyes. Are you alright sir?"

Ernesto was listening superficially. His mind was still dwelling in the dark recesses where Sofia's deposition had placed it. Ernesto straightened his elderly stoop, jutted his chin out and cleared his throat.

"No—I don't think we'll concern ourselves with those gentlemen at the moment. We're going to concern ourselves with something else entirely. Get your coat Nicolas. We're going to police headquarters. And be a good fellow—fetch me a sledgehammer from the maintenance room in the basement."

Ernesto was uncharacteristically silent during the walk to the police headquarters building. But it wasn't overly far, and he held the steady pace of a soldier's forced march, despite Nicolas's badgering.

"Sir—are you absolutely certain such an intrusion into the lair of our police department is absolutely necessary? I don't understand what you have in mind."

"Don't worry lad—if the sledge is necessary, I'll be the one to use it. You can either stay and witness me expose the charlatans, or you can leave—it's up to you."

They faced each other for a moment. "I think I'll stay sir."

"Come on then," Ernesto said, the sledgehammer balanced on his shoulder. He was familiar with the interior of the headquarters building and made straight for Lieutenant Machado's office, where'd he'd assisted with the deportation affidavits from time to time. The detectives he encountered in the hallway weren't surprised at his presence, considering the brouhaha percolating in the holding cells of their basement. If they were curious as to the deal with the sledgehammer—they didn't show it. "Where's the Lieutenant?"

"I'll get him for you sir."

Ernest opened Lieutenant Machado's office door and there it was, exactly as he remembered it, sitting on the orchestral landing in front of him while believing his granddaughter and he were going to die. It sat curiously alone, perched on an otherwise clear desk, as it had on the orchestral platform. Lieutenant Machado was running, shouting from the hallway.

"Don't touch the lunch box for Christ's sake!"

The detectives watched in bewilderment, and then horror, as his intentions finally dawned on them. 'He wouldn't dare—?' But Ernesto could only hear one thing before he swung with all his force, and only he heard it because it was in his head, and that was Sofia Montserrat.

'Why didn't the lunchbox explode?'

'I switched it for a look-alike that was filled with rocks and sand.'

To the collective wince of the detectives that had lurched towards him in a vain attempt to stop the sledgehammer mid swing. It struck the metal lunch box with a resounding crunch, bursting the latches, and it fell to the floor, spilling out its contents. "Your bookkeeper had to save the day for us Lieutenant—because you had no intentions of doing so," he said, facing the dumbfounded group. "But you can leave her be—the allegations in regards an attempt to assassinate Chief Falcon will be dismissed as a foolish woman's fantasy—I'll make sure of it."

Chapter 25
A True Friend

Wednesday, 27 May. Late that evening, Tony made his way to the warehouse, he had a mission. It was dark, but Joaquin and Sofia were there, to his relief. The two were holding hands, sharing conspiratorial glances.

"Thank you, for checking in on us. We seem to be in a pickle."

"An understatement as always. You're already missed at the Social House Sofia—Madam Josefina can't keep up with the business by herself."

"I'm letting her down."

"You can't feel that way. Lieutenant Machado was skulking around. He spoke with Josefina and then Hortense, and then left. You can't go back there."

"We know—we have to go away," Joaquin said. "It's the only way to keep Sofia safe. I've spoken with Pablo. He will look after my warehouse while I'm gone."

"I wish we didn't have to say goodbye like this, but this is best."

"But I have good news—and I want you to be the first to know."

Tony didn't understand how Joaquin could be so upbeat given the depressing situation. "What exactly is the so-called good news?" He was certain Joaquin was playing a joke on him.

"We're going to be married."

"My God—that is good news! Or is it bad news? Sofia what are you thinking?"

"I'm thinking I'm no longer letting this fine man out of my sight," she said.

"Congratulations—I'm pleased for the both of you." But he was thinking the opposite, that they were in serious danger with Lieutenant Machado stalking them. "Can you postpone things until we can celebrate the occasion properly?" Tony's thoughts turned to the lunch box, the bomb, still sitting in Joaquin's office up the stairs.

It had to be removed now, before the police showed up, and they all knew that was just a matter of time. He'd confided some details to his brothers, both of whom were very protective of him, and still hadn't gotten over the death of Tico. They were nearby, waiting for him to bring the item as described—an innocuous looking lunch box. They'd worked out a plan for its disposal, the details of which he couldn't confide to Joaquin or Sofia, only that his brothers, whom Joaquin knew to be tough stevedores, had their ways.

"I have to take the infernal device now Joaquin."

"Are you sure?"

Joaquin had his hand on his shoulder and Tony felt their bond of friendship stronger than it had ever been. They'd been through so much, and their dreams of presenting Tango to audiences had come true!

"I can go with you; I'll carry it until it's put someplace safe."

"No—leave this to me. Your place is with Sofia—go somewhere safe. The sooner you leave—the better." He gave them both a hug, tears falling down his cheeks, and walked up the stairs.

Ernesto walked through the front entrance of the Spanish embassy under the glare of the Civil Guard, eyes shaded under the brim of the black tricorn hat. He'd taken a carriage northward, passing through the upscale houses rising in Barrio Norte, the homes of the elite families of Buenos Aires, gradually leaving the core of the city. 'The city's growth continued to bode well for the Teatro Colon,' he thought, which relied on continued ticket sales to repay its creditors, and to attract the famous tenors and sopranos of Europe.

Passing by the Recoleta cemetery, where President Quintana was entombed, brought his mind back to the political calculus that weighed so heavily on his inquiry. President Alcorta astutely navigated a complex path through a politically fraught period, and he'd gained control of the house of deputies. But he'd made bitter enemies of the provincial governors whom he'd temporarily defanged. Powerful enemies.

This made an unrelated public scandal anathema to the President. His inquiry was now merely an exercise in suppressing its exploitation by the President's foes. He gloomily conceded that the enemies were many, and outweighed the moral assertions of the few. And they were few indeed.

A single woman, to whom he, and his fellow opera goers, owed a debt of gratitude that could never truly be repaid. He couldn't help but feel disappointed with himself. She had believed that those in high office would somehow intervene with Machado and De La Fuente when she exposed them, and she would be safe. But he could do no such thing. It was yet another compromise of his ideals forced upon him by the vagaries of public service, and he knew he had to take the path of least resistance.

He embraced his estranged colleague, and a hobbled ascent of three flights of stairs later, the two men settled into the leather studded chairs in the office. Its polished brass name plate read, 'Miguel Balcazar, Senior Legal Attaché, Embassy of Spain,' in cursive.

"You didn't tell me you were promoted," Ernesto said.

"Did you forget we weren't speaking? I wish you would believe me—we didn't know Gabriel Chavez was a revolutionary."

"It's water under the bridge. A peace offering?" Ernesto gave the bottle of fine Dewars Scotch to Balcazar. "If there was ever a time for a drink, now would be it."

Balcazar nodded. "I agree on the condition we make this a regular occurrence again."

"I saw you at the opera with your wife—lovely as ever."

"And I saw you with your granddaughter. To our loved ones?" They raised their glasses, held each other's gaze sombrely, and took a sip. "Can you tell me the real story? I'm too old to accept the newspaper's version—that it was merely a prank, the perpetrator losing his life for his troubles."

"Police officers don't shoot pranksters Miguel. There is indeed more to the story."

"Was it a bomb then? That didn't explode for some reason?"

"It would have been a bomb—but for the concerns of a courageous woman. A Spanish woman, whose name you most certainly know—Sofia Montserrat."

"The niece of the late Senator?"

"Yes. The Senator made sure she ended up on the dung heap the minute she arrived in Buenos Aires—but it seems she's irrepressible. Lucky for you and I because if it weren't for her actions your wife, my granddaughter and the two of us would be dead."

"Do tell."

"She became a local celebrity, writing articles under the pen name the Enraged Prostitute. Depraved anarchists recruited her into their circle as they needed a woman to make their scheme work, and they believed she would condone their antics. They were wrong. She swapped out the bomb for a dud when no one was looking—including senior officers of the police department."

"What exactly are you saying?"

"There is a small element of corrupt officers. She thought that if she reported it to them, they would coerce her to follow through with the bomb plot—so she took it upon herself to stop the madness. I've confirmed these suspicions of hers to be true. There are two officers in particular—Commissioner Felipe De La Fuente, in charge of the division that investigates political threats amongst other things, and his right-hand man Lieutenant Machado, in charge of its detectives. They intended to discredit Chief Falcon. In my estimation, it would have worked."

"What is it you need from me?"

"You're aware of President Alcorta's tenuous position?"

"Of course."

"Then you'll understand why her accusations against them will have to be denied and suppressed by the ministry. You'll also understand that puts her life in peril. The Lieutenant is known to be extreme in closing his cases shall we say—and protecting the reputation of Commissioner De La Fuente. I'm sure, you see my point. In any case, I believe her safest course of action is to return to Spain—if it weren't for the serious accusations that remain outstanding. She could be sentenced to death if found guilty. I'm asking you for a personal favour—a way out for her. It would help my aging conscience, and we owe it to her."

"My dear friend," Balcazar said, refilling their glasses. "I would gladly draft a testament of character for the young lady, but no such thing is required anymore."

Balcazar pulled a dossier from a desk drawer and unwound the twine holding the contents in place. It was labelled Montserrat, Hugo on its upper right corner. "On occasion, serendipity intervenes—and makes the path forward as clear as the crystal tumblers in our hands. We were inclined to pay Sofia Montserrat a visit a couple of months ago as there were developments surrounding the murder of her parents."

"But in the end a decision was made to sit on this information, I'm afraid. As you said—the President's position is tenuous, and he was closely associated to Senator Montserrat. It would have been yet another scandal. A stable government in Argentina is also in my country's best interests."

"However, the young woman has nothing to fear—the case is now closed.

There was a witness you see, a gypsy child—now come of age. The maid was her friend—she'd hidden the witness in her room, and was sneaking her scraps of food. She was hiding in the wardrobe when the shooting started. She saw the Senator execute her friend—and heard him taunting his brother before he finished the job in the cruellest of fashions. She managed to sneak out without anyone seeing her. The witness's mother wouldn't let the traumatized child bear witness. But eventually the child, now a teenager, recovered and told her Flamenco instructor what she'd seen. The instructor, also a gypsy woman, insisted that the Civil Guard be advised. The dead Senator is guilty as sin—may he rot in hell for his vicious crime."

Ernesto smiled, nodded, and held up his glass briefly. "The problem is solved and my conscience is clear. I'll advise her of this right away." He took a swig, liking Balcazar less and less. He had intended on just letting Sofia Montserrat anguish.

"Since you're here there's another matter. It goes back to late 1904—a few months before the attempted coup d'état by the radical party. I had passed some information along to your deceased colleague Gabriel Chavez. Commissioner De La Fuente had travelled to Spain that year, to a law enforcement conference focused on anarchist terrorism."

"It was organised by our own officials, and when he went missing for a couple of days—it was noticed. This has come to us in bits and pieces, but we followed it up doggedly on our end. He wound up in a disagreeable neighbourhood of Barcelona, where he hired three local thugs known to our spies. Mercenaries really—former infantry soldiers that knew their way around firearms and weapons of all kinds. They were last seen on a steamship bound for Buenos Aires."

"Chavez was following some leads and asked us to brief him on what we knew of the murder of her parents. He asked us to lay off of Sofia Montserrat, although as it turns out, we had not received any request to pursue her extradition. In any case, he never got back to us for obvious reasons. But perhaps you know. Did these three men have anything to do with her accusation of a plot to assassinate Colonel Falcon?"

Ernesto took another sip of scotch, buying precious seconds to ponder this revelation. Why had Miguel given this information to Chavez and not to him? Because he knew Chavez was a revolutionary—because he believed the coup would succeed—because he thought Chavez might be appointed minister of the interior and was currying favour. In any case, he now needed to bury what his inquiry had revealed and clearly couldn't trust Miguel.

"It's the first I've heard of it."

Ernesto was in a hurry. Sofia could safely return to Spain, out of the reach of Lieutenant Machado. But he had to get this information to her and he knew of only one way to do so without attending her brothel and tipping off Machado.

He had asked Sofia Montserrat how he could contact her at the end of the interview.

"Leave a message with Madam Josefina. I can't return there but she'll find a way to get it to me. She takes her tea at the Hotel Metropol."

It had been three decades, he thought with astonishment, that he'd been introduced to her. British, described herself as a cockney that had escaped London's east side, a former actress with a love of Shakespeare, which was a shared passion. The British were a mystery to him for the most part, but he knew they had a penchant for tea in the afternoon, so he'd taken a seat in the ornately decorated restaurant inside the Hotel Metropol at 3 pm, and waited. She arrived one hour later.

He stood and approached her table. "Josefina as I recall. My name is—"

"Don't tell me. I never forget names—it's the key to my success. Let me see," blowing smoke from a cigarette in a holder, "Ernesto Torrente—lawyer at one of the ministries. Have you been waiting for me then? You'll make an old harlot blush."

"I need to pass a message to someone—it's urgent."

"There's only one someone I know that would need that sort of message. What's your business with my Sofia?"

"She has reported concerns about certain police officers."

"Oh my—she'll not have made any friends that way. Now—don't be telling me any information that would make me think poorly of my Felipe— Commissioner De La Fuente as you probably know him—or my Vicente for that matter."

"As you wish—they're not germane to the issue. The message is that diplomatic representatives of Spain have informed me that she is no longer sought by their authorities. She's in the clear and can return without fear of repercussions."

"You're too late, I'm afraid."

"What do you mean," Ernesto said. "Has she been killed?"

"Nobody I know could hurt that girl dearie—she's too bloody smart by half. I think I knew it the day Vicente brought her kicking and screaming to the Social House. He should have known it as well. Knew her numbers that one—and played her attributes to advantage. No—there's nothing the likes of you or I can do for her. She's already on her way home to Spain. They found themselves a steamship with room in steerage. Since I know you're wondering—I don't know the name of it. We thought it best she didn't tell me such information as I might be tempted to pass it on. They'll be in line for boarding by now."

Ernesto sat back in his chair and pondered the resourcefulness of Sofia Montserrat. "She's travelling with someone else you say?"

"Her handsome Tango man didn't you know? They danced their way into each other's hearts while none of us were looking. They'll be bound for Madrid—he has family there."

"I see. Perhaps I'll take a quick walk to the docks then—to see if I can spot her before they board. It's not far—and I'm certain she'd like to know."

Vicente was once again troubled by something that he couldn't quite put his finger on, as things had worked out amazingly well. The allegations put forth by Sofia Montserrat under her alter ego the Enraged Prostitute, had not been picked up by the main newspapers. They apparently wouldn't venture down the path of questioning police officials in good standing on the word of a single brothel worker, as De La Fuente had mused the day before. In fact, when Chief Falcon had heard about the article, he took it upon himself to get to know De La Fuente better.

'When they target you personally, you know you've done your job effectively!' Following a detailed discussion of strategies targeting the anarchist scourge, the Chief had taken to bringing De La Fuente along to meetings with the President, relying on him to provide the details of the rapidly evolving investigation, to help the President fend off the press.

'Things have all worked out Vicente my boy,' De La Fuente had said. De La Fuente, in turn, had relied on Vicente to have the carriage waiting at the police headquarters building every afternoon at 3 pm sharp, in order to arrive at the president's office with plenty of time, and get the investigational details Vicente had acquired that day.

The disappearance of Sofia Montserrat had given them considerable latitude in this regard, as long as the Enraged Prostitute didn't miraculously reappear shouting further accusations. He hadn't had time to put any serious effort into locating her, but that would come in due course. Despite the lawyer's unsolicited advice, certain things could not be forgiven.

The priggish lawyer Torrente had broken open the lunch box with a total absence of fear, with the confidence of someone who knew of its contents. 'He had spoken with Sofia. Another strike against her.'

He dearly wanted to know how the lunch box had come to contain rocks. Clearly Diego Salvador, the stevedore, had believed he'd thrown a bomb in the opera house. He wasn't responsible for the switch. The newspaper publisher Ricci had confessed to the entire conspiracy and had broken down in tears of frustration when he learned the bomb had not exploded and killed his intended bourgeois oppressors. Randazzo had been explicit about building a bomb hidden in a lunchbox. Sofia was the only explanation.

He hadn't had time to spy on Cuéllar and knew too little about him. Presumably they'd disappeared together, as his detective reported that Cuéllar hadn't been at his warehouse or residence in two days. It meant he would have to kill them both, leaving no loose ends. Then the solution came to him—the tango musician from the brothel. 'The three of them were thick as thieves.' He would follow up with this angle tonight, after he'd brought De La Fuente back from la Casa Rosada.' Tony was his name he remembered, and Tony was going to tell him where they were.

'Having thought through his next steps, his concerns should no longer be troubling him,' he thought. But they were. It was 3 pm by his gold pocket watch, and he watched De La Fuente emerge from police headquarters and limp his expanding bulk toward the carriage. He was growing more and more dependent on his cane.

"Let's get moving lad. Day three of the Presidential inquisition—never-ending questions about the bomb plot—which I pretend not to know the answers to. But we're almost free and clear—I can feel it. You've got a half hour—start talking and don't leave anything out."

Vicente nodded. He clambered into the carriage behind De La Fuente and signalled the coachman to get rolling with a sharp whistle. It was an uncomfortable position for Vicente, who preferred to let others do the talking. It took all his concentration to summarise the progress of the investigation, while the carriage shimmied back and forth, bumping eastward along Moreno.

The previous day, his detectives had followed up on the information they'd obtained from the interrogation of Ricci, the publisher of the Worker's Rebellion. They'd located an ironsmith, one Rocco Zabatino, the man he'd beaten at the brothel for torturing one of the prostitutes, but no need to clutter the mind of the President with that particular detail. Vicente described Zabatino as a mindless follower, easily manipulated. He confessed that he'd taken the bomb from Diego Salvador and Sofia Montserrat, and hidden it in the woman's restroom, for Sofia to retrieve. Vicente had just sent detectives back to the Teatro Colon to search the women's restroom, certain that Sofia must have left the bomb there, and handed Diego Salvador a look alike at the last moment.

"If it's found in the theatre, the case is closed," De La Fuente said, "the men will be tried and convicted—although an interview of Sofia Montserrat would be expected."

"Yes."

"But she will not be found."

"She will not be found."

Vicente had been so focused on updating De La Fuente that he hadn't noticed how close the carriage had rolled to the tall building on its cabin door side, effectively closing them in. He only turned his attention to his surroundings when it became apparent the carriage had stopped. The damned coachman apparently didn't understand they had a schedule to respect.

"Why is the bloody fool so close to the building," De La Fuente asked.

Vicente whistled and peered out the window of the door, his head just fitting between the carriage and the building's wall. Why is the coachman running away? He knew the answer of course, and looked upwards. He should have known. The glimmering metallic object dropping quickly towards the roof of the carriage, was obviously the worker's metal lunchbox, the real bomb.

That was about all the time he'd had to consider his imminent death, as the bomb worked exactly as intended. It struck the roof of the carriage, causing the downward momentum of the dynamite to crush the tubes containing nitroglycerin, causing the ensemble to explode with sufficient percussive force to remove heads and limbs from bodies from those closest to it, and kill 50 people within a proximity, with the help of metal pellets and screws projected at high velocity. That is, had there been 50 people as intended, instead of two horrifically, decimated corpses of yet to be identified senior police officials, as the newspapers reported the following day.

9 781035 813032